The Treasure of the Sicarii Gospel

By Randall Gannaway

The Treasure of the Sicarii Gospel

By Randall Gannaway

The Treasure of the Sicarii Gospel

Paperback: (979-8-950072-08-6)
Hardcover: (979-8-950072-09-3)

For my wife and children.

The joy you have given me is immeasurable.

Prologue

Riley Callahan crashed into a trash can and stumbled forward until he fell to the sidewalk. Skidding on all fours, his palms and knees burned, and sweat poured from his brow to form little pools on the pavement. The night was warm for May, even in the early hours after midnight, and his sweat-soaked hair and shirt stuck to his skin.

Rising to his knees, he took a few seconds to plan his next move. The nearby street lamp revealed the 72nd Street and Central Park West street signs. In his panic he had failed to realize he had been running parallel to Central Park. *Fitting location.* John Lennon had been murdered nearby at the entrance to his home in the Dakota Apartments.

Should I take a chance and enter the park?

Echoing footfalls jolted him. He had no time for internal debate. Sucking in a deep breath, he rose to his feet and darted in a direction perpendicular to his previous path. He passed through Inventor's Gate and ran down the path into Strawberry Fields, the two-and-a-half-acre tear-drop-shaped parcel dedicated to Lennon.

As Riley crossed the Imagine mosaic, his pounding steps pierced the silence. *He'll know where I am.* He jumped on the small fence that bordered the path and sprinted through trees and bushes. The softer ground muffled his movement, while the tree cover helped hide his silhouette.

Leaving the south end of Strawberry Fields, he bounded across the junction of West Drive and Terrace Drive and entered Sheep Meadow. Though sheep had not grazed there in almost eighty years, most of that part of the park remained treeless grassland. *Not at all the right place for me. No cover and no one at this hour to help me.* He turned left, crossed another path, and entered a heavily treed area. The thick cover brought a fleeting sense of security but did little to lessen the pounding in his chest.

Weaving through the trees, he focused with myopic precision on what lay directly in front of him. *Why is he after me? I no longer have the gospel. The woman has it.*

Even now Riley could not rid his mind of the image of her face. After she had conned him out of the most significant discovery of his life, he had pursued her from

Cairo to New York only to find someone more frightening also tracking her. He had just managed to elude the giant. *But for how long?*

The thick brush slowed his pace and stung his flesh. His lungs burned, and his heart felt ready to burst. Every snap of a twig communicated a threat. Every rustle of leaves relayed terror. His foot struck something hard. Falling forward, his face scraped across the ground. Rising to his knees, he felt the stickiness of his blood but no pain.

My adrenaline must be operating in overdrive. Where am I?

He saw the statue that had tripped him. *Literary Walk.* It was populated with sculptures of literary figures and a few out of place others such as Beethoven in front of him. He was near the Bandshell. East Drive lay just a little farther to his right. Asian portrait sketch artists and the crowds they attracted might still be there. If he could reach the street beyond, he would be safe. He pulled himself to his feet and dashed toward his salvation.

Am I running the right direction? He slowed at the Christopher Fratin sculpture Eagles and Prey, depicting two eagles attacking a goat. *Yes!*

Reaching East Drive, he followed the curving path until he could see the bright city lights and traffic that marked its end. *I made it.*

No! The outline of a hulking creature expanded between him and his exit and eclipsed the streetlamps. The long shadow crept along the pavement toward him. He turned to run, but before his second step, he heard a puff and saw his right shoulder torn open.

Spinning, he saw a flare erupt from the shadow. Searing pain racked his chest and back, and the blow propelled him to the asphalt. Sprawled lengthwise on the path, he choked and spit up blood, but his coughs did nothing to clear his throat.

After a series of almost silent footfalls, the dark hulk, outlined in a mystical glow from the streetlights, stared down at him. The halo did not encircle a saint.

Sputtering through the liquid filling his mouth, Riley begged for his life. "Please." He tried to raise his head and right arm, but the pain was too intense. Grimacing, he let them fall back to the pavement. He labored to breathe.

The giant bent over him and raised a Glock with silencer extended toward Riley's head. He spoke with a thick French accent. "*Où est l'évangile?* Where is the gospel?"

Riley attempted to respond but could not without drowning in his blood.

The hulk touched the pistol to Riley's forehead. "*Où est la femme?* Where is the woman?"

Riley again struggled to answer. He owed her nothing. She had stolen the gospel and his future. She had played him for a fool. Now he would die because of her. At least he could ensure she would soon follow him. He choked, sucked liquid into his lungs, and spit out a whisper. "Boston antiquities dealers." He coughed up more blood before grabbing breath. "May God curse you for this."

The hulk smiled. "*Brûlez dans l'enfer.* It is I who bear God's curses *a vous.* We will find the woman and the gospel before you fully roast in Hell."

The muzzle flashed.

Chapter 1

"Samson prayed, 'Lord, remember me! Please give back my strength one more time that I may pay back the Philistines for the loss of my eyes. Let me die with them.' Then Samson pushed against the pillars, and the temple crashed down on the Philistines. He killed more at his death than he had killed in his previous lifetime."

Not much reaction. Doctor Shane Randall shifted the weight of his six-feet-four-inch frame from one leg to another and wondered if his situation was not unlike Samson's. In his experience over one hundred disinterested students could get as out of control as any half-drunk Philistines. The seemingly endless rows of seats in Yale's Niebuhr Hall would have been quite intimidating if he had not spoken there hundreds of times before.

Shane pressed his laptop projector remote, and the classroom blinked. The screened filled with the late nineteenth century etching of *Samson Puts Down the Pillars* by James Tissot. It depicted Samson as a long-haired blind man standing alongside a frightened boy between two pillars in the middle of a crowded temple. Samson's extended arms were buckling the pillars around him.

"Though it's not a Christian story, the tale of Samson is a favorite of children throughout Christendom because of Samson's superhuman strength. He killed a lion with his bare hands and slew a thousand Philistines with the jawbone of an ass. He was a sort of a Hebrew Hercules."

The laughter of a group of boys clustered in the back drew Shane's attention. There were always students who found it humorous an ass could have a jawbone. A woman entered the arena through an entrance near the boys. Shane had not seen her for years, but he recognized her immediately. He fought back the memories that could derail his lecture.

He again pressed the remote and the screen flickered to the late sixteenth century engraving by Philipe Galle entitled *Samson Destroying the Pillars of Philistine Temple.* In this image, Samson's arms were wrapped around the pillars such that he could bring them to his body and tear them from their foundations.

"The story of Samson is also a great example of the Bible's numeric code. Note the *five* kings and the *three* thousand Philistine victims. But neither the heroic dimension nor the numerical dimension is the aspect I want to explore. The Samson story is an example of the ancient hatred of Palestinians and Jews and the acceptability of suicide as a weapon of war. Today's suicide bombers throughout the Middle East are examples of the same zealous motivation. It's been occurring for over three thousand years, and it's not about to stop."

The image changed once more to the early seventeenth century painting *The Death of Samson* by Peter Paul Rubens, which had Samson supporting the crumbling pillars just before they crushed him beneath their weight.

"Suicide is an acceptable tactical weapon in a holy war. On a personal level, passing such a test of faith guarantees one's place in the highest level of heaven reserved for martyrs. And from a military perspective, suicide's difficult to defend against. If you're the weaker of two warring factions, someone willing to commit suicide can get to places and people where other means cannot. One suicide usually results in the death of many enemies, as in the case of Samson. He was renowned for killing Philistines throughout his life, but his suicide resulted in the deaths of more Philistines than he'd killed in twenty years before."

Shane's eyes kept returning to the woman waiting patiently against the far wall. He cared deeply about the impact he had on his students, so many of whom were blinded by beliefs with no basis in historical fact. Even so, he rushed the end of his lecture.

"Here's a man who was a Nazirite, a man consecrated to God from birth. Yet he's revered for the way he died more than the way he lived. As we near the end of the semester, it's important we tie the Old and New Testaments together. I want you to question the traditional views of Samson and tell me why this story's as pertinent today as it was over three thousand years ago when Samson lived and two thousand years ago when Christianity was born. Your assignment is to write a five-page comparison of the Samson story to current events. Have it to me next Tuesday. That's all for today."

The students dispersed. A trio of coeds lingered near the front, exuding a desire to talk. He hoped to discourage them by avoiding eye contact.

On the other hand, he was finding it difficult to remove his eyes from the woman waiting in the back. He walked from the projected image to the first row of seats. The three coeds approached him with flirtatious laughter.

He did not turn in their direction. "Please excuse me. Any questions'll have to wait until my normal consultation hours. Or send me an email, and I'll get back to you as soon as I can."

The coeds glared at the woman near the top of the steps but took the hint and left through the lower door. The woman made her way down until she stood in front of Shane.

She was about five feet seven with an athletic body and tan skin. Her hair was darker than he remembered, but the blond highlights acted like windows to those younger years. She wore a navy business suit, but even in the conservative attire, she was stunning. Standing this close to her, he was lost in her brown eyes. His defenses evaporated, and memories flooded his thoughts.

Though it had been over a decade since he had seen her, Shane remembered Lauren as if they had been together yesterday. They had shared a fiery and very intimate junior year at the University of Texas before differing priorities and pressures tore them apart. He had always believed they would get back together, but time had separated them further. Eventually it had just become impractical to renew the relationship.

He thought of all the times he had looked for her in the crowds at the DFW and Austin Bergstrom airports without finding her. After several years he had found her online, but thoughts of contacting her had been separated by long periods of travel, research, and writing that now added up to eleven years. In that time no woman had filled the hole Lauren had left in his life.

"Lauren Mallory. Of all the classrooms in all the universities in all the world, why'd you walk into mine?"

Lauren smiled. "Hi, Shane. I haven't seen you since UT. Or should I call you Doctor Randall?"

"Shane'll do fine."

"I found myself in need of the most renowned expert in early Christian history. Imagine my surprise when I saw your name at the top of the list?"

Shane laughed. "I can't imagine why you'd need someone like that. But I'm glad to see you."

"You look fit, Shane."

"You look great."

Redness filled Lauren's cheeks but quickly faded. "Would you mind spending some time with me? I have something important to show you. And I need your help."

Shane pretended to think about his answer for a few seconds. "I can clear the rest of my afternoon. We can go to my office."

"No, I can't do it now. I don't have with me what I want to show you. I came here now because I saw your name on the course schedule. I wasn't sure you'd be here, and what I have to show you's too precious to risk."

"Then I'll go with you."

"No. Better we do it tonight."

Shane stepped forward until his face was inches from Lauren's. "Do you think I'm going to let you out of my sight?"

Lauren looked up with her eyes full of promise. "Just for a few hours." She rested her hands on his chest. "I'm not going anywhere."

Shane took a step back. "What do you suggest?"

"Do you still like Thai food?"

"Of course."

"Then let's meet at the Thai Taste at seven. My treat." Lauren handed him a business card. "Here's my card. It has my mobile phone number on it."

Shane read the card. "Mallory Antiquities?"

"I'll explain everything over dinner. Call if you're going to be late."

Shane followed her with his eyes as she turned and walked toward the lower door. When she disappeared on the other side, the room seemed a little dimmer.

Chapter 2

As Lauren exited Niebuhr Hall and walked toward the parking lot, she managed her body language to exude confidence and self-assurance. Though she had used this skill many times to beat men at their own games, on this occasion she feared her nerves were showing.

Shane must help me. I'm running out of options.

Lauren flashed back to how she had obtained the gospel. Perhaps she should have given Riley a chance. After all, he had been bright enough to acquire the gospel. And he had turned out to be an adequate lover. But if she had partnered with him, it would only have been a matter of time before he double-crossed her. The potential reward was too important to him. With Riley she would have been afraid to sleep; afraid he would do to her what she did to him.

And a woman my age needs her beauty sleep. She chuckled. *Besides, it's better to be the double-crosser than the double-crossee.*

The gospel was way out of Riley's league. He was far too weak to stand up to the other group pursuing the gospel. She knew the organization well enough to know he was no match for their henchmen. She was counting on her intelligence and swift action to stay ahead of them. Riley would have slowed her down.

Following him from the black market in Alexandria to his favorite restaurant in Cairo had not been difficult. Seducing him had been easier. A couple of sleeping pills dissolved in his whiskey had reinforced what the sex had begun, giving her plenty of time to search his room for the gospel. She had found the gospel in his closet hidden by some dirty clothes. *What a fool! A priceless two-thousand-year-old document hidden under dirty boxers.*

At least he had protected it by encasing the vellum pages in Mylar to minimize damage from the air or anything else that might contact them. Between each of the six Mylar-encased pages he had placed a sturdy sheet of acid free cardboard to provide stability and additional protection. Then he placed the package in a padded leather attaché.

He would be looking for her. The others would be as well. She had called upon all her experience to cover her tracks. In her business the use of false ids was common, so it had not been difficult to book flights, trains, cars, and hotels under aliases. She had done so first to New York, then to Boston, then to New Haven.

The limited number of places she could go for help worked to her disadvantage. Given enough time, anyone pursuing her would pick up her trail. The men she had sought out for help over the last few days had been jokes. But now, with Shane, she had real hope. She swore she would do whatever it took to win his assistance. Then she smiled at what that implied.

That wouldn't be bad, whether he helps or not.

A blur of movement caught her eye. *Idiot!*

She ran the last few steps to her rental car, unlocking it with the key fob. As she grabbed for the door handle, she found the source of the movement. A student was running, perhaps late for class. She scanned the campus in a circle around her and found no other cause for concern. Taking a deep breath, she opened the door and sat behind the steering wheel. Beads of sweat formed on her forehead, which she dabbed with a napkin she found in the passenger seat. She started the car but did not shift out of park. Instead, she rested her head on the steering wheel.

"You better keep your act together. This is too serious to be daydreaming like a schoolgirl."

She raised her head and slowly pulled out in the direction of her hotel.

Chapter 3

Marcus Quinn awoke in darkness. Though he could see nothing, he was sitting upright on a hard, wooden, straight-back chair. He tried to pull himself from the chair, but he could not move. His arms were restrained at the wrists, his legs at the ankles, and his chest to the back of the chair. Rolling his head confirmed he was wearing a hood pulled together around his neck.

Panic permeated through his mind and muscles as he pulled at the ropes with all his strength and shook his head wildly. His increasing difficulty breathing heightened the horror. He tried to rock back and forth but could not get any leverage. His bindings did not loosen, and the chair remained steadfast to the floor.

He gasped for air, but the hood restrained his breathing. His pulse pounded as his blood pressure skyrocketed. *Calm down or you're going to suffocate.* He took a few long, controlled breaths. The pounding lessened, and his mind cleared.

Where am I? What's the last thing I remember? It was late, and I was locking up my store. I heard something behind me and then nothing.

Quinn fumed. He paid dearly to locate his store on Charles Street, the main shopping boulevard in Boston's historic Beacon Hill neighborhood. Muggings were not supposed to happen there. The rich locals and tourists who shopped there preferred crime to happen in other parts of the city.

It must be a robbery. My store is being cleaned out!

He took a mental inventory of his shop, which was divided into two parts. The larger front room housed the antiques he sold to the locals and tourists. It was crowded with china, stemware, statues, figurines, urns, and furniture the typical antique buyer sought. The back room stored his personal collection. It also contained those items involved in transactions that skirted legalities. He had searched the globe for years to find the treasures that now gave him his living, only to have them taken from him by thieves.

He strained once more against his bindings to no avail. He was accustomed to getting his way, and his helplessness infuriated him. *Bastards!*

He heard the door open. Someone spoke in a deep voice with a French accent.

"You are awake, *mon ami*, no?"

"Thief!" Quinn contracted every muscle in his body and pushed with all his might on the ropes and chair, but he only increased his frustration. His heart hammered his chest to the brink of bursting. "Let me out of here! You can't rob me and get away with it. I'll track you down! I don't care how many of you there are. I don't care where you run. There's no place you can hide where I can't find you."

A question interrupted his rant. *"Où est la femme?"*

Quinn did not understand. "This is America. Speak English, asshole!"

"Where is the woman?"

Quinn did not expect that question. There may be more to what was happening than he knew. "What woman?"

"The woman asking about the gospel."

Quinn's mind raced, but the intensity of the moment and the constraint of the hood clouded his thoughts. "I don't know who you're talking about."

A heavy weight came down on Quinn's right foot, and intense pain rocked his body. His foot was broken, probably shattered. He screamed in agony and strained to free himself. As he sucked in air, the hood sealed his mouth and threatened to totally cut off the flow. His screams and moans pushed the fabric from his mouth, but his gasps choked the air his body craved.

"Where is the woman?" his captor repeated. "The woman asking for your help."

A woman asking for my help? An image of a woman fitting that description filled Quinn's mind. *She must be the one.* She visited his shop a couple of days ago wanting information about something with a religious slant. He told her religion was not his area of expertise. She came on to him to change his mind. He thought about finding out how serious she was about bartering her body for his attention, but he was late for a meeting with a big potential client. He told her what she needed was too academic for him.

What was her name? Where did I send her?

Another blow crushed his left foot. Quinn screamed again and sobbed. His face was wet with spit and tears. The hood clung to his skin, and what he could not see terrified him.

His captor feigned sympathy. "*S'il vous plaît, mon ami.* Must I move higher?"

Quinn's situation was futile. Pain racked his body, and there was nothing he could do to prevent more. His captor was obviously mad. No one could do what he was doing otherwise.

At the moment Quinn resigned himself to death, his mind cleared. He yelled the answer that would save his life. "I sent her to Harvard Divinity School! Doctor Samuel Evans! I sell antiquities. She needed a theologian. That's everything I know. Now, let me go."

Quinn hung his head on his chest as his entire body numbed against the pain. *He'll let me go. I haven't seen his face. I'm no threat.* He prayed the man would loosen the bindings before he left.

The French accent moved closer to his ear and became almost a whisper. "*Merci, mon ami.* Now you can rest."

The next crushing blow struck Quinn on the left side of his skull.

Chapter 4

Shane walked up Chapel Street toward the Thai Taste restaurant. It was a pleasant May evening, and the university students and native population were taking advantage. The air was alive and reaching out to seduce his senses. Enticing aromas escaped from the kitchens of the many varying style restaurants. Competing forms of music from open doorways mixed on the sidewalk. And people were everywhere, screaming with laughter. Shane loved college towns and New Haven in particular. It made him feel young.

He had compromised between casual dress and trying to look his best by donning newly washed jeans, a maroon button-down shirt, and a dark blue blazer. In his hand he carried a single long-stemmed red rose. It had been a couple of months since he had been out with a woman. Though Lauren's request had sounded professional in nature, the evening might turn into a date.

He found the street access to the Thai Taste and walked down the steps to the lower level of the Hotel Duncan, which housed the restaurant. Passing through the ornate metal doors, he found Lauren sitting in a booth to the right. She was dressed in light blue jeans and a tucked in darker blue button-down shirt. Her black leather jacket lay to her left in the booth next to the wall. She was staring down at a glass of merlot she was slowly spinning from side to side with both hands on the stem and cup. The level of the wine indicated she had already taken a few sips. Shane motioned to the maître d' he was meeting someone and proceeded to the booth.

Lauren looked up with a smile and greeted him with a purr. "Why Doctor Randall. Whatever are your intentions for that rose?"

He handed her the flower and sat opposite her in the booth. "Just a reminder of younger days."

Lauren brought it to her nose and inhaled deeply. Her eyes looked past him and lost their focus. Shane would have given anything to know her thoughts.

She looked back into his eyes. "Is there a woman in your life, Shane?"

Shane thought for a few seconds about how to respond. *Should I reveal her question targeted the one void in my life?* Shane accepted the hole was there. He had tried to fill it with many varied activities and interests. In general, he was comfortable with the result. After a few minutes with Lauren, he realized how much he had failed.

He decided to go with honesty. "There have been women. But no one serious. It just never felt right. I had too many other passions demanding my time. How about you? Ever married?"

Lauren responded coyly. "How do you know I'm not?"

Shane pointed to her left ring finger. "No ring. Well?"

"Never put it as a priority."

A young waiter walked up to Shane and disturbed their conversation. "Can I get you something to drink?"

He was a student, but Shane did not remember his name. "Woodford Reserve. Neat."

The waiter left the way he had come, and Shane again focused on Lauren. "What does that mean? *Never put it as a priority.*"

Lauren broke eye contact. "I've been busy." She looked back at Shane. "And most people I deal with aren't the kind you want to settle down with for happily ever after."

Shane remembered the card. "Mallory Antiquities?"

"My company. After college I somewhat by chance made contacts in several Middle Eastern countries. I connect sellers there to buyers in the States and take a commission. I have a working knowledge of Arabic and Farsi and a set of balls larger than any man's."

Shane laughed.

Lauren took a sip of her wine. "I'm sure you know how hard it is for a woman to do business in that part of the world. Luckily for me, there's always a war going on, and there're plenty of people who don't care who they have to do business with to make a buck. The War on Terrorism has been a boon. Objects have come on the market that would never've been available before. The trick's determining the real ones from the fakes. And sometimes even that's not all that important."

Shane was surprised. "You deal on the black market?"

"I do what I have to do. Most of the items I trade aren't appreciated in the least in the countries they come from. They're far safer in private collections or museums."

"That sounds like a rationalization."

"Perhaps. But you have an answer to your question. A lot of my days are devoted to not being taken advantage of or trying to convince some character I'm as mean as he is. Not exactly an environment that leads to matrimony."

The waiter arrived with Shane's drink and placed it in front of him. "Are you ready to order?"

Lauren turned questioning eyes to Shane. "What do you suggest?"

"The Pad Thai's their signature dish. Some say it's the best in the country."

"That sounds fine."

Shane lifted the menus to the waiter. "Make it two."

The waiter nodded. "Very good." Then he left again.

Shane chuckled. "I'm not sure back in college I foresaw you becoming an antiquities dealer. And a not so reputable one at that."

Lauren smirked. "I thought you'd still be playing baseball. I carried one of your cards in my purse for years."

"The major leagues aren't very forgiving about a shoulder injury that takes five miles per hour off your fastball. I couldn't handle a return to the minors so I gave it up and went back to school."

"Well, we were young and idealistic. Although in your case, Divinity School might still be considered idealistic. Harvard Divinity School? Where you earned a Doctor of Theology degree specializing in the New Testament and Christian Origins? Followed by two highly acclaimed books, *Jesus, the Revolutionary Rabbi* and *The Twelve Myths of Christianity*. And a number of controversial articles questioning orthodox interpretation of New Testament events."

Shane laughed loudly. "Been spending time on Google?"

"That's how I found you. It gave me the times of your three classes at Yale's Divinity School. The History of Christianity, Biblical Archaeology, and Religion and Politics in Early Christianity."

Shane gave his standard response when explaining his vocation. "It allows me time to explore–physically, historically, and spiritually. Now what's so important that you looked me up after all these years?"

"I may have found something, something extraordinary."

"What do you mean?"

"A couple of weeks ago, I was in Alexandria. I do business with a number of antiquities dealers there. I heard from a source that one of the dealers, named Adjo, had acquired a new find off the black market. As I'm sure you know, the antiquities business has its share of shady and dangerous characters. But Adjo and I go way back. His name means *treasure*."

Lauren lifted her jacket and exposed a leather attaché lying on its side on the bench. "Once I saw the contents of this bag. I felt like I was in the Parable of the Pearl in which a man finds a pearl of such great value he sells all he has to buy it. I bought it on the spot."

Shane could not help correcting her. "In that parable, the pearl's a metaphor for the Kingdom of God. It wasn't meant to apply to an object. On one level it teaches that the Kingdom of God is far more precious than everything we have on earth. On a practical level to the time, Jesus had all of his followers sell everything they had and pooled the money into one common fund."

Lauren rolled her eyes to the ceiling and waved her right hand to the side. "Whatever. You'll see what I mean in about five seconds."

She lifted the attaché upright and pulled from it a page encased in Mylar.

Shane studied the contents. "Looks like animal skin."

"Vellum," confirmed Lauren.

Shane reached for the edges of the Mylar with both hands and pulled it closer. Lauren sat back with an anticipatory and perhaps hopeful expression on her face.

Shane examined the document with a skilled eye. It brought back memories of the many ancient vellum manuscripts he had seen over the years. In fact, he had been shown the honor to examine the three oldest versions of the Bible, known as the Vatican, Sinaitic, and Alexandrian, which dated back to between 300 and 450 C.E. He had also seen the original Dead Sea Scrolls, most of which were on vellum, and he had spent many hours studying their photographs and translations.

His tone exuded authority. "This probably came from a sheep, though it might've just as easily come from a calf or goat. The vellum'll be easy to date, though visually it's hard to do so more accurately than within a few hundred years. Vellum was invented some two hundred years before the time of Jesus because of difficulty getting papyrus out of Egypt. Vellum was easier to write on than papyrus and extremely durable. It was fully capable of lasting centuries or even millennia if preserved properly. Still, for the first few hundred years of its existence it was only used for the most important documents because it was much more expensive than papyrus. Even most of the New Testament books were originally written and distributed on papyrus. It was two hundred years later when they became viewed on par in importance to the Old Testament books that they were transferred to vellum. Vellum eventually displaced papyrus as the dominant medium for writing until it was displaced in turn by paper in the Middle Ages."

Shane paused, and Lauren took advantage. "You sure know a lot about animal skin."

Shane replied with a half-grunt.

The single sheet measured about fifteen inches wide and eleven inches long. The margins were darker than the text-filled middle, though the coloration varied somewhat throughout the sheet. The borders were rough and curled slightly toward the grain. The large block letters were bold, and though they were faded in places, they were still quite legible. There were some stains and a few tears, but the page was in very good condition.

He pointed to the text. "The inscription is Aramaic, the language spoken by Jesus and his disciples. Aramaic, not Hebrew, was the language used by the Jews of Galilee, Judea, and Syria. It's a Semitic tongue, one of the world's oldest continuously spoken languages. At the time of Jesus, Hebrew was a dead language, read but not spoken, much like Latin today. Many of the New Testament books may have been written in Aramaic before being translated into Koine Greek which was the common language of the Roman Empire."

Shane motioned across the page. "Ancient Aramaic was written from right to left filling the page. There was no punctuation or capitalization. Punctuation was implied by the structure. Spacing wasn't used or was inconsistent. Scribes of the first century used a stylus to mark the lines and margins and then filled in the space with straight text."

The page in front of Shane was different. There were two columns of fifteen lines with irregular margins. There was so much empty space, it almost seemed intentionally structured. It was very unusual but at the same time somewhat familiar. Given the quality of appearance and the inaccurate use of space, the document had to be a forgery.

He picked out some Aramaic words and phrases popular at the birth of Christianity, such as *righteousness* and *Kingdom of God.* Someone wanted to pass the document off as an original or copy of a first century text.

Shane did not relish the idea of giving Lauren bad news. "What do you think it is?"

Lauren shook her head. “I’m here because I want you to tell me. I have five more sheets like this one.”

Shane was impressed. “Twelve columns?” He looked back at the scroll. “Many things are consistent with vellum manuscripts from two thousand years ago, but other things aren’t. The vellum and lettering look right and some of the words I can make out are consistent.” He hesitated. “But the spacing and margins are off. They indicate it’s most likely a forgery. The best forgers use real material from the right time. It’s hard to tell much more by just looking at it.”

Lauren did not seem concerned. “My source is very reliable. Why don’t you run it through your own tests and prove it to your satisfaction?”

“I will.” In spite of his better judgment, Shane could not keep his pulse from racing. “You know, there have been other examples of significant finds in recent times. The Gospel of Peter was discovered in 1886 in a monk’s tomb in the town of Akhmimin, Egypt. The most complete Gospel of Thomas in Upper Egypt in 1945. The Gospel of Mary and three other lost works in a Cairo antiquities market in 1947. That same year the first Dead Sea Scrolls near Qumran. The Gospel of Judas in Middle Egypt in 1978. Etcetera.”

Lauren smiled. “It’s hard not to think about the possibilities, isn’t it?”

“Yes, but the likelihood of it being anything like that’s extremely low.”

“Test it.”

Lauren’s confidence indicated she knew more than she was saying.

Shane pressed. “What do you know?”

“Let’s just say I have strong suspicions. I want you to prove them right or wrong.”

He looked back at the page. “Have you translated it?”

“No.”

“Why me?”

Lauren leaned forward and forced Shane to look her in the eyes. “Like I told you yesterday, I need help. And when I asked the best people I could find who I should go to, they sent me to you. I want you to test it, authenticate it, and translate it. Then we’ll decide where to go next. But I don’t have a lot of time. I need you to do it quickly.”

Shane was not satisfied. “What do you know? If you want my help, show me enough respect not to keep me in the dark.”

“It’s not about respect. I don’t want to sway your judgment.”

"Then it *is* about respect."

Lauren seemed to wage an internal debate about how much to say. "What do you know about the Sicarii Gospel?"

Shane was taken aback, surprised by both the reference and that Lauren had used the Latin pronunciation–sih-CAR-ih-ee–rather than the pronunciation most English speakers would use–sih-CAR-ee-eye. Before he could say anything, their waiter returned with their food and placed it on the table. Shane returned the Mylar-enshrouded page to Lauren, who inserted it back in its place in the attaché, covered by her coat.

The waiter looked from one of them to the other. "Is there anything else I can get you?"

Shane replied with a harsher tone than intended. "Bring us two more drinks."

When they were alone again, Shane studied Lauren. She was sampling her food and appeared to be avoiding eye contact. *Was she serious?*

When she looked up, she spoke through a slight grin. "Very good."

"To hell with the Pad Thai! Do you really believe you have a copy of the Sicarii Gospel?"

Chapter 5

Shane sat and waited for Lauren's response.

Before she could speak, their waiter returned with their drinks. "Is there anything else I can bring you?"

Shane's frustration peaked and showed in his tone. "No, we have everything we need. Please give us a few minutes."

The waiter winced and meekly walked away.

Shane's impatience bled through. "Well?"

Lauren repeated her question. "What do you know about it?"

"It's called the Sicarii Gospel because many theologians theorize it contained proof of Jesus' revolutionary intentions. Some believe once Christianity became the Church of Rome, the early church leaders either hid the copies or destroyed them to downplay any intent Jesus and his followers had to rebel against Rome. Or any role Jewish Christians played in the two Jewish-Roman Wars in which Jewish zealots did in fact rebel. I alluded to it in my two books. But you already know that, don't you?"

Lauren flashed a half-smile. "I may have read something about that."

"There were many gospels beyond the four canonical gospels of the New Testament. They form a spectrum with sayings gospels like the Q Gospel and the Gospel of Thomas on the far left and revolutionary gospels like the Gospel of Peter and the Gospel of Judas on the far right. The four gospels in the New Testament are in the center of that spectrum."

He took a bite of his food but continued to talk while he chewed. "When forming the New Testament, the Church censored those gospels too far to the left or right. Some theologians believe there's an undiscovered gospel to the far right which portrays Jesus as a Jewish revolutionary, another in a long line of messiahs wanting to lead the Jews in a war against their Roman conquerors. Some have even claimed a copy of the gospel was found along with the Dead Sea Scrolls but never made public."

Shane paused. "I'm afraid I'm being too academic. It's a curse of having taught college too long."

Lauren shook her head. "No, go on. I want to hear this."

"There's some proof the gospel once existed. There are vague allusions in some of the first Christian commentaries. Then there's a particularly interesting reference in the Gnostic Apocryphon of James, found near the city of Nag Hammadi in Upper Egypt in 1945. The Apocryphon of James states that Jesus confided special knowledge to his brother James before his ascension. James communicated this knowledge in an epistle now called the Apocryphon of James. Some Christians held this special knowledge in such high esteem they formed a new sect called Gnosticism, a powerful competitor to Jewish Christianity and Paul's Christ church in the first century. Gnostics had no use for church leaders because they thought they possessed the knowledge themselves."

Shane took a sip of his drink. "You can imagine what the Roman church leaders thought of the Gnostics. Their gospels were excluded from the official New Testament canon, though some Gnostic beliefs did make it in. For example, parts of the Gospel of John have a Gnostic slant. But back to the Apocryphon of James. In that book, James also references another secret book he sent them previously, only that gospel was so secret he doesn't describe its contents. Some think it may have been the Sicarii Gospel. Have I lost you yet?"

Lauren's eyes beamed. "No, I'm with you."

Shane's excitement escaped in tone and volume. "The Sicarii Gospel was supposed to be in twelve sections, what might appear as twelve columns on a scroll." He gave Lauren a raised eyebrow at the similarity to her document. "It was supposed to lay out Jesus' philosophy, what now might be called his theology, as dictated to his brother James. Supposedly that theology culminated with an appeal for an apocalyptic overthrow of the Romans, similar to what's in Revelation, the last book of the New Testament. Only more explicit."

Shane thought about where to go next. "There were only twelve copies. One was kept in Jerusalem with James. The other eleven were sent to eleven churches established around the world by Jesus' disciples."

Lauren interrupted him. "Twelve copies for twelve disciples?"

Shane had lectured on this topic many times. "There were a lot of disciples that traveled with Jesus. Jesus separated out twelve of them for special instruction. My guess is he chose them for three reasons. First, they were people he could trust. Mostly his bothers, cousins, and best friends. James, his brother, was one of them. It's a common misconception that Jesus' brothers didn't support his beliefs. Second, they were literate, unlike many of Jesus' followers. Third, they spoke multiple languages, a talent very useful in spreading a new theological view among the Jewish communities of the Greco-Roman world. Galilee was the crossroads for many different cultures and languages. In the New Testament, the Galilean disciples demonstrated this capability at Pentecost."

Shane tried not to let his strong opinions take the conversation down a tangent. "The Twelve assumed leadership of the Jewish Christian sect. When Judas Iscariot committed suicide, he was replaced by Matthias, resulting in twelve leaders again. And the leader of the Twelve was Jesus' brother James. Not Peter. Not Paul. James succeeded his brother Jesus, and he distributed the copies of the Sicarii Gospel to the rest of the Twelve."

Lauren broke in again. "What happened to the copies?"

"As the Twelve began to die, the copies were handed down to their successors–to Simon from James in Jerusalem, to Clement from Peter in Rome, to John Mark from Matthew in Alexandria, and so on. Jerome recorded that the Jewish Christians in Pella used a gospel he had just translated to Greek. Epiphanius mentioned the same Jewish Christian gospel and said it was corrupt. Eusebius alluded to a veiled reference by the second century church historian Hegesippus. But most scholars believe if the gospel ever existed, the early Roman Christian Church destroyed any copies. The Jewish Christians of the first two centuries did not believe in the virgin birth and maintained strict adherence to Jewish Law except for the ritual of sacrifice. Not exactly orthodox Roman Catholic beliefs."

Shane leaned back in the booth and gestured with his right arm. "Though who knows for sure what documents remain hidden away in the catacombs of the Vatican museums or in the Vatican archives. Jesus may have been different from the many other would-be messiahs, but he was a revolutionary all the same, and his followers were zealots. He was crucified for sedition against Rome."

Shane threw up both arms as if concluding a point in one of his lectures. "That's why it's called the Sicarii Gospel–after the sicarii, the most feared Jewish zealots. They were assassins who carried small, curved daggers, called *sicae*, under their robes. They were known for leaping out and stabbing their victims in broad daylight in the heart of the city, and then disappearing back into the crowd."

Shane leaned forward and rested his elbows on the table. "The early Church was trying to survive in a Roman world. The Roman historians Tacitus and Sutonius considered Christianity a terrorist movement. Yet a century later it became the official church of the Roman Empire. Having become increasingly non-Jewish, the early Church had no interest in a document that proved its founder to be a crucified Jewish anti-Roman revolutionary. Instead, Jesus became a pacifist, wrongly crucified by the Jews. A copy of the Sicarii Gospel would be potentially very dangerous to the Church, even today."

Lauren smiled broadly. "It seems I came to the right man after all. You *do* know a lot about it."

Shane shook his head. "I know a lot about what it's *supposed* to be. No one knows what it really *is* because no one's seen a copy of it in seventeen or eighteen hundred years. That's probably still the case. What you have here's most likely a forgery. Even if it's genuine, it's probably something else. Another lost gospel or commentary."

"I understand your doubts. That's why I want you to authenticate it."

"It'll take several days just to get a good idea. Perhaps a week. Even then we won't know for sure. The better the forgery, the longer it'll take to disprove it. Are you planning on remaining in town?"

"I'm not going anywhere until we're done. I would like to keep it very quiet though."

"No problem. I understand. Are you staying here at the Hotel Duncan?"

Shane wondered whether his question sounded inappropriate. Lauren did not seem to mind.

"No, I'm staying at the Three Chimneys Inn, just a block up Chapel Street."

"Yes, I know it. All right then. Bring the complete manuscript by my lab right after lunch tomorrow, and we'll put it through the gauntlet. We have space in the Sterling Chemistry Laboratory building up on Science Hill, 124 Prospect Street. Do you think you can find it?"

"I'll find it."

"Let me get the check, and I'll walk you to your hotel."

Lauren signaled for the waiter. "I said it would be my treat. Besides, I probably make a lot more money than you do."

Shane smiled. He loved it when a woman picked up the check.

Chapter 6

Lauren lay in the soft mattress of the mahogany four-poster bed and surveyed her hotel room through the Edwardian bed drapes. The two story 1870 mansion made her feel more like she was visiting a rich uncle than hiding under a false name. The bed rested on a Persian Kashan rug which protected the dark-stained hardwood floors. The furniture in the room included an antique armoire, matching dresser, a table with two overstuffed chairs, and a sofa. A mounted deer's head decorated the wall above the fireplace, and a tapestry of a European hunting scene hung on a side wall.

The room exuded luxury, but it might as well have been a jail cell. Lauren trusted her instincts, and her senses were tingling. She would have felt better if Shane had stayed with her, but she had not tried to seduce him. Too much was at stake for her to risk him not taking her seriously. The gospel was the priority. Anything else was a bonus. Still, if he had pressed to come up, she would have let him.

Upon entering the hotel, Lauren had hurried up the ornate mahogany staircase. She had barely glimpsed the library, parlor, and dining room that gave so much character to the mansion turned hotel. In her room she had changed, checked her many email accounts through the seemingly out of place internet connection, and climbed into bed.

She wondered why she did not feel guiltier about exposing Shane to her danger. *Have I become that calloused, that cold, that hell-bent on solving the mystery of the gospel and reaping its reward? Would I risk the life of a past lover, a man I feel drawn to?* She sighed, rolled over, and turned off the lamp.

Chapter 7

"*Shema Yisrael Adonai Eloheinu Adonai echad.*" Amit David repeated the prayer out loud in English with the utmost sanctity. "Hear, Israel, the Lord is our God; the Lord is One." He emphasized each syllable of his name as he continued. "Ah-meet Dah-veed, this could be it."

He sighed, rubbed his weathered face, and pushed his curly, dark hair back under his wide-brimmed leather hat. He smiled that he had not been fooled by the pleasant Judean Desert morning and had dressed appropriately. The air was already warming, and afternoon temperatures would reach at least thirty-two degrees Celsius.

"Amit David, did you interpret the clues correctly?" He rationalized talking to himself with the belief that anyone who spent comparable time in the desert probably talked to themselves too. Even so, he whispered such that the other members of his team did not hear him. "Yes."

Amit looked past the cliff of his archaeological dig and beyond the light brown, rocky plain to the Khirbet Qumran ruins rising hundreds of meters away. He imagined what the complex was like two thousand years ago when it thrived on a rock-strewn desert bluff overlooking the Dead Sea. Blazoned in his memory was the computer-animated three-dimensional model he had built with the help of some colleagues. He saw the long dining hall used for communal meals, the steps down into the ritual purification baths, and the scriptorium, where some scholars think the Khirbet Qumran residents wrote the Dead Sea Scrolls. Pride surged through him at his role in discovering some of the building foundations and other defining characteristics, such as cisterns, a limestone sundial, a cemetery, and a small pottery jug filled with balsam oil perfume.

Sonic booms interrupted his thoughts as fighter jets split the air above him. A different roar filled the plain beneath him as a line of military vehicles drove down the modern road running about thirty meters below the Khirbet Qumran complex. A tour bus and a few private cars followed.

Amit turned up his nose at the intrusions, and the pressure they symbolized. Standing about sixteen kilometers south of Jericho and forty kilometers east of Jerusalem put him on the West Bank within the borders of a potential Palestinian state. Access may soon be limited. He was running out of time.

He suddenly found it difficult to breathe. He tried not to think about being four hundred meters below sea level and only forty-five meters above the lowest place on earth–the Dead Sea. He found the Dead Sea in the distance merging into the clear blue sky. Then he looked upward and took in the heaviness of the air. On still days, even his two decades of experience in the area did not immunize him from the effect.

He shifted his eyes to the cliffs nearby to the west of the Khirbet Qumran complex. Many difficult-to-reach caves dotted the steep rock walls almost like windows in the rough, eroded sandstone. He could almost see the two young Bedouin goat herders crawling through one of the windows to discover the first Dead Sea Scrolls.

"Doctor David."

Amit turned toward the voice to find Eathan, one of his assistants. The youth stood in his climbing harness with his face contorted into a perplexed expression. Whatever Eathan's issue was, Amit was not ready to focus on it.

"Eathan, did you know the two Bedouin boys who found the first Dead Sea Scrolls had difficulty selling them?"

Eathan's perplexity turned to frustration. "Of course, Doctor David. But..."

"They hung them from a tent for who knows how long before finally selling four of the scrolls for two hundred fifty dollars. In fact, there was so much confusion about the scrolls and who should own and study them that no one knows how many were destroyed by the Bedouins for fuel or sold to private collectors."

"I know, Doctor David, but..."

Amit held up his hand to interrupt Eathan again. "Can you imagine their excitement when the first archaeologists determined the age of the scrolls? And what about their wonder when they first read them? Imagine seeing copies of books of the Old Testament one thousand years older than any texts previously known to exist."

"Doctor David, please." Eathan's eyes pleaded for his attention.

"All right, Eathan. "What is it?"

"We need your help. Please come with me."

Amit followed Eathan toward where four other young members of his team were putting the finishing touches on a rigging that extended over and down the edge of the cliff. When completed, the rigging would hold a ladder down to a platform that would represent the physical manifestation of two years of work, the discovery of Amit's life.

He wondered if Roland de Vaux of the French Dominican École Biblique felt the same pride and apprehension as he entered five caves found by Bedouins and six caves discovered by archaeologists to find about nine hundred documents hidden in clay jars and preserved in the arid climate. He imagined de Vaux's excitement as he read the commentaries on the Old Testament books, histories, hymns, psalms, apocalyptic visions, and rules of behavior for a non-rabbinical aesthetic religious sect.

He whispered to himself as they walked. "Amit David, did you interpret the clues correctly?"

His nervousness stemmed from his break with traditional methods. He could not help but think about it and relive his choices. Like drilling for oil, determining where to dig was as much art as science. Once the location was determined, the real tedium began laying out the dig into grids of one-meter squares with pegs and string, assigning field personnel to grids, selecting the appropriate tools to use, establishing procedures for digging and recording anything found. Most of his digging had occurred by hand. Pickaxes broke up compacted soil. Shovels, spades, and wheelbarrows cleared away the loose dirt. Trowels and paint brushes completed the finer work. These archaeological methods systemically destroyed the dig site layer by layer, many times without finding anything of interest.

Though he had done his job that way for twenty years, for this dig he had used more modern methods. Instead of digging exploratory holes and trenches, he had used ground-penetrating radar. Pushing a small, wheeled cart carrying light weight equipment, he had mapped the entire dig site in a single day. An antenna transmitted short, low frequency pulses into the ground and received and registered their echoes. Using the elapsed time before the reflections returned, a computer system interpreted the echoes and correlated the readings to form a three-dimensional image of a hollow area right where Amit had predicted it would be.

The hollow area was once a cave about ten meters long, three meters wide and four meters high, tapering downward to its most inward end. The entrance had been about five meters down from the top of the cliff and about twenty-five meters from the plain below. Over time, erosion had collapsed the roof of the entrance and filled in the opening with rock and dust.

His uncertainty resulted from immaturity of the technology. Enough clutter remained in the images that he would not know for sure what he had discovered until he dug a hole to reveal it. The rigging and platform would allow him to break through the outer wall.

When they reached the edge of the cliff, Eathan pointed to the rigging. "We are having some issues. We need your approval of the changes we are making."

"Eathan, you can make this kind of decision yourself. I trust your abilities. You should too."

"Doctor David, this is too important."

"Eathan, the treasure has waited two thousand years. It is not going anywhere."

Chapter 8

Shane woke up to the alarm from his iPhone and rolled to a sitting position on the side of his bed. He sat there naked, head in hands, summoning all his strength to stand up and start the day. He had not slept well. All he could think about was the sudden appearance of Lauren and the gospel.

The previous night had ended with a peck on Lauren's cheek at the entrance of the Three Chimneys Inn. He had been conflicted then and remained that way now. Lauren had sent signals an advance might be accepted, perhaps even desired. He enjoyed her touchy-feeliness and the way she bumped and rubbed against him as they walked. But Shane was not comfortable mixing business with a romantic relationship. He might soon have to tell her she had been duped into spending a lot of money on a fake. That kind of news tended to throw water on the fires of passion.

Shane replayed the image of the vellum page again and again as if the two columns of Aramaic characters had been seared on his eyes. One question echoed in his head. *Could the scroll be real?* Each time the answer came back the same. *No way. I'm just torturing myself.*

Shane decided not to follow his daily regimen of a jog to the Yale University fitness center followed by thirty minutes lifting weights and a jog home. *Not today.* He stood up, stretched, and walked toward the bathroom. The air felt good on his exposed body. A shower would feel even better.

Entering the bathroom, he reached into the shower stall and turned on the hot water. Then he went to the sink, turned on the cold water, and splashed it onto his face. Standing up straight, he let the water drip down his body while the sleep cleared. He turned to enter the shower, but before he could do so, he heard the Indiana Jones ringtone from his iPhone on the bed.

"Crap!"

He turned the shower off and returned to the summoning phone.

"Hello?"

A young male voice responded. "Doctor Randall?"

"Yes."

"This is John Willis."

The tone in the voice implied Shane should recognize the name. Shane searched his memory for a face. Nothing came to mind.

"I worked with Marcus Quinn."

Shane remembered. Shane and Quinn had worked some sites in Israel together until Quinn set Shane up to take a smuggling charge. Deserting Shane to take the fall, Quinn had escaped the country with a number of artifacts dating back to the Hasmonean dynasty. Fortunately for Shane, the Israeli authorities proved his innocence. But Shane had lost someone he had considered a friend. Since then, Quinn had been at best a competitor, at worst an enemy.

Shane's top lip curled upward at the thought of what Quinn was now–a *commercial archaeologist*, a treasure hunter backed by big money from investors with the objective of locating gold, silver, and other artifacts for profit. Though Shane recognized there were rare cases when the risk-filled ventures had been successful and immensely profitable, commercial archaeologists like Quinn were known far more for conning investors into projects that never found anything. When they had consumed the money, they convinced their clients the loss was an unfortunate consequence of the risk.

Even when successful, there were often uncommunicated legal issues. Though in international waters the finding team might keep ninety percent of the value of their loot, more often governments entangled the commercial archaeologists with claims of illegal looting, piracy, and theft of the countries' cultural history. Finds within country boundaries involved negotiation in which the country held the strongest position. The percentage retained by the finding team was much smaller, on the order of ten percent. It was a shady stratum of archaeology that Shane found distasteful.

Last fall, Shane ran into Quinn at a Red Sox game at Fenway Park. John Willis was with him and introduced himself. Shane ignored the younger man and, like a boxer before a fight, stood glaring at Quinn while calculating whether he was worth the embarrassment of a public brawl, being thrown out of the game, and perhaps jail. Quinn seemed to recognize Shane's internal debate and sat looking up at him with a half-daring smirk. Above all else, Shane wanted to knock that grin off Quinn's face. Ultimately Shane's good sense won out. He told Quinn he could do something anatomically impossible to himself and walked off.

Shane's voice was dry and emotionless. "I remember you." He wanted no renewed association with Marcus Quinn or anyone close to him.

"I thought you should know Quinn's dead."

"What? How?"

"He was murdered yesterday afternoon. I know you weren't on good terms, but you two were once friends. And Quinn didn't have many friends. And no family. Someone should know."

Shane was torn. A person he knew had died. He should feel something. "How'd it happen?"

"A security guard found him in a warehouse in South Boston near Fort Point. He had been beaten to death."

"That's horrible"

"Yes, it was quite gruesome. The police have no leads, and I doubt they'll find who did it. I'm having the body cremated on Friday. There'll be a short ceremony if you're interested."

Shane was not. "I can't make it." After a brief pause, he continued. "Thank you for calling though."

"Well. I don't want to bother you any more than I have. I just needed to tell someone. Quinn rubbed a lot of people the wrong way, but he was always straight with me. He didn't deserve to go out like this."

The click on the other end of the line indicated the conversation was over. Shane was not surprised Quinn's life had ended in violence. The world was a better place with Quinn not in it. Shane threw the iPhone on the bed and turned back to his shower. He needed one now more than ever.

Chapter 9

Doctor Samuel Evans sat in his Harvard Divinity School office examining the eleventh century commentary on the Exodus from Egypt by the Talmudic scholar Rashi. It was a rare find indeed. His frail body could not contain his excitement. He shook to the point he had to adjust his wire-rimmed glasses back to their correct position on his long, slender nose. His glasses were often falling off because the back of his head was larger than the front, making his face appear small in comparison to the size of this head. He rubbed his hand through his disheveled gray hair that encircled an expanding bald spot like a crown on his bulbous head. Then he wiped his hand on his pin-striped gray suit, the same suit he wore every day with a white shirt and thin black tie.

Facing the window, Evans carefully maneuvered the manuscript on his desk surface between the computer monitor to his left, the stack of ungraded research papers to his right, and the stacks of dust-covered books covering everywhere else. The tall bookcases against the walls to both sides made him feel small but also secure as he labored.

He was so into the work in front of him, he barely heard the door open and close behind him. Waving his arm above his head in recognition he had a visitor, he never took his eyes from the ancient text. "Please come back later. Consultation is from three to five."

He received no response but heard footsteps in his direction. *Was I not clear?* He began a spin around, but before he could complete the turn, a massive black hand reached around his neck from the right side. It held something that reflected the light from the window. Another enormous hand from his left grabbed his forehead and held his head in place against the rock-hard abs of his assailant. He felt the cold pressure of something sharp against his throat, and he sucked in air through clenched teeth. His eyes filled the rims of his glasses.

The man behind him spoke in a strong French accent. "*Où est la femme?* Where is the woman?"

Too terrified to move anything else, Evans' eyes pendulated back and forth. *What is he talking about? This must be a mistake!* He unclenched his jaw and panted a whisper. "What woman?"

It had been decades since he had been accused of improper actions with a woman. Was he a jealous husband? *Surely he can see there's no cause.*

The pressure against his neck increased followed by a sharp pain as his skin separated slightly. He exhaled a series of short screams that turned into whimpers. He froze in place, with every muscled tensed.

The French-accented voice behind him was calm in comparison. "*S'il vous plaît.* Do not make me press harder. I know the woman brought you the gospel. Did she leave it?"

I know who he means! She came to his office much as the man behind him had. He did not stand up, even as she walked up to within a few feet of him. She sought the foremost authority to analyze a supposed lost gospel and thought he might be that person.

She spoke in a deep southern drawl. "Doctor Evans, can ya'll help me with my manuscript. My husband bought it for me, but he's always out of town. He told me it's the real McCoy, but I want to know for sure. It'd be just so wonderful if it were valuable. I've talked to ever so many people, and I'm fixin' to run out of options. I'd be *very* grateful if you'd give me your opinion." Then she bent over and put her hand on his leg just above the knee, exposing some cleavage through the top of her blouse. "Are you the man I need?"

He did not take her seriously. No document acquired in such a way could be worth his time. And her advances were pointless. He had lost interest in such things long ago. He never even asked for her name. He sent her to waste someone else's time.

The man behind him pressed the sharp edge deeper into his throat. *My god, he's crazy!* His time was running out. He shouted the information that would save his life.

"I sent her to Doctor Shane Randall at Yale Divinity School! She seemed to recognize the name. I never saw the gospel."

There was a blur of movement and then no more pressure. As he heard the door close, Evans felt the pain and realized he could not breathe. Grabbing his throat with both hands, he saw the blood gushing through his fingers onto the manuscript and the desk. Panicking, he stood up, turned, and reached for the door. He only took a few steps before stumbling to the floor.

Chapter 10

Having made it through his morning class and a quick lunch, Shane paced in the outer office of his lab. He had plenty of space in the thirty by twenty feet office as long as he avoided the desks and file cabinets. Each time he passed the translucent upper halves of the doors to the hall and adjacent lab he tried to discern any motion behind. After a while he began counting his steps and using the number to mark the passage of time.

The hall door swung inward, and Shane rushed to hold it open. As Lauren entered carrying the leather attaché, he breathed in her perfume. "Glad you could make it."

Lauren gestured to the attaché. "Where do you want me to put this?"

Before Shane could answer, the lab door opened and out walked his young assistant. Shane noted how studious she looked with her thick-lensed dark glasses on her round face surrounded by short, dark hair. She wore jeans, a Greenpeace tee shirt that said *Save The Frickin' Whales*, and latex gloves to prevent the transfer of acid from finger prints to the documents she handled.

"This is my assistant, Jane Roman," Shane said to Lauren. Then in an exaggerated twang, he said, "She speaks Aramaic like you speak Texan." Back in his normal voice he said, "She may be the best Aramaic translator in the world. She also helps take care of the over one million priceless documents in our Beinecke Rare Book and Manuscript Library, even a Gutenberg Bible. Our museum's so protective of our manuscripts it doesn't even have glass windows. It uses translucent marble." Shane caught himself. "I'm rambling. Jane, this is Lauren Mallory."

Jane removed the glove from her right hand and extended it. "Just once I'd like to be introduced without a lecture."

Lauren laughed and took Jane's hand. "I know what you mean."

Shane pretended to have his feelings hurt. "There are a lot of places better than this one I could go to get picked on." Then with a flirtatious smile he said, "Good thing I like strong women."

Jane chuckled and put her glove back on. "You're all talk, Doctor Randall." Turning to Lauren, she asked, "What do you have in the bag?"

Lauren bent over, opened the attaché and removed a cardboard bundle. Between the sheets of cardboard were six Mylar-encased vellum pages. Lauren laid the stack in Jane's outstretched arms and removed the top sheet of cardboard.

Jane's eyes lit up. "*Jubilation, she loves me again!*"

Lauren turned to Shane with raised eyebrows and questioning eyes.

Shane shrugged his shoulders. "Jane has what some might consider a quirk. When she gets excited she quotes Paul Simon lyrics." Shane took a step to stand shoulder to shoulder with Jane. "Explain to Ms. Mallory what you're going to do. She might want to know you're not going to damage her manuscript."

Jane spoke with authority. "We're going to put it through a battery of tests. Carbon-14 dating, ink analysis, pollen analysis, vellum preparation, the shape of the letters, style and method of writing and sentence construction, dialect of Aramaic used, etc., etc."

Lauren's eyes widened and her lips formed a half-smile. "Dialect of Aramaic?"

Shane replied for Jane. "We know what dialect of Aramaic was spoken in Galilee during Jesus' and James' lifetimes. Aramaic has been spoken for over three thousand years. We say *Aramaic* like it's a single language, but really it's more like a group of closely related languages. Like the Romance languages, Spanish, Italian, and French. Or the Germanic languages like German, Danish, and Dutch."

Shane saw a slight frown replace Lauren's half smile. "There were seven dialects of Western Aramaic spoken in and around the Roman province of Palestine in Jesus' time. Galilean Aramaic was different from Samaritan Aramaic which was different from Old Judean Aramaic. They could all understand each other, but they pronounced the words with slight differences. They would have known immediately where the speaker was from. There's an example in the gospels when Peter is recognized by the Judeans because of his Galilean dialect and he is forced to deny Jesus three times. Like modern Judeans we can determine whether the Aramaic on the scroll is consistent with the supposed author."

Lauren's smile returned. "Very impressive. Vellum preparation?"

Jane took her turn to reply. "As you know, vellum was made from animal skin. The skin was soaked in baths of various compositions and then smoothed and dehaired by scraping it with pumice. The wet skin was dried under tension to create a smooth surface which was polished on the flesh facing side as a medium for writing. The composition of the baths varied by region. Traces still existing in the vellum'll tell us where it was made. Also, after the second century, lime was added to the skin as a preservative. Before that time, no lime."

"Extremely impressive. What about the ink."

Jane pumped both fists. "Oh, that's really cool. We'll use micro X-ray fluorescence, a mass spectrometer, and a scanning electron microscope to identify the composition of the ink. Trace elements in the ink'll be like a fingerprint to pinpoint the region of origin and general timing. That combined with the vellum preparation, the carbon dating, and any embedded pollen grains'll tell us quite a story. This is going to be fun."

Lauren seemed pleased. "I've obviously come to the right place."

Shane shook his head. "Well, don't be too impressed. Even with all that, it'll be difficult to tell whether it's authentic or a good forgery. It'll definitely rule out an obvious fake. But the best forgers anticipate those tests and use materials that'll pass them."

Jane scolded him. "Don't be a pessimist." Then to Lauren, she said, "We promise not to damage the pages. Only the Carbon-14 dating requires the sacrifice of a very small piece of the vellum. Much of the analysis will be done with photographs."

Shane put a hand on Lauren's upper arm. "Let's get the manuscript into the lab. Then we can get out of Jane's way and let her get to work."

They turned toward the lab door, and Shane reached around the two women to open it. The light in the lab was bright. While their eyes adjusted, they stood on the sticky mat designed to remove dust and dirt from the bottoms of shoes.

Shane's lab was a great source of pride. He quickly inspected the room to ensure everything was clean and orderly. Extending in front of them, the three long rows of near chest high stainless steel and glass work surfaces contained a variety of different style workstations on both sides of a center divider. Computer screens and microscopes dotted the surfaces, and an exhaust vent for vapors connected one station on each of the three rows to the ceiling. In the center of the far wall was a large vault with its door closed, flanked on each side by storerooms. Along each side wall were different types of large equipment, refrigerated storage areas, and file cabinets. Shane returned the acknowledgement of Jane's three lab assistants. Everything was perfect.

Shane followed Jane and Lauren down the left center aisle about midway through the room to a covered workstation. The examination surface was spotless glass. Next to it lay a tray of archivist tools, including a stainless steel spatula and pincers called finger cymbals because they looked like oversized tweezers with flattened discs on each arm. Jane flipped a switch that turned off the overhead lights in that area. Hitting another switch turned on a black light mounted in the workstation.

"*Hello darkness my old friend!*"

Jane slowly laid the delicate package on the work surface. With even more care, she separated the Mylar-protected vellum pages from their cardboard protectors and laid them side by side. It was the first time Shane had seen all twelve columns, and he experienced déjà vu. Without thinking, he reached out to turn the pages to see them better.

Jane slapped his hand. "*Parsley, sage, rosemary and thyme!* You two get out of here."

As Shane turned to leave, he could see the concern in Lauren's wide-open eyes. Jane must have as well because she began reassuring her.

"Don't worry, Ms. Mallory. I'll be careful with your manuscript. The black light allows me to identify anomalies without the damage white light can do. When I'm done for the day, I'll lock it in our vault. It'll be quite safe."

Shane leaned in close to Lauren's ear. "Let's go. I have something to show you."

"All right."

As they turned for the door, Shane called back to Jane. "We'll check with you in the morning. Try to have some good news for us."

"You know I'll do my best."

Shane led Lauren back through the lab door to the closest desk in the outer office. He sat in the leather chair and logged on to the computer and then to the university intranet. "Your vellum pages are about fifteen inches wide and eleven inches long. They have some staining and some tears along the borders but are generally in excellent shape." He shifted his position and turned the monitor such that Lauren could better see the screen. "Look at this. It's a picture of the early fragments found of the Gospel of Peter. As you can see, they're small, torn, rough, and stained." Using the mouse, he backed out of that image and clicked on another. "And here are some pictures of the Dead Sea Scroll fragments. They're small, just a few inches wide and eight to ten inches long at best. They're stained, worn at the edges, and have holes."

Shane paused and examined Lauren. He was not getting through. "Vellum is animal skin. It's very sensitive to moisture changes. It expands when it absorbs water and shrinks when its water evaporates. The net effect of all this wear is that it wrinkles and puckers. Many of the inks of the time were corrosive, which means over time they would eat into the vellum and fade. Print on vellum doesn't last thousands of years in an easily readable form without very strict climate control."

Shane caught himself before diverging into a lecture on his archaeology pet peeves. "Your vellum document's in pages. It may have originally been a scroll someone cut up, or it may have started as pages organized into a codex like a modern day book. Anyway, here's my question."

Lauren laughed. "I knew a question was coming eventually."

Shane tried to be serious. "Why, if your scroll's genuine, is it in such good condition?"

"I can't explain it. I can only guess someone understood its importance and preserved it."

Shane let his question go for the moment. "The fact is we may never know for sure. Carbon-14 dating can only tell us *when* the vellum was prepared, not *when* the gospel was written. The composition of the soaking baths can tell us *where* the vellum was prepared, but not *where* it was written on. The Shroud of Turin has been through test after test and evaluated by scores of great minds, and scientists are still split. Valid and invalid test results can be explained away. All we can do is go through the entire battery and make our best scientific guess. Then we publish and let other scientists give their opinion. Often authenticity is a matter of belief, or even faith."

"I want your opinion. Then we can discuss where we go next."

Shane understood. "Speaking of where we go from here. How about dinner tonight at the Anchor? I burn a lot of calories when I think."

"Sounds great."

"I'll meet you in the lobby of your hotel at eight, and we'll walk down Chapel Street from there. Tonight's my treat. Dress is very casual."

"I'll be ready."

Chapter 11

The sun was setting as Raphael passed through the door of Our Lady of Victories Catholic Church. Located in the heart of Boston's Black Bay hotel and business district about a block from the Park Plaza Hotel where Raphael and his father were staying, it was a Marist church built in the late nineteenth century by French immigrants. The Marist order of priests, founded in France in 1816 by Jean-Claude Courveille, was so called because of the priests' special devotion to Mary, the mother of Jesus.

After kneeling and crossing himself, Raphael entered the nave, but paused in admiration of the fourteen beautiful stained-glass windows that decorated the sides and depicted the life of Mary. Three more large stained-glass windows adorned the sanctuary at the far end. In the center of the sanctuary was a marble altar brought to the church in 1892. The original wooden ceiling had long since been hidden by a plaster ceiling which gave the church a gothic look.

Raphael had seen many cathedrals designed to show man's reverence for God. He never ceased to be amazed how each of them could be so different yet so equal in their inspiration of awe. But Our Lady of Victories was also a French national church. He had entered France, just as surely as if he had transported to a village in the French countryside.

He had killed three men in as many days, but his conscious was clean. Heretics did not deserve God's love or mercy. Such blessings were reserved for the true believers of God's Church. The Church was the earthly incarnation of Christ's body. Any challenge to the Church affronted Christ, and such blasphemy could not be tolerated. He and his father were doing God's work. It was only appropriate they meet in a church dedicated to the Virgin Mary by whose good graces the Dominican Order was founded.

Towering over the wooden pews, Raphael walked down the center aisle until he reached the third pew on the right where his father sat a few feet from the aisle. Hunched in prayer, his father looked even shorter, paler, and slighter than normal. With his almost bald head, closely trimmed crown of dark hair, and clenched eyes behind wire-rimmed glasses, he looked older than his years. His almost kneeling positioned exaggerated his drooping shoulders. Most people would not have guessed what an esteemed French priest and archaeologist he was.

Raphael sat in the pew, which announced his presence with creaks and groans. While he waited for his father's prayers to end, he remembered how his father had found him as a young teenager on the streets of Fort-de-France, Martinique. At that time, Raphael was more animal than man. He had no family and no name. He lived in filth and stole and murdered to survive. The only women he had ever known were the ones he had raped and killed.

His father had seen the man in the animal. He had seen how the powerful youth's talents could be used for good rather than evil. He had forgiven his sins, converted him, and adopted him into his family. He had become his mentor and taught him right from wrong, when violence was justified and when not. He had given him the name Raphael, after the powerful archangel. The name meant *it is God who heals.* When Raphael took a heretic's life, he was healing the body of Christ. When he sent a heretic's soul to Hell, he was paving the path for other souls to Heaven.

His father opened his eyes but directed them at the altar. "*L'évangile?*"

"*Non,*" Raphael replied. He did not have the gospel.

"*Le professeur?*"

Raphael flattened his right hand and slid it right to left across his throat. His father sighed. Then he continued in their native tongue. "The body count is getting too high. The police will find the connection."

Raphael protested. "She took the gospel to Docteur Shane Randall at Yale University. I will find the woman and the gospel there."

"No, it is time for another approach."

Raphael cursed under his breath. "*Merde!*" Still, he dared not question his father.

"Patience, my son. God will deliver her to us."

His father was always right. The woman was more elusive and street smart than they had expected, but God and his Church would prevail.

His pulse quickened at the thought of finding the woman. He had already played out a dozen different scenarios in his mind, each of them designed to give him intense pleasure and her intense pain. The woman would regret stealing from the Vraie École Biblique.

His father must have sensed his thoughts. "My son, when the Vraie École Biblique broke off from the École Biblique, it did not do so to become a harbinger of death. We are the hand of God."

Raphael knew the story well. The École Biblique, or more formally, the *École Biblique et Archéologique Française de Jérusalem*, came to secular fame in 1949, when the British director of antiquities in Jordan and the Jordanian government entrusted it with collecting, translating, and studying the Dead Sea Scrolls. Founded in 1890 in Jerusalem by Dominicans, the École Biblique was located near an ancient church that since the year 439 had housed the remains of Saint Stephen. Their specialty was the analysis of biblical texts.

The École Biblique exercised so much control over the interpretation and publishing of the Dead Sea Scrolls they came under attack. Their critics charged them with slowing the availability of the scrolls to others for study. They questioned their ethics and whether they were abusing their exclusive rights. They accused them of being biased and anti-Semitic, unfit to handle material that might hold content contrary to Church doctrine. The implication was they were trying to control the translation and interpretation of the scrolls.

The Vraie École Biblique believed such control a necessity. It was imperative only the true interpretation of the Dead Sea Scrolls and other so called *lost gospels* reach the masses. History contained millions of deaths resulting from conflicts over biblical translations.

The Vraie École Biblique became a necessity in the early 1970's when Roland de Vaux died and Father Pierre Benoit of the École Biblique became project director over the Dead Sea Scrolls. He vowed to cooperate with Israeli authorities to bring the scrolls to publication. In opposition, the original leader of the Vraie École Biblique focused his attention on blocking that publication. He succeeded in doing so for another twenty years. The institution's purview now included all non-canonical writings.

"I can make Docteur Randall talk," Raphael insisted. "I always make them talk."

"The Directeur is getting impatient and nervous the situation is getting out of control. These are emotions we do not want from the Directeur. I will go with you to visit this Docteur Randall. He is a teacher of the Bible. He may help us. If we are fortunate, the woman will be with him. If not, one way or the other, he will lead us to her."

Raphael's father was wise, but Raphael was a predator. He was closing in on his prey and craved the kill. Still, he nodded his head to indicate he understood. He honored his father too much to rebel.

He also feared the Directeur. The Directeur was well-connected and held the power of excommunication, Raphael's only fear. As long as he acted as an instrument of the Church, he was guaranteed an eternity in paradise. He could apply his special skills to advance the Church's agenda while satisfying his darker urges. Rewards would be his in heaven. Excommunication meant no paradise in the afterlife and the torment of hell in its place. Raphael had been to hell and had no desire to return.

Chapter 12

Shane and Lauren leaned back in the well-worn black leather booth and waited for their drinks to arrive. Shane had selected the Anchor partially because of its dim lighting, laid-back atmosphere, and juke box music and partially because the liquor-induced clamor and bustle of movement precluded anyone from overhearing private words.

Lauren wore tight jeans with a lighter denim shirt and her wavy hair casually resting on her shoulders. Shane was not immune to the effect. When the waiter arrived with their drinks, Shane asked him to leave them alone until he signaled him they were ready to order.

Lauren raised her glass for a toast. "To discovering history."

Shane touched his glass to hers. "To discovering history."

They each drank from their glass and put them back on the table.

Shane had an agenda. "As you know. I'm prone to lecturing. You, on the other hand, are prone to sharing very little."

"Really?"

"I have a proposition for you."

Lauren eyed him flirtatiously. "This is sounding better all the time."

With not a little discipline Shane continued. "If we're going to work together, we need to exchange what we know. In about fifteen minutes I can give you everything you need to know to understand the significance of the Sicarii Gospel. If I do that, you have to give me at least a few minutes on what you know about your document."

Lauren quipped with a smirk and a twinkle in her eye. "So you're going to give me my own private course? And in exchange you expect me to open up to you?"

Shane nodded, unsure of what her response would be.

"Sounds fair."

Shane exhaled in relief. "Great. The easiest way for me to summarize what you need to know is by way of negatives. Much of what you've heard from the Church over the last seventeen hundred years just isn't true. Or at least it's only one version of the truth. A trait of the early Church was its loyalty to its core ideals while it changed the shell around them."

"What do you mean by that?"

"The first Christian church was one hundred percent Jewish. Then, with the ministry of Paul, it became increasingly Greek and increasingly persecuted by the Romans. A little over two centuries later, it *was* Roman with a new Christian emperor highly involved in what it meant to be a Christian. The Church morphed to survive."

"I see."

"At the Council of Nicaea in 325, the Christians had to give Constantine something he'd accept in order for Christianity to become the official religion of the Roman Empire. On the other hand, they were well-intentioned Christians who wouldn't stray from their founder's teachings. So they stayed true to the core while defining what was orthodox, but they packaged it in myth that appealed to the emperor and other powerful Romans."

Shane paused again. "Do you know my book, *The Twelve Myths of Christianity*?"

Lauren nodded.

"Have you read it?"

Lauren lowered her eyes. "I meant to but I just haven't ..."

Shane raised his hand palm outward to stop her. "Doesn't matter. I'm going to give you a summary version right now."

"You mean like a book on CD?"

"Yes. Only a highly abridged version. Myth number one: Jesus' message was directed to both Jews and non-Jews. Wrong. White supremacists and neo-Nazis might not want to believe it, but Jesus was a Jew, and he directed his teachings to Jews.

"During Jesus' lifetime, the Roman standard and non-Jewish influences were everywhere. The Romans named their province *Palestine* after the Philistines, who had inhabited the coastal areas. Galilee in particular was populated by non-Jews because invading conquerors had long before removed Jews from that region. It had only been a few decades or so before Roman control that the Maccabees had established a number of Jewish settlements in the area. Not unlike what Israel has done in recent years in the West Bank.

"So Jesus' home was a crossroads for every nationality of the Roman Empire and beyond. Jews were the minority. That means Jesus grew up around non-Jews his entire life. Yet, in the gospels, Jesus compares non-Jews to dogs and swine. He tried to avoid traveling through Samaria because he considered them half-Jews. Jesus had to have seen how sinful and lost the non-Jews were, but he had no interest in ministering to them.

"It was Paul who first discovered the receptivity of the non-Jews after being turned away by the Jewish communities of the Greco-Roman provinces. Many Greeks and Romans found Judaism attractive because they found the idea of gaining access to one omnipotent God who created the world, defined morality, and actively participated in men's lives very appealing. And it was inexpensive and easy to convert, unlike many other competitive religions of the day such as Mithraism which required the sacrifice of a bull. The only deterrent was the men had to circumcise their penises. No small hurdle for Paul to overcome.

"But Paul was not the leader of the early Christian Church. So he had to get approval for his non-Jewish mission from James, who knew Jesus better than anyone and was carrying on his ministry. In a historic ruling, James decided the non-Jewish converts did not have to become Jews but they had to follow the rules applied to *god-fearers*. God-fearers were non-Jews who wanted to convert to Judaism but did not want to undergo circumcision of their penises. The rules for god-fearers were established in the Old Testament Jewish Law. They worshipped as a Jew but did not have all the religious rights of a Jew. James stayed true to Jewish Law, and ironically, now every Christian is a Jew wannabe."

Lauren looked puzzled. "Weren't Jews and Christians always at odds?"

"Not at all. Christianity *was* Jewish. And most of the Jewish authorities saw it as a harmless sect. Which brings me to myth number two: Jesus wanted to form a new religion to replace Judaism. Jesus said repeatedly he had not come to replace the Law of the Jews but to fulfill it. He definitely wanted to reform the Jewish Temple-state, but within Judaism. He was one of a growing group of Jews who resented they could only get forgiveness for their sins by paying to sacrifice an offering at the Temple in Jerusalem. Difficult and expensive to do from Galilee or elsewhere in the Roman Empire.

"Jesus and others like him abhorred the way the priests were in league with their rulers who they saw as corrupt and ungodly. The rulers of the province made up less than one percent of the population but owned fifty percent of the land and took in well over half of the province's income. The rulers legitimized the priests, and the priests legitimized the rulers, and both became very wealthy at the expense of the peasants."

Lauren sighed in disgust. "Not unlike many places around the world today."

"Jesus, John the Baptist, and others found the system offensive and began offering alternatives to the priesthood-controlled sacrifices. An alternative would have provided greater opportunity for forgiveness while leaving more money in the peasants' hands. John the Baptist offered immersion. Jesus took it a step further. He wanted Jews to live as if they were already in the Kingdom of God in a direct relationship with God as their father and ruler. But he was still a Jew worshipping within the religion of Judaism.

"In fact, Jesus would have abhorred some common practices and symbols of Christianity. For example, he would have seen a crucifix as a graven image forbidden by God. He would have compared hanging a crucifix in a church or house to idol worship."

The side of Lauren's mouth curled up in disbelief. "If that's true, then why doesn't the Church teach these things?"

"Because religion is like a tree. It grows and changes shape over the years. Sometimes the changes are natural. Sometimes the result of pruning. But at any point in time people see the shape it's in then. They don't see it the way it was decades earlier. And they surely don't care about the roots.

"Myth number three: Jesus was illiterate. Many scholars make that assertion because over ninety-five percent of the population was illiterate and learned orally. They ignore that Luke in his gospel has Jesus reading from the book of Isaiah. They also discount the non-canonical letter from Jesus to the King of Edessa some tie to the Shroud of Turin. And that if Jesus was an Essene, the Essenes educated their children.

"Then there's Jesus' brother James. Josephus recorded James was such a powerful rival to the High Priest he could've become High Priest had he not been murdered. James was so popular that when the Romans destroyed the Jewish Temple, the common belief among the Jewish people was it was punishment for his murder. This wasn't an illiterate man. If James was literate, why wouldn't we conclude Jesus was?"

Lauren reached out and touched Shane's hand. "Why's that significant one way or the other?"

"Because literacy adds a dimension to everything Jesus and the leaders that followed him did that goes way beyond rabble following a peasant. Gospels take on symbolic and hidden meanings the illiterate could never imagine. Religious theology takes on scope and depth that an uneducated peasant could never dream."

"I see your point."

"Myth number four: Jesus wasn't political. The gospels show Jesus was a zealot claiming to be the Messiah. The Messiah wasn't a religious title. It was a political and military title. It was the warrior king in the model of David. Do you know the Messiah is mentioned more often in the Jewish Hebrew Bible than any person other than God?"

"No, I didn't."

"The Jewish Messiah wasn't the Greco-Roman redeeming Christ. He was a warrior who, with God's miraculous help, would free the Jews. In that vein, it wasn't blasphemy to call yourself the Messiah. Defeat the Romans and return self-rule to the Jews, and you were the Messiah. If you didn't, you were just another revolutionary making a false claim. In addition to Jesus, there were at least eleven other would-be messiahs in the first century. Every one of their movements ended with their deaths."

"I had no idea."

"That's not unusual. The Church would have you believe that Jesus was the only messiah claimant and was executed for his claim. But that's nowhere near the truth. The Romans had messiahs springing up all over Palestine. Since Galilee was far away from Jerusalem and the Roman strongholds, it was a major spawning ground for revolutionaries. And would-be messiahship tended to run in families with multiple generations making the claim. Who knows, it's possible Jesus' father Joseph died fighting the Romans."

"You're kidding!"

Shane shrugged his shoulders. "There's no way to know for sure. But if you believe that Jesus was a revolutionary, then it's highly likely Joseph was too."

Shane paused and took a sip of his drink. "My point is claiming to be the Messiah wasn't blasphemy. Even claiming to be the son of God wasn't that unusual. There was already a son of God ruling the Jewish world, and he had ushered in an era of peace that had lasted decades. Since Julius Caesar had been officially declared a god, Augustus Caesar was the son of God. And since Augustus was declared divine, Tiberius Caesar was also the son of God."

Shane took another sip of his drink. "Of course, Jesus presented himself as a different kind of messiah, one who preached the Kingdom of God could be experienced on earth and Jews could be free even while still under the Roman yoke. That if they lived correctly, God would usher in his kingdom, first subtly and then in an apocalyptic upheaval. So while resisting opportunities for violence, at least until the time was right,

Jesus told his followers he had come not to bring peace but the sword. But regardless of how he couched the claim, he knew when he said he was the Messiah he was talking in political terms. That's why he cautioned his followers from calling him the Messiah in public before he was ready to do so. Do you remember when Jesus entered Jerusalem in triumph sitting on the donkey?"

"Passover, I think."

"Good for you. That's exactly what the gospels imply. But it isn't true. He entered during the Jewish Feast of the Tabernacles in autumn. Passover is in spring. That means Jesus was in Jerusalem for at least seven months before his death. We know this because of the description of the palm branches and singing of Hosannas, which accompanied the Feast of the Tabernacles but not Passover. There's also the accompanying story of the barren fig tree, which could only have been expected to bear fruit in autumn.

"But even more important is the Feast of the Tabernacles was the only Jewish feast in which according to Jewish Law the Jewish royal family took part. In essence, Jesus was announcing himself as the Messiah, the King of the Jews. Interestingly enough, this claim is confirmed by the inscription, or *titulus*, placed over Jesus' head at his crucifixion.

"Myth number five: Mary remained a virgin her entire life. The gospels repeatedly speak of Jesus' brothers and sisters. Some of the rationalizations for why brother doesn't mean brother and sister doesn't mean sister are simply ridiculous. Jesus had up to six brothers and two sisters. James, Joses, Jude, Simon are named in the gospels. Lysia and Lydia are sisters named in non-canonical books.

"Nowhere in the gospels does it say Mary remained a virgin. In fact, they say the opposite. Virginity didn't come into vogue until centuries after Mary's death. It wasn't until then that perpetual virginity was applied to Mary."

Lauren leaned forward. "Now you've lost me. Why is Mary's virginity significant enough to make your list?"

"Because understanding Jesus' family's very important to understanding who Jesus was. Which leads me to myth number six: Jesus' family didn't understand or support his ministry. Not true. In fact, Jesus' closest followers, the Twelve, were made up of his brothers, cousins, and best friends. James was his brother. Jude was his brother and looked so much like him his nickname was Thomas, the Twin. Simon the Zealot and Levi were either brothers or cousins. James and John were probably his cousins as well.

"Jesus was so close to the Twelve, he gave them all nicknames. I already mentioned Jude nicknamed the Twin, and Simon nicknamed the Zealot. Of course, there was Simon nicknamed the Rock, or Peter. James and John were the Sons of Thunder. The other Jude, nicknamed Thaddeus in Aramaic or Lebbaeus in Hebrew, both meaning Loved One. And so on."

Shane paused and took another sip from his drink. "I'm half way through. Have I lost you?"

"No," Lauren insisted. "But I don't see the connection to the Sicarii Gospel."

"I'm getting there."

Chapter 13

Emilia Cisneros dumped the office waste basket into the large trash barrel connected to her cart and returned it to its place beside the desk. She had already straightened the desk and credenza and dusted the entire office with a quick pass. The trash was the last task she had to complete in that office before moving to the next.

Emilia liked working at the University. It was quiet, and the repetitious nature of her job allowed her to relax. She loved her family, but time away was also good. At times her feet and back ached, but generally she had little complaint.

Emilia turned off the light as she pulled her cart through the office door. Then she rotated the cart and pushed it down the well-lit hallway to the next door. She put her master key into the lock but found it already open. That result was not unusual. Many of the professors forgot to lock their doors. This professor was especially forgetful.

As she cracked the door open, she cringed at the rank odor of rotting meat strangely tinged with a sweet smell. It was not strong yet, but if she did not clean up whatever was causing the stench, it would get much worse. She also knew she would be blamed.

El profesor estúpido dejó su almuerzo para pudrirse. The professor must have left his lunch to rot. It would not be the first time she had cleaned up his mess.

Leaning into the cart, Emilia used her weight to push it through the door and roll it into the office. She had not gone far when the front wheels of the cart seem to catch and get sluggish. A thought hit her. *¿Por qué están las luces en?* The lights should not be on. Still, it was not that unusual for the lights to be left on. But the door, the lights, the smell.

Chills ran through Emilia's body, and the hair on her arms and neck stood upright. Something was not right. *¿Qué es?* The office looked like it did every night. Then she saw the dark spatter on the papers on the professor's desk. *¿Qué es eso? ¿Es sangre?* It looked like blood.

Emilia stepped to the side of her cart. She did not go any farther. Her hands at her lips muffled a scream, but she did not run. The professor was lying face down in a large pool of blood.

"¿Profesor?" she called lowly.

She bent over to lift his arm. The body was stiff. When she raised his arm, his entire frail frame moved with it, exposing the large gash on the professor's throat, his face still contorted in fear.

Emilia panicked. Shrieking, she rushed to the door and escaped into the hallway. Running down the hall, she screamed again and again as loudly as she could.

"¡Nueve uno uno! ¡Policía! ¡Nueve uno uno! ¡Policía!...

Chapter 14

Shane waited until the waiter refreshed their drinks and walked away with their empty glasses. Then he continued.

"Myth number seven: The Jews murdered Jesus. Jesus was executed by the Romans after they judged him to be a revolutionary. The official charge was sedition against the Roman Empire. He was a Galilean, and there had been so many Galilean uprisings that the Romans equated *Galilean* with *revolutionary*, or *zealot*, or *sicarius*. The mere fact Jesus was from Galilee was enough for Pilate to convict him. But there were lot better reasons. Jesus' followers were zealots. The nickname Iscariot is a variant of *sicarius*, or *dagger-man*. Jesus nicknamed his cousin Simon *the zealot*. He nicknamed James and John *sons of thunder*. These are not pacifist names.

"All Jews knew the Romans had the right to crucify, Herod Antipas had the *ius gladi* or law of the sword, and the Jewish Sanhedrin had the right to sentence people to death by stoning and other equally horrible ways. So if the only crime Jesus had committed was blasphemy, the Jewish priesthood could've had Jesus stoned to death without having to get Roman approval. But they didn't. So if Jesus wasn't crucified for blasphemy, why was he executed? The gospels are very clear. Jesus committed a planned revolutionary act. He cleansed the Temple. Probably with the help of his followers. The book of Mark refers to an even wider insurrection in which people were killed.

"Afterwards, the Romans captured Jesus, determined he was a Galilean revolutionary, and crucified him. Crucifixion was an unbelievably cruel punishment that the Romans were very fond of it for revolutionaries because it carried such public dishonor–hanging nude in a high traffic area until there was nothing left to bury–unless someone like a rich Jew, such as Joseph of Arimathea, paid a high enough bribe to have the body entombed. Revolutionary act. Capture. Crucifixion. Very straightforward.

"Could Caiaphas and the Jewish aristocracy have saved Jesus? Perhaps, if they had wanted to stick their neck out. But Jesus had made it clear he wanted to take down their Temple and replace it with a much more democratic process for absolution of sin. The merchants that Jesus chose for his attack were the source of Caiaphas' wealth. That point of difference is played up in the gospels to the point their theme becomes Jesus versus the Jewish establishment instead of the Jewish zealots versus the Romans."

Lauren leaned back in the booth. "Wow. How many millions of people have lost their lives because of that?"

Shane could talk far too long about deaths brought about in the name of the *Church.* Christianity versus Judaism. Islam versus Christianity. Catholicism versus Protestantism. Shia versus Sunni. All of them worshipped the God of Abraham, and each group considered the others heretics. He chose not to go down that path.

"The writers of the gospels were doing what was necessary to survive in a Roman world. They probably had no idea how some of their words would be interpreted hundreds and thousands of years later. And Paul surely would've been more careful in his letters.

"Myth number eight: Peter and Paul were the leaders of the Christian Church after Jesus died. A misinterpretation perpetuated after the Church became centered in Rome rather than Jerusalem. Of the early Christian leaders, only Peter and Paul ever visited Rome. But make no mistake. James was the leader of the Christian Church. He led the Church from the death of his brother Jesus until his own death some thirty years later. After that, Jesus' cousin or, more likely, younger brother, Simon became the leader. Jesus' brother Jude Thomas was either younger still or had died in India. So what you had was the Jewish Christians establishing a caliphate led by Jesus' heirs.

"This dynastic inclination was so strong in the early days of the Church that the emperor Vespasian tried to eradicate the descendents of David after his destruction of Jerusalem in the year 70. Then when his son Domitian became emperor in 81, he had the grandsons of Jesus' brother Jude brought to Rome with the intention of executing them. Instead, he found them to be simple farmers and released them. All these acts are documented by the second century Jewish Christian writer Hegesippus. Peter and the other apostles took direction from James. Paul started out as an outsider and remained an outsider."

Lauren stopped him again. "Then why don't we know more about James?"

"The answer's coming. Myth number nine: There was one unified Christian Church. There were as many factions of the early Church as there were communities of worshippers, with each group interpreting Jesus' sayings in its own way. There was the Greek *Christ* faction spawned by Paul that became increasingly non-Jewish in its views. It exploited James' god-fearer ruling and threw out virtually all six hundred thirteen laws of Moses. Then there were the Gnostics who represented Jesus as a spiritual redeemer who came to rescue us from the evil of the physical world and return us to the perfection of the spirit world.

"What was *Christian* wasn't defined until at the direction of Emperor Constantine, the Council of Nicaea met almost three centuries after Jesus' death. Romans demanded order. Once Christianity became Roman, there had to be one universal church, undivided and the same everywhere–catholic.

"Though orthodox Christianity mostly resembled Pauline Christianity, it contained elements of all the factions. The New Testament contains books written by Jews, Greeks, and Gnostics. As Christianity gravitated to its new core, the extreme factions became heretical. They were persecuted and destroyed. Even Jewish Christianity, the root of the Christian faith, became heresy. The Jewish Christians were hunted down and slaughtered. The Church in Rome did what was required to distance itself from its revolutionary roots.

"Which brings me to myth number ten: The early Christians were pacifists. Some argue the early Christians left Jerusalem before the first Jewish rebellion against Rome because they were against violence and war. But that's not true. The early Jewish Christians were apocalyptists, much like the Essenes of the Dead Sea Scrolls. In fact, many scholars, and I happen to be one of them, believe the Essenes and the Jewish Christians were one and the same. At the very least, Jewish Christianity was an evolution of Essene beliefs brought about by a radical new teacher named Jesus.

"Jesus wasn't content with the teachings of other apocalyptist leaders, including John the Baptist. They taught repentance, preparation, and waiting for the apocalypse to bring about the Kingdom of God on earth. Jesus didn't want his followers to wait. He taught them to live as if the Kingdom of God was already on earth, and in doing so, they would usher in the apocalypse. Only with the direct intervention of God could the Jews free themselves from Rome.

"So until that day occurred, Christians were not to engage in open warfare against the Romans. They were to give passive resistance only. They were to spread Jesus' teachings, recruiting others into the Kingdom of God. When God intervened, they'd rise as an army and destroy the Romans in one final, horrific, apocalyptic battle.

"After Jesus' death, the Jewish Christians waited on Jesus' return to lead the army. This isn't a pacifist's view. They were militant. They were just conditionally militant. Jesus warned against false messiahs who would come after him and lead many on lost causes. It was because of this warning that most of the Jewish Christians left Jerusalem before the First Jewish-Roman War. They also refused to accept and fight with the messiah-want-to-be Bar Kokhba in the Second Jewish-Roman War. They knew such wars were destined for failure. The only successful war would be the war to end all wars, led by Jesus at his return. Jewish Christians prepared for that battle. Read the New Testament book The Revelation and then try to make an argument that the Jewish Christians were pacifists

"Now, Pauline Christians were different. Since they weren't Jews, they had no interest in a revolution to free the Jews from Roman rule. Their concept of a Messiah was very different. He was a redeemer who could wash away their sins and ensure their passage into heaven. They desired to be like Jesus, selecting his teachings of non-violence and reinterpreting his subversive statements."

Shane paused to take a breath and a dip of his drink. "Myth number eleven: The early Christian Church was poor. Members of the early Christian church had many names before they took on the moniker of *Christians*. One of those names was *The Poor*. The term *Ebionites*, which later was applied to the Jewish Christians, means *The Poor*. This has led many historians to assume they were a bunch of illiterate peasants scraping by on handouts. Nothing could be farther from the truth.

"First century Jews in Palestine were divided into the very rich and very poor. Very seldom did someone cross the immense gulf that separated the two extremes. Yet there's story after story in the New Testament and Josephus' writings about Christians in contact with the wealthiest and most powerful people of their time. Rulers, royal families, high priests, wealthy aristocrats. As the leader of the Jewish Christian sect of Judaism, James was said to have been allowed to enter the Holy of Holies in the Jewish Temple. A poor peasant, I don't think so.

"Also, it's a matter of record that many of Jesus' early followers were wealthy. Joseph of Arimathea was one of the richest men in Jerusalem. Nicodemus controlled the water utility in Jerusalem. Joanna was the wife of Herod's steward.

"So why does that matter? One of the criteria for being a Jewish Christian was to sell all you had and give it to the Church. So these wealthy converts must've given all of their riches to the Church. There's a story in the gospels of a rich man Jesus instructs to sell all that he has and give the money to the poor, but the man refuses and couldn't follow Jesus. *The poor* that Jesus referenced weren't the poor peasant people. He meant the Church—The Poor.

"In Acts, James tells Paul and his churches not to forget The Poor. So Paul, in an effort to show the value of his non-Jewish churches, takes up a collection and brings it to Jerusalem. The Jewish Christian Church wasn't poor. It was probably very wealthy. You didn't do what James did unless you had the power wealth brings."

Lauren smiled broadly. "Now we're getting somewhere. I like this part."

"I can see that. But the Jewish Christians believed in building treasure in heaven, not on earth. So what did they do with the wealth? Did they distribute it to their members and raise the average well-being of all of them? The Jews weren't socialists. Did they distribute it to Jewish peasants and leave themselves with nothing to live on? Jesus had taught there would always be poor. So what was the purpose of collecting everyone's money? I'll tell you. It was a war chest intended to fund the last great war to end all wars. They were going to use it to usher in the Kingdom of God by force when Jesus returned."

Lauren's eyes widened, and her smile became much more mischievous. Shane took a mental note to ask her about it later.

"Myth number twelve. This is the last and probably the most controversial. Salvation comes through faith alone. It's one of the foundational doctrines of the Christian Church. But Jesus never taught it. Jesus spoke of the importance of faith, but it was always followed by action. It's the action demonstrating faith that led to Jesus' miracles. It wasn't enough for the paralyzed man to believe Jesus had healed him. He had to get up, pick up his bed, and walk. Jesus taught in his parables and his healings that the Kingdom of God was made up of people who took faith-based actions, not people who had faith alone.

"It was Paul who introduced the principle of salvation through faith alone. Paul was rebelling against the Jewish Law which no man could live up to. He replaced the chosen race with a new church that once you joined, you were always a member. He became to Jewish Christianity what Martin Luther was to Catholicism sixteen hundred years later. And this Pauline doctrine became one of the divisive forces that split Christianity from Judaism.

"James, the brother of Jesus and the head of the Christian Church, in his epistle contained in the New Testament, refutes Paul's position and reinforces Jesus' teaching over and over. He asks 'What good is faith without actions?' James taught as Jesus did, that the Kingdom of God on earth would be ushered in through people *acting* as if it was already here. The final act would be participation in the final war of good versus evil. And that war would be funded by every Christian member."

Shane raised both arms to signal the end of his lecture. "So if you put all this together, the early Christian Church was made up of and led by Jewish zealot apocalyptists who had the means and desire to lead a war to usher in the Kingdom of God. They were just waiting on Jesus' return as the Warrior Messiah leading the army of God. His return would ignite the rebellion, which they fully expected to happen in their lifetimes. But as they say, 'God works in mysterious ways.' Two failed Jewish revolts and the acceptance of Christianity by Constantine resulted in the conquering of the Roman Empire in a totally different way. It also resulted in the extinction of the Jewish core of Christianity. And we're still waiting on Jesus' return."

Shane examined Lauren for a reaction.

She shifted her weight. Her raised eyebrows indicated surprise. "Not what I expected."

"In what way?"

"When you spoke of myths, I expected to hear about virgin births, miracles, and resurrections."

Shane shook his head. "Those stories are different. Who knows whether Jesus' birth was from a virgin, the result of a consensual union, or the result of a rape or adulterous affair? You don't have to believe one way or another to understand his teachings. As far as Jesus' miracles go, there were other well-known miracle workers around the time of Jesus, all with stories very similar to his. Who knows if they were miracles or magic tricks or made-up stories? They're not important to the core.

"I also can't explain the early Christian Church and the acts of the apostles without Jesus having survived crucifixion either through physical recovery or miraculous resurrection. Radical Essene healers wouldn't have let a Roman seal on a stone keep them from their Messiah. Or perhaps they really were angels. Don't you see? Those things, whether historical fact or legend, are part of the shell of Christianity. The myths

I spoke of go to the heart of the Christian Church. Not what it is now, but what it was when it was several hundred to a few thousand Jews."

Lauren maintained a strong eye contact and spoke firmly. "And the relation to the Sicarii Gospel?"

"The Sicarii Gospel has the potential for proving everything I said is true. That Jesus was an apocalyptist. That the early Jewish Christian Church under the leadership of James was many things, but one of those things was a revolutionary organization waiting for the right time to strike. That they were amassing a war chest to pay for their revolution. That the Church was something entirely different before Paul and his followers morphed it into a religion acceptable to the Roman Empire. The Sicarii Gospel is the key to the truth about the roots of the Church."

Lauren again smiled broadly, but she dropped her eyes to avoid Shane's. "You may be onto something there."

Shane once again sensed that Lauren knew more than she was letting on. "It's your turn."

Chapter 15

Detective Adam Reese had been home long enough to change his clothes and slip a frozen dinner of turkey and mashed potatoes into the microwave. While waiting, he was in the restroom washing his hands and face. He saw in the mirror that his workout shorts and a loose tee-shirt did not flatter him, but he did not care. They allowed him to move without restraint. He had heard from others many times how much he looked like a young Denzel Washington, but he never saw the likeness. All he saw these days were the stress-induced age lines.

He responded to the ding by walking back into the kitchen. Before taking the bland dinner from the microwave, he supplemented it with a glass of merlot from a seven-dollar bottle in his refrigerator. He placed the glass of wine on his small wooden table and retrieved the meager meal. Grabbing the remote, he turned on the small flat screen television in the corner and scanned channels. What he watched did not matter as long as it was not the news. He finally settled on the Red Sox game and returned the remote to the table. After sitting down in one of the two chairs, he could not help but review how he had arrived at this lonely position.

At twenty-eight, Reese had been one of the youngest members of the Boston Police Department to make homicide detective. In the three following years, he quickly rose in rank within the Homicide Unit of Boston's Bureau of Investigative Services. His ability to profile killers and predict their patterns and movements bordered on the psychic and had sometimes drawn strange looks from other detectives in his unit. His abilities, commitment, and the seemingly never-ending caseload had been great for his career. He had even attracted notice by federal agencies and had entertained offers from the FBI. But what had been good for his career had been destructive to his marriage. One year ago, almost to the day, his wife had filed for divorce, taking his two-year-old son, his dog, and his house.

The divorce had led Reese to reassess his priorities. He left Boston and moved to the Cambridge Police Department. He was now head of their Homicide Unit.

Deaths from aggravated assaults and other potential homicides were not major issues in Cambridge. The slower pace allowed him to spend more time with his son, and he hoped the change showed enough commitment to a different lifestyle for his ex-wife to give him another chance.

He was lifting his first bite of turkey when his mobile phone rang.

"Damn!"

Setting the fork back into the turkey compartment of the plastic container, he stood up, walked to the kitchen cabinet, and retrieved his phone. "Detective Reese."

"This is Tony." Reese knew Tony was young and green for a detective, but his voice shook more than normal. "We need you at Harvard."

"What is it?"

"A divinity professor was murdered. His throat was slashed."

A murder? Cambridge averaged only about two or three per year. "Who found the body?"

"One of the cleaning ladies. She's pretty shaken up."

"Anyone else there?"

"There are some paramedics. And the cleaning lady's supervisor showed up just before I arrived. Otherwise, it's just me, sir. I was in the area when the call came in. It's pretty gruesome, sir."

Reese could imagine what everyone was doing to the crime scene and how rattled his young detective must be. "Keep everyone there but keep them away from the body. Don't touch anything. I'm at home, but I'll get there as soon as I can. Until I get there, you're in charge. Stay calm."

"Yes, sir."

Reese hung up. This was precisely the kind of thing he was trying to escape. He looked at the turkey and mashed potatoes on the table.

Oh well, there's another one where that one came from.

He turned down the hall to get changed back into something more suitable to a detective investigating a homicide.

Chapter 16

Lauren was feeling the effect of the alcohol. She welcomed the waiter returning for their food order. She could not afford to lose control of her senses or her words at this juncture.

Both she and Shane ordered burgers and fries from the Anchor's meat and potatoes menu. She knew Shane was anxious for her to tell him something. She had used the time while he was talking to think through how much that would be. A fine line separated the appearance of honesty from revealing more than necessary. Share too much and he might begin questioning her motives. If that happened, she would lose the ability to direct him where she wanted. Fortunately, she made her living walking fine lines.

Shane pressed for an answer. "Well?"

"You're a hard act to follow. Especially when all you've been doing is talking and all I've been doing is drinking."

"Try. I'll catch up on the drinking."

Lauren intentionally hesitated. "I'm not sure where to begin."

"Just say the first thing that comes into your mind and go from there."

Lauren was not about to say the first thing to come into her mind. "Brussels," she began as if the location had just popped into her head. "I heard from a friend about an unveiling at the Royal Art and History Museum."

"What was the occasion?"

Her tone was serious now. "Artifacts from a dig in Jericho. Archaeological social events are a great source of information." She shifted her weight in her seat in a gesture of false modesty. "A nice looking woman can work a room, ask seemingly unrelated questions to a lot of different people, splice the answers together, and come away with almost any information she wants. And no one has a clue she has it. I thought I could get information on what artifacts may not have made it to the museum and might be available for sale on the side."

Shane interrupted her. "Let me get this straight. You wrangled an invitation to an unveiling at one of the most prestigious museums in the world in order to get information about artifacts you could buy and sell on the black market."

Lauren's response exuded pride more than embarrassment. "That about sums it up. I always have a plan before entering the room. Who I'm going to approach. The order. What questions I'm going to ask. How long I'm going to stay with each person. Basically all the puzzle pieces jumbled up but in a way I can put them back together later. But in the process of working the room, I heard something better."

Shane's eyes opened wide. "You went there for artifacts from Jericho and stumbled onto what might be a copy of the Sicarii Gospel."

"Exactly. I was talking to a handsome Belgian archaeologist near the intersection of two hallways when my ears picked up a conversation from around the corner. There were three men, but I was careful not to be seen. The last thing I wanted was to have them aware I was listening."

"And they were saying?"

He's hooked.

"They were speaking in French so I couldn't pick up every word, but I understood enough to get the gist. One man was giving a report to the others. A black market antiquities dealer named Adjo in Alexandria had come across what they thought was a genuine copy of the Sicarii Gospel. They were sending an agent to acquire it. The man getting the report seemed very insistent their agent get there quickly. As I told you before, I have known Adjo for years so I got on the earliest flight I could to Alexandria and beat them to it."

Lauren elected to leave out Riley and other details. *It'd only complicate things to tell everything.* She saw the waiter coming with their food and stopped her story until he had placed their plates in front of them, exchanged his brief pleasantries, and left.

Before she began again, Shane asked a question that relayed he had doubts. "It was just that simple?"

"There was nothing *simple* about it. It wasn't easy putting the pieces together. And it sure wasn't easy to beat them to Adjo. Then I had to smuggle it into the States."

"Do you know who the men were?"

She lied. "No." She took a bite of her burger and reached for her drink. While doing so, she studied Shane. His gestures seemed to indicate he was satisfied with her explanation. *Now for the icing on the cake.*

She spoke with a tone of wonder. "The first time I saw it, I knew there was more to it than anyone knew. It had an aura about it. It was like I'd been looking for it my whole life. The dealer Adjo didn't seem to know what it was. And that's unusual. Normally the dealers know more about what they're selling than the best archaeologists. If anything, they lie to make you think what they're selling's more valuable than it really is. In this case he seemed in a hurry to get rid of it. It didn't make any sense."

Shane's face scrunched. "Why would he do that?"

"I don't know. He may have thought the authorities or someone worse was after him. There are a lot of ruthless people in this business who believe life to be cheaper than antiquities. They'd quickly trade the life of a dealer for the Sicarii Gospel."

"I'm sure that's true. Is there anything else you can tell me?"

Lauren lied again. "Not much. I got the document back to the States and began looking for someone to authenticate it."

Lauren and Shane took a break from the conversation while they ate their burgers and fries. Lauren had learned long ago that once the sale was completed, anything else she said only had downside risk. Shane seemed to be digesting her story with his food.

When they finished their meal, Shane signaled their waiter for the check. It did not take long to settle up because the Anchor only accepted cash. Lauren was somewhat taken aback by the suddenness of the evening's end. *Did I say something wrong?*

Shane must have noticed her concern. "We don't want to stay too long after we've finished. The owner's known for publicly berating people who take up his space without eating or drinking." Shane laughed. "If you try to stay to closing time, you take your life in your own hands."

Lauren felt better. *He must've accepted my story.* But then as they stood to leave, Shane stood in front of her and looked her in the eyes. "What I still don't understand, Lauren, is why you need someone like *me*."

Lauren felt sincere admiration for the man in front of her. She had underestimated him. He was truly bright. He had already figured out there had to be something more.

When she did not answer right away, Shane continued. "What I mean is, if I prove the document a forgery, you lose a very significant amount of money. Enough to keep me in *my* lifestyle for the rest of my life. If I prove it genuine, then there'll be pressure to sell it to a museum. And as it becomes public, there quite probably'd be a major legal battle with Egypt and/or Israel over ownership. Either way, your life becomes more complicated, and the amount of money you get for the document's dramatically reduced. Given your line of work, you know many people who'd pay top dollar, without authentication. And if they wanted it authenticated, they'd use their own person. No matter what happens from here, my involvement makes your situation worse. So I ask again, why do you need *me*?"

Lauren was not often surprised. She stood there quickly processing all the alternative answers she could give. She could say she had seen the evil in her ways and decided to do something good for the world. *There's no way he'll buy that.* She could say it was not about the money but something more important. *No.* She could say she wanted to spend time with him in hopes of rekindling their past romance. *No.*

Shane became impatient. "Well?"

There was nothing to do but play the honesty card.

"Shane, there's more to the gospel than I've told you." She watched as Shane seemed to relax. Perhaps he was relieved she was finally opening up. "I didn't tell you because I really don't know what it is. I believe in my heart, the gospel's genuine and is the door to something truly amazing. But I don't know what the key to the door is. I need your help to find it. Just trust me a little longer."

Shane looked at her for what seemed like hours but was only seconds. "I will. I'll do everything I can to help you." Then he took her hand in his own and spoke calmly. "I can tell it's no longer in your nature to tell the complete truth, but I need you to try."

"I will, Shane."

Even she did not know if she was sincere. At that moment, she knew she meant it, but she also knew her limited capacity to keep promises.

As Shane walked Lauren to her hotel, they made plans to meet the next day to check Jane's progress. The evening ended as had the one before. Shane walked Lauren to the door of her hotel and placed a peck on her cheek. Lauren entered her hotel and watched through a window as Shane walked away. She had not been that disappointed in a very long time.

Chapter 17

Raphael lay on his bed daydreaming of Martinique. His simple mind was divided. At the same time, he knew one day he would return and feared he never would. He loved his home island. It was beautiful with lush green tropical forests surrounded by white sand and turquoise water. It was also a volcanic island that had grown from a series of violent eruptions. It basked in West Indian warmth, but its core was an active volcano, Mount Pelée, which in 1902 erupted to kill over thirty thousand people. It provided its residents with a paradise but at any time could spew forth death and destruction.

He and his father shared a two-bedroom suite in the Park Plaza Hotel in Boston. His father had spent most of the evening in the central living area on his mobile phone with the Directeur. They were discussing the trip to New Haven tomorrow. Raphael seldom listened when his father worked. When he did, the result was always the same–a splitting headache. Fortunately, the conversation was ending.

"Oui, nous ferons attention." His father promised to be careful. "Adieu."

Raphael sat up on the side of his bed. As expected, his father came through his door and sat beside him. His face was worn, but he spoke to Raphael calmly as a father does to his son just before bedtime.

"Our plans are set for tomorrow. The Directeur wants us to tread lightly until he gives us further direction."

Raphael nodded to show he understood. His father patted him on the leg and stood up to leave. Before he was out the door, he turned and spoke to Raphael again with genuine affection.

"I am going to bed. Sleep well."

Raphael watched his father leave and listened as he crossed the living area into his bedroom on the other side. He lay back down and dreamed again of Martinique.

Chapter 18

Amit David had pursued the treasure of the Copper Scroll over half of his life. He had discovered many other relics, some of them treasures in their own right, but nothing had come close to satisfying his lust for what lay at the end of the Copper Scroll's clues. It was not the treasure itself that drove him, though the idea of being set for life definitely was not a deterrent. It was the idea of deciphering a puzzle no one else could solve. After two decades, his obsession had made him one of the foremost authorities in the world.

"Are you ready, Doctor David?" Eathan looked nervous standing in front of the other four members of the team near the edge of the cliff.

Everyone wore safety harnesses equipped with dual lanyard lifelines which allowed them to relocate one connection to another spot on the rigging while still connected with the other line. They had tool belts around their waists.

Amit nodded and strode toward the rigging. "Let's do it."

He looked over the cliff edge and followed the rigging to its end. His eyes continued down the rough wind-hewn rock face to its abrupt meeting with the plain some thirty meters below. He did the calculation in his head. A falling person would take only two and half seconds to travel the distance to the plain. He would be traveling at almost ninety kilometers per hour when he hit bottom. Amit was willing to face much greater danger to solve the mystery he knew so well.

The first time he read the story of the odd scroll now displayed in Jordan's Archaeological Museum of Amman was in his first class at the Institute of Archaeology of Jerusalem's Hebrew University. Archaeologists found the Copper Scroll in 1952 in the third Dead Sea Scroll cave, about two kilometers north of bill. Since it was the fifteenth scroll found in the cave, it was given a name that belied its significance–3Q15–cave three, Qumran, fifteenth scroll.

Behind a large boulder near the cave wall were two pieces of copper scroll, one on top of the other. The copper was highly oxidized and broken into two rolled sections.

In total it was about thirty centimeters wide, two and a half meters long, and one millimeter thick.

How to open the oxidized rolls without shattering them and damaging the text proved to be a tough problem. Finally in 1955, the team took one piece of the scroll to England where a professor at the Manchester College of Science and Technology sliced it into twenty-three sections using a one tenth of a millimeter saw. The second piece followed in 1956.

With the scroll opened, scholars from many different sciences began intense analysis of the language, content, and construction of the scroll. The more they studied it, the more they realized it was very different from the other Dead Sea Scrolls. It was so different that no one then or since has effectively explained why it was at Qumran.

The language, though odd in style, was Mishnaic Hebrew used in the first to fourth century CE. Most scholars dated it to between 50 and 100 CE, later than they placed the other scrolls. Multiple translations soon competed for prominence, but the École Biblique tightly restricted their publication. No universally accepted translation was ever produced.

To everyone's surprise, the Copper Scroll was essentially a treasure map, an inventory of gold, silver, jewelry, perfumes, and other valuables, with detailed directions to sixty-four locations across a broad area. Sixty-three of the locations pointed to treasure. Disregarding the historical value, the tons of precious metals inventoried had a modern day market value of between half a billion and three billion dollars, depending on how the units of measure were translated.

The École Biblique, who had quickly determined the residents of Khirbet Qumran had no interest in earthly wealth, thought the treasure was an ancient hoax. They controlled information to keep would-be treasure hunters from their dig sites. For decades, only an early drawing and poor quality photographs were available outside of the inner circle. Only in the last few years had new methods to clean and see through the corrosion made high quality images available for greater study.

Amit knew every Copper Scroll theory, and there was no shortage. Some thought it Egyptian treasure from the time of Moses. Others thought it an inventory of first Temple treasure the prophet Jeremiah hid from invading Babylonians. Still others thought it second Temple treasure hidden by Jewish priests from Roman legions surrounding

Jerusalem during the first Jewish revolt. Contributing to some of these theories was that the writing on the Copper Scroll appeared sloppy as if done in a hurry.

Amit did not hold firmly to any theory, but he in no way thought the treasure a hoax. As important as they were to the residents of Khirbet Qumran, the Dead Sea Scrolls were written on vellum and papyrus. The contents of the Copper Scroll were engraved into an extremely valuable copper alloy sheet. The reason had to be to ensure the scroll's long-term survival. A hoax made no sense.

Still, Amit had many unanswered questions. How could Jews of the time have hidden successfully an immense treasure from the greedy Hasmoneans, Herodians, and Romans? Why would a community that held worldly possessions to be no value care that much about a list of treasure?

Many treasure hunters over the last several decades had claimed to have deciphered a code embedded in the Copper Scroll. But every treasure hunter pursuing the wealth of the Copper Scroll came to realize it would not give up its treasure easily. The issue was the writers of the Copper Scroll wrote their directions with obscure references as if the reader already knew the landmarks. It was like *turn right where the barn used to be and go where Aaron and Miriam married.* Expedition leaders and conspiracy theorists had collectively raised many millions of dollars and euros to finance digs. They had dug holes all over the Judean Desert and near Mount Gerazim in ancient Samaria, but not one item from the treasure had been found.

Since his university years, Amit had engaged in almost every significant Copper Scroll expedition. He published four books and many articles documenting his accumulated knowledge, and he became a regular on the History International television channel as an expert spokesman. His renown began attracting wealthy donors who financed his own digs. Among those digs were four unsuccessful searches for the Copper Scroll. He knew this time would be different.

Though the Copper Scroll documented sixty-four locations, Amit's experience told him the number was a code. The number sixty-four in Jewish numerology was equivalent to the number one. He was convinced the items of treasure lay in a single location. Scattering the treasure increased exponentially the probability of losing valuable items and made reclaiming the treasure at some future time almost impossible. Other indications of a code seemed embedded in the Copper Scroll's unique features–the strange Greek letters following seven sections, the strange landmark references, the odd use of personal names, and the foreign units of measures.

Amit had written a computer program to decipher the code and run through hundreds of potential locations ranked from most probable to least likely. He input into his program combinations of key letters from locations to get angles and turns, and he used the lengths and volumes as a guide on relative distance. Word of his model spread quickly, and a financial backer soon entered his life. He was a French Catholic collector with a consuming interest in the Copper Scroll.

Three previous locations indicated by Amit's program had yielded nothing viable. Following each attempt, he had tuned his model. On the fourth attempt, in the predicted location, the ground penetrating radar had picked up a hidden cave containing what appeared to be dozens of small chests. Amit knew he had found it.

While the other team members watched, Amit stepped out onto the rigging. It was ricketier than he liked, but he had little doubt it would hold.

He took a few steps down and looked up at Eathan. "Be careful. Wait until I'm securely on the platform before you follow. Take your time. I don't want you falling on top of me and taking us both to the bottom."

Eathan looked over the edge. "No problem. I'll wait right here."

Amit laughed and continued down. His heart pumped pure rapture into his arteries. He was about to solve one of the largest mysteries in the history of archaeology–the Copper Scroll.

Chapter 19

Yousif Al-Jamal sat in his office in Nablus, West Bank, sixty-three kilometers north of Jerusalem, and listened to a telephone report from one of his field soldiers. As the Sunni Muslim head of the Shudada Allah, the Martyred Followers of Allah, he had many such operatives. His mind wandered during the report, and the pictures on his desk and credenza shouted all the reasons he hated the Jews and their financial backers in the West.

His grandfather died in the Six Day War of 1967 and his father in the 1982 War between Israel and the Palestinians in South Lebanon. Without a father, Al-Jamal was forced into a Palestinian refugee camp in Lebanon with his mother and sister until the Israelis murdered them. A so-called *surgical strike* against *terrorist targets* went awry and struck noncombatant refugees. Since then he had been on his own, connecting with others like him who shared an intense hatred of Israel and the Jews who occupied it.

Ultimately, he joined Harakat al-Muqawama al-Islamiyya, the Islamic resistant movement better known by its acronym, *Hamas*. Hamas was founded by Sheik Ahmed Yassin in 1987 as an arm of the Muslim Brotherhood, a religious and political organization established in 1928 in Egypt. Yassin, like many other Palestinian freedom fighters, was assassinated in 2004 by an Israeli pilot of a helicopter gunship.

Today Hamas received most of its funding from the government of Iran, wealthy private donors in Saudi Arabia and other oil-rich Persian Gulf states, and even the United States. Such donations paid for Al-Jamal's education at Stanford University where he majored in archaeology.

Hamas' original objective was the destruction of the state of Israel, but as the organization became increasingly political, it had to become more pragmatic. Most of Hamas' leadership acknowledged the destruction of Israel was unlikely. Their true objective now was the establishment of a Palestinian state in the West Bank and Gaza. This modified objective dictated two very different faces and associated methods. On the one hand, Hamas had to morph into a political organization and overcome the suspicions and criticisms of Western governments. On the other hand, until the Palestinians achieved independence, they were still at war with Israel. War required a militia.

The military wing of Hamas, called the Izz ad-Din al-Qassam Brigades after the Palestinian nationalist sheik of the same name, provided Al-Jamal with his military instruction. They attacked Israeli military and civilian targets, and Palestinians who collaborated with the Israelis. Their attacks had killed well over one thousand of their enemies over the last twenty-five years.

The label of *terrorism* was unfounded on any level. No method of attack or weapon of destruction was too horrendous if it furthered their holy cause. They shot, stabbed, launched short-range rockets, and deployed suicide bombers. Of course, it was not really suicide if one sacrificed himself in defense of Islam. And the families of the bombers received between three thousand and five thousand dollars for their son's martyrdom.

As Hamas became more inclined to accept normalized Israeli relations as a tactic to achieve an independent Palestinian state, Al-Jamal became less willing to follow its directives. He rejected the idea any diplomatic or political process with the Israeli government would result in an independent Palestinian state. Jews could not be trusted. They would stall as long as they could, and when forced into an agreement, they would renege at first opportunity. History was full of such examples.

Al-Jamal broke from Hamas with some of his most trusted friends to form his own organization. They struggled for a while, but several well-executed attacks on Jews in shopping centers, bus stations, and schools in Jerusalem attracted the attention and support of a few radical, wealthy Saudis.

Al-Jamal's vision was to displace Hamas and become the leading Palestinian liberation organization. Palestinian independence was at the tipping point, and someone needed to push it over. Hamas had already proven they could not do it. There was too much history, too much hate, and too much disorganization. Whoever provided the final push would play an important role in ruling the resulting state. Perhaps he would become such a powerful tool of Allah he might one day lead his entire people.

Al-Jamal knew different tactics were needed. Traditional methods of terror had become passé. Blowing up supermarkets and subways and killing a few people had become absorbed into life's norm. Such acts were the equivalents of a fatal car accident everyone accepted as part of the price of driving cars.

He had devised a new, ingenious approach. Instead of destroying what could be rebuilt, he would destroy what could not be. He would attack the heritage of the Jews and their American and European allies. He would erase their history. Once the Jewish and Christian trees began losing their roots, the trunks and branches would weaken very quickly. The Jews and their friends would give the Palestinians their homeland to keep their heritage from disappearing.

Al-Jamal had selected his first target as Qumran. It was remote, and security was laughable. Then he would move to Masada, the last Jewish stronghold in the first Jewish-Roman War. Though all the Jewish resistors died at Masada, the fortress ruins concentrated Jewish pride. Following Masada, he would target sites in Jerusalem–the Western Wall and the tomb of Christ. As his followers increased, he would send them to other parts of the world to attack cathedrals, synagogues, and museums.

He would make what the Taliban did to the Buddha's of Bamyan seem trivial. The international outcry after their destruction was intense, but it did not have the passion that would accompany a similar act in Israel or a Western country. Al-Jamal intended to bring the war with the West to an end by driving them to their knees. He might get the Noble Peace Prize.

Al-Jamal smiled and refocused on his phone call. He would have already set off his first explosive message had his man in Qumran not discovered a bigger target about to be unearthed. The archaeological team on site should reach the discovery later that day.

He provided simple instruction. "Report back to me immediately with what they find. If the value is as you suspect, I will send in help to do what must be done. If it is nothing, at your first opportunity return to your original mission."

Al-Jamal hung up the phone. He was a patient man. He could wait a day or two for the world to tremble at the name Shudada Allah.

Chapter 20

Jane focused on cleaning up the images of the vellum sheets.

"*Momma, don't take my Kodachrome away!*"

The bell rang, signaling someone had come through the outer office door. She looked at the other workers, but they shrugged their shoulders. Before Jane could move toward the door, it opened, and Doctor Randall walked in.

"Doctor Randall, I didn't expect you until much later."

"I'm too antsy to not be involved. The semester's almost over. My teaching assistant Paul's going to take my classes."

The first time each day Jane saw Doctor Randall she could not help but smile. It had been the same for the four years since she had won him over in her interview. She sang Paul Simon's Mrs. Robinson in Aramaic. He laughed so hard at the *koo koo ka-choo* he almost fell out of his chair. He offered her the job on the spot.

She respected Doctor Randall more than any man she had ever known. It would have been easy for him to take advantage of her admiration, but she knew Doctor Randall would have considered it a violation of trust. And trust was very important to him. She had thought more than once about initiating a different sort of relationship herself. But such a move carried with it significant risk of ruining the happiest, most rewarding part of her life.

"How's it coming?" he asked.

"So far, everything's checking out. Vellum, ink, Aramaic, everything. No obvious signs of forgery. If it's a fake, whoever did it's very good. Of course, the results are very preliminary. We could study it for months."

"Do you have a translation?"

"Yes, though that too may not be one hundred percent accurate."

The outer office bell rang again.

"*Still crazy after all these years!* We're unusually busy this morning."

Jane followed Doctor Randall through the lab door into the office. Two official-looking black men in dark suits and ties greeted them.

One of them spoke to Doctor Randall. "Are you Doctor Shane Randall?"

"Yes." Doctor Randall gestured toward Jane. "This is my assistant Jane Roman."

"I'm Detective Adam Reese. I'm with the Cambridge, Massachusetts Police Department." He turned to the other man at his side. "This is Detective Ben Taylor from the New Haven Police Department. He's been nice enough to help me find you. I have a few questions if you don't mind."

"What about?"

"Did you know Doctor Samuel Evans of the Harvard Divinity School?"

"*Did* I know him?"

"A cleaning lady found him in his office last night. With his throat cut."

Jane gasped. "*The borders of our lives!*"

She sat behind one of the nearby desks and found a napkin to dry her watering eyes.

Detective Reese apologized. "I'm sorry to just blurt it out that way. In Cambridge we don't get many murders. We could use your help."

Jane could see by the look on Doctor Randall's face he was wondering what any of this had to do with him.

The detective explained. "Doctor Randall, let me get to the point. We found the imprint of your name on a pad of paper in Doctor Evans' office. We think he wrote your name on the top sheet and gave it to someone. We hoped you might be able to shed some light on who that was."

Doctor Randall shook his head. "I'm sorry, but I can't help you. Of course, I knew Doctor Evans. We are... were in the same field. But I didn't know him well. I have no idea who may've done this."

Detective Reese persisted. "You weren't working on anything together?"

"No. I haven't talked to him in months. I really wish I could be more help."

Detective Reese handed Doctor Randall a card. "My mobile number. Please call me if you think of anything."

"I will."

Detective Taylor also extended his card. "You understand why we had to talk to you."

Doctor Randall nodded.

The two detectives turned to leave. Jane found it hard to believe the two men could drop such a bombshell and then leave with so little explanation. "Wait."

The two men stopped and turned back to look at her with questioning eyes.

She summoned the courage to continue. "Do you think the murderer could be after Doctor Randall?"

Detective Reese spoke in a comforting tone. "I doubt that very much."

"But you think the murderer has his name."

Detective Taylor spoke in a more matter-of-fact manner. "We're just following up on all leads."

Jane looked to Doctor Randall. He shook his head as a signal for her to let it go.

"We'll catch the bastard," declared Detective Reese. "All the same. Be careful. Vary your routine and your route home. If you see anything that concerns you, call one of us immediately. Doctor Randall, Ms Roman, thank you for your time."

The two detectives turned and left through the door. Jane looked up at Doctor Randall as she often did when she needed answers. He walked to her side, leaned over, and put his arm around her. Jane buried her face in his chest.

Chapter 21

Lauren was walking down the hallway toward Shane's lab when she saw two men in suits exiting his doorway. She had seen enough law enforcement officers across the globe to know a cop when she saw one. She darted into an open door to her left. Silently closing the door behind her, she watched with apprehension through the door's opaque window as two shadows passed by.

Did Riley figure out who I am and call the police? Did they tell Shane what I did? Did he tell them where I am? Her mind continued to race for a few minutes. *There's only one way to find out.*

She opened the door, found the hall empty, and continued to the lab. She paused at Shane's door, took a deep breath, and confidently turned the knob. When the door opened, she saw Shane with his arm around Jane, rocking her as if she was a child.

Here goes. "What's going on?"

Shane released Jane. "Two police detectives were here asking about a murder at Harvard. They shook Jane up pretty badly."

A murder? "What does that have to do with you?"

"I knew the victim. He was a divinity professor by the name of Samuel Evans. They don't know who did it."

Lauren was stunned by the name but remained stoic.

Shane continued as if trying to figure out a mystery. "It's very odd."

Lauren was afraid he might be drawing a connection to her. "What?"

"This is two days in a row I've been told about someone I know being murdered in Boston."

The revelation surprised Jane. "Who else?"

"Marcus Quinn. He was apparently beaten to death."

Lauren kept her composure but inwardly was in turmoil. *It can't be a coincidence.* Her knees felt like they would buckle, and she feared if she did not say something she might collapse. Her voice cracked a little. "Was he a friend of yours?"

Shane waved the question off. "Not for a long time."

Jane spoke with more certainty. "Marcus Quinn was human slime." Then she softened her tone. "The police think Doctor Randall may be next."

Shane reached out and gripped Jane's shoulder. "That's not what they said. In fact, they said the opposite."

Jane reached up and grasped Shane's hand. "They told you to be careful."

Lauren casually turned her face from Shane and Jane as they continued their mild argument. Her thoughts raced. *Someone's after me, and they're close. How'd they find me so quickly? Riley. But Riley wouldn't kill anyone. It must be the Frenchmen.*

She had no answers except she was in danger. And now Shane and his staff were in danger as well. *Should I warn them? Or should I let the police warning suffice?*

The question she asked herself was difficult. She would not decide something so important while the rush of adrenaline coursed through her veins.

Shane tried to put it behind them. "Well, the police have it now. I'm sure they'll figure it out. Lauren, Jane was just about to show me the preliminary translation. You arrived just in time."

Lauren's instinct was to get off by herself to plan her next move, but she very much wanted to hear Jane's results. She saw Shane turn to enter the lab and felt her body follow in subconscious response.

Chapter 22

As the two detectives exited the building and entered the parking lot, Reese was getting one of those feelings that told him he was in the right place to catch his murderer. "Ben, I can't tell how much Randall knows, but there's something going on here."

"I agree."

"How about you and me watch Randall for a day or two and see what happens?"

"No problem. I'm not sure I can get us much help, but *I* was ordered to cooperate. I guess that makes me available."

Reese smiled. He knew Ben was doing him a big favor. Ben had to have a long backlog of cases. Babysitting an out of town detective would not get him through them any faster. "I know you're a busy man. As soon as either one of us thinks this a waste of time, I'll get out of your hair."

"No problem."

Reese's reading of Ben was that he was well-trained. A detective could do worse for a partner.

Ben stopped and turned toward Reese. "Since we know where he is, we might as well start now, don't you think? I'll call it in from the car."

"Get his home address, the make of his car, license number, and any other personal information you can. If we lose him, it'll make it easier to find him again."

"I'll see what I can do."

Reese believed in being thorough. "You probably should check him out a little. See if he has any priors. Or if he associates with anyone dirty."

"No problem."

Reese knew he was pushing, but he might as well take it as far as they would let him. "And it wouldn't hurt to at least ask for some relief and backup. All they can do is say no. Can't eat you."

Ben laughed. "I can tell you haven't worked in New Haven before."

Chapter 23

Amit felt the wall of sandstone in front of him give under the weight of his favorite hickory-handled, alloy steel handpick. For seven hours Amit and his team had attacked the cliff face in shifts of two to shave centimeter by centimeter from the entrance of the hidden cave. The result of their ordeal was a sturdy tunnel a little less than two meters wide and high and about a meter long.

Amit struggled against his lanyard which was stretched as far as it could go. He struck the stone again and a small hole opened. The stale air of the cave escaped to mix with the heavy desert air outside.

Eathan felt it as well. "We did it!" He backed out of the tunnel and shouted upward. "We're through!"

Cheers rained down from above.

Amit was not immune to the exhilaration. "Help me! We need to widen the opening."

Trying to control his emotions, he inserted the wide edge of his handpick into the opening and began expanding the edges. Eathan quickly swept away the dust and rubble as it fell. As soon as the hole was the size of a soccer ball, Amit could wait no longer. *To hell with safety!* He released his lifeline and pulled himself directly next to the remaining wall of rock.

Retrieving a small flashlight from his tool belt, he shined the light through the hole and maneuvered his head to see past the flashlight into the cave. A light cloud of dust reflected and diffused the beam. Amit strained until he saw some small chests in the back half of the cave.

His heart quickened. Dropping the flashlight behind him, he began ripping at the remaining barrier. Eathan picked up on his leader's excitement. Releasing his lanyard, he pulled himself forward to help.

Amit moved to the side to make room. "Help me push."

Together they used their shoulders to push against the thin remaining wall of rock. Amit felt it give.

"Again!"

They pushed together again and some of the larger stones separated and fell to the floor.

"Again!"

Once more their shoulders contacted the stone, and the wall collapsed around them. Some of the rougher and sharper rocks scraped Amit's face and came down hard on his arms and gloved hands. Amit coughed from the resulting dust and raised his shirt to his mouth to filter the air.

A cry came from above. "Is everything all right?"

Eathan again backed out of the cave to the outer edge. "We're fine."

Amit felt behind him for his flashlight until his fingers found the round casing. Rising to a crouch, he stepped through the opening into the main part of the cave. The height of the ceiling allowed him to stand upright.

The light from outside filled most of the space around him, but enough of the wall remained to shade the sides of the cave and its inner depths. Stepping forward, he searched fervently for the chests with his flashlight.

His heart sank.

Stacked in front of him were dozens of ossuaries. The rectangular limestone boxes, between fifty and sixty-five centimeters long and about thirty centimeters wide and high, had flat lids to facilitate stacking them on top of each other. These ossuaries belonged to Judean Jews, who used them as secondary burial bone boxes for their dead. They did not originate in Khirbet Qumran.

Following the death of a loved one, the Judean Jews washed, perfumed, and wrapped the body. Then they laid it on a stone shelf in a tomb or cave where they allowed it to decompose. Tombs were expensive, and space had to be optimized. When nothing but bones remained, the relatives collected the bones and placed them in an ossuary. Then they placed the ossuary in a loculus, a niche carved into the side of the tomb. Judean Jews only used ossuaries for the two centuries before the Roman destruction of the Temple in the year 70. These ossuaries were approximately two thousand years old.

Khirbet Qumran residents did not use ossuaries. They placed their dead in the rocky ground according to very strict ritualistic practices. Archaeologists had found over a thousand graves in the area. They were individual use shafts dug about a meter and a half deep into the rock. Single bodies were placed in the shaft, with the bodies oriented north to south. Their feet were always at the north end, and their heads were turned to the east. What Amit was looking at was nothing like a Khirbet Qumran cemetery.

Sometimes lying at awkward angles, the ossuaries appeared to have been stacked in a hurry. Amit surmised Judean residents escaping Jerusalem ahead of Roman legions had relocated the ossuaries to the cave. Some scholars had proposed the same theory for the hidden locations of the Dead Sea Scrolls, though many others disputed that theory.

Amit's discovery could potentially support or refute positions of many scholars relative to what was happening around Jerusalem just before the Romans crushed the Jewish rebellion and destroyed the Temple. He understood the significance of finding ossuaries near Khirbet Qumran, but they were not what he wanted. Again, the Copper Scroll's treasure had eluded him. He stood dejected with his arms hanging at his sides and the flashlight directed toward the cave floor.

Eathan stepped passed Amit and kneeled down to examine the ossuaries. He began dusting off the side of one of them to better read the inscription.

Amit stopped him. "Do not disturb anything."

Eathan looked up at him with questioning eyes.

Amit explained. "We need to report the find and wait for guidance. The Israeli government takes a dim view of excavating cemeteries. Myriad regulations make breaking the law very easy."

Eathan stood up and gushed with pride. "Doctor David, this is a great find."

Without responding Amit turned and walked toward the light.

Chapter 24

As Shane approached the lab door, his mind churned over the two murders of Samuel Evans and Marcus Quinn. They had absolutely nothing in common. *Did Quinn involve Evans in one of his cons? No, Evans would've thought Quinn a waste of his time. Then what's the connection? Is it really just a morbid coincidence?*

What Shane knew was that he had two shaken up ladies. He had to divert their attention. He reached for the door, but Jane corrected him.

"I've uploaded images and my preliminary translation to the university intranet. I can show you both from here without removing the gospel from the safe. My translation's not final, but it's pretty close."

Lauren seemed to snap back into focus. "What makes it preliminary?"

Jane hesitated as if determining where to start. "Well, there are many possible translations for Aramaic words. What I may think means *landowner*, someone else may translate as *master*. I may choose *hate* when someone else would use *put aside*. You get the point."

"Yes, I see."

Jane was not through. "But that's not all. Ancient Aramaic writing didn't use vowels."

Lauren's face lit up. "Like ancient Hebrew. They're implied in the context."

The volume in Jane's voice increased. "Right. It can be as much art as science, especially when it comes to proper names."

Shane took a sheet of paper and took out his pen. "Let me show you an example."

He wrote three sets of letters across the top of the paper–S-H-N, L-R-N, and J-N. Then he began writing words under each set.

"SHN could be Shane, Shana, shine, or shone. LRN could be Lauren, Lorna, or learn. JN could be Jane, June, Joan, or Jon. The more letters you have in the word, the more possible combinations you have."

Lauren's face scrunched. "Sounds impossible."

Shane smiled with pride. "It almost is. That's why there are so few Aramaic gunslingers like my Jane here. Jane, let's see the translation."

Jane nodded and walked behind the central desk. She sat down and entered characters on the keyboard of the desktop computer. Shane and Lauren watched over her shoulder while she accessed the Archaeology Department's document library. She opened a folder with the name of *Sicarii*, and a list of documents appeared–six images of the vellum pages and an English translation.

She opened the translation. "Look at this. It starts with a statement attributed to James, the brother of Jesus."

Shane was taken aback. "That's promising."

He leaned over such that his chin almost rested on Jane's shoulder. He began reading.

> *These are the words of Jesus as heard and transcribed by*
> *James, his brother. Whoever hears these words and embraces*
> *their meaning will never die.*

It sounded like what one would find in first century gospels, but a forger would mimic the form.

Jane looked back at him. "Then it continues with seventy verses. Starting with four beatitudes and ending with two more.

Shane read the first four beatitudes.

> *Jesus said,*
> *Blessed are the poor; they will experience God's kingdom.*
> *Blessed are those who weep; they will find happiness.*
> *Blessed are the hungry; they will be fed.*
> *Blessed are those who suffer, for they will find life in the*
> *Kingdom of God.*

Again, Shane found the words believable. They could easily be authentic words of Jesus. He asked himself the key question. *Could this document be real?*

Jane interrupted again. "And look at this verse."

Shane looked lower on the screen where Jane was pointing.

> *Jesus said, "Some may tell you the Kingdom of God is in*
> *the sky. Others may say it is in the sea. But I say to you the*
> *Kingdom of God is both outside of you and inside of you."*

Jane waited several seconds. Then she used the mouse to scroll down and highlight another verse. "There are other Kingdom of God statements like this one."

> *Jesus said, "The Kingdom of God is like a treasure hidden in a field owned by a man who did not know the treasure was there. When the man died, he left the field to his son, who also knew nothing about the treasure. Another man found the treasure in the field and covered it up. Then in his joy he sold everything he had to buy the field."*

A short gasp escaped Shane's lips. "It's a sayings gospel."

Lauren pushed her way closer to the monitor. "What do you mean?"

Shane did not take his eyes from the screen. He moved Jane's hand aside and took control of the mouse.

"Sorry," he said as he studied the monitor. "The earliest gospels were just lists of Jesus' sayings. They had no plot and often little or no order. What was important to the early church was what Jesus *said*, not what he *did*. An example is the Q Gospel, which was a source for the Gospels of Matthew and Luke. *Q* stands for *Quelle*, which means *source* in German. That's one reason why they're so much alike. Another example is the Gospel of Thomas. Most theologians now consider it to be a legitimate fifth gospel.

"Narrations describing what Jesus did came later in the second half of the first century, decades after Jesus' death. The basic narrative plot appears in the Gospel of Mark. Sayings gospels were later combined with the narrative plot, lists of miracles, and a passion narrative addendum to give us the gospels we have today. An example of a passion narrative is the Gospel of Peter discovered in 1886. It describes Jesus' trial before Pilate, crucifixion, resurrection, and ascension."

Shane paused to read a few more Kingdom of God verses. Then he stopped and looked up at Lauren. "What Jesus said was precious to the early church. Leaders recited his words in early Christian services as if they were words directly from God. But as with all words repeated over and over, they began to morph ever so slightly. Recognizing Jesus' sayings could be lost over time or, even worse, distorted by people seeking to manipulate their followers, the early church leaders wrote them down. Sayings gospels rank with Paul's letters as the earliest and purest first century Christian sources we have.

"Still over time, as the sayings were woven into narratives, the message changed. Jesus' message of *blessed are the poor* became *blessed are the poor in spirit* because while the early Jewish Christians gave all that they had to the church, later gentile Christians didn't."

Jane fought for control of the mouse again and pushed Shane's hand away. "This sayings gospel seems to be ordered roughly by theme. And while some of the verses are very consistent with other New Testament sources, the words in some of the verses seem a little extreme. Look at this verse."

Jane scrolled down farther, and Shane read where she highlighted.

> *Jesus said, "The Kingdom of God is like a sword used by a man to kill a more powerful man."*

She paged down and highlighted another area. "And look at these down here."

> *Jesus said, "Perhaps you think I have come to bring peace to the world. I have come to cast dissension on the world—fire, sword, and war. If there are five in a house, three will be against two, and the son will be against the father."*
>
> *Jesus said, "I have set a fire on the world, and I am guarding it until it becomes an inferno."*
>
> *Jesus said, "No one can enter a strong man's house and steal his treasure unless he first binds the strong man. Then he can take what he wants."*

Jane paged backed up. "And here's a verse you'll find interesting."

> *Jesus said, "If you want to follow me, sell your possessions and give the money to the poor. You will have treasure in heaven."*

Jane scrolled to the end. "Then it goes on and ends with a section on Jesus' return and the final beatitudes."

> *Jesus said, "If a householder knows in what part of the night the thief will break in, he guards his house to prevent the break-in. You must be like the householder, for the Son of Man is coming when you do not expect."*

> *Jesus said, "When I return, it will be like the days of Noah. In those days before the flood people went about their lives, eating and drinking, marrying and giving in marriage, until Noah entered the ark, and the flood came and destroyed all of them."*
>
> *Jesus said, "Blessed is the man who perseveres in times of hardship, because when he has passed the test, he will receive God's treasure."*
>
> *Jesus said, "Blessed are those who have heard my words and have kept them in their hearts."*

Jane and Lauren looked at Shane. He could tell they wanted his opinion. Shane walked away from the desk. He knew there could only be one conclusion.

"This can't be the Sicarii Gospel."

Chapter 25

Shane was tired. Driving home in the late afternoon sun in his Lexus LX570, he found the thirty mile per hour speed limit of his neighborhood almost unbearable. His eyes pressed on their sockets like lead spheres, and his head felt three times heavier than normal.

He had spent all day with Lauren and Jane analyzing the document's images and translation. Lauren insisted he was missing something and that the document had to be genuine. It might yet prove to be a genuine sayings gospel, but Shane had found nothing to support it being a copy of the Sicarii Gospel. Though there were some strong verses describing the subversive nature of Jesus' movement, they were no more strongly worded than what appeared in the four canonical gospels or the Gospel of Thomas. There was nothing about rebelling against Roman authority or about a war chest, nothing to prove the early Jewish Christians were zealots awaiting an apocalyptic war to usher in the Kingdom of God. The document was too mainstream.

A newly discovered sayings gospel would be big news. In addition to the academic fame that would accompany such a find, there would be television interviews, speaking engagements, and books. Once an archaeologist had his name associated with a discovery of that magnitude, he would be asked to give his opinion on any related discovery from that point forward. The potential ongoing income was significant. *So why I am so disappointed.*

He pulled into his driveway in the Prospect Hill neighborhood, home to the Yale Divinity School just north of the main university campus. He knew his two story, dark wood-trimmed Tudor style house was typical of the type that attracted prosperous academics who wanted to live near campus, but he loved it anyway.

He parked his car next to a side door, grabbed his laptop bag, and climbed the three steps to the door. He entered through the breakfast nook and input the code to turn off the security system. Straight ahead was his kitchen separated by a hallway that led back to his bedroom and a guest room. To the right was a small parlor-style living room containing a brown leather couch, matching leather chairs, and cabinets containing clutters of religious artifacts. It opened to an entryway for the front door and a large walnut staircase to the second floor. On the other side of the entry way was a library with rows of books topped with others at odd angles.

He dropped his laptop by the breakfast table. He needed a shower. He had promised Lauren he would pick her up at her hotel for dinner. He started down the hallway but had only made it halfway before the doorbell rang. Retracing his steps, he saw through the leaded glass two silhouettes of dramatically different sizes. Shane unlocked the door and swung it open.

In front of him and to his right was a slight, white man about five feet four inches tall with an oval face and receding, thin hair. The man to his left stood much larger. He was darkest black, nearly seven feet tall, and had to weigh over four hundred pounds. His head was very round and clean shaven, and the sunlight reflected off the top of his cranium like a freshly cleaned mirror. Both wore black suits, white shirts, and thin black ties. They looked as if they had just stepped out of a B-movie.

The smaller man spoke with a strong French accent. "You are Docteur Randall?"

"Yes."

"May we come in? We have something to discuss I trust you will find... que est le mot... interesting."

"Surely."

Shane stepped aside, and the two men followed the light into the living room. "Please, sit down."

The smaller man sat in the chair closest to the entry way and sank back into its cushion. The larger man took the couch but sat rigidly upright on the front half. Both pieces of furniture groaned as leather will do under pressure. Shane was surprised the couch survived.

He looked from one man to the other. "Would you like something to drink?"

The smaller man raised his hand palm outward and then waved to the remaining chair. "Non, Docteur Randall. S'il vous plaît, sit down."

Shane sat, leaned back, and silently waited for the purpose of the visit.

"I am Docteur Andre de Vaux," announced the smaller man. "This is my son Raphael."

Shane eye widened. "De Vaux? Of École Biblique fame?"

The man shook his head. "A fortunate coincidence."

"Nice to meet you."

"As it is for us. We have heard much about you."

Something about de Vaux made Shane uncomfortable. "Me? Really?"

"You are too modest, Docteur Randall. We share similar interests in Biblical archaeology. You sate your interests at the université. I sate mine in Israel."

Shane resented the Frenchman's arrogance. "How I can help you?"

"Oui, forgive me. I sometimes forget you Americans like to... comment vous faire le dit... get to the point." He leaned forward in his chair. "We have reason to believe Mademoiselle Lauren Mallory will be contacting you."

Shane's eyes reflexed into large saucers again.

De Vaux's face reflected satisfaction. "Voilà! I see you know her, Docteur Randall."

The larger man's lips parted slightly to show a glimpse of white teeth. It was the first time he had moved or reacted in any way.

Shane tried to recover. "We knew each other for a short time in college."

"Oui, we know."

Shane wondered what else they knew. "I'm not sure I like the idea that you've been invading my privacy. Isn't personal privacy big in Europe?"

De Vaux's tone deepened. "Mademoiselle Mallory has something that belongs to my institution."

Shane knew the Frenchman had finally revealed the purpose of his visit. "Which is?"

"We prefer to remain private. We just want back what belongs to us."

Shane pressed. "What is that?"

"It is an extremely rare vellum scroll, insignificant except for its age. It holds great sentimental value to my organization."

Shane's face remained flat though internally he was shocked at the scroll's mention. He hoped the Frenchman would add to what he already knew. "What's on the scroll?"

"It is just an Aramaic document from the time of the Essenes. It is similar to the Dead Sea Scrolls found in Qumran. But insignificant in its content."

"Has it ever been made public?"

"Non, it would add nothing to what is already known about the period."

De Vaux's words struck a nerve of one of Shane's pet peeves. "Shouldn't the public make that determination?"

"Surely, Docteur Randall, you must know the Church of Rome has hundreds, if not thousands, of documents that would add greatly to the world's knowledge of the early church period. But it chooses to hide them away in its libraries."

"I don't approve of *their* actions in this regard either."

"Mon ami, like the Church of Rome, we do not seek your approval. The scroll is ours. We simply want it back. Has Mademoiselle Mallory contacted you?"

Shane lied. "No." He watched the Frenchmen for any sign he knew otherwise.

"Are you certain, Docteur Randall? We mean no one harm. We just want our property back."

"I'm sure."

The Frenchman stood. "Pity. We do believe she will." He reached into his inside coat pocket and pulled out a card. "Please call when she does."

Shane and the silent giant stood in response. Shane took the card. It contained only the man's name and mobile number.

"De Vaux stared into Shane's eyes with an intended force. "You will find us very grateful to anyone who helps us and a formidable foe to anyone who opposes us."

Shane understood de Vaux's message very well. "Is that a threat?"

"Docteur Randall. Like you, we are teachers of the word of God. We want to be your friends."

"I'd prefer that as well."

"Then please contact me if you can help us."

Shane did not reply.

"Merci for your hospitalité, Docteur Randall. Come, Raphael, we have bothered Docteur Randall enough."

De Vaux turned to the door followed by his giant companion. Shane moved ahead of them to get the door. He opened it and held it until they were outside. He was glad they were leaving but unsure of what to say. "Perhaps we'll talk again."

Without turning back, de Vaux replied, "Perhaps we shall. Au revoire."

Shane closed the door. *What kind of trouble has Lauren brought on herself, and now to me?*

Chapter 26

Raphael followed his father down the walkway to where their rental car was parked. Hearing his father speak of Lauren Mallory had brought back his immense hatred for the woman. She had humiliated him by getting to Adjo and the gospel before he did. No woman made a fool out of Raphael and lived very long afterward.

Even his encounter with Adjo had been unfulfilling. The black market thief was normally a reliable resource to the Vraie École Biblique, and the Directeur had expressed his desire to keep him alive. Raphael had hoped Adjo would give him an excuse to go beyond his orders, but the Egyptian had sold out Riley and the woman so quickly that Raphael did not get the pleasure of torturing and killing him. Adjo swore he had not received confirmation of the Vraie École Biblique's interest in the document until after Riley had purchased it and the woman had visited him.

His father subtly signaled him not to say anything. Words were unnecessary. Raphael knew the meaning of all his gestures. They stopped at their car.

His father was frustrated. "He either knows where she is or knows she will contact him. I hoped he would be reasonable, but he will not help us. He will warn her and help her get away. He may even go to the police."

Raphael nodded in response. Randall was not cut from their cloth. His faith was more in science and history than God. He was suspicious of their motives, and he would trust the woman over them. Even if he knew her sins, his misguided American gallantry would not allow him to turn her over.

His father raised his arm and accented key words with short down strokes. "The Directeur made it very clear how much he wants the gospel. He is understandably uneasy with continued violence, but he does not want the gospel to slip away from us again. We are too close. You will pay Docteur Randall a visit tonight. Get him to tell you what he knows. If you get the woman's location, you know what to do with him. If not, we need him alive. Nothing is more important than finding the woman."

Raphael nodded again. He could not completely hold back a slight smile.

"Be careful, Raphael. We have given him notice."

Being careful was imprinted in Raphael's DNA. He was going to enjoy tonight.

Chapter 27

Reese sat in Ben Taylor's unmarked car about a half block from Doctor Randall's house and watched the odd couple of men who had entered the house and now talked by the curb. He was too far away to hear what they were saying. They could have no relation to his case, but Reese's instincts were telling him otherwise.

Ben must have been thinking the same thing. "These guys look promising."

"Absolutely. Call in their rental car. Let's see what we can find out about them."

Ben reached for his radio. "If they're staying in New Haven, it shouldn't be too hard to find their hotel. Do you see the size of that guy?"

"How could I miss him?"

As Ben called in the license plate of the Hyundai Santa Fe rental car, Reese continued to watch the two men. The big man's face reacted to whatever the smaller man was saying with intense satisfaction. His eyes transformed from dark and dead to bright and alive. Reese had seen the look before on the faces of murderers who thought they were smarter than the detectives who pursued them. It did not portend good things.

Reese saw the two men preparing to leave. "If your men can't find their hotel, we're going to lose them. You take the car and follow these guys. I'll stay here and watch Randall."

"All right."

"Just don't forget about me."

Ben laughed. "I'll call for another car to come pick you up. With any luck, I can get someone to relieve you."

"Thanks. If you get anything on these two, pass it on to me."

Randall's two guests began pulling away in their car. Reese stepped out but leaned back in and looked his new friend in the eye. "Be careful. These guys may be killers. And that big guy looks like a pro."

Ben acknowledged the warning with a slight downward head cock. "You do the same. I'll check in with you later."

Reese shut the door and watched as Ben drove away. Suddenly, he felt very exposed.

Chapter 28

Shane stared out his window and watched the Frenchmen drive away. He was no longer tired. His adrenal glands pumped new energy into his bloodstream with every heartbeat. He knew he had to get to Lauren.

Does she know she's in danger? How much of what she told me's a lie?

The only way to get the answers was to convince Lauren to share them. He turned and walked down the hall to his bedroom. He turned the water in his shower on hot, undressed, and immersed himself in the spray. Once out and dressed, he reached for his iPhone and dialed Lauren's mobile number.

She answered right away. "Hello."

"Lauren, this is Shane."

"I know who you are, Shane."

"I don't think we should go out to dinner tonight."

"You're not coming?"

"That's not what I mean. I have some things to talk to you about, and I'd rather do it in private. I'll meet you in your room. Is that all right?"

"That sounds great." She gave him her room number.

"Order room service. I'll be there in twenty minutes."

"See you then."

Shane took a brisk pace through the hall into his breakfast nook. On the way to the door, he caught his foot on his laptop bag. He had not intended to work tonight, but looking at his laptop bag made him reconsider. *Better to be prepared than not.* He picked up the bag, set the alarm, and left the house.

Chapter 29

As Reese sat on the curb watching Randall's house a red glow brightened the driveway. *Just my luck.* Randall was backing out his Lexus. Reese had known there was a chance of losing Randall if he and Ben split up. He had rolled the dice, and he was about to crap out.

He rose to his feet and began running toward Randall's house. He did not know what he was going to say, but he would think of something. He was still two houses away when Randall's car entered the street. He shouted, but Randall gave no indication he heard him. *Damn!* Reese crossed the boundary of Randall's property but could do nothing but helplessly watch as Randall sped away.

Reese kicked at a small clump of tree twigs at his feet. "Shit, piss!"

He turned back toward his original position and had only taken a few steps when he saw a car pull up exactly where he had been sitting. Though it was unmarked, he knew it contained two of New Haven's finest. *Perfect timing!*

Reese waved his arms at the men inside, and the car crept forward. When it reached him, Reese leaned over and supported himself on the passenger door. The window opened.

The detective in the passenger seat greeted him. "You must be Reese."

"Yes."

"I'm Peters and this is Longwell." He pointed to the driver. "Ben Taylor told us to meet you here and help you any way we can."

Reese opened the back door and slid into the back seat. He remained silent for several seconds and fought his anger. The situation was not their fault. When he spoke, he did so in a calm and even tone.

"Thanks. Problem is Randall just left, and we don't know where he's going. If he doesn't come back soon, I may need you to take me to my hotel and then come back here to watch. Are you guys able to do that?"

Peters threw both hands in the air in a shrug. "We can stay as long as no one orders us off."

"Thanks."

Reese leaned back, rested his head on the seat, and closed his eyes. He began thinking he should call the FBI, though he had little hard justification to do so. He could not make the decision alone.

I'll discuss it with Ben tomorrow.

Chapter 30

Lauren greeted Shane at her hotel door with a smile so sincere he would have forgotten the two Frenchmen had he not been so angry. He had accepted she was hiding information. Now her half-truths and omissions had put him and his staff in danger.

As he entered her room, she placed her hands on his chest and pulled him down to plant a kiss on his cheek. He pulled away and walked past her.

She read his nonverbal message. "Is there something wrong?"

He carried his laptop bag to the far side of the room and set it down next to a small round mahogany table with two overstuffed upholstered chairs. The table was already set with plates covered with stainless steel domes surrounded by napkins and place settings. A bottle of Zind Humbrecht Riesling wine from the Alsace region of France decorated the center of the table.

He deflected her question. "What are we having?"

"Since you live in New England, I thought you'd like to start with some clam chowder," replied Lauren. "Then because I know you're a Texan and like simple, fried food, I ordered us fish and chips. It arrived right before you did."

Lauren seemed very proud of her choices. Shane sat at the table and removed the chrome cover. Lauren joined him in the chair opposite. They began picking at their food.

Lauren was first to break the silence. "Are you going to tell me what's wrong?"

"I was visited by two friends of yours."

Lauren looked surprised. "Really? Who?"

"Andre de Vaux and his giant son Raphael."

Lauren's expression flickered from surprise to shock before going flat. "What did they want?"

"Oh, I think you know exactly what they wanted."

"What did they tell you?"

"They told me you stole the gospel from them."

Lauren reacted with passion. "That's a lie."

Shane was surprised by the emotion. "Lauren, do you think you can tell me the entire truth? It sounds like you need my help more than ever."

Lauren put her fork down on her plate, stood up, and paced between the table and the bed. "All right, Shane. Here it is." She sat down on the side of the bed. "As I told you, I overheard a conversation at the Royal Art and History Museum and used what I heard to locate and acquire the gospel. But I left out a few details."

"Such as a couple of dangerous men tracking you?"

Lauren hung her head as if ashamed. If the situation was not so serious, Shane would have laughed. *How can a woman with so much talent and beauty be so incapable of honest emotion? I don't remember her being that way.*

Lauren almost wept the answer. "The men are members of the Vraie École Biblique?"

"The True Bible School?"

"They're a radical group whose mission is to perpetuate lies about the Dead Sea Scrolls and other non-canonical works. They protect secrets they think could undermine what they consider the true message of God. They'll do anything to protect those secrets. They may have killed both Marcus Quinn and Dr Evans."

Shane could not believe what he was hearing. "Are you serious? What would make them do that?"

"I went to Marcus Quinn and Doctor Evans for help before coming to you. They must have followed me."

"Then you brought them to me?"

Shane stood up. He was fuming. He searched for something to punch or kick, but everything looked too expensive. That made him seethe even more.

Lauren reached for him. "I would've told you sooner. But I thought the less you knew, the safer you were."

Lauren inserted so much misdirection into everything she said Shane could not tell how much of what she was saying was true. *Perhaps I'll never know. How did I get involved in this mess? A pretty face from the past? Stupid ass!*

As Shane cursed himself, a thought surfaced from under the emotion. *The reaction of the Vraie École Biblique doesn't make sense. Unless…* "Do you really think they'd kill two people to keep a forged sayings gospels hidden?"

"These men aren't innocent Bible school leaders. They're bad men intent on two things: hiding the message of the gospel from the public and using the treasure to extend their power."

A very large missing piece just moved into place. "What *treasure*?"

"I didn't tell you before because I thought once you translated the gospel it'd be clear. You were the one talking about Jewish Christian zealots and war chests. I was going to tell you tonight over dinner. I overheard the Frenchmen say the gospel contained an encoded treasure map."

"So the Vraie École Biblique is killing its way to what they think's a treasure map? And now I'm in their crosshairs?"

Lauren hung her head. "Apparently. Doctor Evans must have told them he sent me to you before they killed him."

"Obviously."

Lauren stood up and faced away from Shane. "Do they know I'm here?"

"I don't think so. But if you're getting ideas about running away ..."

She turned dejectedly and sat down hard on the bed. "Of course not. I'm in too deep."

"Perhaps, if we prove to them it's not the Sicarii Gospel, they'll leave us alone."

"I seriously doubt it. They seemed so sure it was genuine. I don't think they're going to believe otherwise. I doubt they'll smile, say thank you, and leave."

"Is that it? Have you told me everything?"

"Yes, that's all I know. I was so sure it was the Sicarii Gospel. When you said it wasn't, I didn't know what to do. I had to think."

Shane did not know why he had asked his last question. He was increasingly certain Lauren was incapable of telling the entire truth. He knew she was only telling him what she wanted him to know. Still, he did not think she was lying. *Some puzzle pieces are still missing.*

Shane cleared the table by putting the plates and utensils on the floor. Then he lifted his laptop out of its bag and turned it on. "It doesn't make sense."

"What?"

"I would like nothing more than for this document to be the Sicarii Gospel. But it's nowhere near radical enough."

When his laptop sprang to life, he established a virtual private network connection and logged on to the Yale University intranet. He called up Jane's folder and opened the images of the gospel and Jane's translation. The images again brought a strange sense of déjà vu, but he shrugged it off. Instead, he leaned forward, supporting himself with his elbows on the table, his thumbs under his chin, and his hands cupped in front of his mouth.

Lauren walked behind him and began rubbing his shoulders. It felt great. But no matter how much stress Lauren rubbed away, Shane could find nothing in the images or the translation to indicate the gospel was anything other than what he thought it to be.

"There's nothing here. I don't see anything to indicate a treasure map. And the theme's no more subversive than the four gospels of the New Testament. There *are* some verses that mention treasure. I wonder if that's how this whole misunderstanding began."

Lauren responded by leaning over and kissing his left ear and neck. Then she worked around to his lap, wedging herself between Shane and the table. Her arms encircled his neck, and her eyes looked directly into his.

She spoke with the most genuine emotion Shane had seen her display. "Thank you." She leaned in and kissed him.

Shane pulled away. "This isn't a good idea."

What he was truly thinking was she could not be trusted. She had put his life in danger without as much as a warning. He knew she would do so again if it served her purpose.

Lauren pressed forward and kissed him again. She was not taking *no* for an answer.

Shane put his hands on her shoulders and once again pulled away. "Lauren what is this? You lie to me and expose me to murderers, and your solution is we should sleep together?"

Lauren looked hurt and ashamed, but she did not give up. "You have no idea how afraid I've been. I'm sorry I got you into this, but I need your help. I didn't know they were this close. I thought we had more time. You know how I felt about you in college. Feelings like that never go away. When I first saw you, I knew we'd be doing this."

She kissed him again. She pressed her breasts against his chest and slowly grinded her lower body against his left leg.

Shane's resolve began melting away. Though he tried to control his thoughts, his memories took over. He became a college kid again, throwing caution to the wind. *What the hell.*

He put his arms around her and kissed her back. Their lips pressed into each other until they were as one set connecting the two lovers. Their tongues danced. Shane forgot all about the gospel and the danger. He forgot about her lies.

Lauren separated and stood up between the table and the bed. "I don't want to be alone tonight. Stay with me."

Shane joined her and pulled her to him in another deeply passionate kiss. He brought his hand up to her breast. Moaning, Lauren lifted her hand up his inner thigh to his belt and began unbuckling it. He separated from her lips and began unbuttoning her blouse. Soon their clothes cluttered on the floor, and they lay intertwined on the bed.

Chapter 31

It was after eleven o'clock, and Detective Ben Taylor slowly sipped his coffee in his car outside the Omni New Haven Hotel. He had followed the two men there from Randall's house and now sat about one hundred feet from their car.

He and Reese had spoken several times during the evening. Ben had told Reese the name of the hotel and where it was. He had also told him, as strange as it seemed, the car had been rented to an account belonging to a religious school located in Jerusalem.

After waiting over two hours for Randall to return, Peters and Longwell had relieved Reese, and he had gone to his hotel. Ben had not yet found similar relief.

He thought about his wife having to go to bed alone and his two young daughters wondering when their dad would be home. At ten and eight years old, the girls still got excited when he walked through the door. Certainly, it was not the first time he had worked late on a stakeout, but he preferred to minimize the evenings and nights away. Being at home in the early evening added a sense of normalcy to his job and took his wife's mind off the inherent dangers. Even after all this time, the light in her eyes and smile on her face signaled her relief when greeting him in the evening. After all, she had not signed up for this life from the beginning.

Ben often thought about the early days. When he and his high school sweetheart graduated, he had aspirations of going to college and then law school. She intended to accompany him to college and perhaps go to medical school. As fate would have it, the summer before college, she had become pregnant, and both of them modified their plans.

Deciding to serve the law in a different capacity, he entered the New Haven Police Academy and worked his way up the ranks to detective. She had attended junior college part time, entered nursing school, and now worked at the Yale New Haven Hospital as a neonatal nurse. Different paths but life was still good. And Ben wanted to get back to it.

He spoke his frustration into his radio. "Where's my relief? I'm out here without backup, and I'm tired as hell."

The voice on the other end cracked a little. "Sorry, Detective Taylor. We're swamped tonight. We'll have someone there as soon as we can."

Ben went back to sipping his coffee and debating with himself how much longer he would remain.

Out of the corner of his eye he picked up a shadow moving to his right. *What the . . . ?* Before he could find the source, he saw a muzzle flash and heard a muffled puff from a silenced handgun. Simultaneously, the passenger side window shattered, followed by the driver side window.

Something propelled his head against the driver side door frame and lower third of the splintered window. Beads of glass covered him, and his thoughts were dazed from the concussion to his head. Unconsciously responding to his training, he reached for his weapon, but he never pulled it from its holster. Instead, he was overcome by searing pain from the bottom of both sides of his face. He felt for his chin, but his chin and a section of his lower jaw were gone. Reacting to both the shock and the pain, he filled the night with his screams.

His instincts took over. He knew he had to get out of the car. He had to run, hide, and regroup. He pulled on the latch and felt the door give way. He dislodged himself from under the steering wheel such that he could roll out of his glass-filled seat.

A second muffled shot rang out followed by a powerful blow to his shoulder, as if a hot poker had been thrust into his flesh. The force thrust him through the door onto his face and stomach on the pavement of the parking lot. Blood pooled beneath him as he gasped for breath. He screamed his wife's name in unformed syllables.

A shadow darkened the pavement around him. He could not see who it was, but he heard someone speak.

"*Idiot stupide.*"

Chapter 32

Amit sat in his tent staring at his laptop monitor in the early morning light. A portable generator provided electricity to keep his laptop charged and feed everything else in the tent that required electricity. The screen displayed one of the many translations of the Copper Scroll. Because of the variables involved, no one really knew exactly what the Copper Scroll said. Some of the engraved letters were difficult to read, and some of the spellings were unusual. Also, the translator had to interpret the vowels and proper names.

Is that my mistake? Do I have an error in the translation?

The sixty-four sections of the scroll followed a pattern. First came the hiding place. Then an instruction followed, usually to dig or to measure a specified distance. Then came a description of the treasure to be found there. In some cases there were additional comments, and in seven occasions there appeared Greek letters.

Amit read one of the sections from the fifth column out loud in hope that hearing the words would make their hidden meaning clearer.

"A water channel is on the northern side of Sekak. Dig under the large stone at the head of this water channel to a depth of three cubits to find seven talents of silver."

He scanned column to column and locked in on a section in the second column.

"In the cave behind the Old House on the third terrace rest sixty-five bars of gold."

Then he read the next section that followed.

"A wooden container in the cistern below the burial chamber in the Courtyard holds seventy talents of silver."

Amit refused to believe the author expected the reader to know where the Old House and the Courtyard were. The proper names were not specific enough to be helpful. They were more like reminders. Only the author of the scroll or someone very close to him would know where to find the treasure. *No, the proper names, the distances, and the directions must be parts of a code.*

The logic in his program must have an error. One small misinterpretation had the potential of introducing an error of kilometers. *What am I missing? Is there a key I don't have?*

Amit's focus was so intense the ringtone of his satellite phone momentarily brought intense pain to his head. He uttered a guttural groan both from the pain and the frustration of having to stop what he was doing. He looked at the satphone's display and recognized the number. Another groan escaped his lips. Amit's financial backer was not a patient man.

He lifted the phone to his ear. "Amit David."

The speaker replied in English with a mixed French and British accent, a sure sign a British teacher had taught the Frenchman English. "Docteur David, have you found the cause of our latest setback?"

"No. I was working on it when you called."

"That is very disappointing, Docteur David."

"We mustn't forget that we made a significant discovery."

The voice expressed his disgust. "Ossuaries? I have six in my personal collection. I was told you were the best, Docteur David. Was I misinformed?"

"No, monsieur, you were not. But as we have discussed many times, the Copper Scroll is not a child's riddle. It's very complex. We're missing something."

"Missing something?"

Amit grew more confident in his conclusion with every word. "Oui monsieur. There must be a key we don't have. Until we have it, we're guessing."

The backer's tone turned to revulsion. "I thought the purpose of your program was to eliminate the guesswork. I do not like to *guess*."

"Neither do I. But there you have it. I'll try again soon."

There was a pause before his backer replied. "No need."

Amit was afraid he might have lost his financial support. "What do you mean?"

"You will soon get the help you need."

Amit was taken aback. No one else should be brought in without first consulting him. *Financial backing be damned. I'll find someone else.*

"What help? If you'd asked me, I could've told you involving someone else will be a waste of my time and your money."

"Pull in your horns, Docteur David. I have involved no one."

"But you said..."

"I said help will be coming your way soon. When it does, accept it, Docteur David."

The backer hung up. The odd conversation left Amit wondering what kind of help he was going to get.

Chapter 33

Gilbert de Clisson hung up from the Israeli archaeologist and clicked a window on his desktop computer. While the screen filled, he could not help but admire his reflection in the monitor. Though his square head was now covered with graying hair and his once thin frame had given way to a stocky build, he was still handsome for someone in his mid-fifties. In his youth, he had been quite the ladies' man, and though he was married with grown children, he still maintained a young mistress in a nice apartment not far from his residence. Of course, even with a wife and mistress, he did not pass up the occasional dalliance with a model or young starlet when opportunity arose. After all, wealth and power had their rewards, and Parisian society demanded a certain lifestyle from the wealthy.

The computer window he pulled up displayed his customized Copper Scroll application containing an inventory of the treasure. Each gold and silver item was linked real-time to the commodities market to determine the street value of the precious metals. Other items were tied to past auctions for similar finds.

Recent economic woes had sent the commodity markets to new highs and the value of the Copper Scroll treasure along with it. The total appearing near the lower right corner of the screen was just over one point seven billion euros. The application then multiplied that total by a factor to indicate the treasure's intrinsic historical value. The grand total flashed in large numbers. It was thirteen point six billion euros.

Clisson sat behind his ornate, bronze-trimmed Louis XV Boulle desk with a large smile on his face and bathed himself in his superiority. His plush flat in the seventh arrondissement neighborhood of Paris exuded his wealth. Located on the Left Bank of the Seine River, the seventh arrondissement was one of the most expensive neighborhoods in the world. He could see the nearby Eiffel Tower from his balcony which overlooked a private garden.

Clisson could trace his aristocratic heritage back to the thirteenth century. His family tree included both advisors to kings and pirates on the high seas. The family's historical wealth came from their lands in western France which contained both castles and manor houses, but Clisson had built on the wealth bestowed upon him at birth through his shrewd investments and his uncanny ability to read people.

The large room in which he sat was one of nine rooms in his flat that encompassed the entire top floor of his high rise residence. It was his favorite because it housed his impressive antiquities collection. Matching glass-shelved cabinets lined the walls, with each cabinet containing items from a specific period of Holy Land history.

One cabinet contained Bronze Age weapons, sculpture, and pottery. Another contained coins and jewelry from the time of the Hasmoneans and Herod the Great. Still another contained bones from three of the twelve disciples, wood and a nail from the cross of Christ, and other Roman period relics. Others represented periods of occupations by the Assyrians, Babylonians, Persians, Greeks, Byzantines, Arabic Caliphs, Crusaders, Mamluks, and Ottomans. Bronze and marble statues stood in open spaces or sat on cylindrical pedestals. The weight of the room was so great the floor had required special steel rod reinforcement. Protecting it all was a security system rivaling the best museums.

Clisson loved the chase. He loved exerting his will on the world. What he did not like was depending on any single source. Too many people had disappointed him with their incompetence and lack of vision. Now he always had multiple gambits in play.

Clisson snapped back to matters at hand. He was in a great mood. After nearly a decade of searching, he was finally close to solving the Copper Scroll's secrets and claiming its treasure. Though confident in the outcome, he knew his complex network of plans required constant care lest they unravel. He picked up the phone again and dialed another long distance number. It connected him to the personal number of the Directeur of the Vraie École Biblique. Clisson was not one to waste time talking to operators or assistants.

"Allo."

Clisson was pleased Directeur Edmond Neuville answered the call. He knew if the call had come from a lesser person, there was a high probability Neuville would have let it go to voice mail. By answering the call, Neuville showed he understood the hierarchy in their relationship.

"Bonjour, Directeur Neuville." Then continuing in their native French, he applied the pressure that was the reason for his call. "Are you making progress on our endeavor? I am paying a lot of money for results. I trust you are committing the appropriate resources."

Multiple gambits always in play.

Chapter 34

Peters adjusted his weight in his seat and let out a groan. "What time is it?"

Longwell looked at his watch. "Just after midnight."

Waiting down the street from the professor's house had literally become a pain in Peters' backside. "I can't take any more of this. I have to stretch my legs."

"When you get back in, we're getting the hell out of here."

Peters opened his door and stepped into the grass. He turned and leaned at a forty-five degree angle against the car to stretch his calf muscles. A flurry of motion caught his eye. *What the hell?* His pulse quickened. Some fifty yards behind the car, a large dark form was quickly darting back and forth within the shadows.

"Longwell, get out here. Something's going on."

While Longwell scrambled to respond, Peters drew his Glock 22 .40 caliber police pistol from his shoulder holster. He pointed the weapon, but the amorphous mass closed on his position more quickly than he thought humanly possible. A blow from what felt like a spinning elbow to his jaw jarred the handgun from his grasp and sent him reeling onto his back. Peters raised his head to see the dark form was not a phantom. It was just a large man in black sweats and ski mask.

Longwell had one leg in the street and contorted his body to aim his weapon over the car. The roof of the car blocked Longwell's line of sight, but the man in black angled to take advantage of the open passenger door. After two flashes accompanied by muffled puffs, Longwell grunted and fell backward on the concrete in a crumpled heap. Peters was an ex-Marine and had seen people die from gunshots. Longwell was gone.

Peters' blood surged with anger and self-survival. Searching the darkness, he found the killer's weapon in his gloved hand and kicked it free. Almost simultaneously, he reached with his right hand for his ankle holster which held his backup .38 special revolver. Before he could reach his .38, a giant hand engulfed his own hand in a crushing grip. A massive weight came down hard on his chest and knocked the wind from his lungs. Another weight came down on his left arm and broke both bones in his forearm.

Peters let loose a primal scream. Pinned by the knees and grip of his giant attacker, he lay helpless and barely able to breathe. The weight on his arm was agonizing. All he could see was the reflection of a distant streetlight off the killer's teeth and whites of his eyes. A strobing gleam to the side indicated that the killer had something metal in his hand.

Peters yelled curses and struggled with all his strength, but he was left with no options. He hoped the end would be quick. It was not.

Chapter 35

Lines and columns of Hebrew and Aramaic swirled in Shane's mind. One minute the dark writing arranged into two sets of letters, and the next minute the characters morphed into irregular shapes. The pattern kept repeating, as if sending Shane a message he should understand.

Shane's ringing iPhone interrupted his dream. Rolling over, he found the Indiana Jones theme emitting from his crumpled pants on the floor. He pulled the phone from his left front pocket. It was after one o'clock in the morning.

"Hello."

"Shane Randall?"

"Yes."

"This is your security service. We have received an intrusion alert on one of your back windows. Do you need assistance?"

"I'm not at home."

"Would you like me to send the police?"

Shane was still half-asleep, but he was awake enough to know the last thing he needed right now was the police asking him questions. He might have just figured out the code of the Sicarii Gospel.

He sat up on the side of the bed. "No. I'm nearby. I'm sure everything's fine."

"You're sure?"

Shane lied. "I've noticed a loose sensor on one of the windows."

"May I have your code word?"

"Zealot."

"Thank you, Mr. Randall. Sorry to have disturbed you. I'll deactivate the alarm."

Shane disconnected, and turned to find Lauren still asleep. There was no reason to disturb her. He stood up, gathered his clothes, and dressed. He found one of the room's hotel notepads and wrote Lauren an explanation. Then he picked up his laptop bag and quietly left.

A short drive later he slowly turned into his driveway. Pulling up to his normal spot, he kept the car idling while he examined the house and yard. Seeing nothing concerning, he stopped the engine, opened the car door, and shut it noiselessly. He crept around to the back and immediately saw the reason for the alarm. The lower pane in a corner rear window was shattered. The hair on his neck stood on end, and goose pimples rose on his arms.

Shane instinctively crouched to make himself smaller while he walked back to his side door and inserted his key. The door was already open. A shadow passed over the white door from left to right. The flickering shades of gray formed a hand extending its long fingers in Shane's direction.

Shit!

In an adrenaline rush he backed away from the door. He looked both directions, but he saw nothing. The shadow moved again. Looking up toward the side porch light, Shane found the source. A spider had crossed its web and was now paralyzing and wrapping its victim. Shane fell back into a leaning position against the car.

He hated his huge fear of spiders. *Arachnophobia*–Shane took some solace in the fact the fear was common enough to have a name. He often relived that early fall day in Texas when he was ten years old. He and some of his friends were playing in a creek bed looking for turtles. The boys began roughhousing, and Shane ran through a narrow portion of the creek's ravine. Turning a sharp corner, he ran directly into a three feet diameter web with a large spider resting head downward in its center.

Shane tripped and hit his head as he fell. When he awoke, the web encircled his face, and he was staring through the spider, still clinging to the silver filament. The gold and black bulbous body of the golden garden spider was three inches long with legs extending even longer and wider. The thicker zigzag patterned portion of the web, called the stabilimentum, extended from Shane's nose to the spider. Shane looked directly into the spider's two anterior median eyes, two posterior median eyes, and the two orange pedipalps extending from each side of the spider's face.

At his young age Shane had no way of knowing that golden garden spiders did not bite, and even if they did, the bites at most would cause an itchy bump similar to a mosquito bite. He panicked and began screaming deliriously. The other boys came to his rescue and pulled the web and the spider from his face, but the damage to Shane's psyche had been done. The spider on Shane's porch light appeared to be a similar breed, but at this time of year, it was much smaller, perhaps a half inch long.

Keeping a wary eye upward as he moved forward, Shane returned to the door and opened it. His house was a shamble. Whether the intruder was still there was the question that Shane's pounding heart wanted answered. As Shane walked through the breakfast nook into his living room, he had difficulty finding places on the floor not covered by his possessions. Looking back at the side door, he saw the alarm box ripped from the wall and hanging by its wires. The visitor or visitors had responded with an act of brute force and rage rather than intelligence.

As Shane continued to inspect the damage into the library, he saw golden coins dating back to the time of King Herod scattered on the floor. Framed antique maps once on the wall were now on the floor with their protective panes of glass shattered. The break-in had not been a burglary. They had been after *him*. It had to be his two French guests.

I guess they weren't willing to wait for my answer. A thought struck him with the force of a sledge hammer. *They know what the gospel really is.*

Shane reached for his billfold and pulled from it the cards of the two detectives who had visited him. He first keyed in the number for the New Haven detective, Ben Taylor. He waited while the detective's phone rang and eventually went to voice mail.

"Detective Taylor, this is Shane Randall. I need to talk to you. Please call me."

Shane left his mobile number and disconnected. He flipped to the next card and punched in the number. After two rings, a sleepy voice answered.

"Hello?"

Shane struggled to hide the panic in his voice. "Detective Reese?"

"Yes, who's this?"

It was obvious Shane had disturbed the Cambridge detective's sleep. "This is Shane Randall. I'm not sure if you're still in town, but I need help. I tried Detective Taylor, but he didn't answer."

"What is it?"

"Someone broke into my house."

"There's a car down the street. Stay there. I'll call them."

A car down the street? Are they watching me? Shane thought for a minute. "Are you sure? I just drove in and didn't see anyone."

"Hell! They may have left. Stay there. Someone'll be there soon. I'm on my way."

Detective Reese hung up, leaving Shane to assess his situation. He knew when the police arrived they would secure his house and everything in it. He would not be able to do anything or go anywhere alone. He needed time. *I'm not going to stay here and wait for anyone.*

Shane hurried into his bedroom and packed a rollerboard suitcase with about a week's worth of clothing and toiletries. He found his passport and put it in his back pocket. Then he reached for his home phone and called Lauren in her hotel; that is, he called Elizabeth Phillips.

When Lauren picked up the phone, she did not speak right away but continued to breathe heavily. Under other circumstances, Shane would have laughed at the image he had of her in his mind–gorgeously nude under the covers with eyes still closed and the phone held limply to her ear.

"Lauren, wake up. You have to listen to me."

"Shane, is that you? Why aren't you here?"

"I'll explain all that later. You have to get out of there."

He could see in his mind that Lauren was instantly alert. "What is it?"

"You need to pack and check out of the hotel. I have a professor friend of mine who's out of the country. Write this address down." Shane gave her the address. "Get there as soon as you can. If you get there before I do, look in the flower bed to the right of the front door. There's a spare key under the stone hedgehog."

"I understand." Lauren hung up.

Shane stood for a moment longer in his demolished house. The damage filled him with a deep sense of loss. He knew there was nothing he could do about the invasion of his house, but he also knew how to hurt the ones who did it. He would solve the mystery of the Sicarii Gospel and take from them what they wanted most.

Chapter 36

Reese arrived at Randall's house with three New Haven detectives and a half dozen uniformed policemen. He had not been able to contact Ben, but he ultimately had convinced Ben's captain something very wrong may have occurred. Once on board, the captain had responded with impressive speed and force.

They searched the ransacked house but did not find Randall. As Reese walked a second time from room to room, he played out possible scenarios. *Was he abducted? No, Randall called me after the break-in. But why would he leave on his own? He must have reconsidered police involvement in whatever he is doing.*

Reese exited the house through the front door. A commotion down the block drew him to the car he had sat in with Peters and Longwell. Several detectives surrounded one of the uniformed policemen, who was using a crowbar to open the trunk.

A detective noticed Reese. "We found a lot of blood on the grass, street, and trunk."

The trunk popped open and everyone gasped. The bodies of Peters and Longwell lay haphazardly on top of each other in a dried pool of blood. Longwell's upper torso was caked in blood, and Peters face, throat, and chest were slashed.

Reese could not hide the rebuke in his tone. "Did anyone notice they hadn't checked in?"

The detectives looked at each other with confusion before one of them replied. "We were unusually hectic last night. I guess they got lost in the churn."

Reese could not believe what he had just heard. "Lost in the churn! That's the best you can come up with? Anyone find Ben yet?"

The detectives shook their heads.

"Lost in the churn as well?"

Reese was getting less popular with every biting comment. One of the detectives stepped within in inches of Reese's face. "Look! They were *our* friends. And this isn't your jurisdiction. We'll get who did this. Perhaps *you* should go home."

Reese glowered at him, but then a thought struck him. "You're right. You're fully capable of handling this. I need a car to get back to my hotel."

Another detective tossed him his keys. Reese hit the unlock button on the fob and located the car. Without speaking, he turned toward the Dodge Charger and left the others behind him. Any time he spent with them would be wasted. They knew what had occurred could have happened to any of them. They were operating on sheer emotion. They were a family. The size of New Haven made them a close family. Reese was a distant cousin at best.

Protocol would have him leave the case to them and sit back and watch. But he had seen this situation before. The sound bites would be full of outrage. The New Haven law enforcement fraternity would swear revenge. But it would take time to form the task force, get the structure in place, and hand out the assignments. Reese's senses told him for this case that approach was too cumbersome. There was not enough time to follow the book. Reese would not wait.

Chapter 37

Lauren stepped from her rental car not looking anything like herself. After getting Shane's call, she had thrown on some jeans and a T-shirt. She had wrapped her hair in a scarf and had kept out an overcoat and her sunglasses. Everything else she had packed. She had not bothered to checkout. No one knew who she was, and there was no longer any evidence she had stayed in the hotel.

Lauren's survival instinct had told her to run and leave Shane as a diversion. Something was wrong. Shane had obviously experienced something that had frightened him. But leaving Shane meant leaving the gospel.

She stood by her car with the door open and the engine running and stared at the upper middle-class house. The deep darkness of the early morning sky was just beginning to lessen with the faintest rays of light. She must have arrived before Shane. She scanned both directions along the houses and shrubbery but saw nothing in the shadows. She reached into the car and turned the key. The engine went silent.

She walked up the sidewalk leading to the front door. The house had a large tree to each side of the sidewalk and low shrubs of various sizes and textures along the front. She stopped short of the porch and searched the flower bed to her right. Exactly where Shane said it would be sat a small stone hedgehog, its rough gray body partially covered by the limbs of a Chinese holly bush. She bent down, avoided the thorny leaves, and lifted the small round sculpture to find a bronze-colored key.

As Lauren reached for the key a large hand gripped her right shoulder. Her heart almost stopped, but her training took over. She dropped the hedgehog, reached up with her left hand, and grabbed across the top of the hand firmly. Then she twisted it to the outside as she rose to her feet. The action took her attacker to the ground with a thud and a groan of surprise. Bringing her right hand in to help, she continued to twist and pull until the entire arm was extended and distorted. Then with the thumbs of both hands she directed all her weight down on the back of the hand and bent the attacker's wrist back toward his arm. She knew it would snap in a matter of seconds.

"Lauren! It's me."

Lauren let up on the pressure but did not release the hand. "Shane! Are you trying to give me a heart attack?"

Shane's voice was strained, with a higher pitch than normal. "More likely the other way around." He nodded toward his arm. "Do you mind?"

Lauren released Shane's hand and began composing herself.

Shane rose to his feet rubbing his wrist. "Where'd you learn that?"

"I took a self-defense class a few years ago. A girl can't be too careful."

Shane reached up and rubbed his shoulder. "Well, you're good at it. You just about separated my bad shoulder and almost broke my wrist."

Lauren struggled to regain her breath. "Where'd you come from?"

"I parked in the back. I came around front to get the key and saw you."

Lauren's pulse slowed enough for her nerves to settle. She reached down, retrieved the key, and handed it to Shane. As she did, her hand trembled a little. She took advantage of the momentary weakness by exaggerating the shake for effect.

Shane took the key with one hand and held her hand with the other. He pulled her to his chest and wrapped his arms around her. Lauren reciprocated and pressed her breasts and the side of her face against him. She had to admit the position felt great. Maybe she had made the right decision to meet him after all.

Shane was first to break the embrace. He raised his hands to her shoulders and held her in place about a foot in front of him. Lauren kept her head down to communicate with body language how sorry she was for involving him in a life-threatening situation. Shane moved his right hand to her chin and raised her head such that their eyes met. His blue eyes communicated great confidence. There was no blame, no despair.

He held up the key. "Let's go in. I have something to show you."

Chapter 38

Reese pulled into the parking lot of the Omni New Haven Hotel. As far as he knew, he was the only one Ben had given the location. He searched for Ben's car but could not find it. He had a bad feeling his friend had joined the ever-increasing list of victims in this bizarre case.

Reese got out of his car and entered the hotel. He found the front desk and walked up to where a very young clerk was processing paperwork. The clerk looked up with a puzzled expression. People approaching him so early in the morning must have been a rare occurrence. Reese flashed his badge, not giving the clerk time to read the city. The clerk's eyes widened more.

Reese pressed his advantage. "I have a couple of questions about two men staying here."

The clerk shrugged his shoulders. "I work nights. I may not've seen them."

"If you've seen them, you'll remember. One is an older white man. The other's a giant black man, much younger. He looks like a football player. Very tall. He must weigh four hundred pounds."

Recognition brightened the clerk's face. He seemed eager to share what he knew. "I haven't seen the older man, but a giant black man matching that description came in a few hours ago."

"Do you know his room number?"

"No, I don't, but I could get my manager."

Reese knew he was out of his jurisdiction, and he had no evidence to justify barging into a hotel room. "That won't be necessary. I'm going to wait for them here."

Chapter 39

As the morning light forced its way through the slim openings in the shuttered windows, Shane and Lauren huddled in front of Shane's laptop computer. They sat in the kitchen of the spartan house belonging to one of Shane's single academic friends. Shane was confident they would be a long way from New Haven before anyone figured out the connection and looked for them there.

Shane reestablished his network link to the university intranet and accessed Jane's folder. Instead of reading the documents online, he saved the images and translation to his laptop hard drive. Then he downloaded another folder containing images, a translation, and other supporting commentaries on the Copper Scroll.

Lauren seemed intrigued. "The Copper Scroll?"

"Yes. What do you know about it?"

"I know it's an ancient treasure map found with the Dead Sea Scrolls. I also know a lot of people have tried to find the treasure without one piece of it ever being found."

"That's right."

"You think that's the treasure the Vraie École Biblique is after?"

"That's exactly what I think. Look at this."

Shane split his screen and pulled up the first two columns of the Copper Scroll on the left side and the first two columns of the alleged Sicarii Gospel on the right side. He adjusted the images of the two documents to equivalent sizes. Then he sat back and looked at Lauren. "Notice anything?"

He watched the excitement of recognition brighten her eyes.

She pointed from one document to the other. "They're the same shape!"

"Yes. I'm an idiot for not seeing it earlier. I knew there was something odd about the shape of the gospel. I just didn't link the two. Now watch."

Shane pulled up the remaining columns of the two documents, two columns at a time. The number of lines in each column, the associated margins, and therefore the shape of the columns were identical.

Shane exuded his pride in his discovery. "The odds against this happening have to be a billion to one. One of the oddities of the Copper Scroll is its shape created by all the unused space. First century Jewish scribes normally wrote from right to left filling every bit of the available space. They didn't leave margins or indent paragraphs. It's been demonstrated the Copper Scroll could've been written in only seven columns rather than twelve. So given the value of copper at that time, why would a scribe waste so much space?"

"Makes you wonder."

"And then to find the same waste on a vellum document. It can't be a coincidence."

"So what are you thinking?"

Shane spun around to look at Lauren. "If the Essenes of Khirbet Qumran and the early Jewish Christians were one and the same, then isn't it likely the Copper Scroll written by the Essenes and the Sicarii Gospel written by Jewish Christians were really both written by the same sect?"

"Makes sense to me."

"And what if when the École Biblique translated and studied the Dead Sea Scrolls it found texts that looked Christian but in places were inconsistent with the four canonical gospels? Like a Teacher of Righteousness who was also a revolutionary. Wouldn't it be natural for them to explain it away with the mysterious and obscure sect of Essenes? When people heard *Essenes*, they just yawned and went about their business. But if the École Biblique had said *Christians*, then the news would've made headlines. The Church would've had to explain the differences."

Lauren caught on quickly. "So by referencing the Essenes, the École Biblique began a cover-up that has lasted over sixty years."

Shane nodded. He hid the document images and pulled up their translations side by side. Then he paged down to the end of the Copper Scroll translation. *That's it.* "What a lot of people don't know, even people familiar with the Copper Scroll, is only sixty-three of the sixty-four locations in the Copper Scroll describe treasure. The last section is different. Look."

Shane waited for Lauren to find the section. Then he read it out loud.

"Buried at the mouth of a dry pit with smooth rock walls and its opening pointing northward is a copy of this document, with an explanation of the locations and their measurements, and everything in the inventory."

Shane knew he was closing in on the answer. He gestured to the screen with a voila wave of his arm. He looked at Lauren, but she appeared confused. He knew he had not connected the dots for her. "Its position as last in the Copper Scroll's list is very significant. It describes the greatest of the treasures listed because it promises a way to decode the Copper Scroll. The exact wording's not meant to be taken any more literally than the rest of the locations and instructions. What's important is the Copper Scroll says very plainly there's a second document the reader needs to interpret it."

"So you think our gospel's the second document. The key."

Her voice still lacked the excitement Shane expected. *No wonder. There's a lot more to my hypothesis.* "Most scholars assume the second copy to be another copper scroll. But what if it isn't? What if it's a document in disguise, such a good disguise that multiple copies of it could be written and distributed without anyone knowing what it is?"

Lauren was catching on. "You mean like a sayings gospel."

"Exactly. What if the secret book of knowledge referenced in the Apocryphon of James was so secret because it was the Sicarii Gospel, which held the key to finding the early Christian war chest? And what if that secret book is the same scroll referenced at the end of the Copper Scroll?"

"You think the treasure of the Copper Scroll is the war chest?"

"Imagine what must've been going on when the Jews first rebelled against the Romans and took Jerusalem. Zealots dancing in the streets celebrating their independence. Temple priests, having lost their Roman sponsors, defending themselves from their own people. Ignorant peasants watching confused, unsure of what to do. Religious scribes afraid that if their scroll libraries burned, the entire religious heritage of the Jews could be lost."

"Chaos."

"Yes, and in the middle of all the chaos, a small Jewish sect stood apart, having been told by their executed leader that false messiahs would lead their people into wars with no chance of success. The Jewish Christian leaders know in their hearts the Romans'll soon triumphantly return. The fate of their entire sect depends on what they do next. What would you do?"

Lauren used her best Texas twang. "I'd high-tail it out of there."

"Right! You wouldn't commit your resources to a lost cause. You'd run away to fight another day. The leader of the Jewish Christian sect at that time was Simon the

Zealot. Ironically, you have a man so radical that Jesus nicknamed him *the Zealot*, but instead of fighting the Romans, he leaves. It's a testament to how strong the beliefs of these early Jewish Christians were, and how much faith they had in the words of their founder Jesus."

Shane paused.

Lauren put her hand on his thigh. "What is it?"

"You're Simon the Zealot, and you've decided to leave Jerusalem. What do you do with the war chest you've amassed from your converts?"

"I'd take it with me."

"Of course. Why would you leave it behind for the Romans to find? That has to be what happened. The Jewish Christians left right under the noses of the celebrating Jewish revolutionaries and took their wealth with them. And no one has seen the treasure since. The treasure of the Copper Scroll is the war chest of the Jewish Christian church."

Shane paused again. All kinds of thoughts swirled in his head until they coalesced on one central question. "What if Jesus never came back to lead that final war?" He answered his own question. "Over the decades and centuries, the Church morphs. The Jewish Christians are wiped out. Secrets are lost. Even if you have a copy of the Sicarii Gospel, you think it's a sayings gospel. Wouldn't the treasure still be waiting?"

Lauren squeezed his leg hard. "Unless someone stumbled onto it."

Shane studied the two documents. *There's a connection. What is it? It must be right in front of me.* His eyes went back and forth between the images.

Lauren must have seen his struggle. "You *do* know how they connect, don't you?"

"Not exactly."

"What do you mean? I thought you'd figured it out."

"No, I'm hoping now that we know the two documents connect, it won't be that difficult to figure out the rest."

Lauren leaned back in her chair and pinned her chin to her chest. "That's what thousands of other people have thought over the last half century."

Shane leaned over and rested his hand on her forearm. He looked deeply into her eyes.

"*They* didn't have the Sicarii Gospel. Thanks to you, *we* do. I promise you. I *will* find the connection."

Chapter 40

Jane walked down the deserted hallway toward the lab. It was not a rare occurrence for her to be the first one on the floor in the early morning. The lab was the only place she felt complete, felt totally alive.

As usual when first to arrive, she questioned her lifestyle and her focus on work. But her personal life was not totally uneventful. She went on the occasional date. Her parents and brother and sister lived in the area. And for company at home she had Pearl, a solid white, short-haired, puma-shaped house cat. Regardless, wherever she was or whatever she was doing, she was biding time until she could return to work.

At the hallway door to the lab, she reached into her purse, found her key, and slid it into the keyhole. The door moved. *Restless in anticipation!* The light was on. *Was I last to leave? Didn't I turn the light off?*

She put the keys back in her purse and pushed the door inward. She saw the door frame splintered and knew someone had struck the door lock with more force than the surrounding wood could take. Her pulse quickened, and she hyperventilated. *Should I get help?* She weighed the risk, and anger replaced her fear. *Hell no! This is my lab!*

She slowly leaned forward, put her head through the increasing space, and turned it both ways to search for the intruder. The outer office was a mess with papers, books, and drawer contents strewn everywhere across the floor. Computer terminals lay crumpled on the floor as if they had been picked up and thrown with intense anger. Desks lay on their sides with cavities where drawers once were.

No one was there.

She stepped across the threshold and walked to the lab door. She repeated the process of slowly opening the door and peering inward to see if anyone was there. The lab was dark, but she did not see any movement. She reached in and turned on the lights.

What she saw was utter destruction. She weaved her way through the debris in utter shock. *Slow down, you move to fast! You got to make the morning last!* When she finally made it to the vault at the far side of the room, she saw the strength of the steel had severely frustrated someone. Small dents and scratches indicated someone had repeatedly beaten the door with whatever he could find in the room.

Jane wept. She could not even imagine the extent of the damage to the various projects in process. *Who would do such a thing?* She could think of only one place to go for answers. She reached for her mobile phone and nervously pulled up Doctor Randall's mobile number. She listened while it rang once, and then a second time.

"Hello, Jane?"

His voice was like pure adrenaline. He would know what to do. She began blubbering into her phone.

"Doctor Randall, someone broke into the lab." She could control her grief no longer. *"When you're weary, feeling sad, when tears are in your eyes!* They've destroyed everything."

She accentuated her report with sobs.

Doctor Randall spoke in a soothing tone. "Jane, calm down. What about the gospel?"

"No, it's safe. It's in the vault. They couldn't get in."

"Listen, Jane. Get out of there now. Leave everything as it is."

"But Doctor Randall..."

"Jane, I have to get off the phone. I only answered it because I saw your name and wanted to know you were safe. Don't worry about anything. Get out of there and stay away until you hear from me. Call everyone else and tell them the same thing. Do you understand?"

"No, but I'll do it." As she spoke she remembered the visit from the police detectives. Something more fearsome than her damaged lab filled her thoughts. "Are you ok? Is someone after you?"

"Don't worry about me. I'll be fine. Just get out of there. I have to go."

The line went dead. Jane wiped her tears with her hand and then her hand on her jeans. She would be brave for Doctor Randall.

Chapter 41

Lauren could tell Jane's call had shaken Shane. After hanging up, he had leaned back away from the documents on his laptop monitor, lost in thought.

She reached out and rubbed his shoulder. "Is Jane ok?"

"Yes, but the lab's lost." He saw Lauren's eyes widen. "Don't worry. The gospel's safe in the vault." He paused. "These guys aren't going to stop until they get it, are they?"

"No, I'm afraid not."

"I might give it to them if I thought they'd just leave."

"You know that's not the answer. We have to get what's at the other end of the gospel."

Shane leaned forward and stared at the monitor again. Lauren leaned in beside him. They remained that way without anything said for several minutes.

Lauren's patience ebbed. "Shane, I can't read your mind."

"Really? Seems to me you've been doing a great job of it."

Lauren ignored the reproach. "Seriously, Shane. Tell me what you're thinking. Saying it out loud may help."

He exhaled loudly. "All right. I'm frustrated. I don't know what I'm missing."

"Go through it with me."

"There are a lot of different opinions on how to unravel the Copper Scroll. You and I are guessing the only way is to have both the Copper Scroll and the Sicarii Gospel."

"That's right."

"The thing is, if we have both documents, why isn't it more obvious. We have both the lock and the key. We shouldn't have to pick the lock."

Lauren knew sometimes solving a problem was easier if you came at it from an oblique angle. "How much do you think the treasure's worth?"

Shane stared at her as if he found the question random. "I don't know."

"Guess."

"Where are you going with this?"

"I want to try something."

Shane backed away from the monitor. "All right. Let's do some math. Let's assume Jesus had two hundred followers at his death in around the year 30. We know the year at least roughly because Pontius Pilatus ruled from 26 to 36 C.E. and Joseph ben Caiaphas ruled from 18 to 36 C.E. Ironically, both of them were removed from office in the same year because of various acts of wrongdoing the Romans couldn't tolerate any longer."

Lauren laughed. "Of course you'd know that."

"Unlike core Judaism, Jesus' sect was a proselytizing religion. That is, Jesus sent his disciples out to actively convert other people. So let's ignore the three thousand men converted on Pentecost and assume the church grew ten percent per year for the forty years between Jesus' death and the destruction of the Jewish Temple. What that means is during the entire year after Jesus' death, his two hundred followers only had to convert twenty others. In the year 32, they would've only had to convert twenty-two new believers. And so on."

"That doesn't sound like a lot."

"Not until you perform the calculation and realize that conversion rate would lead to the number of Christians growing to over nine thousand by the year 70."

Lauren wanted to keep him down this line of thinking. "That's incredible. It's like compound interest on an investment."

"Exactly. Now let's assume only one percent of those converts were wealthy Jews, split evenly between the very wealthy with the equivalent of fifty million today dollars and the fairly wealthy with the equivalent of five million today dollars. The resulting war chest would be worth about two and a half billion dollars. That amount just happens to be within the range of market valuations for the treasure."

Lauren whistled. "That's a lot of money. What would it be worth to museums?"

"It'd be subjective, but probably five to ten times that amount."

"That's even more money."

Shane looked at Lauren, and she could feel him penetrating into her soul. She answered him with her eyes. *Of course I'm driven by financial reward. You're not immune to numbers that big either.*

In an instant Shane's facial expression changed. She knew he had experienced an epiphany. He turned to the images again.

"What is it, Shane? What have you figured out?"

"Since no one knows our gospel exists, traditional methods to interpret the Copper Scroll focused solely on that document. I'm afraid I've been letting that way of thinking influence me."

"How so?"

"To find the connection, I shouldn't be thinking about what's the same between the two documents. I should be thinking about what's different."

"What do you mean?"

Shane continued to speak while he worked the keyboard and shifted the images on the screen. "What are the differences between the two documents?"

Lauren thought for a few seconds. "One's copper, and one's vellum?"

"True, but that's not it."

"One's in Hebrew, and one's in Aramaic."

"Also true, but that's not it either." Shane laughed. He was having fun at her expense.

"What, Shane? Tell me."

"Look at this." Shane pointed to the images. "As you noticed yourself, the documents are identical in shape but not in words. Any number of substitution codes could link the two documents, but I think a code like that is far too complex. As I said, we have both the lock and the key. Why make it overly complicated?"

Lauren's optimism spiked. "So what am I looking at?"

"You're looking at the first two columns of both documents. Are they the same?"

Lauren's excitement dissipated. "We've been over this. They're the same."

"Look again. Look closely."

Lauren leaned her head closer to the screen. She stared for several seconds. There it was. It was obvious. Why had they not seen it before?

Chapter 42

Raphael sat on his made-up bed and leaned back on the headboard. A pillow supported his lower back, but the weight of his upper torso distorted the headboard such that it rested against the wall and groaned with his every move. His father's phone rang in the other room. Raphael felt a headache coming.

His father answered. "*Oui?*"

Raphael could tell by his father's tone that the Directeur was on the other end.

"*Non.*"

They did not yet have the gospel.

"*Oui. Trois.*"

The Directeur must have asked whether there had been more killings. The long silence meant the Directeur was not happy.

"*Surveiller des détectives.*"

The fact that the three men killed were police detectives would not make the Directeur any happier.

"*Je sais.*"

His father was agreeing with whatever the Directeur was saying.

"*Nous aurons l'évangile aujourd'hui.*"

His father just committed they would have the gospel today. They had found the woman's hotel. Their net was closing in on their prey.

"*Je comprends.*"

The conversation must have been accentuated with a threat. His father understood the consequences of failure.

"*Adieu.*"

Raphael heard his father's footsteps coming toward his room and stood up.

"Come," his father said. "We must finish this."

Chapter 43

Shane waited for Lauren to see them.

Lauren pointed to a spot on the image of the Copper Scroll. "They're the same except for these extra characters."

Shane nodded. He was smiling with pride. "They're Greek letters. Sixteen in total. They appear in seven different places in the Copper Scroll."

"What are they doing in a Hebrew scroll?"

"There are a lot of theories about that. Some scholars think they're the initials of the scribes or metalworkers who etched the Copper Scroll. Others believe the letters spell out a name of a person or a location, and they've played with all sorts of anagrams. Greek is used very sparingly in the Dead Sea Scrolls and nowhere else like this. Until now, they've been one of the Copper Scroll's mysteries."

Lauren spoke with an anticipatory tone. "Until now?"

"I should've seen it before. Write down the Greek letters as we find them."

Lauren reached for a pen and paper and wrote down the first letters that appeared in the margin of the fourth line of the first column.

Κ Ε Ν

Shane pointed to the margin three lines from the bottom of that same column. "Don't forget these."

Lauren wrote three more Greek letters next to the first three.

Κ Ε Ν Χ Α Γ

Shane continued to direct her. "There are six more in column two. Two in the second line, two in the fourth line, and two in the ninth line."

Jane dutifully wrote them down in sequence.

Κ Ε Ν Χ Α Γ Η Ν Θ Ε Δ Ι

Shane scrolled to the third and fourth columns.

Lauren found them herself. "There are two more right in the middle of the third column."

Shane pointed. "And look at the size of that margin. There must be a reason. The last two are in the second line of the fourth column."

When Lauren finished writing them down, she looked at Shane for the rest of the story. "Now what?"

Κ Ε Ν Χ Α Γ Η Ν Θ Ε Δ Ι Τ Ρ Σ Κ

Shane's smile kept getting broader. "What do you make of it?"

"Nothing. It doesn't spell anything."

"Not even a Greek word?"

"No."

Shane laughed. "That's because they aren't letters."

Lauren grew tired of the runaround. "Shane, No more games. Explain it to me right now!"

"They're numbers. Since long before the first century, the Hebrews and Greeks used letters of the alphabet to express numbers. This concept's better known to us today with the Roman numeral system."

Shane took the pen and wrote some Roman letters and their numerical values.

1
5
10
50
100
500
1000

Lauren seemed impatient. “Of course. Everyone knows them.”

“What everyone doesn’t know is Greek letters and Hebrew letters were used the same way. Using letters to represent numbers was practical, but it also allowed a writer to work magic with numerology.”

“What do you mean?”

“If every letter in the alphabet is also a number, then every word or phrase has a numeric value.”

“I guess so.” Lauren paused, apparently letting the words sink in. “If every letter is a number, then letters together would also be a number.”

“Right. When doing this in Hebrew, it’s called *gematria.* In Greek it’s called *isopsephy.* Both are forms of numerology that allow words to contain symbolism associated with a number. The Bible adheres to a numeric code, and both the Old and New Testaments are full of this sort of symbolism. But unless I miss my guess, what we have here’s much simpler. These are just numbers that look like letters.”

Shane reached into his laptop bag and pulled from it a laminated sheet. On the sheet were two tables. In the top table were the Hebrew letters and their corresponding numerical values. In the bottom table was the Greek counterpart.

Tet	Het	Zayin	Vav	Heh	Dalet	Gimel	Bet	Aleph
ט	ח	ז	ו	ה	ד	ג	ב	א
9	8	7	6	5	4	3	2	1
Tsade	Pe	Ayin	Samekh	Nun	Mem	Lamed	Kaf	Yod
צ	פ	ע	ס	נ	מ	ל	כ	י
90	80	70	60	50	40	30	20	10
					Tav	Shin	Resh	Qof
					ת	ש	ר	ק
					400	300	200	100
Tsade-F	Pe-F	Nun-F	Mem-F	Kaf-F				
ץ	ף	ן	ם	ך				
900	800	700	600	500				

Alpha	Beta	Gamma	Delta	Epsilon	Stigma	Zeta	Eta	Theta
Α, α	Β, β	Γ, γ	Δ, δ	Ε, ε	ς	Ζ, ζ	Η, η	Θ, θ
1	2	3	4	5	6	7	8	9

Iota	Kappa	Lambda	Mu	Nu	Xi	Omicron	Pi	Koppa
Ι, ι	Κ, κ	Λ, λ	Μ, μ	Ν, ν	Ξ, ξ	Ο, ο	Π, ϖ	ϟ
10	20	30	40	50	60	70	80	90

Rho	Sigma	Tau	Upsilon	Phi	Chi	Psi	Omega	Sampi
Ρ, ρ	Σ, σ	Τ, τ	Υ, υ	Φ, φ	Χ, χ	Ψ, ψ	Ω, ω	ϡ
100	200	300	400	500	600	700	800	900

Shane read Lauren's face. "You'd think I'd know these without having to look."

"I can't believe you know this at all."

Shane got the jab. He was on thin ice of being a nerd. "You see, with the Copper Scroll written in Hebrew, adding other Hebrew letters as reference numbers wouldn't work. But Greek letters work just fine."

"If you say so."

"Okay then, let's see what we have with our Greek letters."

Shane wrote the numeric values below the corresponding Greek letters.

Κ	**Ε**	**Ν**	**Χ**	**Α**	**Γ**	**Η**	**Ν**	**Θ**	**Ε**	**Δ**	**Ι**	**Τ**	**Ρ**	**Σ**	**Κ**
20	5	50	600	1	3	8	50	9	5	4	10	300	100	200	20

Shane reviewed them with an expert eye. "What we have are sixteen separate numbers."

"How do you know the groupings of letters aren't large numbers? How do you know KEN doesn't represent seventy-five?"

Shane was impressed Lauren had picked up the concept so well. "Because large numbers are formed by selecting the letter with the largest numeric value less than the number to be written. Then the largest valued letter less than the remainder would be selected, and so on. If KEN were seventy-five, it would be OE. If XAΓ were six hundred four, it would be XΔ."

"I see. So what do we do now?"

"We start in the Sicarii Gospel at the same place as these numbers appear in the Copper Scroll. Then we count the number of characters corresponding to the numerical value of the Greek letters. If we write the corresponding letters in the Sicarii Gospel, we may find a message. Check me as I go."

Shane began counting and writing.

Lauren moved closer to the characters Shane wrote. "That looks like scribble to me."

"I'm afraid my writing of Aramaic isn't very good."

One by one, Shane found and wrote the sixteen Aramaic letters indicated by the Greek numbers. Then he began dividing them into words.

Lauren's impatience was bubbling over. "What does it say? Can you read it?"

"My reading of Aramaic isn't much better than my writing."

"Shit!" Lauren brought her hands down hard on the arms of her chair. "What do we do now? Take it to Jane?"

"I said my Aramaic isn't that good, but I know what it says."

Lauren straightened up and shoved Shane forcefully in his shoulder. "You asshole!"

Shane guffawed. He was ecstatic.

Lauren shoved him again. "Well?"

"It's a combination of Aramaic and Greek place names from the time the Copper Scroll was written. It says *Yegar-Sahadutha Dekapolis Rihabis.*"

"Is that one place or three?"

"Both."

"Shane! Do you want me to hurt you?"

He laughed again before letting the high settle in. He had deciphered a code that had remained hidden for two thousand years. "Yegar-Sahadutha is Aramaic and means *the Mount of Gilead.* Gilead was an Old Testament region on the eastern side of the Jordan River between the Dead Sea and the Sea of Galilee. It was home to three of the twelve tribes of Israel."

Lauren repeated what she heard. "So the first word refers to Gilead. How about the next word?"

"After Alexander the Great conquered the region, the Greeks founded ten cities in and around Gilead. They came under Hasmonean rule when the Jewish Maccabees conquered the area and then under the Romans when Pompey conquered Judea in 63 B.C.E. Since the ten cities were Greek rather than Jewish, they welcomed Pompey as a liberator. It was in the Romans' interest for the cities to grow and thrive so they left them in place as semi-autonomous city-states. The region became known as *Dekapolis* which in Greek means *Ten Cities*. It's mentioned in the New Testament. Jesus traveled there."

Lauren seemed doubtful. "That still sounds like an area too large. Does *Rihabis* narrow our search?"

"Definitely. Do you remember us talking about the Jewish Christians fleeing Jerusalem just before the Romans arrived to destroy the Temple?"

"Of course."

"The fourth century church historian Eusebius reported the Jewish Christians received a revelation from God that they should go to one of the Dekapolis cities–Pella. But there's no hard archaeological evidence of the Jewish Christians taking refuge in Pella before the second Jewish-Roman War, when Hadrian totally destroyed Jerusalem and banned Jews from the city."

"So where does that leave us?"

"Rihabis was a smaller city in Dekapolis. It was within the jurisdiction of the city-state of Pella. What if the Jewish Christians were afraid to move to a large Roman-friendly Greek city at a time when the Jews and the Romans were at war? Wouldn't it make sense they'd move to a smaller city instead? Later reports of the Jewish Christians fleeing to Pella in the first century may have been referring to the city-state of Pella rather than the actual city."

"Shane, you're doing it again."

Shane laid it out for her. "The Jewish Christians moved their church to Rihabis, which lies within the Old Testament region of Gilead and the New Testament region of Dekapolis within the city-state of Pella. Rihabis is the Greco-Roman name for what's now Rihab, Jordan. I know exactly where we need to go."

Lauren jumped up and leaped into action. "I have ten different passports and sets of credit cards in each name. We'll do everything we can in my name. I know you probably have just the one passport so we'll have to use it. It makes traveling without being followed a little more challenging, but I know ways of dealing with it. Throw away your phone and credit cards. We're going off the grid."

Chapter 44

Amit David sat at his laptop after having worked all day with the Israel Antiquities Authority on the disposition of the ossuaries he and his team had discovered. The issue with the ossuaries was what they contained–the bones of first century Jews. Israeli law dictated that before the ossuaries could be removed for study, any bones, bone fragments, or remaining tissue must be removed with the appropriate respect and ceremony and reinterred by the Orthodox Jewish authorities. Over the years the Israel Antiquities Authority had numbered and cataloged about one thousand ossuaries.

Amit was excited because he had found several adjustments to improve his computer model. As he was inputting one of the parameter updates, his satphone rang beside him. "Amit David."

"Docteur David, how are you?"

"Bonsoir, Monsieur Clisson."

"How are your ossuaries?"

Amit picked up on the sarcasm. "The Antiquities Authority is here. You know how that goes."

"Yes, I do. How are you proceeding with the search?"

"I've made some adjustments. We'll be ready to dig again quickly."

"You can stop your efforts, Docteur David."

"What do you mean? Are you pulling your support?"

"Far from it. In fact, I will be coming there soon to assist your efforts."

"I'm confused."

"No reason to be. As I told you. Help is on the way. Accept it when it comes."

"I don't understand."

"You will." Clisson disconnected.

The call left Amit perplexed. There were times when he did not understand Clisson's eccentricity. He returned to his model, but after only a few minutes his satphone rang again. "Amit David."

"Amit, this is Shane."

Hearing from Shane always made Amit feel better. Shane and he had worked many projects together throughout Israel. The tough conditions had resulted in a special bond forged from respect, dependability, and similar interests. Though they were separated by an ocean and did not talk to one another for weeks at a time, Shane was one of his closest friends.

The two often debated their different beliefs. Shane's special interest was first century Christianity, and he had some radical positions on early Judaism and Jewish Christianity. Amit thought Shane extrapolated too much without hard facts. Shane accused Amit of relying so much on facts that he had disconnected his common sense. It was great fun.

"It's good to hear you, Shane."

"It's good to be heard. Look, Amit, I don't have long to talk. I need a big favor, but it's one you may find very rewarding if you can do it."

If Shane was in, Amit was in. "You know I'll help you any way I can."

"Another friend of mine and I are on our way to Israel. I know it's short notice, but can you pick us up in Tel Aviv tomorrow afternoon?"

"I'm in the middle of something outside of Qumran. Does it have to be tomorrow?"

"Yes. It's important."

It was unlike Shane to be so mysterious. "What's going on?"

"I'd rather not discuss it over the phone. I'll tell you when we meet. Until then, I'm asking you to trust me."

"Of course. I guess I can hand off what I'm doing here."

"Qumran. That brings back good memories."

Amit grunted. "Right now it's not going well."

"Well get ready for a change. I'm on the verge of something big, and I want you to be part of it. More than that, I need your help."

"All right. What time do you arrive?"

"3:10 PM on Delta Airlines."

"I'll be there."

Shane was not done. "Bring a four-wheel drive SUV big enough to seat three, and put some tools in the back."

"Are we going on a dig?"

"I wouldn't be at all surprised. One more thing. You might want to be a *cautious fellow.*"

Amit sucked in a breath and held it. Shane had just used a code phrase. It was part of a famous Indiana Jones line. He used it right before throwing his revolver into his suitcase. They had spent many nights testing each other's trivia quotients on the Indiana Jones movies. There was no doubting Shane's meaning.

"I understand."

"Good. I look forward to seeing you."

"Same here." Shane disconnected.

A rather boring day had just turned otherwise.

It's getting crowded in the Holy Lands.

Chapter 45

After hours of waiting in the hotel lobby, Reese tried to quell his impatience with the thought he did not know what he was going to do with the two men if he found them. He entered the small hotel novelty shop and bought a small bag of salted peanuts. He was not hungry, but he had to do something to keep busy. While eating them in small handfuls, he perused the magazines, always keeping one eye toward the lobby. The scantily clad women on the covers attracted his attention, but the articles left him wanting. *How do people read this crap?*

As he emerged from the shop, his mobile phone rang.

He answered in a monotone. "Reese."

"Detective Reese, I'm glad I found you. This is Captain Reginald Turner."

"Yes?"

"I thought you'd want to know we just found Ben Taylor's body."

"Where?"

"Near Yale University in a parking lot a couple of blocks from Science Hill. A patrolman spotted his car. We found him in the trunk. He was shot twice and left to bleed out."

Reese sighed. "He was a great guy."

"Yeah, and he had a wife and two girls at home."

"I didn't know."

"So Detective Reese, you want to tell me what's going on?"

As Reese was thinking about how to respond, the elevator opened and a short white man stepped out followed by a giant. They crossed the lobby toward the front door.

"Captain Turner, I'm at the Omni Hotel. I just found the two men who may be behind all this. Ben Taylor was here before he disappeared."

"Stay there. I'll send as many men as I can get."

"I can't wait. They're leaving. Get your men on the road. Stay on the line. I'll follow them and relay our position."

Reese ignored the warnings from Turner coming through the speaker. He kept the phone on but put it in his pocket. Exiting the lobby, he found the two men nonchalantly getting into their car. Reese looked away and took a direct path to his own car.

By the time he started his engine, the two men were already pulling out of the hotel parking lot. He allowed them a significant lead before following. When on the road he reached into his pocket for his phone. "Captain Turner, are you still there?"

"Yes. I hope you haven't done anything stupid."

"I can't promise that. We're headed westward on Chapel Street. Where are your men?"

"They're close."

To Reese's surprise, after only four short blocks, the Hyundai slowed and pulled into a hotel, the Three Chimneys Inn.

"Better hurry."

Chapter 46

Raphael smiled at the irony. While they had been searching for the woman all over the city, her hotel had been within walking distance of their own. He was glad it would soon be over. His instinct told him it was time to leave.

He wished his father was not with him. His father's code of morality would restrict the acts of defilement he could employ. Killing a woman should not be rushed. Their extreme emotional responses and obvious bodily advantages made killing them the ultimate experience. Such an act offered opportunity to satisfy both mind and body.

Raphael followed his father into the hotel lobby. Behind the registration desk stood a well-dressed young man, not much older than a college student. The youth watched them from the entrance to the desk. His wide smiled greeted them with the warmth he had been trained to exude. "Welcome to the Three Chimneys Inn. Checking in?"

Raphael's father waved off the question. "Non."

The desk clerk's smile faded upon hearing the French accent.

Raphael's father spoke with a confidence founded on his advantage. "We are looking for someone. A woman. Taller than I am. Shoulder-length brown hair. Attractive. Professional."

The desk clerk seemed happy the request was such a simple one, with a standard response. He replied with an enthusiasm inappropriate to his words. "I'm sorry, but we cannot give out information on our guests."

The three men stood silent for about thirty seconds.

The desk clerk twitched. "Is there something else I can do for you?"

Raphael's father replied with a single word. "Raphael."

Responding to the command, Raphael thrust his massive hand over the front desk and seized the desk clerk by the knot of his tie. He lifted him off the floor and halfway across the desk surface. The clerk's eyes bugged out in terror. His face turned a deepening shade of red.

Raphael's father spoke with a deliberate enunciation. "Perhaps with my accent you did not understand me. We want the woman's room number."

The desk clerk gasped for breath. Raphael looked into his eyes and smiled. It would be so easy to crush his throat.

"Raphael, let the young man talk."

Raphael loosened his grip. The desk clerk sucked in air to his full lung capacity.

Raphael's father leaned in closer to the clerk. "Room number."

The desk clerk spoke as if he had gravel in his throat. "Number 5."

Raphael's father pressed him further. "Key."

The desk clerk reached into his pants pocket and pulled out a key ring with a dozen keys. He played with the keys until he found one in particular. "Master."

"Raphael, keep the young man comfortable while I retrieve our friend."

Raphael's father pulled his Glock from his shoulder holster and climbed the stairs to the second floor. Raphael continued to support the desk clerk effortlessly and stared at him with all the intensity he could muster. It was fun.

The youth closed his eyes and begged for his life. "Please don't hurt me. I'll do whatever you want."

Raphael grunted and gave the clerk a little shake in response. The clerk's whimpers transformed into sobs. To Raphael the tears were beads of satisfaction.

After only a few minutes, he heard footsteps returning down the stairs. He turned to see his father. His weapon was hidden again, and he was frowning.

His father addressed the youth firmly. "Has the woman checked out? Her clothes are gone."

Tears streamed down the youth's cheeks. "No. I don't know."

As Raphael squeezed the youth's neck harder, a command came from the hotel entrance. "Police! Stay where you are!"

Raphael did not look in the direction of the voice, but he sensed the location of four policemen. He spun around, pulling the desk clerk with him. A shot rang out. The bullet struck the youth in the back near the shoulder, exiting his chest inches from Raphael's face. With both hands Raphael flung the limp desk clerk toward two of the policemen. With continued motion he dove to the ground and somersaulted in their direction. Two shots rang out from behind him, and a policeman fell. Another shot from in front of him whizzed over his head.

As Raphael completed his somersault the body of the clerk collided against its two-man target. Raphael followed it with a body roll of his own, leaping sideways into the air and coming down on the same men. He brought his elbow down on the temple of one of them and his knee to the face of the other, crushing his nose.

The lone remaining officer turned his weapon on Raphael, but another shot from near the hotel desk knocked the officer's legs out from under him and drove him face down to the floor. Raphael looked out the entrance and saw uniformed and plain-clothes policemen charging the door. Some wore assault gear and carried Heckler & Koch UMP submachine guns.

"Raphael!" It was time to go.

Raphael leaped to his feet and ran to catch up with his father, already near the rear entrance. As they emerged from the back of the hotel, shots rang out in their direction. The police had stationed men behind the hotel. Raphael and his father did not slow down.

An unsuspecting hotel resident pulled his car into the parking lot to their right and stopped. With bullets ricocheting off the pavement, Raphael and his father turned toward the car. Reaching it in seconds, they hid behind the vehicle near the driver's door. The hail of bullets ceased.

Raphael ripped the door open and pulled the driver tumbling to the asphalt. His father jumped into the driver's seat. Raphael opened the back door and sprang in behind him. His father backed up the car, shifted, and sped forward. Bullets struck the rear of the car and shattered the rear window. Beads of glass rained down on Raphael as the tires squealed and the car sped to safety.

Chapter 47

Adam Reese entered the Three Chimneys Inn with Captain Turner. The once inviting lobby looked like a war zone. Blood spatter covered the floors, glass, and walls. Men were running everywhere. Moans of the injured and cries for help from officers treating them filled the air.

Reese was having difficulty hiding his feelings, and he could not help but mumble under his breath. "What a fuck-up."

Captain Turner had insisted his men were capable of controlling the situation. Now there were two men, including the young desk clerk, on the floor with jackets covering their faces. They would soon be filling body bags. Two more men lay semiconscious on the counter awaiting an ambulance and paramedics. A group of officers hovered around them and struggled to keep them alive. A fifth man holding a bloody cloth to his face sat leaning against a wall.

Reese turned to the captain and stared. He must have had contempt all over his face because the captain reacted by shaking his head and holding up his hand. "I know what you're going to say. But there was no way for me to know they were that good."

Only that they've been murdering people in at least two cities with impunity. What a waste of manpower. What a waste of life. We had them, and this fool let them escape.

Reese turned back to the lobby door. *Should I leave?* He had not decided when sirens announced the arrival of a fire truck and two ambulances in front of the hotel. Men emerged from all three vehicles. The paramedics carried stretchers and orange-colored kits that looked like a cross between a suitcase and a briefcase.

As the first paramedics rushed through the door, Reese got their attention and showed them the two men requiring the most urgent care. A couple of the paramedics behind them peeled off in different directions, one to take care of the officer with the bloody rag and one to confirm the dead. Reese stayed with the paramedics at the counter and watched with amazement their skill and technology. With nimble hands and dizzying dexterity, they removed clothing, examined the men's eyes, hooked up IVs to restore fluids, and treated open wounds.

"He's bleeding out!" The paramedic attending the officer who had sustained a gunshot to his right thigh shouted his frustration. "The bullet snapped the femur! The muscle spasmed, and the sharp edge of the bone has nearly severed the femoral artery!"

Reese knew the femoral artery was located in the muscle of the thigh and was one of the largest arteries in the body. Because of its size, severing it could cause death in as little as three minutes.

The paramedic continued to yell his instructions. "We have to get him in a traction splint! I have to repair the artery!"

The paramedics began pulling the leg straight and applying the splint. Even in his semiconscious state, the man groaned as they manipulated his leg. Reese turned to the other injured officer.

The lead paramedic there was more sedate. "He has a subdural hematoma. His skull's filling up with blood, and the pressure's destroying his brain tissue. Get me the drill. We have to give the blood somewhere to go."

As Reese watched with morbid curiosity, the paramedic took a small drill and placed it next to the back of the officer's skull. Then he pressed the trigger and began digging into the man's head. Careful not to go too far, the paramedic withdrew the drill. Then into the hole he inserted and secured a catheter. Immediately, blood began flowing from the wound.

The paramedic seemed satisfied. "Let's get him out of here."

While other team members prepared to move the officer to a stretcher, Reese returned to the officer with the broken leg. The paramedic there was shaking his head. "We were too late. There was too much damage."

Reese spun around and walked back to the lobby entrance. One man with an injured brain had survived, at least for now. Another man with a broken leg had died. He had to get his mind on something else.

He began playing out the two fugitive's next move. *They have an entire police force after them. Would they head out of town? No.* Reese's instinct told him they had not finished what they had come for. *Where then?* As if a bright spotlight turned on and illuminated his otherwise muddled thoughts, the answer came to him.

Randall's lab.

Chapter 48

Jane stared at the splintered lab door frame and hesitated. Doctor Randall had told her very clearly not to come back. As instructed, she had called the other staff members and told them not to come in. But while sitting idly at home, her guilt over leaving her lab in a demolished state had compelled her to return.

Whoever did this has been here and gone. They're a long way from here now.

Jane pushed the door open and entered the outer office. It was just as bad as she remembered. *And the vision that was planted in my brain still remains!*

Jane uprighted the central desk and stacked strewn papers and books on the surface. As she got into the work, her nerves settled, but the sorrow remained. With tears in her eyes, she resigned herself to what seemed like a never-ending challenge. *Do it just like you restore a large manuscript—one page at a time.* After she had straightened the office enough that she could move freely, she decided to get to what really had brought her back. She entered her precious lab and closed the door behind her.

Her eyes overflowed and tears streamed down her cheeks. *Come on, girl. Suck it up. You can do this.* She threw herself into the task. She worked her way down the right center aisle picking up the larger items. She repositioned chairs and lifted various pieces of lab equipment back to the work surfaces. Some of it could be salvaged. Best of all, the lab staff had been disciplined about returning their work in progress to the vault. She was glad she had come back.

When she reached the end of the aisle, she turned back down the left center and repeated the process. As she neared the lab door end of the aisle, noises from the office froze her in place. Her hair stood on end, and her heart pounded in her chest. She dropped to her knees to hide below the work surface. Terror squeezed her into as small a ball as she could make.

She tried to talk herself into opening her eyes. *Perhaps it's building security, or the police, or even a curious student.*

After no one attempted to enter the lab, she composed herself enough to creep to the door. She slinked into the office. No one was there.

Just as she noticed a dark silhouette behind her, another silhouette appeared in the translucent upper half of the hall door. The door opened and a short, pale, balding man with wire-rimmed glasses entered the office. His sudden entry shocked Jane into forgetting the shadow behind her.

The man smiled in a way that sent a chill up her spine. "Bonjour, mademoiselle. My son and I were wondering why no one reported your break-in to the police."

The lab door creaked behind her. She realized too late that it was swinging closed. She attempted to run, but she was enveloped in darkness. She felt two large coils of flesh squeezing her like an anaconda, tighter and tighter until she could not breathe. Her lungs burned, and her head felt on the verge of exploding.

Air! I have to get air!

She struggled, but her head and arms were pinned. She found hard surfaces behind her and kicked with all her might, but the blows had no effect. Her mind gave into the futility, and she felt her body go limp. *I'm going to die.*

Before she lost consciousness, the coils lifted her in the air and swung her over and down forcefully onto a chair. In front of her was the largest man she had ever seen. Stepping out from behind him was the meeker, smaller man. Jane whimpered as she continued to catch her breath. "Why are you doing this?"

The smaller man spoke with an upbeat tone. "Pardonnez-moi. I merely want the pleasure of talking with you."

"Did you do this to my lab?"

The smaller man laughed. "Oui, though we thought it was Docteur Randall's lab."

Jane jumped to her feet but was roughly pushed back into the chair by the larger man. His glare communicated she better not move again.

Jane responded with anger. "He's my boss."

The smaller man laughed again. "Très bon. Very good. We are looking for a gospel."

Tears flowed freely down Jane's cheeks. "Why ask me? I'm just a lab geek."

The smaller man's voice took on a very serious quality. "Something tells me you know where it is. If you give it to us, we may leave you in peace. If not ..."

Jane broke eye contact. *Why didn't I listen to Doctor Randall? Now I've ruined everything.*

Chapter 49

Shane glanced at Lauren's open British passport while they stood in the security line at Boston's Logan International Airport Terminal A. The picture was hers, but the name appeared as *Lauren Bridges*. Shane shifted his eyes to his own passport with the correct name. It was a significant exposure they hoped to overcome with speed and misdirection. Lauren exuded coolness and confidence. Anyone seeing her would think she was embarking on a vacation with her boyfriend and nothing more.

Once through the security entrance, Shane and Lauren walked to their gate. While they waited, Shane's iPhone vibrated and rang. Lauren glared at him as he pulled the phone from his pocket. She reached for the phone, but Shane blocked her attempt. It was Jane.

"Hello. Jane?"

The voice on the other end was Jane's, but she did not sound like herself. "Doctor Randall, I had to give them the gospel. *He was a most peculiar man!* They were hurting me badly. Please forgive me."

Shane's blood pressure spiked, and his skin flushed. "Jane, what's wrong? Who was hurting you?"

Turning to Lauren, Shane gestured the seriousness and opened the face of the phone from his ear such that Lauren could hear the conversation. There was a rustle and then another voice, with a French accent. "Docteur Randall, we have the gospel."

Shane recognized the voice as that of the older Frenchman who had visited him. *What was his name? Andre de Vaux.*

De Vaux spoke with arrogance. "Do us a favor. Save us the effort of chasing you. We have the gospel. We have your assistant. And we will soon have you."

Shane felt a mixture of anger and helplessness. "Let her go. She can't give you anything more."

An announcement broadcasted over the gate's public address system. "Welcome to Delta flight #5855, service to New York JFK Airport."

Shane quickly muted his iPhone, but it was too late.

De Vaux laughed. "We know where you are and where you are going. Give up."

Shane unmuted his phone. "I am afraid I can't do that. You may have the gospel, but you don't have the answer. I do."

Lauren signaled Shane to stop talking and disconnect the call. Shane refused.

De Vaux pressed further. "Docteur Randall, give up this foolishness and come back to us. We are men of God. The woman is leading you astray."

"Men of God don't murder people."

"You are a New Testament scholar. You should try reading the Old Testament. Return to us and tell us what you know, or we will kill everyone close to you, starting with your assistant. Raphael, show him we are serious."

Shane heard Jane begging a short distance from the phone. "No!" A shot rang out simultaneously with a scream.

Shane hung up the phone. He turned to Lauren in angst. "They've killed Jane. What have I done?"

Jane put her hand on his arm. "It's not your fault. If it's anyone's fault, it's mine."

"No, I should've known they would get to me through Jane. In my fever to get to the treasure, I let her down. What a self-centered ass I am."

"You got into to this to help me." Lauren took his iPhone, separated it into its pieces, and threw it into a nearby trash receptacle. "They won't hurt anyone else. They'll use their energy to come after us now. We have to hurry to get to our other flight. They won't know where to look for us."

"What do you mean?"

"We had to use your real name so I purchased three different sets of tickets. We have to get to Terminal E quickly to catch our Iberia flight. If they look for us in New York, they won't find us there."

Lauren walked away, but Shane did not move. *Can I really leave Jane lying on the lab floor and go on a treasure hunt?*

Lauren returned. "Shane! We have to go now."

She grabbed his hand and pulled. Shane stopped thinking and followed where Lauren led.

Chapter 50

Reese felt foolish as he tried to find his way back to the building of Randall's lab. The only time he had been there he had relied on Ben Taylor to guide him. On this return trip he had found his way to Yale's Old Campus easily enough, but he had been wandering up and down streets for some time since.

There it is. He saw it to his left just a little farther up Prospect Street. It was a massive building. He again felt foolish for not finding it earlier. He turned into the parking lot and found a space close to the door.

Pulling his Glock 23 from his shoulder holster, he checked the clip. He had thirteen shots without having to change clips. His backup Glock 39 at his ankle gave him another six. *What am I doing? I have no backup and no jurisdiction.* He had left the local law enforcement and gone on a wild goose chase. If he was right, it might turn into a wild tyrannosaurus rex chase.

He snapped the clip back in place and returned the weapon to its holster. *Gut up, man. These guys killed Ben Taylor and who knows how many more.* He stepped out of the car and jogged to the front door.

Reese entered the building trying to remember his way. A gunshot echoed from one of the hallways to his left. He ran to the hall entrance and saw the two men he was after rounding the corner at the far end. They did not see him.

Reese pulled his weapon and sped after them. As he passed the entrance to Randall's lab, he heard a loud moan coming from inside. *Someone's hurt.* He stopped and backed up to the doorway. Pushing the door open, he saw Randall's assistant lying on her side with a small pool of blood around her head. She was not moving except for the shallow expansion and contraction of her chest. *She's alive!* Another moan escaped her lips like an unconscious call for help. Reese knew if he stopped to help her, he would lose the two men. He had no choice.

He ran to her, sat beside her, and supported her head in his lap. Around and through the blood on her head he could see singed hair and tattooing of her scalp from powder burns. She had been shot at close range. Pulling back her hair, he examined the slightly bleeding wound. She moaned again in reaction. It did not appear the bullet penetrated. Reese guessed she had shifted her head and the bullet had struck her at an obtuse angle, bouncing off her skull. Even if he was right, she could be suffering from damage to her brain not visible on the surface. She needed a doctor now.

Reese reached for his phone and called 911. When the operator answered, he announced himself as a police detective, gave his location, and requested an ambulance. He also told the operator to find Captain Turner and tell him where he was.

While he waited, he did what he could to control the bleeding and comfort the young woman. He also grimaced with frustration at losing the two murderers again. *How will I ever catch them now?* As he planned his next step, the woman shook and struggled to speak, but no words escaped. He lowered his ear to her lips.

After several pain-filled seconds, she managed a whisper. *"Time, time, time, see what's become of me!"* She stopped as if to muster more strength. "Doctor Randall." She paused again. "Logan airport." Another gap. "Leaving country."

Reese squeezed her closer to his body. "Hang in there. Help's on the way."

"Slip sliding away!"

Reese was afraid the young woman was giving up. He spoke directly into her ear. "Stay with me. I'm here. I'm not going anywhere. I need your help. Doctor Randall needs your help. You have to be strong for Doctor Randall."

The young woman seemed to return from where she was going.

"I am a rock!"

Her body went limp, but her breathing was more regular. *She has to live.* She was his last lead to Randall and the two fugitives.

Chapter 51

Raphael followed his father through an exit at the rear of the building. His father carried a soft-sided attaché containing the gospel. They had completed their mission, and by the grace of God, neither of them had been injured. Raphael should have been pleased. He was not.

They had not found the woman. He did not get to defile her body before torturing her to death as he had planned. They had not found Randall either, and he was looking forward to beating the superiority off the Yale professor's face. Even the killing of Randall's assistant had happened too quickly. There had been no time to extend her death with intelligence and skill.

His father looked back at Raphael. "We need another car. We will have to drive a long distance before flying home. They will be looking for us at nearby airports and train stations."

Getting another car would be no problem. Raphael had stolen many cars.

His father's phone rang. "Oui?" After a pause, his father continued. "Oui, we have the gospel." Another pause. "Oui, very likely he has broken the code and has the location." Another pause. "We know their flight, but they may have changed it by now." Another pause. "Oui, we are returning now. There may be a delay while we sort through the details." Another pause. "Merci."

His father disconnected and returned the phone to his coat pocket. "The Directeur is pleased. He says there is no reason to pursue the professor and the woman at this time."

The Directeur was *pleased.* Raphael was *not.*

His father must have noticed his disappointment. "Raphael, the Directeur knows what he is doing. It is not over."

Raphael nodded. Trust did not come easily. He swore to himself there would be another time and place.

Chapter 52

Shane handed his boarding pass to the gate attendant and proceeded to the awaiting Airbus A340. Lauren followed. The flight attendant at the loading door greeted Shane with a big smile, but Shane just nodded in response.

The four-engine wide-bodied Airbus A340 seated well over 300 passengers, but Shane and Lauren would not have to worry about crowded flight conditions. Lauren had purchased first class tickets. Shane turned left down the aisle and stopped at the back row of the first class cabin on the left window side. He stowed his rollerboard suitcase in the overhead storage bin and then helped Lauren with hers. He waited in the aisle while Lauren entered in front of the two oversized seats and sat by the window. Shane sat beside her in the aisle seat and put his laptop under the seat in front of him.

Lauren weaved her right arm around Shane's left and grasped his hand. She placed her left hand on his bicep and tucked her head into his shoulder. Shane knew she was doing her best to get his mind on something else, but all he could think about was Jane. He was sitting in first class, and Jane was dead on the floor.

"Shane, it wasn't your fault." Lauren lifted her head from his shoulder and made him look her in the eye. "These are bad men. You can't hold yourself responsible."

Shane pressed his head back against his seat and clinched his eyes. "Jane *was* my responsibility."

A flight attendant interrupted them with an announcement over the plane's intercom system. She was urging everyone to take their seats so they could have an on-time departure to Madrid. She did so both in English and Spanish. Lauren's alternative flight plan had them landing early tomorrow morning in the Spanish capital. After a three-hour layover, they would continue to Tel Aviv. Ultimately, they would arrive in the afternoon a short time later than their original plan.

Lauren patted his arm. "Shane, get some rest. You'll feel better after you've slept."

Shane knew she was probably right. Jane's death had taken away the joy of his discovery. He needed to get back his motivation. He had to get past blame and move on to revenge.

A flight attendant walked down the aisle handing out DVD players and movies. Another flight attendant spoke over the intercom and announced they would be taking off soon. Shane went limp in the comfortable seat.

Lauren spoke softly into his ear. "Shane? Are you all right? I need you to be all right."

"I *will* be."

Sleep came so quickly he barely felt the plane lift from the runway and begin its steep climb.

Chapter 53

Reese struggled to maintain his balance as the ambulance darted though traffic. Though he was sitting down, he extended his arms in both directions and pressed against the side and rear of the cabin. The sudden shifts in centrifugal forces did not seem to faze the two paramedics laboring over Jane, who was held in place by three tightly secured straps. She had an IV in her arm and an oxygen mask strapped to her face.

Reese had not remembered her name until he found her driver's license in her jeans pocket. Knowing her name was important because the paramedics constantly used it when talking to her. It was a simple approach used to focus her brain's attention, even while unconscious. Experiments had shown unconscious patients often had normal auditory function. Hearing someone talk to them gave them hope of recovery. Not hearing anyone translated to their brains as loss of hope and often resulted in the patients drifting into a deeper unconsciousness, coma, or death.

"Jane, stay with us."

"Jane, we have you."

"Jane, you're going to be ok."

"Jane, you're with friends."

"Fight for us, Jane."

Reese had shown his badge to the paramedics in order to ride to the hospital in the back of the ambulance. There was no denying he felt a sense of ownership of the young woman. Being the one to find her, he had taken on the responsibility to see her to the hospital. The paramedics had his card along with Jane's information. The hospital could contact him later with updates on her condition.

She must live. He needed what she knew to determine where the two men he chased may be heading. He doubted Randall was an accomplice to the murders in any way, but a connection was there. If he found Randall, he would find the two men.

The trip to the hospital ended much sooner than Reese had expected. After only ten minutes, the ambulance pulled into the emergency entrance of the Yale New Haven

Hospital. An emergency room orderly greeted the ambulance and opened its back doors. Reese leaped to the pavement and backed out of the way. The two paramedics with help from the orderly on the ground pulled and rolled the gurney from the ambulance. While they ensured the IV and oxygen mask were secure, Reese walked up beside Jane and put his hand on hers. Her fingers curved around his and tightened.

Her reaction caught Reese off guard. *Did I imagine it? No, she's definitely grasping my hand.* Reese put his other hand on top of their two hands and looked up to her face. Her eyelids fluttered open ever so slightly. Her expression indicated she wanted to say something.

One of the paramedics interrupted them. "I'm sorry, detective. You need to move. We have to get her inside."

"One minute."

Reese leaned over and put his ear to Jane's face. He lifted the oxygen mask slightly.

"Detective!" insisted the paramedic.

"One minute!"

Jane gasped seven words divided by breaths. "Israel. Amit. David. Friend. Save. Doctor. Randall."

Jane's hand went limp. Reese returned the oxygen mask, and condensation from Jane's breath immediately formed on the inside.

Reese used his fingers to brush her hair to the side of her face. "I will, Jane. Thank you. Hang in there."

The paramedic was becoming irate. "Detective! If you don't move..."

Reese straightened up and stepped away from the gurney. The paramedics rushed it forward through the automatic glass doors of the entrance. Reese watched until they passed through an interior set of aluminum doors and disappeared.

Chapter 54

Shane looked across Lauren at the scattered clouds and plain below. They had taken off for the second leg of their itinerary. Having slept much of the first leg from Boston, Shane felt better. They were scheduled to land in Tel Aviv in a little over four hours, later than he had told Amit by forty minutes. He hoped his friend would still be there to meet them.

When the flight attendant announced they could access their electronic equipment, Shane reached for his laptop and powered it on.

Lauren leaned into him. "What are you doing?"

Shane pulled up a translation of the Copper Scroll and turned the laptop slightly in her direction. "The instructions in the Copper Scroll are very cryptic. I'm reacquainting myself with the landmarks and directions."

"But you know where we're going, right?"

"I do, but some of these directions may be helpful once we're there." Shane wanted to be sure Lauren understood. "Just because we know where to go doesn't mean it's going to be easy. I don't expect we'll find the treasure lying out waiting for us."

Lauren grabbed his bicep with both hands. "I have faith in you."

Shane smiled. "Of course, Amit's the real expert. No one knows the Copper Scroll like he does. He has multiple translations memorized."

"Give me an example of what's bothering you."

Shane took his cursor and scrolled down the translation column by column. "There are too many directions for all of them to be correct. Sixty-four in total. Most of them have to be diversions."

"I see."

"Everything about the Copper Scroll is coded within a veil of context. It's like you telling me you left me a present in the house you were living in when you saw your favorite movie. I'd have to know you extremely well to identify the house. Then I'd still need to know to look in the attic, the basement, a crawlspace, or under the back patio."

Shane paused for a couple of minutes. An idea was forming in his brain. He took out a pad of paper and a pen. “The Copper scroll contains sixty-four instructions in total. If you add the six and the four, you get the number ten.” Shane wrote the numbers as he spoke. He circled the number ten. “Then adding the one and the zero, you get the number one.” Shane circled the number one. “*One* is the number in the Bible’s numeric code that symbolizes God and acts of God.”

Lauren interrupted him. “You’ve mentioned a code before. What is it?”

“It is a simple code the writers of the Bible used to build symbolism into scripture.” Shane reached into his laptop bag and pulled out one of his laminated cards. He handed it to Lauren.

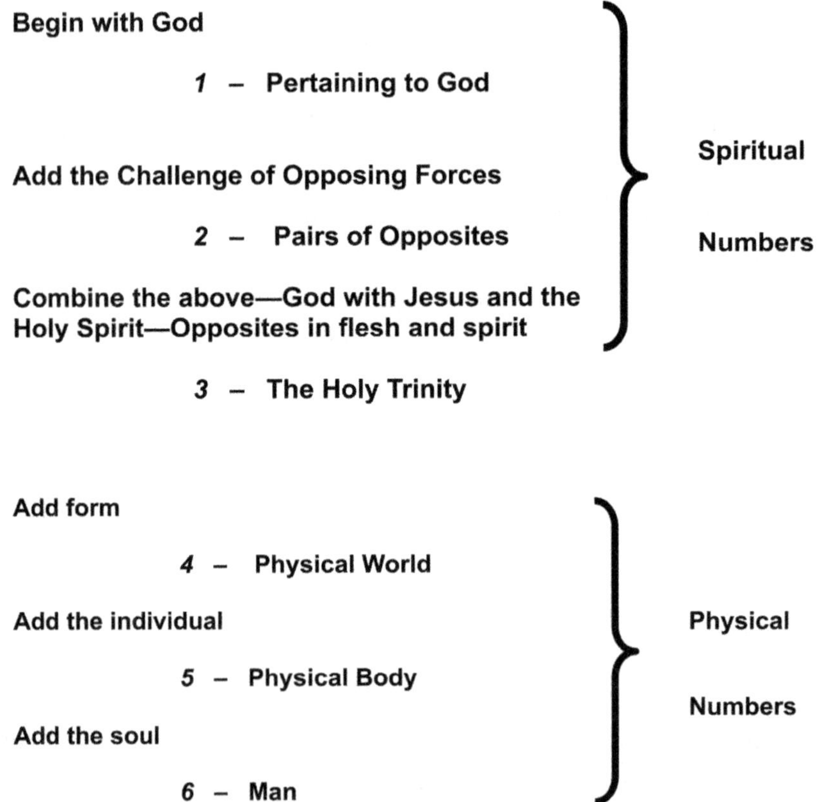

Add the grace of God through salvation		
7 – Perfection		
Complete the development of mankind		**Completion**
8 – Completed Evolution		
End		
9 – The Ending		

Shane pointed to the numbers in succession. "Each number builds on the one before in a very logical manner. The first three numbers are spiritual. They begin with the one God and end with the Holy Trinity. The second three numbers are physical beginning with the world around us and ending with the number of man. And the last three numbers are all different facets of completion—perfection of the soul, completion of our evolution, and the end of it all. Virtually every significant number in the Bible adheres to this code."

Lauren rolled her eyes. "If you say so."

Shane laughed. "So as I was saying, the sixty-four instructions result in the number *one*, and *one* symbolizes God and acts of God. I can see where that number would apply to a war chest to usher in God's kingdom through a final apocalyptic battle. If you just take the sixty-three instructions applying to the treasure rather than the second scroll and add the six and three together, you get nine." Shane circled the number nine. "*Nine* symbolizes the end. It could mean the treasure would be used to bring about the end of this age."

Lauren responded with concerned. "It's dizzying."

"It gets worse. The Greek letters only appear in the first four columns. *Four* symbolizes the physical world, God's creation, in which the treasure is hidden. There are twelve columns in total. Adding the digits together gives us the number *three. Three* symbolizes the Holy Trinity, especially acts of Jesus and the Holy Spirit. The first four columns make up one third of the total number. That also gives us the number *three.* And those four columns contain twenty-one of the sixty-four instructions. Adding the digits of twenty-one again gives us the number *three.*"

"So what does all that mean?"

Shane thought for a few seconds. "It means we only have to concern ourselves with the first four columns. Everything else is meant to misdirect us."

"Are you sure?"

Shane shook his head and leaned back in his seat. "Not at all. I may be applying too much meaning to coincidental numbers. Even if it's true, it may only be part of the solution. We won't know until we get there."

Shane leaned forward to continue his analysis of the translation. Another thought struck him. He began paging through the Copper Scroll again.

Lauren must have picked up on his body language. "What is it?"

"Look at this. The Greek letters appear in seven locations of the first four columns. *Seven* is the number of perfection."

"So?"

Shane pulled up Jane's translation of the Sicarii Gospel. He searched the document for the word *treasure* and highlighted the verses. There were seven verses in total. "That can't be a coincidence. Seven locations for the Greek letters in the Copper Scroll, and seven treasure verses in the Sicarii Gospel."

"What does it mean?"

"I'm not sure yet."

He stripped away all of the non-treasure verses and read the seven remaining verses in sequence.

> *Jesus said, "If you want to follow me, sell your possessions and give the money to the poor. You will have treasure in heaven. For where your treasure is, there your heart will be also."*
>
> *Jesus said, "The Kingdom of God is like a treasure hidden in a field owned by a man who did not know the treasure was there. When the man died, he left the field to his son, who also knew nothing about the treasure. Another man found the treasure in the field and covered it up. Then in his joy he sold everything he had to buy the field."*

Jesus said, "No one can enter a strong man's house and steal his treasure unless he first binds the strong man. Then he can take what he wants."

Jesus said, "The gate is wide that leads to death and destruction. Follow the narrow path instead. It leads to the treasure of life."

Jesus said, "Do not store up treasure on earth, where moths and worms consume and human hands can take it from you. Sell your possessions, and give the money to the poor, thereby storing up for yourselves treasures in heaven, where moths and worms cannot consume and where no human hand can reach it."

Jesus said, "The Kingdom of God is like a treasure hidden under a light for all to find."

Jesus said, "Blessed is the man who perseveres in times of hardship, because when he has passed the test, he will receive God's treasure."

Shane knew the four hours to Tel Aviv would pass quickly.

Chapter 55

Adam Reese sat in front of his gate at Logan Airport. His frustration was as high as his blood pressure. He had been unable to get on a flight before 11:15 this morning. That meant he would not arrive in Tel Aviv until 9:15 Sunday morning. He had arrived at the airport very early to try to get on the standby list for the 7:30 flight, but it was oversold. Regardless, he could not find an earlier connection out of Newark than the 3:55 PM flight. He was losing the better part of a day in picking up Randall's trail, and he still had at least three hours before he could expect to board. The wait was killing him.

He was not entirely sure why he was going. Even flying coach, the fare was quite expensive for his salary, and he doubted he would be reimbursed. The only lead he had was the name of an Israeli. Chances of success were poor to say the least.

He stood up and walked up to the gate agent. She appeared flustered and continued to type with frenzied strokes on her keyboard.

"Can I help you?" she asked without looking up.

"Yes. Can you tell me if the 11:15 flight to Newark is on time? And the 3:55 connection to Tel Aviv?"

"We're very busy working the next flight from this gate. If you'd take a seat, I'll look it up when we close the door."

Reese reached into his jacket pocket and pulled out his badge. He put it in the line of sight of the gate agent. "Please."

The gate agent sighed but began pounding the keyboard with even more force and speed. "Yes sir. Both are on time."

"Thank you. You wouldn't want to upgrade me, would you?"

The gate agent frowned. "Sorry, sir. Now if you'll excuse me, I have a lot of work to do."

"Certainly." Reese turned with a smirk and walked back to his seat.

Just as he was about to sit down, his mobile phone rang in the jacket pocket opposite his badge. He removed it and answered. "Hello."

"Detective Reese?"

"Yes."

"This is Doctor Abrams from the Yale New Haven Hospital. I have you as the police contact in the case of Jane Roman. I hope I didn't wake you."

"Yes, that's right. And no, I was awake. I'm at the airport about to take a long flight to find the people who put her in your hospital. How's she doing?"

"She may have a few tough moments in the coming days, but it looks like she's going to make it. I thought you'd want to know."

"That's great doc. Thanks for calling."

"No problem. I probably shouldn't say this, but if you find the guys who did this, pistol whip them for me. Or whatever you guys do to criminals when you catch them. She seems like a nice lady. She didn't deserve what they did to her. Good luck."

The line disconnected, and Reese sat down to wait for his flight. *At least something is going right.*

Chapter 56

Gilbert de Clisson sat comfortably in his plush private office adjacent to the hanger housing his Falcon 7X three-engine jet. The forty-million-euro long-range business jet symbolized how Clisson wanted the world to see him. It incorporated fighter plane technology and could fly nonstop from Paris to Tokyo at an altitude of over fifteen kilometers and a speed of nine hundred kilometers per hour. He could go anywhere and do anything in total luxury.

Clisson's private hanger resided in Le Bourget Airport. Le Bourget was located eleven kilometers northeast of Paris and catered to private aircraft. It had a rich history and was most famous as the landing site for Charles Lindbergh's historic solo transatlantic crossing of 1927. In addition to stoking his French pride, Clisson enjoyed Le Bourget's private terminals and customized hangers which ensured the confidentiality and luxury the French elite desired and deserved.

Outside of the crew, only his bodyguard Gustave would accompany him. Gustave had left to ensure everything was ready for departure. Clisson knew it was. The only thing missing was his destination.

Clisson patiently sipped his Mariage Frères tea, arguably the best tea in the world. This specific blend was *Red Moon,* a green tea from the hillsides of an ancient caravan route to Tibetan monasteries. It had a flowery, spicy taste with a honey flavor balanced by ginger and scented with rose. It reminded him he could afford the best things in life.

He was reading one of the latest books on the Copper Scroll. It was espousing one of the many theories that the treasure no longer existed and therefore could not be found. There was always an expert claiming the treasure had been stolen by the Romans, the Babylonians, the Seleucids, or the Egyptians. Clisson found it amazing publishers would print such rubbish. He stood up, threw the book down, and talked to it as if it was a physical manifestation of its author.

"Imbécile! Anyone can write about where the treasure is *not.* True greatness is demonstrated by identifying where the treasure *is.* Tas de merde!"

The entrance of his bodyguard interrupted his cursing. Gustave looked like he could have once been a bodybuilder, with his short hair, broad chest, and massive biceps and quads. He wore dark slacks and matching shirt and a gray sports jacket with the tell-tale bulge of a shoulder holstered weapon.

"Monsieur Clisson, Capitaine Fournier is curious as to when we will know our destination."

Clisson waved off the question as irrelevant. They would know when they knew. He hardly had the time to satisfy every whim or curiosity. He took another sip of his tea. As he sat his cup down, he looked up at Gustave still waiting and thought better of ignoring the captain's need. Small minds required linear data and structure.

"Tell Capitaine Fournier we should know within the hour."

"Très bon, Monsieur Clisson."

Gustave turned on his heels and left to relay the message. Clisson knew as soon as he had the location, the real game would begin. Like the general manager of a professional sports team, he was confident he had put together a winning game plan. Picking up the book, he sat back down and continued his reading and his tea.

Chapter 57

Basim Fayyad wiped the sweat from his brow as he labored in the Judean Desert sun. As a Palestinian grunt at a Jewish archaeological dig, he was given the worst, most manually intensive jobs—lugging hundreds of pounds of tools, clearing away buckets of rubble, running from place to place on errands. He hated working next to these arrogant Jews. Since he was Palestinian and willing to work for low wages, they assumed he was ignorant and not to be trusted with substantial assignments. He was an afterthought, only drawing attention when they needed someone for a dirty job.

Though he found working with Jews extremely repulsive, he had done so for over a year at various digs around Qumran. He kept a smile on his face always, and he did anything and everything they asked him to do. The façade was necessary. He believed in Yousif Al-Jamal's vision. He had come with him from Hamas to Shudada Allah. He would gladly give his life for their cause, for their people. Fortunately in this case, that level of sacrifice would not be required.

Security at the dig was so lax that smuggling in and hiding Semtex plastic explosive had been surprisingly easy. Following the collapse of the Soviet Union, Semtex had become available on the open market and a favorite of many freedom fighters around the globe. Many countries supporting the Palestinians, such as Iran and Syria, were accommodating sources for the explosive. Shudada Allah had a large store.

Since most chemical detonators did not react well to the jostling and heat associated with an archaeological dig in the Judean Desert, Fayyad had decided to use a blasting cap. A timer would set off the blasting cap, and the resulting explosion would ignite the Semtex.

Fifteen ounces of the plastic explosive would result in a highly destructive blast especially effective against people. The resulting pressure wave would collapse lungs, create internal bleeding, and concuss the brain of anyone it encountered. Flying debris would penetrate and rip apart their bodies. The blast wind would throw them great distances. And it would be loud. It was the perfect weapon of terror.

Though the Jews did not expect him to understand their language or their science, Fayyad had absorbed everything happening in the camp. The ossuaries had not been what David had expected. He could read the disappointment on his face. David had expected something much more significant and valuable. But this morning David had left mysteriously, and the look of promise was again on his face.

Showing great interest in David's departure, Al-Jamal had ordered Fayyad to take advantage of David's absence to plant his explosive and then abandon the camp. Al-Jamal would find David.

Fayyad had little problem getting his explosive, detonator, and timer. He was nearly invisible to the Jews in the most organized times. It was even easier now David was absent. The camp was in disarray. The Israel Antiquities Authority were running David's young assistant ragged. And it was the Sabbath.

Fools! Their strict observance of the Sabbath meant he would have little difficulty getting to the cave unseen. Fayyad retrieved an empty bucket and placed the explosive, detonator and timer inside. He covered them with a rag and spread some soil over the rag. With the bucket in hand, he walked casually to a location near the ladder to the cave.

He kneeled down as if working and gauged activity descending and ascending the ladder. In the span of fifteen minutes only one team member returned from the cave. No one else was around. He picked up his bucket and walked to the ladder. The thirty meters of openness to the plain gave him a little vertigo, and he did not have a lifeline. One slip and his mission would fail very violently. *At least I won't feel anything.*

Fayyad knew the longer he delayed the more likely he would be discovered. He put one arm through the bucket handle and stepped out on the ladder. He clung to the rails firmly with both hands and quickly descended the five meters to the cave. As expected, the cave was empty.

Once inside, Fayyad deftly went about his gruesome task. He proceeded to the back of the cave where he found the ossuaries spread out on the stone floor. Selecting the ossuary closest to the rear wall, he kneeled next to it and molded Semtex to the rear side of the limestone box. After inserting the detonator, he connected the timer set for a thirty minute delay.

Fayyad checked his work a final time and returned to the cave opening. He threw some stones into the bucket and readied himself for the ascent. His pulse quickened again as he stepped from the cave onto the ladder, but once safely on the rung, he ascended without incident.

As his head emerged above the cliff edge, he saw one of the young members of David's team walking toward him. He was dressed in a harness and appeared about to descend the ladder. Fayyad controlled the panic rising in his throat. He put on his most subservient face and continued up the last few rungs to the level surface.

The Jew scolded him in Hebrew. "What are you doing?"

Fayyad bent over and bowed his head as if embarrassed. He pointed confusingly to the bucket.

"Fool!" continued the Jew. "You do not even have a safety harness. You could have been killed."

The young Jew must have assumed Fayyad was running an errand for one of the other team members not wanting to violate the Sabbath. Fayyad nodded a few more times, smiled crazily as if he was too stupid to understand, and twisted out of the young Jew's path. He gestured to offer his assistance with whatever was needed.

The Jew waved him off. "No, I do not need anything. Go help someone else."

Fayyad nodded again and backed away. He watched as the Jew attached his lanyard, stepped out onto the ladder, and disappeared down the ledge. Fayyad dropped the bucket and scurried from the site.

Chapter 58

Amit waited outside the security gate of the state of the art Terminal 3 at Ben Gurion International Airport in the city of Lod, Israel. The airport was less than twenty kilometers southeast of Tel Aviv and fifty kilometers from Jerusalem. Arguably the most secure airport in the world, no hijacking of a plane departing Ben Gurion International Airport had ever occurred.

Amit accepted security as a way of life in Israel, but it made flying a major hassle. Before entering the airport, he had driven through a preliminary security checkpoint where guards armed with mini-Uzi submachine guns conducted a visual and verbal examination. Then at the terminal entrances he had passed through other armed security personnel who engaged with anyone they found suspicious.

Once inside the terminal, security was everywhere in both visible and invisible forms. All departing passengers were checked through Interpol and interviewed, and their luggage was both scanned and pressure tested to trigger any explosive devices. A passport containing a recent stamp from a country threatening to Israel could easily lead to delays or prevention of an incoming passenger's entry.

Amit hoped that had not happened to Shane. He looked at the arrival board again. Shane's plane had landed over forty minutes ago. Amit paced in varied directions. Many other travelers exited to exclamations of joy, laughter, and hugs from their friends and families, but not Shane.

Amit's mobile phone rang in his pocket. *Finally.* Pulling out the phone, he looked at the caller id. It was Eathan. *At least an update from the camp will kill some time.*

"Yes, Eathan?"

Eathan sounded frantic. His breathing was so erratic he had trouble getting his words out. In the background Amit heard a jumble of strange sounds. Shouts and screams mixed with rustling of activity.

Amit backed away from the crowd around him. "Eathan! Can you hear me?"

"Doctor David! We need you to come back now. Please hurry."

Amit felt Eathan's panic rising in his own throat. "What is it, Eathan? Calm down and tell me."

He could hear Eathan fighting back tears before blurting out his message. "There's been an explosion!"

"An explosion! What do you mean?"

"One minute everything was fine, and the next minute the world was shaking and breaking apart."

From the confusion Amit could hear in the background, he could imagine what his young assistant was going through. "Eathan, you're not making sense. Stop what you're doing and talk to me."

Ethan's breathing slowed. "It was the cave. We think one of the Palestinian laborers planted a bomb."

"Why would anyone want to blow up a cave of ossuaries?"

"I don't know, but it was horrible. The cave entrance acted like a muzzle. The ossuaries blasted out like cannonballs. And, Doctor David, Lev was in the cave. He's dead. Vaporized and rained out over the plain." Eathan broke down again. "Doctor David, the stone above the cave gave way. The landslide caught one of the Antiquities Authority representatives and slid him off the cliff. I can still hear his screams."

Eathan paused again and Amit took advantage. "What about the rest of the team?"

"Some of the stone shot upward like shrapnel. And some of it just turned in on itself. The force knocked us all to the ground. Nathan was caught up in collapsing stone. We're still trying to get to him. I'm not sure how badly he's hurt. Hadasa was knocked unconscious. She's cut badly. Doctor David, I can't handle this."

Amit heard the despair in Eathan's voice. *How could I have left him? If I had stayed, perhaps none of this would've happened.*

Amit's first reaction was to head back to the camp. He took several steps toward the terminal exit before remembering why he was there. He stopped. He could do nothing to change what had happened at the camp. "Eathan, listen to me. Are you listening?"

"Yes, Doctor David."

"I'm sorry this happened, but you can handle it. I wish you didn't have to, but you do. And you can. This is what you do. First, remain calm. You must be a source of strength for the rest of the team. Organize them to get to Nathan as quickly as they can. Minutes can make a big difference in a cave-in. Second, call Emergency Services and request medical assistance. And third, find the men from the Antiquities Authority. Have them get in touch with the Security Agency. They'll know what to do about the bomb. Can you do that for me, Eathan?"

"Yes, Doctor David." His voice still sounded weak.

"Play it back for me, Eathan. I need to know you get it."

Eathan spoke the words slowly. "Nathan. Emergency Services. Security Agency."

A rush of pride in his young assistant coursed through Amit. "Eathan, you can do this. I'll get there, but it won't be today or tomorrow."

"I understand. You can count on me."

"I know I can. Keep me informed about Nathan and Hadasa. And anything the Security Agency turns up."

"I will."

Amit disconnected. *Why would anyone attack my camp?* A hand grasped Amit's shoulder. He jumped and turned to see Shane smiling. A woman was with him.

Shane's brows arched and his eyes opened wide in surprise at Amit's reaction. "Sorry. We had an issue and had to change airlines."

Amit lashed out. "Shane, what the hell's going on?"

Shane smiled. "You're digging in the wrong place."

Amit normally would have found the Indiana Jones reference humorous. Not this afternoon.

Chapter 59

Milak Siyam stood several meters from the Jewish archaeologist. He had used a taxi to penetrate the airport compound, but he had still taken quite some time to clear security. Israeli security forces employed profiling. While civil rights groups in some parts of the world argued the potential dangers of prejudice, Israeli Security maintained it was the passengers more than their bags that needed to be examined. In Israel, profiling meant airport security subjected Arabs and citizens of unfriendly countries to intense questioning while Israeli Jews proceeded without nearly the same scrutiny. The weakness of profiling was that the targeted groups knew they were targeted. Milak had not been surprised.

Milak watched the Jew answer his phone and react with horror. Basim Fayyad had succeeded in sending their message. *Subhan'Allah! Glorious is Allah! Allah be praised!* They would soon take responsibility, and their name would reverberate around the world.

The Jew turned to leave but stopped. *Why stop?* The phone conversation ended, and an American couple came up behind the Jew. The man seemed to know the Jew well. *The Jew places a higher value on what the American knows than his camp.* Milak moved even nearer.

The Jew was speaking. "Sorry, Shane. I just got some bad news. I'll tell you about it later. How are you doing?"

"I'm doing well." The American stepped back a half step and brought the woman in closer. "Amit, this is Lauren Mallory. Lauren, meet my good friend Amit David."

The Jew and the woman exchanged pleasantries.

"Lauren," continued the American, "did you know the Jewish Talmud says there are always thirty-six just men in the world going about doing God's work and keeping the world from destruction? If that's so, then Amit's one of those men."

The Jew waved aside the complement. "Shane, what's going on? Why are you here?"

The American spoke in almost a whisper, but Milak could still hear the words. "Lauren and I think we have discovered something big. We need your help."

"Does it have something to do with the Copper Scroll treasure?"

Milak's eyes widened. The reaction was enough to get the attention of the woman. He cursed himself for being so careless.

The woman stepped between the two men and took each one by the arm. She spoke with firmness. "Gentlemen, perhaps we should discuss this on the road."

The American scanned the area. "Of course. Amit, let's get to your car. We have quite a drive. I'll explain everything on the way."

The Jew reached for the woman's rollerboard, "Right."

The Jew and the two Americans headed out of the terminal. Milak cursed himself again for not getting more information, but he had heard enough to know it could be well worth their time to follow them. He had to get back to Al-Jamal.

Chapter 60

Lauren sat in the back seat of the Toyota Land Cruiser listening to the two long-time friends. She was tired and jet-lagged from the long flight. The motion of the car was not helping her stay awake, but she would not permit herself to sleep.

When Shane had told Amit to head toward Rihab, Jordan, Amit's eyes had widened, but he had not questioned his friend. Shane had not seemed to feel the need to explain further right away. Lauren knew that sort of trust came only from a long relationship of working together, building credibility, and having each other's back.

After the normal catching up conversation, Amit told Shane about the explosion at his dig site. The account was a grim reminder to Lauren of what part of the world she now traveled. It was arguable the holiest land on earth, but danger lurked everywhere. *Life is cheap. And people are just no damn good.*

Shane told Amit about the Sicarii Gospel and the men who were after it. His voice cracked somewhat when he described their willingness to murder to get it. "They shot Jane while I was on the phone just to send me a message."

Amit seemed horrified. "I can't believe she's gone. Jane was great."

"Yes, she was."

There was a pause in their conversation. Amit was first to break the silence. "Why Rihab?"

Shane explained how he had identified Rihab after connecting the Sicarii Gospel and the Copper Scroll using their shapes and the Greek letters. He also took Amit through his theory that because of the positions of the Greek letter-numbers, they only had to concern themselves with the first four columns of the Copper Scroll. Finally, he quoted the seven treasure verses from the Sicarii Gospel.

Amit was not convinced. "Seems like a stretch."

Lauren perked up. "Why a stretch?"

Shane looked back at her and smiled as if he knew what was coming.

Amit continued to speak in a matter-of-fact tone. "Because from what you've told me, the gospel you found sounds like a Christian sayings gospel. The Copper Scroll was found with Essene scrolls. There's no reason the two documents would be linked."

When Amit turned and saw Shane smiling, he got a pained expression on his face. "Oh no. Don't tell me I'm headed to Jordan because you're trying to prove you're right."

Lauren's pulse quickened with every word. "What do you mean?"

"Shane believes the Essenes and early Jewish Christians were one and the same. I don't. We've been fighting about it for years."

Lauren could feel the treasure slipping away. "Explain it to me."

Amit alternated looking back at Lauren and looking forward at the road. "The Essenes were one of three sects of Judaism mentioned by Josephus. The other two are better known from the New Testament–the Pharisees and the Sadducees. The Pharisees were religious leaders and teachers. They evolved into today's rabbis. The Sadducees were the aristocratic class of temple priests. They disappeared after the Romans destroyed the Temple. None were Christians."

Shane jumped in with energy. "Only three writers from the period mention the Essenes. And they were all from the first century. Nothing earlier. The first one was the Jewish philosopher Philo of Alexandria. He names the sect and says there were four thousand of them spread across the Roman province of Palestine. The second was the Roman historian Pliny the Elder. He mentions them living next to the Dead Sea. And finally, as Amit said, you have Josephus. To understand the Essenes, you have to put all three accounts together, along with the Dead Sea Scrolls."

Amit grimaced. "Josephus never connected the Essenes with the Christians. But he did mention prominent Essenes before the emergence of Jesus and James."

Shane pressed with even more vigor. "I'm not arguing the Essenes didn't exist before Jesus' arrival. My argument is the Essenes gave birth to Christianity following what they saw as the fulfillment of prophecy. They saw their role to be preparing the way for the Messiah's arrival. Their mission was fulfilled with the ministry of Jesus."

Amit just shook his head. He seemed to be getting tired of the argument. "There's just not enough scientific foundation to connect the two."

Shane seemed to know he had him going. "There's as much foundation for that as there is to say some mysterious cult wrote the Dead Sea Scrolls as the École Biblique argued. The Dead Sea Scrolls are full of Christian phrases, like *righteousness*, *grace*, *faith*, *forgiveness of sin.* They called their founder the *Teacher of Righteousness.* He was persecuted and perhaps crucified to satisfy the wrath of a *Wicked Priest* in Jerusalem. Who does that sound like to you, Lauren?"

Lauren sat back not knowing how she should respond to the nerdfest.

Amit answered before she could figure out what to say. "Don't answer that, Lauren. He's distorting the facts. The dates don't match. There was a Teacher of Righteousness serving as their leader well after the time of Jesus' death."

Shane was not about to give up. "*Teacher of Righteousness* was a title. After Jesus death, the title was handed down to his brother James, the new leader of the Jewish Christian Church."

Amit's face and muscles tensed. "One stretch after another."

Shane directed another question toward Lauren. "The Dead Sea Scroll known as the Community Rule describes a ritual meal in which their leader blesses bread and wine in the name of the Messiah, who is present in spirit, and then the entire community eats a communal meal. Does that sound like the Eucharist, or Holy Communion, or Lord's Supper, or whatever name you give to the ritual re-enactment of Jesus' last supper with his disciples?"

Lauren looked to Amit but did not answer. It sounded the same to her.

Amit over-enunciated his words. "Two sects having ritual meals do not make them the same."

Amit's obvious irritation did not slow Shane down. "Christianity and the Essenes have too many features in common to be chance. Even the root words in the various native languages for the sect names–Essenes, Messianists, Nazarenes, and Christians–all mean the same thing–belief in the Messiah."

Lauren's growing curiosity drew her into the conversation. "What else?"

"They both saw the Temple as the physical manifestation of the *Old Covenant,* or *Old Testament.* They saw it oppressing the Jewish people and wanted to bring about a *New Covenant,* or *New Testament,* with God. They both believed in baptism as a replacement for animal sacrifice to purify themselves of sin. They both believed everyone was equal in the Kingdom of God and practiced that belief in their rituals. Neither group would swear an oath. Both practiced silent, inward prayer. Both believed in resurrection. Both looked to the Kingdom of Heaven for pleasure and possessions rather than during their life on earth. They both were apocalyptists but did not believe in war. And most relevant to our situation is they both put all of their possessions into a common fund."

Amit interrupted. "How do you know someone didn't forge the gospel in a way to connect it to the Copper Scroll as you did? It'd make it appear more authentic, wouldn't it?"

Shane hesitated. "I guess it would. And I *don't* know for sure."

Lauren's pulse quickened again. *We haven't even started. Can't stop before we start.*

Amit allayed her fears. "Look Shane. You know I don't agree with you. But I'll help you see this through. Your data's more concrete than anything I have. And worth a shot."

Shane smiled. Then he got serious. "I've tried to tell you how dangerous this is. Have you ever heard of the Vraie École Biblique?"

"I've heard a few things. But there are so many fanatical religious groups in and around Israel it's hard to keep them and their agendas straight."

"They're bad men, and they're after us. If they catch us, we may not make it out in one piece. I'll understand if you don't want to take this on."

Amit looked at him. "I just lost team members at a discovery of ossuaries. If I had been there instead of here, there's a good chance I'd be in pieces already. I'm in."

Shane smiled again and put his hand on Amit's shoulder. "Thanks, Amit. I mean it. Even if you *are* wrong about the Essenes and Jewish Christians."

Lauren laughed. Amit laughed too. He came across as honest, intelligent, and passionate. She liked men of passion. She knew how to get them to do what she wanted.

They drove down the road a little while in silence before Amit asked a question Lauren had wanted to ask for a long time. "Rihab spans a large area. Where in Rihab are you thinking?"

"Where would you go?"

"St. Gorgeous Church."

"That's exactly what I was thinking."

Lauren perked up again. "St. Gorgeous Church?"

Shane turned to look at her. "St. Gorgeous is a third century Byzantine church located in Rihab. As you can probably guess, it gets its name from St. George. It's the oldest place of Christian worship built to be a church in the world. Before the third century, Christians worshiped primarily in large rooms and patios of private homes. I bet you don't think of Jordan when you think of old Christian churches."

"No, I don't. But the third century's too late."

Amit seemed impressed. "She's sharp."

Shane laughed. "More than you know. Do you want to explain it to her?"

"All right. St. Gorgeous was constructed in the year 230. That date we know with some certainty. There's an inscription with the construction date that still survives inside the church ruins. But as you've already figured out, it's about one hundred sixty years newer than what we're looking for."

Lauren through both hands in the air. "So I don't get it. Why are you two smiling?"

Amit continued. "Because a little over a year ago. Jordanian archaeologists found another church beneath St. Gorgeous. Not a nice, pretty, stained glass windowed church, but a church none the less. It's in a cave."

Lauren put her hands on the two front seats and pulled herself forward. "How old's that church?"

Shane leaned his head sideways with a slight shrug to his shoulders. "There's a lot of debate about that. But there's evidence to support it dates to the time when the Jewish Christians first fled Jerusalem. For example, they found a small number of silver half shekel coins dated to the year 66 or 67. The faces had a branch of three pomegranates and Hebrew letters translated to *Holy Jerusalem*, and the reverses specified the half shekel denomination. The half shekel coin was used to pay the annual Temple tax that all Jews had to pay."

Amit jumped in to help. "So you might ask what coins meant to pay the Temple tax are doing in Rihab. And of course, those years were during the First Jewish-Roman War. We know the Byzantines built their churches on sites known to be sacred since the first century or before. In addition to St. Gorgeous, there are twenty-nine other Christian churches nearby, constructed in the time between St. Gorgeous and the advent of Islam. That explains why little Rihab is called *the town of thirty churches*."

Shane summed up. "My theory, and I believe my friend here concurs, is that St. Gorgeous is built on top of an even older church that dates to when the Jewish Christians left Jerusalem. And inside that church, we'll find our treasure."

They may really have solved it. But she needed more. "Why hasn't anyone tied all this together before?"

Amit spoke with a matter-of-fact tone. "The Copper Scroll treasure's supposed to be in Israel. No one would've even remotely tied this cave to the Copper Scroll.

And the site's so new it hasn't been completely explored. Most religious archaeologists think the Jordanians are trying to turn it into a tourist attraction for religious pilgrims."

The tenor of Shane's voice was much more upbeat. "But now we have two other historic documents that may be corroborating the church's authenticity."

Lauren was fascinated. "So, you're saying that while others are debating the authenticity of this church, we're going to prove it's legit by uncovering a two-thousand-year-old treasure?"

Shane raised one eyebrow. "That's about it."

Lauren was still uncomfortable. "Won't the Department of Antiquities in Jordan have an issue with that? After all, we don't have a permit or permission, do we?"

Shane and Amit looked at each other and smiled before Amit answered. "That's why we're going tonight."

"We'll ask for forgiveness later," added Shane. "It's easier than asking for permission."

Lauren could not believe what she was hearing. "It sounds like this isn't the first time you guys have done something like this."

Shane feigned confusion. "Not sure what you mean. Amit, how long will it take us to get there?"

"Several hours. It's less than two hundred kilometers, but the trip won't be easy. We'll go north and skirt the West Bank the way Jesus used to do when avoiding Samaria. Then we'll cross the Jordan near Pella and cut across to Rihab. We'll have it pretty easy as long as we're in Israel. Good roads not too crowded because of the Sabbath. The roads'll get worse once we get into Jordan."

Chapter 61

Directeur Edmond Neuville of the Vraie École Biblique hung up the phone in his Jerusalem office. He had just ended the second of two important conversations. The first conversation had come from Gilbert de Clisson. He had called from his jet in the air and spent the next thirty minutes barking orders.

It was obvious Clisson had no respect for Neuville's rank or the institution he led. He saw Neuville as beneath him in class and expected Neuville to see it too. Neuville was accustomed to others underestimating him based on his appearance–fifties, average height and looks, slender, and dark, thinning, conservatively cut hair. But when it came to matters of God, he was anything but average. He took those matters very seriously.

Some church leaders thought his opinions too extreme, but Neuville knew God spoke to him directly. His relationship with God began when he was very young in France. God spoke to him in his father's vineyard and told him to prepare himself for a higher purpose. He entered the service of the Church in his early twenties, and God directed him to the Vraie École Biblique in Jerusalem. It was there, while he worked for the first Directeur, that God revealed to him his purpose–to protect God's message until his son returned. With sponsorship like that, what anyone else thought did not matter.

Neuville kicked himself many times daily for getting involved with Clisson. He personified everything wrong with the French elite. They professed to be Christians, yet they used their wealth to commit every form of sin. They lauded themselves as leaders, yet they reinforced a class structure that treated their fellow man with disrespect. They considered themselves cosmopolitan, yet they considered anything not Parisian as second class.

Even so, Neuville knew why he tolerated Clisson. The Vraie École Biblique had suffered financial hardship in recent years. Without donations from benefactors such as Clisson, it could collapse.

Neuville had no intention of letting the Vraie École Biblique fail in its mission. It was more important now than ever to control the official doctrine of the Church.

Television routinely presented alternative views of the gospels and exalted false gospels. Web sites and blogs across the internet devoted cyberspace to proving false what the Church had taught their flocks for two thousand years. Books everywhere explored the *historical* Jesus and tried to prove their false claims at the expense of the Church. It seemed the more outlandish the assertion was, the more the media spread the heresy.

Neuville was in a battle with evil forces for the souls of humanity, and it was a sad fact money was needed to wage the war successfully. He considered his relationships with Clisson and others like him as deals with the devil, necessary for now but not permanent.

Neuville's second call had come from Andre de Vaux. He and Raphael were safely on their way to Tel Aviv. They had crossed into Quebec and had been able to get seats on a plane flying as French Canadians. Neuville had prayed for their deliverance, and God had answered his prayer. *Praise be to God!*

Still, Neuville knew he would need to enlist other help for tonight. Clisson had told him the location indicated by the gospel. He had demanded Neuville meet him in Amman, Jordan and provide armed support. *Armed support!* The Vraie École Biblique was a religious school dedicated to the true gospel of God. It was not composed of mercenaries. *Clisson will bring the Vraie École Biblique to ruin.*

The more Neuville thought about the conversation, the angrier he got. *A l'enfer avec Clisson! Dieu me pardonne.*

Neuville picked up his phone and dialed the number of an acquaintance within Jordan's Department of Antiquities. The Department of Antiquities supervised all fieldwork conducted by Jordanian and foreign archaeological expeditions within the borders of Jordan. They also safeguarded close to twenty thousand Jordanian archaeological sites by any means necessary, including the deployment of armed guards.

Mikhail Al-Kayed was a senior official within the Department of Antiquities and worked directly for the Director General in Amman.

"Alo."

"Assalamu alaykum," said Neuville. "Peace be upon you."

"Wa Alaykum Assalam. And on you be peace. What can I do for you, Director Neuville?"

"I have reason to believe some people are headed to your country to conduct an unauthorized dig."

"How do you know this?"

"Some members of my school have been following up on information we came upon accidentally. They are on their way back now, but I am afraid they will not arrive in time to prevent a raid on one of your sites tonight."

"Which site is it?"

Neuville could not let Al-Kayed move on the site without him. "I would rather not talk about it over the phone."

"What do you propose?"

"I will come to Amman tonight. After I arrive, I will provide you with a detailed explanation. Then we can decide the appropriate course of action. Is that acceptable?"

"Yes, I will make arrangements. And I will contact the Mukhabarat to assign us a few of their men."

Neuville swallowed hard. Dairat al-Mukhabarat al-Ammah was Jordan's General Intelligence Department, otherwise known as the secret police. It was one of the most powerful and respected enforcement organizations in the Arab world. Some saw the institution as an impediment to democratic reform. Others saw it as a necessity to preserve the country's security. It was not an institution to be taken lightly.

Neuville had no choice but to agree. "That is a wise move."

They disconnected, and Neuville stood up to prepare. The stakes had just risen.

Chapter 62

Shane knew his way around Israel fairly well, but in the deepening shadows of dusk he was having difficulty determining where they were. "I'm glad you're driving."

"Me too." Amit had just left the highway for a much rougher road.

After stopping briefly for sandwiches and soft drinks, they had driven northward on *Kvish Shesh*, or Road 6. The newly constructed north-south corridor cut through rural Israel with the Coastal Plain to the west and the West Bank and the Judean Hills to the east. Plans had it eventually connecting to major highways in Egypt to the south and Lebanon to the north, but no one knew when the political situation would allow those connections.

After following Road 6 as long as he could, Amit had exited off onto Highway 65, which connected the coastal plain with Galilee. The highway minimized having to traverse hilly terrain by passing through Iron Valley and its many small Arab villages until intersecting Highway 71 at Afula just north of the West Bank boundary. Then they had turned southeast and descended through the Jezreel Valley toward the Jordan Valley and the Jordan River Border Crossing.

Shane knew the border crossings well. The Jordan River Border Crossing was the northernmost of three border crossings between Israel and Jordan. It connected Beth She'an, Israel with Irbid, Jordan, one of Jordan's largest cities. Known as Arabella before the advent of Islam, Irbid was about a half hour from Pella and an hour from Rihab. On the southern end of Israel, connecting to Aqaba, Jordan was the Arava Border Terminal, recently renamed to the Yitzhak Rabin Border Terminal. The central crossing, which was the shortest route to Amman from Jerusalem and other central Israeli cities, was the Allenby Bridge, also called the King Hussein Bridge by Jordanians and the Al-Karamech Bridge by Palestinians.

Shane found the hardship crossing Middle Eastern boundaries to be needless and disproportionate to the countries' sizes. He could only imagine what crossing state lines in the United States would be like if the country had taken a different path. "It's ironic how much easier it was to get around two thousand years ago."

Amit agreed. "Without a doubt. The Pax Romana, combined with Roman road construction, opened up everything. It was like your interstate highway system."

Shane had often taught how the Pax Romana was the Roman Peace brought about by the conquest of the Roman Empire and the absolute rule within its boundaries. Caesar Augustus ushered in the period, and its relative calm lasted for two hundred years.

Amit smiled broadly. "And for a while it was great to be Jewish."

Lauren leaned forward. "Why?"

"Jews held protected status within the Roman Empire," Amit explained. "From the time they came to the aid of Julius Caesar in his conquest of Egypt until they rebelled over one hundred years later. Judaism was the only foreign religion in the empire which enjoyed the status of *religio licita*–tolerated religion. It could be practiced openly in accordance with Jewish Law."

Shane joined in. "And since Paul was both a Roman citizen and a Jew, he could preach just about anywhere without interference. Today, we can't even go a few kilometers without facing border guards checking for the wrong stamp in our passport."

His words must have struck a nerve with Lauren. "Are we going to have trouble getting into Jordan this late?"

Amit shifted his weight in his seat. "We would if we were going through the border crossing."

"What do you mean?"

"The Jordan River Border Terminal will be closed. It closes early on Saturday. There'd be too many questions anyway."

Shane had anticipated Amit's plan. "Do you intend to ford the river?"

"Exactly."

Shane laughed inwardly at the look on Lauren's face.

"Is that possible?" she asked.

Amit's weight shifted again. "I'm not one hundred percent sure."

Shane burst into laughter. "At least we won't have to pay the Israeli exit tax."

Chapter 63

"Ibn haram!" cursed Hamdi Adwan. "You lost them!" Hamdi brought his fists down hard on the back of the driver's seat of the Honda Accord sedan.

Ahmad Habib extended his shoulders up around his head as if hiding in embarrassment. "I was too close. I had to back off."

Milak Siyam sided with Hamdi. "You let them get too far ahead."

Al-Jamal knew his men were frustrated. Some time ago they had lost the Land Cruiser they had been following. After hours of pursuit they now found themselves wandering in the darkness in hope of spotting the vehicle's lights. But there were no lights. Ahmad stopped the car and sheepishly waited for instructions.

Al-Jamal was not worried. He knew the area well. They were only forty kilometers from his home. There was still hope. "It is no good. We will not find them here."

Hamdi brought his fists down on the seat back again and screamed curses at Ahmad. "Akho shlickeh!"

Al-Jamal laughed inside. Ahmad's sister was not really a whore. "Leave him alone. It is not his fault."

Handling such varied personalities was one of his greatest leadership skills. Just keeping them from killing each other would have been a challenge for most leaders. "I know what they are doing. We could not follow them anyway."

Milak's eyes opened wide. "Ya Sidi, where are they going that we cannot follow?"

"They are going to cross one of the Beth She'an fords."

This time Hamdi's curse was mumbled under his breath but loudly enough to hear. "Lahis zubi!"

Al-Jamal laughed loudly, and his men joined him. "Go back to the highway and head for the crossing. I'll call for help to cross the border." He pointed to their AK-47s. "It would not serve Allah for us to get caught with our weapons, much less what we have in the trunk."

Ahmad nodded. "Yes, Ya Sidi." He shifted gears and turned around.

"I know where they will most likely emerge," Al-Jamal assured them. "Do you know that *Beth She'an* means *house of tranquility*? So do not worry. With the help of Allah we will find them yet."

Chapter 64

Amit continued first over rough roads and then without roads toward the location he had chosen to ford. As he neared the river he turned off his headlights. "We don't want to draw the attention of the Magav," Amit knew Shane was very familiar, but he thought Lauren might benefit from an explanation. "The Magav are the Israeli border guards. They have been known to shoot and kill both Israelis and foreign nationals attempting to cross the border illegally. With good fording locations nearby, they are especially active around Beth She'an."

Lauren cocked her head. "Like patrolling fording spots along the Rio Grande River in Texas."

"Exactly. The fords have made Beth She'an a strategic location for millennia. Egypt established a large military base there three thousand five hundred years ago. When the Romans established Dekapolis, they made Beth She'an the capital though it was the only city west of the Jordan. At that time, it had the Greek name Scythopolis, because Scythian mercenaries had settled there. The Romans kept it as a major territorial hub for the next seven hundred years through the Byzantine period until Muslims conquered the area.

"The reason these powers thought Beth She'an so important was its location. Sitting at the junction of the Jezreel Valley with the Jordan River Valley, Beth She'an connected a major trade route called the King's Highway passing through Gilead on the eastern side of the Jordan River with another major trade route called the Great Trunk Road which followed the Coastal Plain of present day Israel through Gaza into Egypt. Trade caravans or armies could travel through Gilead and cross the Jordan River to access the Jezreel Valley that led to the Great Trunk Road. Whoever controlled Beth She'an controlled traffic between the interior and the coast. Whoever controlled Beth She'an and both trade routes monopolized the entire region from Mesopotamia to Egypt."

Amit focused on the path ahead in the ever-deepening darkness. With Shane and Lauren helping him, he slowly guided his SUV southeast of Beth She'an. Ultimately, they passed through some thick brush onto a widening section of level land opening up ahead of them.

Stopping the car, Amit rolled down his window. He could hear the river. He turned to Shane and saw his own look of excited anticipation reflected in Shane's face. After ensuring the interior light was set off, he opened his door and stepped outside. He left the car idling and walked to the rear of the Land Cruiser. Shane and Lauren joined him on the rocky soil.

Amit opened the hatch and pulled out two flashlights. "Don't use them unless you have to."

He reached in again and pulled out night vision goggles. He saw Shane's surprise. "I brought these in case we ended up underground. I have another set if you want to try them out."

Shane reached for the goggles. "I would."

Amit pulled out the second set. Designed for cave exploration, the night vision goggles fit using straps that went over the head and around the forehead connecting to a chin strap that extended around the back of the head. The goggles focused both eyes through a single ocular tube that fed an infrared illuminator. The monocular could be adjusted for various levels of brightness to improve vision, and it could flip upward to facilitate normal vision.

Lauren must have felt left out. "What about me?"

"Sorry," replied Amit. "I don't have a third set. I'll look out for you."

Looking like characters from a spy movie, Amit and Shane walked toward the river with Lauren holding on to Shane's belt. Amit was amazed at how well he could see in near total darkness. The footing was rough, but they found the water without mishap.

Lauren stepped around between them. "Can we get across?"

Amit scanned the river. "We wouldn't be here if I didn't think we could. But it's a risk. Shane, how much of a hurry are you in? And how secret do you want to keep this? We could always go through the border crossing tomorrow."

"No, you're right," Shane affirmed. "It's best to take care of this tonight. How far across do you think it is?"

"Fortunately, we had a dry winter. I'm guessing the river is about fifty meters across and well less than a meter deep. We won't know until we're in it."

Shane's tone expressed both expertise and concern. "The current looks strong. And it seems to be swirling. Can we pass fifty meters without being swept downstream?"

"Well, that's the question, isn't it? You know, Christians come here from all over the world. They bathe themselves in this river and talk about John the Baptist and Jesus. To us, the Jordan River is just dirty, smelly water."

Chapter 65

Even before his Dassault Falcon 7X touched down at Queen Alia International Airport, Gilbert de Clisson was dialing the mobile phone number of Director Edmond Neuville. While he listened to the ringing, he thought about how amusing it was that a government with such repressive laws and policies would name their international airport after a woman, the third wife of King Hussein.

Clisson's amusement did not last long. Neuville did not answer. When Clisson's call went to voice mail, he refused to leave a message. He dialed Neuville's office number but met the same response. He tried his home number but nothing.

Clisson fumed. He was unaccustomed to people not being where they were told. *Where is that bastard?* The unpleasant answer came readily enough. Neuville had double-crossed him. Clisson had not thought it possible. Neuville had never come across as having the backbone to do something like this. It was another example of why he would never trust his fate to a single individual. *I was a fool for sharing the destination.* In situations involving money, betrayal should be expected and contingencies available.

"Gustave," he called.

"Oui, Monsieur Clisson."

"It seems we have been left to fend for ourselves."

Gustave raised an eyebrow.

"You know a few men in the area that could come to our aid, correct?"

"Oui, Monsieur Clisson. I know men who for the right price will be our best friends. Before we left, I took the liberty of letting them know we were coming."

"Very good. Do you think they might also provide us with a vehicle suitable to our purposes?"

"Oui, Monsieur Clisson. That should be no problem."

Mercenaries were not always controllable, but they had their uses. The trick was having them thinking at all times they could make more money with you than without you. The relationship had to be kept basic and simple–specific tasks and no information beyond what was necessary for their assignment. Then the relationship had to be severed and moneys transferred before the balance of power shifted. Expecting mercenaries to be loyal was a shortcut to disaster.

"Have three men meet us at the terminal as quickly as they can. Make sure they know to come heavily armed. Promise them a lot of money to do whatever I want with no questions asked."

"Oui, Monsieur Clisson."

The jet turned slowly into place.

Clisson smiled. "See you soon, Directeur Neuville."

Chapter 66

"What are you doing?" Lauren asked Amit and Shane.

Shane and Amit had removed their night vision goggles and were securing a tarp to the front grill of the Land Cruiser.

Amit was first to answer. "We're using the tarp to create a bow wave. It'll minimize the amount of water that gets behind the bumper and enters the engine compartment. That reduces the water spray off the radiator fan and means it's less likely water'll impact the air intake and stall us."

Whatever. She had paired up with an ex-boyfriend divinity professor and now found herself with two crazy adventurers. *How'd I get so lucky?* She knew from experience *good luck* came to people who had their act together. She had stayed ahead of the Vraie École Biblique henchmen long enough to find the perfect help. "Can we make it?"

Amit finished his side of the tarp. "Four-by-four SUVs can ford water axle deep without issue. That means we can easily ford up to sixty centimeters. Uh, that's just less than two feet. Higher than that and there is a risk of us floating off. With the water as high as a meter, this may be your chance to get baptized in the Jordan River."

Shane completed his end of the tarp. "Already done that. Don't need to do it again. The tarp looks good."

Amit took a few steps toward the river. "With the river as wide as it is here, the current'll be less than in other places. But it'll be strong enough to be a challenge."

Shane moved up alongside him. "The surface looks relatively smooth. That means the bottom should be the same."

Amit turned back to the car. "No time like the present to find out. Everybody in."

Lauren joined Shane and Amit in the SUV. A last moment of nervousness coursed through her body. "You *have* done this before, right?"

Shane smiled broadly. "Of course he has." Then to Amit he said, "You have, haven't you?"

Lauren laughed and expected Amit to laugh as well, but he remained stoic. "Normally I'd turn on the roof lights. But I guess we'll have to get by with night vision."

Amit and Shane slipped their goggles back on. Amit started the Land Cruiser, put it in first gear, and directed it to the river's edge. He entered at a forty-five degree angle with the front of the Land Cruiser pointed upstream. The SUV immediately shuddered. Lauren tightened her grips on the overhead handle and armrest.

Amit explained his actions. "I have to drive upstream as we cross. It'll take us a little longer, but the current'll hit us at a smaller angle. That lessens the force along our side and makes it less likely we'll be swept away. The resistance of the current'll drive us toward the far bank."

The Land Cruiser shook and bucked as it moved forward, hit a wall of water, then released to repeat the cycle. Amit maintained a slow, steady pace. Lauren looked to her left and saw what appeared in the darkness to be a flashflood attacking them but in reality was just an unending ribbon of river. She looked to her right and saw what appeared to be the release from under a dam. "I'm getting dizzy."

Amit strained to speak through his concentration. "Don't look at the water. Keep your eyes on the far bank."

Shane acted as navigator. 'We're over halfway!"

Lauren began to relax, but the tension in her muscles did not have time to fully release before the car tires lost contact for a moment and the SUV slid downstream. The sensation of being out of control filled the cabin until a wheel found traction, then another. Amit regained control, and they began moving across again.

Shane gripped Amit's shoulder. "Good job!"

Amit wiped his face. "That was too close."

No joke. Lauren could sense the relief in his tone. She released her grips on the overhead handle and armrest to let a little blood return to her fingers.

The closer they came to the far riverbank, the more the traction returned. Lauren could tell by the angle of the car they were ascending to shallower water. She exhaled deeply. As the front tires gripped dry ground, the current pushed on the rear half of the SUV until it was almost parallel to the river. *Here we go again.* But the steady grinding of the four-wheel drive dug into the soil and pulled the Land Cruiser from the river before it could be thrown back into the water.

Amit continued up the level terrain that bordered the ford until they were a safe distance from the river. He stopped but kept the engine running. Water drained from all sides of the car. Amit hung his head with his chin in his chest. It was the first time he had given in to the pressure he was feeling.

Shane opened his door and stepped outside. "Never a doubt!"

Lauren followed him. Firm ground never felt so good. Amit was last to exit the SUV. While Shane removed the tarp, Amit opened the hatch and began moving things around. He was apparently searching for something. Lauren joined him to see if she could help.

Amit pulled out two Jordanian license plates. "Here they are. No reason to be stopped for something as stupid as the wrong license plate."

Lauren was impressed. "What else do you have in there?"

Amit laughed as he bent down to swap the plate.

Shane joined them in the rear of the vehicle. "The tarp is clear."

Lauren looked up at Shane and hoped she was communicating with her eyes the amazement she felt.

"We're home free," Shane told her. "We have to ascend to the top of that plateau in front of us. Then it's straight to St. Gorgeous Church."

Chapter 67

"Uhibu layla. I love the night." Hassan Jabir said aloud as he stepped from the guard shack and looked up at the night sky.

He often lost himself within the millions of stars. They made him feel a part of something greater, something vast, perhaps even something holy. He wished he had taken time to learn their names.

Jabir enjoyed being a security officer for the Jordanian Department of Antiquities. Even if all he was guarding was a bunch of stones, the uniform demanded respect. His weight gain over the years now stretched his uniform shirt around the buttons and under the arms, but people knew it represented the Jordanian government. And if the uniform was not enough, the AK-47 assault rifle he carried provided sufficient reinforcement. Though he had never found cause to fire it, the weapon had hung from a strap around his neck so long it felt like an appendage of his body.

Not bad for a short, over-weight, balding nobody from nowhere. Time for another round.

As he walked, a cool draft filled the space between his uniform shirt and jacket. It felt great. This time of year the warm thirty degree centigrade days gave way to cool sixteen degree nights. Jabir's tolerance of the heat had waned with age, and now he much preferred the cooler temperatures. Even on the coolest nights, the light jacket kept him comfortable. He pulled the jacket as far around his girth as it would go. The fact the edges did not meet made no difference.

The cool temperatures were just one of many reasons why Jabir preferred working nights. Working the night shift at archaeological sites gave him a lot of time to himself. While some might find the solitude lonely, he reveled in it. He had no reason to be home. His children were grown, and his wife had long ago lost interest in sharing his bed. Their arguments had given way to acceptance and even comfort with their respective roles. Still, working nights made the situation easier for both of them.

Best of all, nothing ever happened. There was nothing of value to steal. *Who would risk imprisonment or his life to run off with a shard of stone?* Every night was as uneventful as the previous one, and Jabir took great comfort from the monotony.

Jabir walked to the edge of the wire fence that surrounded the light-colored stones of the church ruin. The parallel strands of dark wire did little to deter anyone wanting to penetrate the boundary. The fence mostly just marked the line the Jordanian government said not to cross.

The site was not well lit. Indirect lighting from surrounding areas cast shadows that could play tricks on the mind of the inexperienced. As Jabir placed his feet in the impressions he had made in previous trips, he complemented himself on his mental discipline.

A shrill sound suddenly split the night. Jabir jumped in panic. He dropped to a knee and fumbled for the safety of his AK-47. The high-pitched sound erupted again. It was just the ringtone of his mobile phone. *Who is calling at this time of night?* No one ever called him.

"Alo."

"This is Mikhail Al-Kayed. Do you know who I am?"

Jabir stood up straight and snapped to attention. *Why would such a senior member of the Department of Antiquities be calling me?* "Yes, I know who you are."

"What is your name?"

"I am Hassan Jabir, night security."

"Very good, Hassan. Listen to me carefully."

Jabir trembled. *Have I done something wrong? Am I in trouble?* In all his years of service he had never spoken to anyone this powerful.

"We have reason to believe there are some people on their way to penetrate the perimeter of your site. We want you to let them."

Jabir thought he had misheard. "You want me to let them break in?"

"Yes. I am sure you are very good at your job. If you need verification, call this number back. My assistant will get you what you need."

Jabir knew better than to question Al-Kayed. "I understand."

"Do you, Hassan? This is important. Go about your job as you would every other night. Just stay out of their way. I will be there soon, and I will have the Mukhabarat with me. We will deal with the intruders."

The Mukhabarat! Jabir shook worse and stammered. "I-I-I will do as you say."

"Very good. Jazak'Allah. May Allah reward you."

The line went dead.

Jabir was not concerned with reward. He just wanted to survive the night.

Chapter 68

Shane kneeled between Lauren and Amit within the cover of a grove of trees and examined St. Gorgeous Church. They had taken a little over an hour to cover the last twenty-five miles. Having parked the Land Cruiser well out of sight, they had crept through the shadows and now held their destination in view.

Amit whispered. "Almost eighteen hundred years old. What an amazing sight."

Lauren was almost giddy. "Beautiful. It looks like it could be hiding a secret."

Shane was intent on finding their true objective. He had seen pictures of the site many times, but he had never been there. The trees that hid them grew near some houses about thirty yards from the church. The distance and the lack of electric light around the church frustrated Shane in his search. He put on his goggles and heard Amit do the same.

He hoped Amit was having better luck. "Do you see it?"

"Not yet."

From their perspective they looked into the church longwise with the altar at the far end. In front was a large brown sign with white lettering in Arabic and English:

Saint George The victorious Church.
The oldest Church in the World (230 A.D.)

Interesting capitalization.

St. Gorgeous looked as if a titan had taken a giant saw, sliced through the church, and removed the upper half. What remained was a bottom section of stone block walls surrounding partial Roman columns and a floor covered in mosaics. The walls that outlined the shape of the building stopped abruptly at about ten feet high. They were uniform and level at that height around the entire perimeter. The remnants of the square Roman columns varied in height but averaged about half the height of the wall. Each stone block was about a foot and a half high by two feet long by one and a half feet deep. They were separated by mortar and stacked like bricks. The stones were light colored with shades varying from cream to pink to gray.

It was not a large church. Shane estimated its dimensions as about thirty feet wide and seventy feet long. The overall design followed a basilica plan, generally rectangular in shape, squared off at the near end and indented and extended with a semicircular area at the far end. The columns separated the central nave from the outer aisles. The semicircular far end formed an apse which held the altar.

Even from their distance, Shane could appreciate the well-preserved beauty of the mosaic floor. It consisted primarily of a simple combination of lines to form squares shifted ninety degrees into a diamond pattern. Other geometric designs marked the borders of the aisles.

Something's missing. "Do you see any security?" Shane asked Amit.

"No. No lights. No dogs. No cameras. Nothing but a wire fence."

Lauren sighed in disgust. "These countries don't realize what they have."

Shane knew that was changing. "They're beginning to. They're starting to realize how much money they can make from them." He paused. "There has to be a guard."

Amit pointed to a small building inside the compound to the right of the church. "My bet is he's in that shack over there. From the flickering light, it looks like there's a television."

Lauren seemed concerned. "So where do we go?"

Shane scanned the area around the church again. What they were looking for was not in the ruin of St. Gorgeous. It was beneath it. A little over a year ago, a workman at the site struck a spot with his shovel, and it sounded hollow. He reported it to his employer, a Jordanian archaeologist. Together they dug down a couple of feet and found an ancient air shaft. When they shined a light into the shaft, they realized they stood atop a subterranean cave. They excavated the cave and discovered it had been hollowed out and shaped into a series of rooms, including an altar. It was a church, considerably older than St. Gorgeous, which was later constructed directly above it.

"There!" Shane pointed to a deeper shadow outside the left wall of St. Gorgeous. He drew the Beretta 92 semi-automatic pistol Amit had brought for him and started forward. Lauren and Amit followed. They stayed low as they half-jogged the short distance to the fence. *So far so good. No alarms or cries of warning.*

Amit produced wire cutters and began working on the fence. Once severed, the wires sprang back in both directions. A gap of three wires created enough space for Amit to scoot through, followed by Lauren and Shane. They were now officially trespassing on a Jordanian archaeological site. If they were caught, the subsequent experience would not be enjoyable.

Shane took the lead. "Over here."

He led them along the side wall of the ruin to series of steps carved into the rock. The steps, about five feet wide, led down perhaps fifteen feet below the surface. At the bottom were two wooden doors that met in the middle of the cave opening. Shane quickly descended the steps until he reached the doors. Lauren and Amit soon stood shoulder to shoulder with him. The doors opened inward but were secured with a padlock.

Amit turned to Shane. "Do we break the lock?"

'That might make enough noise to attract attention."

Lauren gripped Shane's wrist. "Let me try."

She searched the steps until she found a slender piece of sheet metal, probably torn from equipment being hauled into or out of the site. She folded and shaped the metal to her liking and inserted it in the keyhole of the lock. She moved it back and forth, applied pressure, and snapped the lock open.

"Impressive," Shane declared.

Lauren removed the lock from the doors and pushed them open. "Just pulling my weight."

The air was heavy and dark. Wearing his night vision goggles, Shane cautiously entered through the doors. More steps led a few more feet down to the cave floor. "Careful, there are three steps."

Shane held Lauren's hand, and she made it down unscathed. Amit followed. Shane did a three hundred sixty-degree turn in the room and was momentarily overcome. *I'm standing in the first Christian church ever constructed. I'm walking in the footsteps of people who knew Jesus and James personally.*

Chapter 69

Hassan Jabir watched as two men and one woman cut through his fence and disappeared into the lower church. He was extremely proud of himself for using the television in his shack as a distraction. He was not watching television. He was hiding behind a pile of rock and metal to the side of the church. He had dug a cavity in the rubble such that he was hidden on three sides. From his vantage point, he could easily see the intruders, but they could not see him. He had always been smarter than people thought.

Jabir grew increasingly more courageous with every wave of pride that swept over him. He rubbed his AK-47 and fantasized about confronting the trespassers.

"Stop where you are!" he would cry in his deepest voice. "Put your hands on your head."

Of course, they probably did not speak Arabic.

He would have to gesture to them with his weapon they were his prisoners. He would hold the AK-47 with one hand while roughly turning them with the other. He would frisk them, taking his time with the woman. Then he would herd them to the wall of the ruin and make them sit down. When Al-Kayed and the Mukhabarat arrived, they would see him as a hero.

Who knows? They might even ask me to join them. Jabir wondered what his wife would say about that. *Who cares? I will get a new, younger wife who will appreciate me for the man I am.*

What am I waiting for?

Jabir rose up from his hiding place and crept along the ruin. He gripped his weapon with both hands, turned the safety off, and rested his finger near the trigger. He stopped every few paces and listened to make sure the intruders were not coming back up the steps. His hair stood on end, and his skin tingled. He did not want to kill anyone. But he would do what he had to do to defend his site.

When Jabir reached the steps, he twisted over in a quick, jerking motion and pointed his weapon toward the open doorway at the bottom. He saw no one. There was only darkness. He did not lower his weapon. With the door open someone could emerge at any time.

Jabir hesitated. He never went into the lower church cave. He was claustrophobic. The only time he had gone down there, his lungs had nearly shut down, and his heart had almost exploded. Just the thought of entering the cave now caused his body to react with an intense sweat. The pace of his breathing increased, and his pulse raced so quickly he thought his veins might jump out of his skin.

What was that? Shuffling noises in the cave. The intruders were in the main room. They might have heard him approach. They might be looking at him from the darkness even now.

What am I doing? There are three of them. At least one of them is armed. Perhaps all three. A couple of flashes from the darkness and his life would be over.

Jabir backed away and retraced his path. He was hyperventilating and sweating through his uniform. Al-Kayed had specifically ordered him not to interfere. Perhaps more was going on than he knew. *Why did Al-Kayed ask me to ignore my duty? Is there something in the cave he wants? Were the intruders his partners?* Regardless of Al-Kayed's motives, Jabir knew it was not a good idea to upset someone that high in the Jordanian government.

He returned to his pile of rubble and sat down. He reset the safety on his AK-47, released his grip, and let it swing to his side.

Chapter 70

Lauren was becoming increasingly frustrated. "I can't see a thing."

Only faint indirect lighting penetrated the circular air shaft above them. It did little to soften the deep blackness.

Amit's voice echoed about the cave. "You can use your flashlight now. I doubt anyone will see it down here. As long as we don't look directly into the light, we can adjust our goggles to compensate. Just be careful not to point it at us, out the door, or up the air shaft."

Lauren pushed the button on her flashlight and instantly felt better. The beam brought the cave into focus. The stone floor was surprisingly smooth, but the ceiling and walls were rough-hewn. The height from floor to ceiling varied between nine to twelve feet. In places, stacks of mortared stones filled in and reinforced the walls.

Lauren estimated the cave chamber at about forty feet long and a little over twenty feet wide. To the right of the entrance was a large open space, and to the left was a circular area almost twenty feet in diameter. The round part of the cave contained several large oval stones about three feet in diameter and flat on top. They appeared to be sculpted into seats. A few other longer stones of similar height appeared shaped into benches. All-in-all, the cave looked like a place where Fred Flintstone would have been comfortable.

Shane stood near the seats and benches. "We're in the chapel. The circular area's the apse where the altar would have been. This room's where the congregation met to worship."

Amit walked up to one of the walls and rubbed his hand down the rough stone. "*In the ruin under the steps. Concealed by sediment is a cave.*"

The statements seemed totally out of context. Lauren looked to Shane. "What does that mean?"

"He's quoting two of the directions from the first column of the Copper Scroll. I told you he had it memorized."

Then that's good. "We're in the right place."

"Perhaps."

Amit left the wall for the middle of the room. "We need to see if there's a cistern. If you're right about focusing exclusively on the first four columns, they repeatedly mention a cistern. The inhabitants would've needed one to hold fresh water. It'd be a great hiding place."

Lauren saw nothing that looked like a big pit dug into the rock where rain water or spring water would channel and collect for use by the inhabitants. *How much larger can this cave be?*

Amit seemed to be searching for something. "*In the tunnel which is to the south.* It's supposed to lead to an underground cavity, perhaps a cistern."

Shane explained again. "Another Copper Scroll direction. This one from the fourth column." Then to Amit, he said, "Since the apse points east, south would be to its right."

Lauren pointed her flashlight in that direction. There was a doorway complete with a doorsill composed of squared off stones laid on top of one another and held in place with mortar. It was positioned almost directly opposite the cave entrance.

Shane approached the doorway. "Must be the living quarters."

Lauren followed Shane and Amit through the doorway where they found three separate rooms constructed from partitions of stone blocks surrounded by rough cave walls. They were each about twenty feet in length parallel to the chapel and thirty feet wide.

Shane leaned in and peered into one of the rooms. "The Jordanians think these three rooms were separate living quarters for men, women, and children."

Lauren's excitement was trying her patience. "So where's the cistern? Or the tunnel?"

Amit answered. "*It lies on the third level in the cave.*"

Shane reached out for Lauren. "I think that's from the second column. The cistern's at a lower level."

Lauren pointed her flashlight on the far wall of the living quarters. There she found another doorway framed by stacked stones. The threshold was larger than normal, about eighteen inches high and two feet deep. It was composed of a single stone block.

Amit seemed entranced. "*The cistern's entrance is under the large stone threshold.*"

"Also from the second column." Shane pointed. "What's on the other side?"

Lauren walked to the doorway and directed the beam of her flashlight into the void. "Unbelievable. It's a tunnel angling downward."

Shane and Amit came up behind her. The tunnel was about six feet wide and eight feet high. The walls were pockmarked and abrasive. What really bothered Lauren was the tunnel was not totally clear of rubble. It was partially filled with sand and rock that seemed to get gradually deeper as the tunnel descended. Apparently the Jordanian archaeologists had focused on the chapel and living areas and were just now in the process of clearing the tunnel. Though passing through the tunnel looked like it might be doable, Lauren was not looking forward to the attempt.

Shane must have had similar concerns. He turned to Amit. "How long do you think it is?"

"According to the fourth column, it should be about forty-one cubits. That's about nineteen meters."

"A little over sixty feet. That's a pretty steep angle. It goes deep."

"The inhabitants had to have a water source. They must have widened a pre-existing passageway to a point where water seeped through cracks in the rock. Then they dug a cistern to collect the water. They'd walk down to the cistern, collect the water in vessels, and carry it back up to the living quarters. The Jordanians found pottery fragments at this level."

Shane rubbed his hands together. "Right. Well, if we're translating the Copper Scroll correctly, we're not going to find anything up here."

Lauren had never experienced claustrophobia before, but this was a little ridiculous.

Shane seemed to sense her discomfort. "It'll be all right. These walls have been here two thousand years. They're not going to suddenly collapse today. Just keep your eyes straight ahead, take your time, and follow me. It's going to get tight."

Shane stepped across the threshold and began weaving his way through scattered stones. Amit seemed anxious to follow, but Lauren could see he was waiting on her.

Oh, all right. I've come too far to chicken out now.

Chapter 71

Leaning against the pile of rubble, Hassan Jabir was half dozing when an unexpected brightness roused him. He rose up enough to see car lights coming down the road toward the complex. It was an unusual sight for the area. The front vehicle was a limousine. Behind it was a Humvee.

When the two vehicles stopped near the entrance, four men dressed in dark uniforms and assault gear rushed from the Humvee to surround the limo. They wore helmets with visors, and they carried AK-47 assault rifles. When the driver opened the door of the limo, two men in suits stepped out. One was average height and build and looked like an administrator. The second was taller and stood proud and erect with a thin face, chiseled features, and piercing eyes. He buttoned his suit coat as if he was on an afternoon outing. *He must be Al-Kayed.*

Jabir slowly revealed himself from his hiding place and began walking toward the gate entrance to the compound. He knew enough to approach the Mukhabarat as if they were wild animals that could turn on him and tear him to pieces. He released his weapon and kept his hands up and visible.

The Mukhabarat reacted immediately to Jabir, but the man he assumed was Al-Kayed quickly called them off. Jabir unlocked the gate, swung it open, and stood motionless except for the knocking of his knees.

The man in charge strode to Jabir. "Hassan Jabir?"

Though the man smiled as he spoke, Jabir trembled under his stare. He was surprised a man as important as Al-Kayed would remember his name. His words cracked as he spoke, "Yes, I am Hassan Jabir."

"Good. I am Mikhail Al-Kayed. And this is Director Neuville. Were we right? Have you had visitors?"

"Yes."

"How many?"

"Two men and one woman."

"Did you interfere with them?"

"No. I did as you asked."

Al-Kayed seemed relieved. Perhaps he expected to hear Jabir had acted against his wishes. Jabir looked up and thanked the stars his good sense had prevailed.

Al-Kayed put his hand on Jabir's shoulder and began walking with him as he spoke. "Very good. Where are they now?"

"Inside the cave below the ruin."

"How long have they been inside?"

"Perhaps thirty minutes."

"Excellent. Please take us to the entrance, and we will take it from there. You have done very well, Hassan. I will ensure you are rewarded."

Jabir liked the sound of that. He relaxed. *My wife will never believe it.* He pointed toward the lower church entrance. "This way."

He led them to the steps leading down to the cave.

Neuville spoke in broken Arabic. "It is paramount we not interrupt them until they complete their search."

Al-Kayed turned to the Mukhabarat security agents. "Take positions in the cave just inside the entrance. Very quietly. Safety your weapons. We must take them alive. Anyone who shoots one of them, I will shoot."

The four Mukhabarat agents began down the steps in formation. When they reached the door, they paused to look inside. Then they silently disappeared into the cave.

Jabir's adrenaline pumped into his veins again. It was the most excitement he had experienced in many years. "What would you have *me* do?" He was very much afraid of what Al-Kayed's response might be.

"Stay here. Let us know if anyone else comes."

Al-Kayed and Neuville descended the steps slowly. Jabir had no problem remaining behind.

Chapter 72

Shane squeezed through the far end of the tunnel and slid down a pile of sand, stone dust, and rocks into a large open room. As he did, he failed to see some cobwebs and passed directly through them. Looking down awkwardly with his goggles, he saw the thick fibers across his stomach and arms. The presence of webs did not necessarily mean spiders, but the webs on his skin and clothes gave him a major case of heebie-jeebies. He knew Israel had six species of widow spiders, two species of recluse spiders, and a redback spider that was not only dangerous to humans but quite scary looking.

His heart pounded, and his sweat glands gushed their liquid. He franticly began brushing and pulling the webs from his body. His response was all reflex, and no matter how embarrassed he knew he would be in a few minutes, he could not control the nervous chant he made with each motion of his hands. When he finally concluded no spiders crawled over his arms, hair, or neck, he bent over and took a few deep breaths.

"What's going on?" Lauren asked from the tunnel.

"Nothing."

Shane helped Lauren and then Amit into the room. Amit stood staring at Shane. "Cobwebs?"

"Major. How'd you know?"

"You must be kidding. You awoke the dead."

Lauren laughed out loud. Shane was glad no one could tell how deeply he was blushing. "Is everyone all right?"

The trip through the tunnel had not been easy. At one time, Shane had feared the far end would be blocked. As it turned out, a few open feet of space remained.

"A few scrapes," Lauren replied. "But otherwise all right."

"Likewise," agreed Amit. "Where are we?"

Shane looked from side to side and realized they stood in an exitless room of stone. It was roughly square with each side measuring about fifteen feet. The ceiling rose about twelve feet above the floor, though the rough cave features varied that height a couple of feet in places. As expected, the room was dominated by a cistern in its center.

Each side of the cistern was about eight feet long. Its depth was difficult to determine because it was partially filled with sand and stone dust. About seven feet of depth remained visible. As Shane approached the side nearest the tunnel, he saw a steep set of stone steps descending into the sand. Presumably the steps allowed the inhabitants to reach the water when the level was low.

Amit burst into another quote. *"Enter into the staircase of the stone reservoir.* The first column."

Lauren moved to the edge of the stairs. "It looks like people's feet were smaller back then."

Shane pushed past her. "Well I'm going to give it a try."

Shane began down the steps sideways with his feet running longways on the steps. To support himself, he leaned back and held onto the steps behind him. When he met the surface of the sand, he tested it and found it to be firm.

He called up to Amit. "What am I looking for?"

"The second column says to look for *a sharp edge in the rock on the eastern wall in the cistern.*"

Knowing the orientation of the chapel allowed Shane to calculate the steps were on the northern wall of the cistern. He searched the wall to his right for sharp edges. The surface was abrasive. Almost anything could be considered sharp. "Get down here."

As Amit made his way down the steps, Lauren sat at the top with her legs over the edge and her feet on the first step.

Shane feared finding the edge may be more difficult than they could manage. "I don't see anything. What if it's beneath the surface of the sand?"

Amit moved closer to the wall and kneeled down in the sand. "What's this?"

There protruding about an inch from the wall was a geometric design. It was only about three feet above the sand and about two feet in diameter. The lines of the design were so covered and filled with sand it was almost invisible when looking at it straight on. Shane was amazed Amit had picked it out from the background.

Together they began wiping the sand from the lines. To Shane's surprise, the lines giving the design its shape were the edges of metal bands embedded in the stone wall. The exposed design looked like a bicycle wheel complete with spokes. "It's an ichthus symbol."

Amit concurred. "Yes, I think so."

Lauren called down from the steps. "I can't see it. Is it shaped like a fish?"

Shane stood upright. "No, but you're right. In the second half of the first century, the Christians used the fish as a symbol of their sect. Jesus had made them *fishers of men. Ichthus* is Greek for *fish*. Its letters can be used to form an acrostic."

Lauren interrupted. "Yes, I know. The first letter in ichthus is

Iota the first letter in *Iesous*, Greek for *Jesus*.

The second letter is

Chi the first letter of *Christos*, Greek for *Christ*

The third letter is

Theta the first letter of *Theou*, Greek for *God*

The fourth letter is

Upsilon the first letter of *Uios* (or huios), Greek of *Son*

And the fifth letter is

Sigma the first letter of *soter*, Greek for *Savior*."

The volume of her voice increased. "That is why I asked about the fish shape. The fish symbol replaced the acrostic in the second half of the first century when Christian persecution began under Nero. A member of the Christian sect identified whether another person was truly a member by drawing half of the symbol of the fish."

She drew the shape in the air.

"If the other member knew the secret symbol, he would complete the fish." She finished her shape in the air.

Shane was impressed. "Yes, but what everyone may not know is that before the symbol of the fish, the ichthus symbol was expressed differently."

"How?"

"The Greek letters were written over each other to form a wheel."

Shane walked to the staircase and drew a wheel in the sand of one of the steps.

"Now watch. First *iota.*"

Shane redrew the wheel after each letter.

"Now *chi.*"

"Now *theta.*"

"Now upsilon."

"And finally sigma."

"All of them together result in a wheel." Shane drew the letters one at a time on top of each other.

Amit interrupted. "Well this wheel has a couple of broken spokes."

Shane rejoined Amit by the metal figure. "What do you mean?"

"Look for yourself."

Shane examined the wheel more closely and saw what Amit had discovered. Two of the spokes were out of place. While the other spokes were set, the two misplaced spokes seemed less secure. There appeared to be a narrow track carved into the stone to the inside of each misplaced spoke.

Shane was puzzled. "It shouldn't be like this."

Lauren spoke his thoughts. "So is it an ichthus wheel or not?"

Shane took both hands and pushed the top spoke down. He felt an immense sense of satisfaction when it moved. As the sand buildup behind the spoke gave way, the friction lessened and it moved more easily. When the spoke reached its proper position, it snapped into place.

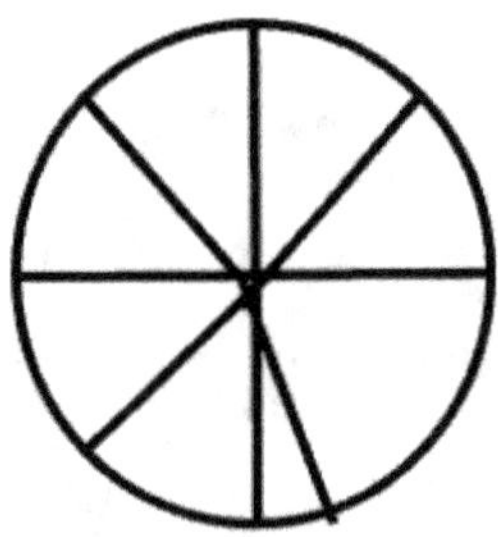

As the spoke locked into position, the staircase under Lauren shuddered. Dust rose in the air, and sand fell through cracks appearing in the wall on both sides of the steps. The cracks continued at right angles on the surface above the steps.

Lauren let out a cry of surprise. "What the hell!"

Amit spoke with excitement. "The third column says to look *beneath a secret door in the cistern in the north-east end.* The second column also says to look *under the stairs.*"

Shane knew he was onto something. He lifted on the last spoke to pull it up into place, but it did not move. "Help me."

Together Shane and Amit pulled on the spoke. It resisted. The two men adjusted their position for greater leverage and pulled upward again. Slowly the metal spoke rose counterclockwise and locked into place.

A loud, dull noise rocked the room. Shane could feel the vibration of a counterweight freeing and falling into a pit. The steps shook again. Lauren hurried down far enough to jump into the sand just as the staircase moved backwards into the wall. Sand near the steps drained into an opening that appeared between the staircase and the side of the wall. Stale air escaped into the chamber. The purpose of the mechanism was obvious. *The treasure's on the other side.*

Shane rushed to the gap in the stone and found it was large enough for him to squeeze through. Without saying anything to the others, he slipped behind the stone steps. He had to jump the last few feet to the bottom of what appeared to be another corridor inclining upward.

"Come on!"

Chapter 73

Shane led Lauren and Amit through the newly discovered corridor. It was about eight feet high and six feet wide with smooth walls, floor, and ceiling. It appeared sculpted from a once natural tunnel. The cream-colored stone floor inclined upward several feet in elevation in a matter of just a few yards. At the top of the incline, the passageway bent back level and remained so until it dead-ended into a wall of stone some forty or fifty feet away.

The corridor was squared off at the floor and ceiling. Seven staggered openings, four on the right and three on the left, looked like doors in the wall. From Shane's vantage point, the passageway looked like a hotel hallway.

When Shane entered the first such doorway, he saw it opened into a large room about twenty feet deep and ten feet wide. Several stone shelves dotted the floor, and niches carved into the stone sat empty in seemingly random places along the walls. The room reminded Shane of a first century Judean tomb.

"This is it," Amit declared. "This is the place the Copper Scroll describes."

Lauren's tone was less certain. "Are you sure? There's nothing here."

"It's in the second column. *You will find the vessels in the underground burial chambers.*"

Shane felt a rush of anticipatory excitement. He walked through the room to be sure it was as empty as it appeared. Then he crossed the hallway to the second room. It was similar in appearance, and just as empty. He went to the next room and the next.

After examining six of the rooms with the same result, Shane had ridden an emotional roller coaster down to total dejection. "Someone must have found the treasure after all. I didn't want to believe it."

He entered the seventh chamber followed by Lauren and Amit. Like the others, it contained nothing but sand and air.

Lauren's spoke with utter disappointment. "This can't be. My sources were so certain."

Shane knew different. "No one knows for sure what happened two thousand years ago. Facts become distorted. Truth becomes legend. Legend becomes myth. It's obvious something was here once, but it's gone now. There's no way of knowing what it was or where it went."

As Shane spoke, he saw faintly glowing spots reflecting Lauren's flashlight beam from the ground near the rear wall of the chamber. He walked over to them and bent over to pick up three small coins partially covered in dust. They were gold.

The fact that gold retained its shine and did not tarnish with time was one of the reasons the ancients valued it so much. They thought the metal to be miraculous, a piece of heaven fallen to earth. Looking at the glimmer of these coins after two thousand years, Shane could understand that conclusion. He handed one to Lauren and one to Amit.

Amit confirmed Shane's view. "Definitely from before the destruction of the Temple. The treasure could have been here."

Shane's heart sank even more. "If it was here, it's not here now. And we're at a dead end." Shane flipped the coin in the air and caught it in his hand. "At least each of us got a souvenir."

Lauren turned and with her flashlight examined the room's floor and walls. Shane followed the path of her light, which ended on the wall in front of them. "Satisfied? No more hidden openings or secret passageways?"

She had not given up. "What's that on the wall?"

Shane examined the wall in front of them above where he had found the coins. Lauren steadied her light on a place where markings appeared to be etched into the stone. The image was blurry in Shane's goggles. He adjusted his monocular for the intensity of the light reflecting off the stone. The image came into focus. "That's just ancient graffiti. People can't resist drawing on surfaces. Pictures. Words. Been that way since caveman days. You find that kind of stuff all over the walls of caves and catacombs."

Shane turned away from the wall. He had been so sure he had unraveled a two thousand year old puzzle. Now, there was nothing to do but go home.

Amit called him back. "You better look again. This graffiti may be a message."

Shane turned back to the wall and saw Amit standing only inches from the rock. He had raised his monocular, and in his left hand he held Lauren's flashlight. He was tracing the pattern with the fingers of his right hand and cleaning it gently as he went.

Lauren was leaning in on his shoulder and watching intently. Shane crowded in behind them and lifted his monocular. Instantly, everything went dark except the circle of light.

Amit looked back at him. "Is this what I think it is?"

The carved pattern was about a foot long and five inches wide. Amit traced it again with his fingers. He was a little over halfway complete when Shane's jaw dropped. *I cannot be seeing what I'm seeing.* "I don't believe it."

Lauren pushed her way in closer to Shane. "What? Tell me."

"I'm not sure what it was called two thousand years ago, but today it's called the Messianic Seal."

Amit completed his trace. "Can it be true?"

Lauren reacted with authority and anger. "Someone better start explaining."

Shane reached up and began tracing the pattern as Amit had done. It was real. "It's a symbol from the second half of the first century. No one knew it existed until about fifty years ago."

Shane drew two pictures separately on the ground

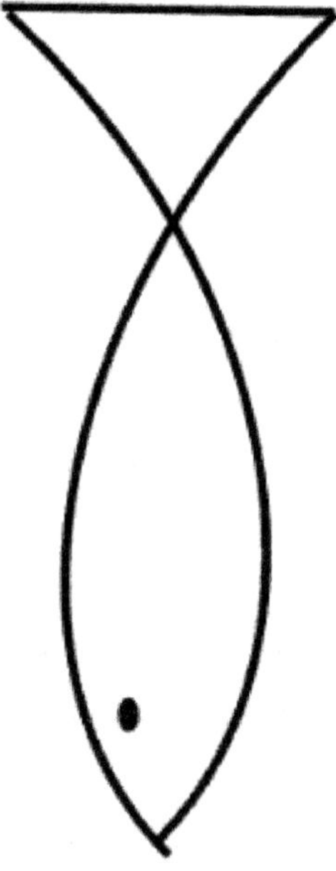

.

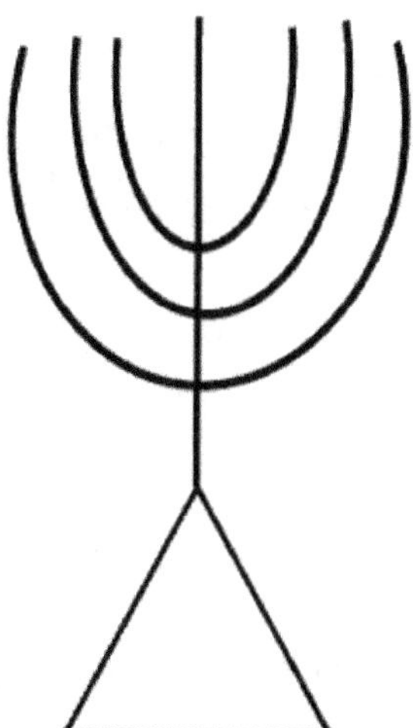

After completing the drawings, Shane continued his explanation. "The ichthus symbol is obviously Christian, and the menorah is obviously Jewish. Now, watch what happens when I put the menorah on top of the ichthus."

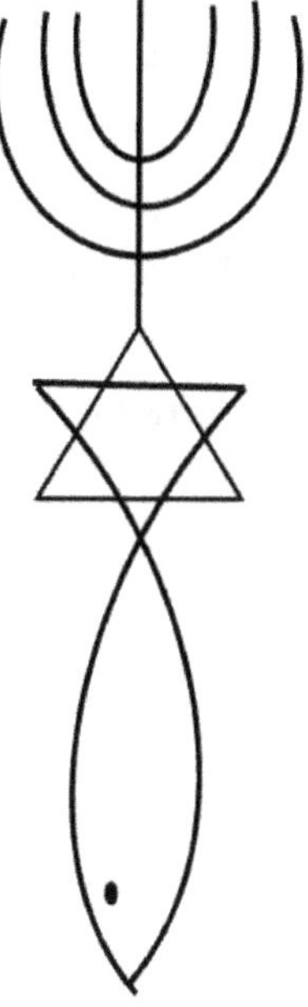

"That's a Star of David!" exclaimed Lauren.

"Yes, it was dubbed the Messianic Seal because it was used by the Jewish Christians who thought Jesus was the Messiah, a descendant of David. It symbolized they were both Jewish and Christian, that they could still be Jews and also believe Jesus was the Messiah."

Lauren seemed to recognize she had only heard half the explanation. "Okay. So why are you two guys so excited?"

Amit traced the drawing again. "Because no one has ever found one of these symbols outside of Jerusalem."

Shane suddenly remembered the first treasure verse from the Sicarii Gospel. *If you want to follow me, sell your possessions and give the money to the poor. You will have treasure in heaven. For where your treasure is, there your heart will be also.* "More specifically, every artifact to bear this symbol came from one specific location. Mount Zion." He looked at Amit. "The treasure wasn't looted. They moved it."

Amit nodded.

Lauren was flustered. "Who moved it?"

Shane could barely contain his excitement. "The Jewish Christians." He quoted the first treasure verse and then added his commentary. "After the war with the Romans, they moved the treasure to where the heart of their movement was. And *we* know where that was."

Shane reached for Amit's hand and gripped it in a firm handshake. They both roared laughter. Shane stopped when Lauren did not join in. "You looked confused."

"I am. *Where* did they move it?"

Amit answered the question before Shane could respond. "We have to get to Jerusalem."

Chapter 74

Though more people were on the site than any night Jabir could remember, all was quiet. He knew his senses were deceiving him. He was standing atop a time bomb. That many armed people in close quarters in the dark required the least spark to set off an explosion of violence. His nerves could not take the waiting, and he did not like the idea of two groups in a gun battle charging up the steps in his direction. *Why am I standing here?*

He decided to make another round of the site. He could put some distance between him and the cave and justify his action by saying he was doing his duty. Besides, doing something normal might reduce his anxiety.

Jabir walked along the stone wall heading toward the entrance to St Gorgeous. After a left turn, he passed the entrance and proceeded toward the far side. He heard a stir inside the ruin. A chill passed through his body leaving goose bumps and standing hair in its wake.

He turned back toward the church entrance and dropped to a knee in the sand. Pushing himself forcefully against the wall, he tried to make himself invisible in the shadow. He was too scared to think straight. *Had the Mukhabarat left someone behind? I do not want to point my weapon at one of them.* Then a more positive thought entered his mind. *It could have been just a rat. It would not be the first time.*

He took his AK-47 off safety and rose to a crouch. He held the assault rifle with both hands in front of him and crept toward the entrance. With a jerking motion, he snapped into the entrance with his AK-47 poised to take on any threat. Everything looked normal atop the mosaic.

As I thought. A rat.

Then he saw him hiding behind one of the shortened columns. "Who is there?" he cried in Arabic. "Come out with your hands on your head!"

An uncomfortable few seconds passed, and Jabir feared he would have to root out the intruder. His anxiety waned when the man stood up, said something in French, and put his empty hands in the air near his head. Jabir kept his AK-47 pointed in the man's direction and marched up to him.

The man was not what Jabir expected. He was middle-aged and dressed in a dark suit and tie. He did not appear armed.

Jabir threatened with his weapon. "What are you doing here? Are you alone?"

Again, the man said something in French. *Enough of this. Al-Kayed will know what to do.*

Suddenly he saw the blur of something swing over his head and down to his throat. He gasped as the wire tightened around his neck and began cutting through his flesh. He could not breathe. He dropped his weapon, which dangled from the strap at his side. He began struggling, but he felt himself lifted off the ground by someone much larger and stronger. He grasped at the wire and kicked with his feet to no avail. The last thing he saw was the suited man smiling.

Chapter 75

Amit pulled himself through the tunnel behind Shane and Lauren. The journey back to the living quarters chamber was much easier. With each body length he progressed, the space in the tunnel increased. Soon he was crawling, then walking hunched over, then weaving upright through the rubble.

As Shane and Lauren emerged from the tunnel, multiple flashlights snapped on in the chamber. Amit groaned and raised his monocular. Seeing silhouettes of Shane and Lauren with their hands behind their heads, he reached behind his back and gripped the Desert Eagle semi-automatic pistol in his belt. He did not pull it free. Unknown arms pulled Shane and Lauren to the side. In their place stood a Jordanian with an assault rifle. Amit knew the Mukhabarat both in appearance and reputation. He released his grip.

The Jordanian in front of him mumbled something in Arabic and reached in to grab him. He pulled Amit roughly over the threshold and threw him to the stone floor. Amit landed on his shoulder and slid on his side before rolling to his back. He looked up at Shane, who shook his head slowly as a warning not to do anything rash.

A very well dressed Jordanian stepped into the light and spoke in English. "Doctor David. I hope that was not a weapon you were reaching for. It would be a shame for such an educated man to go out like a common cowboy."

The Jordanian nodded at one of the Mukhabarat. The security agent grabbed Amit by his collar and yanked him to his feet. The agent stood behind him and frisked him roughly. He pulled the Desert Eagle from Amit's belt. He also collected the night vision goggles and the wire cutters. When he was done, he pushed Amit against the wall.

The agent moved to Shane next. He lifted Shane's arms and searched him top down, retrieving his Beretta and goggles. Then he pushed Shane back next to Amit. A quick frisk of Lauren resulted in a grimace as the agent took too many liberties. Though Lauren quickly recovered, Amit could tell Shane was not taking the Jordanian's mistreatment of Lauren well.

Another man stepped forward, also dressed in a suit and tie. He was not Jordanian. He looked European. He walked up to Lauren and slapped her across the face, causing her to twist around and let out a muffled cry. Shane lunged forward, but two of the Mukhabarat restrained him, ultimately pressing their AK-47's under his chin.

Lauren held up her hand to stop Shane. "I'm all right." She held her other hand to the side of her reddening face.

The Jordanian stepped in front of the European. "Control yourself, Director Neuville," The tone was casual but carried the weight of a command. "There is no reason to be rude."

The man called Neuville backed away.

The Jordanian signaled the Mukhabarat to release Shane. "Doctor Randall. It is very nice to meet you."

Amit could not help but wonder how he knew their names. The Jordanian reached out his hand in greeting. Shane shook his hand but responded tersely. "You better control your man."

The Jordanian remained nonchalant. "With all due respect, you are in no position to make demands. And quite frankly, Doctor Randall, based on your reputation, I expected you to have more control of your emotions." When Shane did not reply, the Jordanian continued. "I am Mikhail Al-Kayed of the Jordanian Department of Antiquities. The rude gentleman behind me is Director Edmond Neuville of the Vraie École Biblique."

Amit and Shane exchanged glances when they heard the organization's name. This man had sent his henchmen to New Haven. They had murdered Jane. Amit slowly edged in front of Shane to block his path.

Al-Kayed's tone became harsher. "You and your partners have been caught in the act of raiding a Jordanian archaeological site. I am afraid the punishment for such a crime is severe. Of course, if you decide to be civilized and tell me what you discovered, you may find me to be a very understanding man."

Shane stepped clear of Amit. "I'm not sure what you mean."

"Insulting my intelligence is not a good way to start our relationship." Al-Kayed looked at Amit. "I do not suppose you want to be reasonable?"

Amit shook his head. "Send your own men through the tunnel. You'll see there's nothing there."

Neuville charged forward. "You lie! You either found the treasure or know where it is."

Al-Kayed turned back to Shane. "Is this true?"

Shane stared directly into Al-Kayed's eyes. "I don't know what he's told you, but there's nothing here." Shane's lips pursed in a visible message he would not say more.

Al-Kayed looked Shane up and down as if assessing what kind of man he was. "Very well. I see no reason to search the cave. But Director Neuville is quite right. You do have information. You know, or think you know, where the treasure is. Perhaps we should continue this discussion in a more appropriate venue."

He signaled the Mukhabarat to close in on their captives and herd them toward the cave entrance. Amit did not think he would like where they were going.

Chapter 76

Al-Jamal watched with intense interest the scene unfolding at St. Gorgeous. From their hidden perch on the second floor of a house about thirty meters away, he and his men had the perfect vantage point. It had been a busy night.

Al-Jamal did a mental count–the archaeologist and his two companions, the four heavily armed Jordanians led by an elite Jordanian and a European, and three heavily armed mercenaries led by two Europeans, one of whom had professionally strangled the guard for the enjoyment of the other. Fourteen people in all, and at least eight of them very dangerous. Lesser leaders may have thought the smart tactic to be retreat. There were too many of them for Al-Jamal and his three men to take. But Al-Jamal was not a small-minded leader.

His instincts told him that the fourteen people were actually three opposing factions. The numbers would level out. And with that many factions after the same objective, the prize had to be great.

Al-Jamal felt completely certain that no matter the odds, Allah would protect him. Allah was always working miracles in his favor. One such example had occurred earlier in the evening. Al-Jamal had known there were only a few routes out of Irbid for the archaeologist and his two companions to take. He had selected one and, *Allah be praised*, he had been right.

Al-Jamal also knew Allah rewarded men who took initiative. Al-Jamal had done so by bringing with him an equalizer. It was a shoulder-launched missile weapon, more commonly called a rocket propelled grenade launcher or RPG. The RPG-28 fired a twelve kilogram grenade projectile across an effective range of two hundred meters with enough power to penetrate one meter of armor or three meters of brick.

Milak was getting impatient. "Ya Sidi, what should we do?"

"Get the RPG ready, but do not fire until I give the order. We must wait for Allah to reveal the time."

As if on cue, the mercenaries standing on the St. Gorgeous mosaic shifted into action. They ran along the ruin and began taking up positions along its side wall. Al-Jamal knew Allah was talking to him. He was listening.

Chapter 77

Shane asked a question for which he did not expect an answer. "Where are you taking us?"

This instance was not the first time he had found himself in a life-threatening situation. He knew how critical to survival it was to identify who was in control and then grasp any reason to delay his captor's plans until an escape opportunity revealed itself. Al-Kayed was obviously in charge, and he would be the one who decided whether to torture them, kill them, or let them go.

Shane pressed on any advantage he could find. "Two of us are U.S. citizens. Do you really want to find yourself in an international incident?"

He had also assessed the Mukhabarat agents and concluded they had orders not to kill them until Al-Kayed commanded otherwise. There was no immediate danger as long as they had information Al-Kayed needed.

Al-Kayed moved inches away from Shane's face. "It is you and your friends who have caused the international incident. Who is to say we found you alive. Perhaps you died in a cave-in during your trespass onto our site. Perhaps we never found your bodies."

Shane thought back to the first time he faced death at the hands of another man. It was in Belize while digging for a pre-Columbian Mayan jade sculpture of Hunab Ku, the creator god. A local village leader took exception to what he perceived to be grave robbing and went after Shane with a machete. The one advantage of having the attack occur in Belize was the threats and curses came in the official language of English rather than the Spanish used in other countries of the region. Shane ducked a sweep of the machete, barely avoiding decapitation. In the same motion, he picked up a fallen limb from a ziricote ironwood tree and used it to knock his attacker unconscious.

Following that attack, Shane took shooting lessons and began carrying a handgun on his journeys. The Beretta was his favorite make. He rationalized whatever was good enough for the U.S. military was good enough for him. He also took a keen interest in martial arts, participating in a tae kwon do class at the university. And while on a trip to the Amazon, he had learned a little capoeira, the dance-like fighting style developed by Brazilian slaves. The name literally meant *chicken coop* because the owners thought the slaves looked like chickens fighting as they practiced.

Like the Brazilian slaves, Shane was often underestimated. "Surely there's some arrangement we can come to. You're an educated man."

The second attempt on Shane's life had come in Nigeria, where he found himself between two warring tribes. The Ibo and the Yoruba continually fought over oil lands and the money they generated. The Yoruba captured him during his search for a legendary ivory altar to Chuku, the great god of creation. They threatened to remove his limbs but reconsidered and kept him alive for ransom. Shane escaped in the middle of the night after rubbing the ropes that bound his wrists in the slop he had been given to eat and then letting a goat chew through the bindings.

Neuville spoke lowly into Al-Kayed's ear. "Do not trust him. Force him to tell us the location."

Giving them the location's a sure way to sign our death warrants. We won't be seen again until Jordanians archaeologists discover our remains.

The last attempt on Shane's life had occurred two years ago in the Philippines. He had discovered some two thousand year old earthenware anthromorphic secondary burial jars. They were formed in the shape of human figures with complete facial features. Unfortunately, he had come to the attention of communist Guerillas. Shane ran for his life through the dense jungle and ultimately eluded his would-be captors by burying himself in mud and leaves and remaining that way through most of the night. He would never forget the absolute terror that spiders might be crawling across his body.

Al-Kayed stepped back. "I am afraid my friend does not want to negotiate. Bind them."

One of the Mukhabarat lowered his weapon and pulled three nylon locking straps from his pocket. They were cheaper than handcuffs, stronger than rope, and quick. In a matter of seconds the agent pulled the straps tight around the three sets of wrists. At least he allowed them to keep their arms in front instead of pulling them more uncomfortably behind.

One thing Shane knew with certainty was they had to escape. The Jordanians were well-known to employ very persuasive means to get information from their captives—drugs, torture, threats on family and friends. One of them would eventually talk.

Al-Kayed's mouth morphed into a devilish grin. "I hope you enjoyed your visit to Rihab. What happens from this point forward is not written about in most tourist guidebooks."

Chapter 78

Amit thrust an elbow at the Mukhabarat agent behind him. "Take it easy." A barrel to his back had just sent a shock down his right leg. The agent replied an obscenity in Arabic and poked him again.

When they reached the wooden doors of the cave entrance, Al-Kayed seemed to grow cautious. He stopped, stepped to the side, and spoke to the two closest agents. "Make sure it is clear."

The two men raised their weapons and proceeded warily up the steps. When they reached the top, they disappeared. After several seconds of silence, Al-Kayed backed away from the entrance. In doing so, he no longer had line of sight up the steps. "Report!"

There was no reply.

Neuville walked around to where Al-Kayed stood. "What is happening?"

"Something is not right." He stared at Shane, Amit, and Lauren as if they had set him up. Amit knew otherwise.

Neuville picked up on his suspicions. "I told you not to trust them. What do we do?"

Al-Kayed remained silent for several seconds before calling out once more. "Hassan Jabir!"

Again there was no response.

Neuville looked like he had been punched in the stomach. "I do not like this."

"Neither do I." Al-Kayed turned to one of the remaining Mukhabarat agents. "Hand me a weapon."

The agent quickly pulled out a Heckler and Koch USP9 semi-automatic pistol and handed it to Al-Kayed.

The Jordanian leader chambered a bullet and pointed to Amit and the other captives. "Take them up first. We will follow."

The Mukhabarat agents prodded their captives toward the doorway. Amit had no intention of making it easy to use him as a human shield. He leaned back in resistance. The pace was so slow one of the agents took the butt of his AK-47 and brought it down hard against the back of Amit's head. Shane stepped between Amit and the agent and took the weapon to his ribs.

Amit staggered forward and stumbled up the steps. When he reached the top, the pain overcame him. He hunched over, supporting himself with his hands on the steps. He could feel blood running down his neck from a cut opened in his scalp. Crawling onto the stony ground, he heard Lauren gasp behind him. Adrenaline pumped into his veins, carrying with it the effect of lessening his pain and clearing his vision.

A horrific sight greeted him. Lying one to each side were the two Mukhabarat agents. Their throats were slashed, with blood still pumping from the wounds.

Chapter 79

Standing between Amit to his right and Lauren to his left, Shane saw the bodies of the two Mukhabarat agents and reacted instinctively. In one motion he grabbed Amit with his bound hands and pulled, while pushing Lauren with his shoulder. His target was the space between the steps and the wall of St. Gorgeous. As soon as they hit the ground the first shots rang out.

Bullets ricocheted off the steps and nearby ruin. Dust clouded the air. Splinters of stone rained down on their backs. They needed more distance between them and the stairs.

Shane shouted as he crawled away. "Come on!" He felt Lauren follow but Amit hesitate. "What are you doing?"

Shane saw what his friend was after. The slain agent nearest them had conducted the frisks. He still held in various places the weapons and goggles he had taken. Risking the gunfire, Amit grabbed the items with his bound hands. Then he lunged back alongside Shane and Lauren.

Shane shouted at his friend over the gunfire. "You're crazy!"

Amit smiled in response.

They scrambled on their bellies and pressed against the nearby wall of stone. Shane flinched and winced as bullets ricocheted all around them.

The two remaining Mukhabarat agents crouched at the top of the steps and returned fire. It appeared from the muzzle flashes that four men were firing on the Jordanians from protected positions within the compound. The Mukhabarat agents took out one of the men firing on them, but they were not in a strong position. One of them soon collapsed, falling forward on the stone. Multiple bullets propelled the other agent backward through Al-Kayed and Neuville midway down the steps. Al-Kayed and Neuville retreated to the darkness of the cave.

With no one remaining on the steps, the shooting stopped, and Shane had time to check on his friends. "Is anyone hit?"

They both shook their heads.

Lauren rose to a sitting position. "What's going on? Who's out there?"

"I don't know. But I think we're about to find out."

With their resistance eliminated, the three remaining men who had fired on the agents left the protection of their cover and began walking in Shane's direction. Two of them looked like Jordanian military. One looked like a European body builder. They did not threaten Shane and his friends. Instead, they hugged the wall of St. Gorgeous, with weapons pointed at the cave.

When they arrived, the bodybuilder issued commands in French-accented English. "Get up! All of you! Come with us!"

Shane, Lauren, and Amit rose to their feet. The Frenchman took the pistols from Amit but let him keep the night vision goggles. He gestured instructions to stay close to the wall for their safety and led them back toward the main church entrance. One of the Jordanians remained near the steps to ensure no one emerged, and the other Jordanian fell in behind them.

None of this made sense to Shane. "Who are you?"

No one answered him. Another man emerged from the far end of St. Gorgeous. He was dressed in a suit and tie and did not look the type to be involved in a gun fight.

Amit gasped. "I know him."

The man walked up to the larger Frenchman. "Bon travail, Gustave. Good work." Then to Amit, he said, "Hello, Docteur David. I told you I was going to pay you a visit." Turning to Shane and Lauren, he said, "You must be Docteur Randall. And of course, Mademoiselle Mallory. Enchanté. Very glad to finally meet you both."

Shane looked at Lauren, but she shrugged her shoulders. "How do you know our names?"

Amit spoke in a low monotone. "He has his ways."

"Oui," the man agreed. "My name is Gilbert de Clisson. As Docteur David is aware, I know everything there is to know about the people I am interested in."

Amit continued. "He financed my last dig. His passion is the Copper Scroll."

Clisson corrected him. "More precisely, the *treasure* of the Copper Scroll."

Lauren raised her still bound hands. "How about cutting us free?"

"Of course. Gustave, would you?"

Gustave pulled a large knife out of a sheath strapped to his ankle. In seconds, he had sliced through the nylon straps.

Shane rubbed his hands to speed up the return of circulation. "Thanks."

Clisson moved closer to Shane and spoke to him as if he had known him for years. "Since that is the second favor I have done for *you*, perhaps you will do one for *me*?"

"Such as?"

"Tell me, is the treasure in the lower church, or must we go elsewhere?"

Chapter 80

Clisson stood waiting for the answer to his question with extreme satisfaction. He had the cowardly double-crosser Neuville and his Jordanian accomplice pinned in the lower church like the vermin they were. He had eliminated the Mukhabarat agents at the cost of a single mercenary's life. And he had done it all in a way that made him appear the rescuer of the people who had the information he most needed. The most important challenge in front of him now was to build trust. He smiled and gave them time.

Randall shrugged his shoulders. "It's not here. It may have been here at one time, but if it was, it was either stolen or moved."

Now we're getting somewhere. Their demeanors and the tones in Randall's words told him more than intended. *The treasure is not here. But it was not stolen. They know where it is.* He tried to speak with innocent curiosity. "Was there a marker suggesting a new location?"

David nodded. "Yes. But there's no way of knowing whether the treasure's there."

Clisson did not miss the exchange of looks between David and Randall. It was clear they would not share much quickly. "And what about you, Mademoiselle Mallory? Are you confident in the location?"

"Yes."

Lauren Mallory. Even covered in the filth of the cave and marred by a deepening bruise on her cheekbone, she is absolutely stunning.

Without warning the limousine parked in the street exploded and burst into flame. Rapid fire scraped the grounds. Randall, Lauren, and David hit the ground again and pressed themselves against the wall. Clisson followed their lead. If he had not, he would have been hit by multiple rounds instead of the mercenary standing nearby. "Gustave!"

Gustave kneeled in front of Clisson to shield him. "Where are they?"

No one knew. Then as they watched, another missile launched from a house some thirty meters away. The Humvee exploded.

Randall pointed. "The house! They're in the house."

Who is in the house? Clisson thought through the possibilities. *Did Gustave and his men miss some Mukhabarat agents? Had the Jordanian summoned nearby reinforcements from the cave?* He was accustomed to being in control. The emotions he felt now were uncomfortable.

Gustave signaled the remaining mercenary. He handed Randall and David their weapons. "Stay here."

Gustave and the mercenary leaped to their stomachs and crept forward, taking advantage of whatever cover they could find. They returned fire in the direction of the house. Clisson saw the bullets piercing the wood, but he knew it would be total luck to hit anyone hiding there. The same luck was all that was keeping him alive as mini-explosions of sand and stone erupted around them.

Another missile flew from the second story window, and the Yukon SUV which had carried Clisson and his men flew off the ground in a burst of flame.

This is crazy!

Randall shouted over the gunfire. "Amit, let's make a break for the back fence."

It sounded like a good idea. "Gustave! We must go!"

Gustave and the mercenary turned toward Clisson's call, first crawling and then running. Clisson watched the mercenary scream and fall to the sand. Fortunately, Gustave was unharmed.

Just before they rounded the end of St. Gorgeous, Clisson heard a hissing sound and knew another missile was on its way. Before it reached them, it veered off course and tore into the wall of the church. Stone erupted from the wall leaving a large crater with a hole in its center.

The force of the blast knocked Clisson off his feet. He felt a burning sensation in his lower right calf muscle. Screaming, he reached for it and felt the sticky wetness of his blood. Randall turned to help him, and Gustave lifted him from behind. They each grabbed one of his arms and supported his weight on their shoulders. After a few paces, they rounded the church.

David and Lauren were working on the fence when they arrived. While they waited, Gustave examined Clisson's injury. Clisson looked at the horrific gash only briefly before turning away. He feared he could be crippled for life.

Gustave deftly attended the wound. "Ce n'est pas aussi mauvais qu'il regarde. It is not as bad as it looks. I will wrap it tightly. The pressure should stop the bleeding, but you will need to get stitches as soon as we can get you to a medical facility."

Gustave used his knife to cut some material from Clisson's pant leg. Clisson winced as the cloth pressed against the wound. To take his mind off the pain he reached out to Randall. "Where is your car?"

"It's a hike up the road. Why?"

Clisson winced again as Gustave tied off the makeshift bandage. "Mine just blew up. I hope yours will hold five."

Chapter 81

Al-Jamal put his hand on Hamdi's shoulder opposite the RPG-28. "Let them go."

Hamdi protested. "Ya Sidi, why?"

"They serve Allah and us alive." Al-Jamal addressed all three of his men in a victorious tone. "Get down there before the two rats emerge from their hole."

Milak and Ahmad picked up their assault rifles and flashlights, and Hamdi gently placed the grenade launcher on the floor. They rushed downstairs and out the front door. Al-Jamal pulled his Glock and followed.

The groups at the ruin were careless. They should have checked the surrounding area. That is what I would have done.

Confidently, he strode the thirty meters to the St. Gorgeous compound. He had to act before others arrived. Even in a village like Rihab, there was authority. The gunshots and explosions would have been reported. Still, it would take time to get the local authority out of bed. And there would be hesitation to engage an unknown force with the kind of firepower being reported.

By the time Al-Jamal arrived at the steps to the lower church, his men were in position to storm the door. Al-Jamal did not like risking their lives for the likes of the men in the cave, but he did not have time to wait either. He had to know whether the prize the archaeologist was after was here or elsewhere.

"We live under Allah's protection. We will capture them without firing a shot."

Chapter 82

Shane saw the Land Cruiser and slowed to a walk. Amit and Lauren followed his lead and took a moment to recover their breath. Trailing with Gustave's support, Clisson looked like he was about to have a heart attack. His face was red and his breathing labored.

Shane took advantage of the moment. "Monsieur Clisson, who exactly are you?"

Clisson wheezed with his inhales and gasped with his exhales. He raised his hand as a request for more time before speaking.

Amit answered for him. "Monsieur Clisson owns the largest private collection of archaeological artifacts from Israel in the world."

Clisson seemed uncomfortable with Amit as his advocate. He forced out words. "And like many wealthy Parisians, I became bored with what I possessed and began obsessing about what I could not have–the treasure of the Copper Scroll."

That does not explain his presence. "How'd you know we were here?"

Clisson had recovered enough to walk on his own. "In addition to funding Docteur David, I partnered with Directeur Neuville on a number of initiatives."

Shane had sensed there was something wrong about Clisson. "You were in league with the Vraie École Biblique?"

Clisson reacted to the emotion in Shane's voice. "Calm down, Docteur Randall. Fanatics have their uses. But you don't have to be a fanatic to use them."

"And how did *they* know where we were?"

Clisson shrugged. "Perhaps they know more about the Sicarii Gospel and the Copper Scroll than anyone thought possible."

How does Clisson know about the Sicarii Gospel? Shane signaled Lauren and Amit with his eyes to say nothing. He in no way trusted the Frenchman.

Clisson must have been reading him. "Docteur Randall," he said calmly. "I may be arrogant, and I am no saint. But I have never given Docteur David cause to doubt me. And don't forget, I just saved you from probable torture and death."

Amit's expression told Shane all he needed to know. His friend had worked with Clisson, but he did not like him. It was one thing to let a wealthy aristocrat fund your expedition. It was something totally different to trust him with your life.

They reached the Land Cruiser, and Amit stepped into the driver's seat. Shane had a decision to make. *Should Clisson go with us, or should I strand him here?* With Clisson's bodyguard in the mix, the wrong decision could get messy quickly. His internal debate did not go unnoticed.

"Docteur Randall," Clisson began. "I have money. I can bribe our way into places you could not get to on your own. You and Docteur David have brains. You can interpret the codes we may encounter. Gustave has brawn. He can protect us. Lauren Mallory has...well, let's just say she is resourceful. The treasure is big enough for all of us."

Shane looked at Lauren. She nodded and said, "Come on, Shane. We need to get out of here." She opened the door behind Amit and pulled herself into the seat.

Shane nodded to Clisson. "All right, get in. We're going to Jerusalem."

Shane hurried around the car with Clisson and Gustave. Shane sat in the front seat, and Clisson and Gustave sat behind him with Clisson by the window.

Clisson pressed Shane for information. "Where in Jerusalem?"

"We'll explain on the way."

Amit started the car and accelerated quickly down the road. "We can't risk fording the river at the same location."

Clisson leaned forward such that his head was between Amit and Shane. "Am I to understand you forded the Jordan River on the way here?"

Shane was already tired of the arrogant Frenchmen. "Yes, it was exhilarating."

Clisson was aghast. "My heart is still recovering from our escape. I am afraid it could not take that much excitement."

"Do you have a better idea?"

"Let me demonstrate my value. I have a man who for the right price can get us across the King Hussein Bridge before it opens. No one will know."

Amit looked relieved. "That would save us a lot of time. We could make it to Jerusalem well before sunrise."

Shane still did not trust Clisson, but if he was going to turn on them, he would not do so until they reached their destination. "All right. King Hussein Bridge it is."

Chapter 83

Neuville stood next to Al-Kayed in the lower church. He had no way of knowing what had happened above them since he and Al-Kayed had retreated down the steps. What he had heard had not sounded good. *I will not die in this cave. God has a greater plan for my life.*

Al-Kayed still held the USP9, but Neuville knew the weapon was not enough. Their only option was to surrender and hope they were returned to the Jordanian government. If Al-Kayed decided to go out in a last act of heroism, it was highly likely Neuville would also pay the price.

Sounds of men coming down the steps stopped short of the doorway.

"Drop your weapons!" one of the men outside cried in Arabic. "If you fire on us, you will die very painfully."

Neuville had no doubt the man meant what he said. Neuville looked at Al-Kayed still standing erect with the weapon in his hand. He could not make Al-Kayed do anything, but he prayed Al-Kayed would be reasonable.

"Last warning!" cried the voice outside. "Throw out your weapons!"

Al-Kayed did not look at Neuville or ask his opinion. He just sighed heavily. Swinging his arm backward and then forward, he threw the USP9 outside the wooden doors. Neuville thanked God for hearing his prayers.

Three men descended the remaining steps and flooded into the room. They appeared to be Palestinian. While two of the men pointed their flashlights and assault rifles in the direction of the two captives, the third frisked them to ensure they did not conceal other weapons.

When satisfied, the man conducting the frisk shouted up the steps. "Clear, Ya Sidi!"

A fourth Palestinian entered the chamber. He had a pistol in his hand. Shadows veiled his face as he walked in a straight line to Al-Kayed.

Al-Kayed erupted. "What is the meaning of this? I report to the ..."

The leader of the Palestinians raised his weapon and fired one shot into the forehead of Al-Kayed. The Department of Antiquities official's knees bent, and he fell straight backward on his lower legs to the ground. The Palestinian then lifted his pistol to Neuville's face. Neuville closed his eyes and waited for his life to end. He prayed God would transport him quickly to heaven.

The handgun did not fire. Neuville cautiously opened his eyes. The end of the barrel was still there, but instead of pulling the trigger, the man spoke. "Jordanians take a dim view of killing other Jordanians. *You* are not Jordanian."

As if an angel was sitting on Neuville's shoulder and translating the words, Neuville understood the Arabic and formed a response. "No. I am French."

"Tell me, Frenchman. Why should I not kill you too?"

"Treasure!" Neuville swallowed hard. "With a value beyond belief."

"He lies," one of the other Palestinians said. "Let's kill him and get out of here."

The leader shook his head. "The others were looking for this treasure?"

"Yes."

"They did not find it?"

"No."

"Then what value are you?"

"They discovered the location of the treasure. I know the treasure and the people. I can help."

The Palestinian leader lowered his weapon. "What led them here?"

"They are following a map. It led them here. Now it leads them somewhere else."

"Where?"

"I do not know. We were about to find out when you attacked us."

"We did not attack you. Another group led by a European aristocrat killed the Mukhabarat and freed their prisoners. We attacked *them*."

The leader's words surprised Neuville. *Clisson!* "I know the man. He is a Parisian. Do you have him and the others?"

"No. He and your prisoners escaped."

Neuville thanked God Randall and David had escaped. He prayed for God to strike down Clisson before he reached the treasure.

Another of the Palestinians spoke. "I agree we should kill him. We do not need him."

Neuville swallowed hard again. He was sweating through his clothes, turning the dust into thin rivulets of mud. *Surely it is not God's plan for me to die here. God would not reward a man like Clisson at my expense.* Neuville's faith once again restored his courage. "If you get me close to them, I will get the destination."

The leader spoke with confidence. "We can get you close. We placed a tracking device on their car. And we made sure it was the only car running."

Neuville was impressed. He had thought the Palestinians to be brutes, but the leader, at least, was an educated and rational man. "Then take me with you. I will find the treasure."

The leader's eyes bored into him. Neuville could see his internal debate. He prayed God would soften the man's heart.

"Bind his hands," the Palestinian leader ordered. "Bring him with us."

Chapter 84

A couple of hours remained before dawn when Shane and the others in the car entered Jerusalem. No matter how many times Shane had been there, each time was as magical as the first. He could easily understand why it was the heart of so many cultures and religions and had been for thousands of years. Looking out the window at the Jerusalem skyline under the night sky, Shane could not help but recall the prophecies on the mind of every first century Jew.

The *Star Prophecy* was a favorite of Jewish zealots and early Christians. It was a Messianic prophecy from the book of Numbers, one of the five books of Moses known as the *Torah*. The prophecy referred to a *Star* to emerge from Jacob, the patriarch of the Jews. The Star would become the King of the Jews and destroy their enemies. The Torah, or *Pentateuch* to first century Greek speakers, held a special significance and made the Star Prophecy extremely important. It was so connected to the Jewish Messiah that every Messiah-want-to-be in the first and second centuries had some association with a star.

The Star prophecy was referenced often in first century religious writing. The Qumran Dead Sea Scroll known as the War Scroll described an apocalyptic war between good and evil. The Star in the form of the Messiah redeemed the Poor and defeated their mighty enemies. In the Gospel of Matthew, the Star of Bethlehem marked the arrival of Jesus–Messiah and King of the Jews. Since the Messiah was supposed to be a descendent of David, even the Star of David had messianic connotations.

Shane looked out the window at the stars and found the brightest star. He turned his head and found Lauren and Gustave awake and Clisson asleep. "Jupiter. The Star of Bethlehem."

Lauren's brows lowered into her scrunched face. "You believe there really was a Star of Bethlehem?"

Shane nodded. "There are many explanations, but the one I like involves Jupiter, Venus, and the star Regulus. Jupiter was the *king* of planets. Venus was associated with various mother goddesses. And Regulus was the star of *kings*. It begins in August of 3 B.C.E. with a conjunction of Jupiter and Venus in the constellation Cancer, the last sign of the zodiac, continues with three conjunctions of Jupiter with Regulus, and ends in June of 2 B.C.E. with another conjunction of Jupiter and Venus in the constellation Leo. Leo was the constellation associated with *royalty*. This last conjunction would have produced the brightest star in three thousand years. It would have definitely attracted the attention of astrologists all over the world, such as the Magi in Babylon. Their founder Zoroaster in 1000 B.C.E. had predicted a king would arise who would raise the dead and usher in a kingdom of peace. The king would be a descendent of Abraham."

"An unbelievable coincidence."

"Or heavenly miracle, if you believe in that sort of thing. And the Romans, who did believe in that sort of thing, had a totally different interpretation of the heavenly events. They saw them as an affirmation of their Empire and their emperor Caesar Augustus, the son of the god Julius Caesar. The year spanning 3 B.C.E. and 2 B.C.E. marked the seven hundred fiftieth year since the founding of Rome. It coincided with the twentieth fifth year of the reign of Caesar Augustus. That's probably what the census of Luke was about. It was a census of allegiance to Caesar Augustus from the Roman Empire's people. Descendants of King David had to swear an oath of loyalty."

Lauren seemed to accept Shane's explanation. "It's amazing how the same events can be used by different groups to support totally different conclusions."

Shane understood very well. "And there were probably many more interpretations. As many as there were different peoples on the planet."

Shane looked out the window again at the narrow streets and thought of other prophecies. "Zechariah prophesized the Messiah would ride into Jerusalem on a donkey's colt, and many Jewish religious scholars calculated the timing of the Messiah's arrival as the first century from Daniel Seventy Weeks prophecy. Jesus knew exactly what message he was sending when he entered Jerusalem on a donkey's colt during the Feast of the Tabernacles."

"So you're saying the Jewish revolutionaries were like a bomb and the prophecies were like a fuse."

"And all it took to light the fuse was someone credible claiming to be the Messiah."

Amit interrupted. "There's our hotel."

Shane looked at the giant building ahead of them. He had never stayed at the historic King David Hotel. He had never been able to afford it. *At least there's some benefit in having Clisson along.*

Chapter 85

Reese's head swung down to his chest, and the weight sent a sharp pain down the back of his neck. He awoke with a start. He checked the time to see how much longer remained before landing and grimaced in both physical and mental anguish after seeing they still had an hour in the air.

This flight will never end.

Reese sat squeezed between passengers in the middle coach seat of the middle section of a full flight. His legs cramped, and his seat felt like concrete. He was not experienced at working the adjustable headrest, and he never slept long before his head slid to one side or the other. His butt cheeks had been asleep more than he had.

The lack of comfort did not seem to affect the men to each side of him. The man to his left snored like a lion roaring, and the obese man to his right thought it totally acceptable to sleep with his weight on Reese's arm and his head on Reese's shoulder. To complete the triangle, the man in front of Reese had leaned his seat as far back as it would go, giving Reese a direct view of his bald spot.

The cherry on the top of Reese's pain was his bladder crying out for relief. Reese thought he had better deal with his bladder now before the pilot ordered everyone to stay in their seats. Ignoring the pilot and going anyway would attract the attention of the flight attendants, who ruled the cabin like strict third grade teachers.

Reese looked to his right and easily saw there was no way through the massive passenger. His only escape route was crawling over the snoring man to his left. He had so little space that he pulled himself up using the top of the seat in front of him. The pressure of his weight on the seat brought an angry reaction.

"Sorry," Reese said with a mixture of sincerity and frustration.

He lifted his leg and stepped over the still sleeping man to his left. He almost made it cleanly but made just too much contact with his inner thigh on the sleeping man's legs. The man awoke with a snort and Reese's buttocks in his face.

"Sorry," Reese said again.

Swinging his other leg over the man now glaring at him, Reese freed himself to the aisle. He stood for a moment to let the blood return to his legs. Then he proceeded up the aisle toward the restroom between the coach and business class sections. He pulled open the folding door to the rest room but stopped before entering.

There, coming toward him down the business class aisle was one of the two men he was after. The smaller, older man mostly looked down as he walked. Instinctively, Reese leaned in and hid as much of his face as he could behind the restroom door. Though he thought neither of the men had seen him well, he saw no reason to risk recognition. He repositioned himself to subtly look farther down the aisle. As he expected, when he found an empty seat, he also found the hulk sitting next to it.

Reese entered the restroom. While he purged his bladder, his mind raced. *How can this be?* The answer came to him. *Of course. They left from another city, but their plane connected through Newark. We began apart but came together.*

Reese looked in the mirror and gave himself a fist pump. Hours earlier he had thought the late departure had doomed his gamble on a trip to Israel. In fact, his roll of the dice had come up a winner more quickly than he ever imagined.

I can't arrest them. I have no jurisdiction. Is there an air marshal on board?

Even if there was, Reese knew he could not take a chance the two men had smuggled a weapon on board. He debated whether to call ahead and have Israeli authorities meet him and take them into custody. *That would be the smart thing to do.*

No, he was not following them in an official capacity. This was personal. His gut told him more was going on than two men on a killing spree. Someone was pulling their strings. He decided to follow them to their handler.

Reese flushed the toilet, washed his hands, and opened the door. The man was there waiting. While seemingly upset by the wait, the man did not look Reese in the face. Reese turned away as much as possible as he exited. The man huffed and pushed by him into the restroom.

When Reese heard the door shut behind him, he did not return to his seat. Instead, he spun around and entered business class. He signaled to the flight attendant.

She walked in his direction with a frown on her face. "Really sir. You must return to your seat in coach."

Reese pulled out his badge and showed it to the flight attendant. Her attitude changed immediately. Reese pushed his advantage, speaking to her in a low but firm tone. "I'm Detective Reese of the Cambridge Police Department. I'm tracking two men in relation to multiple homicides. The two men are sitting in business class." Reese gestured in the direction he wanted her to look. "One of them's in the restroom. The other's the big man over there."

The flight attendant's face morphed through shock and then fear. "You mean the two Frenchmen?"

Frenchmen. Reese had no idea. *Why did two Frenchmen go on a killing spree in the United States? And why are they flying to Israel? The religious school that had rented their car!* "Yes. It's too dangerous for me to arrest them on the plane, but it's imperative I not lose them when the plane lands."

"I'll inform the captain to call ahead."

"No, it's important they not be arrested until they lead me to their boss. Do you understand what I'm saying?"

"But sir, we need to alert Israeli authorities."

"Please, I just need to be able to follow them off the plane without losing them. A friend of mine's in danger."

The flight attendant thought for a moment. "We have one empty seat in the back row of business".

Reese found the seat.

"You could sit there," she continued. "And leave when they do."

"Perfect. You don't know how much I appreciate this. You may have just saved my friend's life."

The beam on the flight attendant's face contorted when she heard the restroom door opening. Reese looked her in the eyes and gestured subtly with this hand for her to do nothing.

Reese and the flight attendant turned inward as the man squeezed past them down the aisle. When they faced each other again, the flight attendant did not look comfortable.

Reese tried to reassure her. "Just act normally. Everything'll be fine."

The flight attendant took on a professional demeanor. "Please take the seat. Do you have a carry-on?"

"Yes."

"I'll get it and stow it up here. What's your seat number?"

Reese told her where he had stored his bag, and the flight attendant quickly left to retrieve it. Reese made his way to the empty business class seat and sat down. The woman next to him gave him a look like he did not belong there, but he did not care. He was lost in the comfort. He leaned back, stretched out his legs, and let the seat envelop him. *This is the life.*

Chapter 86

Al-Jamal, his men, and the Frenchman Neuville sat in their parked car down the road from the King David Hotel. Hotel security made it impossible for them to park closer. Hotels like the King David, which attracted celebrities and foreign dignitaries, took a lot of pride in their security. A lapse in security leading to an explosion or an assassination could permanently damage a hotel's reputation. Earning a five-star rating was difficult if people were dying on your property.

The King David Hotel understood this reality very well. It had experienced such a breach of security in 1946, when a bomb exploded in its basement. The explosion collapsed the western half of the hotel's southern wing, killing ninety-one people and injuring forty-six others. Ironically, the source of the terrorist attack was a radical Jewish organization striking out against the occupying British. Though the King David Hotel had gone to extremes to prevent a recurrence of such an attack, it still could not completely escape the legacy.

Al-Jamal had sent Hamdi into the hotel to verify the archaeologists were still there. He now lay back in his seat with his eyes closed.

A mobile phone rang and snapped him to alert. It was the Frenchman's phone. He watched him hit *Ignore* to avoid the call. Al-Jamal saw the suspicion on his men's faces. "Who was that?"

Neuville replied without hesitation. "Clisson,"

"What does he want with you?"

"He and I have shared information on the treasure. He probably wants to know if I am still available to him to be used in some way. He cannot be trusted."

Al-Jamal thought for a few silent seconds. "If he calls again, answer. Let's see what he wants."

He saw the puzzled look on the Frenchman's face. "We know he cannot be trusted. If we are careful, we can use him as he would use us."

Neuville smiled in realization and nodded in agreement.

Al-Jamal returned the smile. *Allah rewards those who translate his guidance into good judgment.*

Chapter 87

Raphael looked outside the window and watched the plane glide gently onto the runway. He had slept well, with dreams of what he was going to do to the woman when he finally caught her. He had seldom craved a woman so much. She was becoming more than a target, more than a victim. She was becoming an obsession. Finding her was going to be pleasurable in so many ways.

His father turned on his mobile phone. Raphael thought of his own phone in his pocket. It was housed in a special cover that allowed him to conceal his straight razor in a manner that avoided detection by security scanners. He was eager for an opportunity to use it.

His father sat anxiously with the phone to his ear until disconnecting. "Strange. The Directeur knew our arrival time but did not answer."

Raphael did not reply. His father often said things when he really did not expect a response.

As the plane continued taxiing to the gate, Raphael's father called the Directeur's number again. When the call again went to voice mail, Raphael could read the worry in his father's face.

His father put his hand on Raphael's. "I have no doubt the Directeur needs our help. We will go to the school."

Raphael found the idea of the Directeur in danger difficult to believe. He felt the rush of adrenaline in his veins. He knew the sensation well. It often drove out whatever made him human. On this occasion, it conveyed an emotion he not often experienced. He put his other hand on top of his father's. "We will find him."

A thought crossed his mind that brought a smile to his face.

If the Directeur is in trouble, perhaps the woman is nearby.

Chapter 88

Gilbert de Clisson stood in the living room of the three thousand dollar per night Presidential Suite of the King David Hotel. His leg still ached, but some sleep had appreciably calmed his nerves. Standing amid the opulence of the King David, he was in his element.

The King David had a very capable medical staff known almost as much for their discretion as their skill. Clisson was certain they had experienced many emergencies with their wealthy customers much more serious than his jagged gash. A nice young doctor accompanied by a more mature nurse had treated his wound with fifteen stitches and a tight bandage. There was no more danger of bleeding, but the stitches pulled when he moved in certain ways.

He limped to the window and looked out at the Temple Mount. The view was dominated by the Dome of the Rock. Clisson knew its history well. The Islamic shrine was constructed over the sacred stone where the Prophet Mohammed ascended to heaven–the same stone Jews believed was the place where Abraham took his son Isaac should God demand his sacrifice, the site of the Holy of Holies of both the first and second Temples. Completed in the year 691, fifty-four years after the Muslims took Jerusalem from the Byzantines, the twenty meter high by twenty meter diameter dome was said to have received its exterior from one hundred thousand melted gold dinars.

Shifting his gaze to the foreground, he saw Jews mingling and praying along the Western Wall. Also known as the Wailing Wall, it was where for centuries Jews had come to pray and mourn the destruction of the Temple, the closest they could get to the opening to heaven. Palestinians maintained the wall had no association with the Jewish Temple. They called it the Al-Buraq Wall because Mohammed tied his winged horse Buraq there. Clisson shook his head in amazement at both the vileness and gullibility of men. To him the wall was a visual metaphor for the willingness of religion to ignore and distort facts to push their own dogma.

Clisson dialed the number of a man he thought he would never ask for help again. He had tried to call him earlier without success. Clisson did not know if he was still alive, but a few seconds to confirm one way or the other could prove extremely valuable. Randall and David were smart and cautious. Clisson needed an edge.

He listened to the first ring and then the second. He was about to hang up.

"Monsieur Clisson," Directeur Neuville said with surprise in his tone. "You must need something badly to call *me*."

"Directeur Neuville, quite the contrary. I was worried for your well-being. I am glad to hear your voice."

"No thanks to you."

"I never sought to hurt you. Quite the contrary. It was *you* who betrayed *my* trust."

"Do you think I am so foolish I would not see with you there is only one side?"

Clisson thought about the question. Yes, actually he *had* thought Neuville a fool. To some extent he still did. Experience had taught him that in spite of what people thought, fooling someone a second time was often easier than fooling him the first time. "I apologize if I offended you. I still could use your help."

"I have new partners."

Neuville said the words firmly, but Clisson heard an inflexion in his voice that implied he was not happy or secure in his new relationship. *Who are these partners?* He needed more information. "I understand. But the *Jordanians* cannot help you in Israel. I can."

There was a pause before Neuville answered. "The Jordanians are no longer involved."

Clisson heard a muffled voice in the background. *Ah, his new partners are either Israeli or Palestinian. The accent sounded Arabic. Palestinians. Yes, I am sure of it.* He almost laughed at the thought of Neuville held by militant Palestinians. "Regardless, you and your new partners do not have the location."

Clisson heard more muffled conversation in the background.

"Do *you*?"

"I will very soon. If I send it to you, can I count on assistance from you and your *partners*? I propose a three-way split of whatever we find. Is that acceptable?"

Another pause ensued. Neuville was not in control.

"Oui, Monsieur Clisson. We will help you."

"Très bon. Watch for the location and instructions."

Clisson disconnected. He felt better now he had multiple gambits again in play.

Chapter 89

Raphael found it difficult to get comfortable in the tight confines of the taxi's back seat. Fortunately, traffic was good on Highway 1 to Jerusalem, and they had already driven over half of the fifty-kilometer trip.

His father's mobile phone emitted a tone indicating he had received a text message. Raphael watched his expression change from confusion to relief to concern.

Raphael could not remain silent. "What?"

"The Directeur sent me a text."

He held the phone such that Raphael could read the message.

Le Roi David Hôterl. Attente. Pruidence. Aucune réponsde.

The Directeur was at the King David Hotel. He had instructed them to wait, take caution, and not to reply. Raphael found it odd that a few of the words contained typographical errors.

His father seemed to feel better. "It is as I suspected. The Directeur is being held by others. He found a way to send us this message, but we cannot call him. He has told us where to go to help him, but we must wait until he contacts us again."

The King David Hotel was very large. The grounds around the hotel were even more expansive. The intent of the message had to be to position them nearby. The next message would tell them more specifically where to go.

His father leaned forward and spoke to the driver in a mixture of French and English. "Pardonnez-moi. We need to change our destination s'il vous plait. Take us to the King David Hotel. Merci."

The driver nodded in response.

Chapter 90

Lauren opened her eyes and for a moment did not know where she was. Her surroundings had her briefly wondering if she was still dreaming. Then she remembered. She was resting in a king size bed in one of the deluxe suites of the King David Hotel in Jerusalem. The rate for the room ran well over two thousand dollars per night. She vowed one day she would have that kind of money. For now she was perfectly willing for another to pay.

Since its opening in 1931, the King David Hotel had attracted the wealthiest and most powerful people in the world. Kings and queens of many nations had stayed in its rooms. Every U.S. President since Richard Nixon had spent nights there, as well as British Prime Ministers since Winston Churchill. Actors and actresses, industry tycoons, and many other members of the world's elite had made the King David their temporary home. Lauren smiled. *Madonna may have slept where I'm lying right now. Or even Kim Kardashian.*

Lauren lay nude under the plush sheets. Looking to her right, she saw Shane's exposed upper body. He lay sleeping on his side with his back to her. For a moment she just took in his form and listened to his rhythmic breathing. Earlier that morning they had made love. Both were on edge following their near deaths in Rihab, and the sex had a therapeutic effect. Lauren enjoyed making love to Shane. He was open and sincere, unlike so many of the other men who had passed through her life.

She had tried to get more specific information about where they were going next, but he had put her off, telling her it was for her safety. She knew there would come a more opportune time. Men usually opened up after a night of passion.

Lauren silently rose from the bed and stood nude in the spacious bedroom adjoining an even more ornate living area. She walked past the original paintings and stopped at a large mirror hanging on the wall. She admired her naked form with pride.

She reached into the armoire and pulled out one of the hotel robes. After slipping into the robe and tying the belt around her waist, she walked across the room to the balcony door. Making as little noise as possible, she opened the door and stepped outside. The weather was perfect, and a slight breeze blew through her loose hair. Church bells rang in Christian churches so she pushed the door nearly closed behind her.

Lauren had heard many times about the amazing views of the Old City from the balconies of the King David. What she saw now lived up to the reputation. She leaned on the stone wall that lined the balcony and gazed into the most cherished and fought over two hundred twenty acres of real estate on earth–the Islamic Quarter with its Dome of the Rock, the Christian Quarter with its Church of the Holy Sepulchre, the Jewish Quarter with its Western Wall, and the Armenian Quarter with its Church of St. James.

Lauren could also see the Jaffa Gate, which served as the main entrance to the Old City. It was built by Suleiman the Magnificent in 1538. In total there were eleven gates into the Old City, but only seven were open. Some had been sealed over time for various reasons. One of the closed gates was the Golden Gate on the eastern side. Jewish tradition held that the Messiah would enter Jerusalem through the Golden Gate. Suleiman the Magnificent did what he could to prevent the Messiah's coming by sealing it.

The hotel telephone rang and snapped Lauren back to reality. She lifted the handset from the telephone on the table just outside the balcony door. "Hello."

It was Clisson. "Bonjour, Mademoiselle Mallory. I am calling because it is after noon. Is the good professeur there beside you?" An almost wicked laugh escaped his lips.

Lauren lied. "Yes, he is. Do you want to speak to him?"

"Non. Just tell him we should get underway while we still have daylight."

Lauren knew Clisson was being careful. In Israel, hotel security officers routinely listened to telephone conversations. One had to assume no conversation was private. "We'll get ready and be right down."

"Merci, Mademoiselle Mallory. I bet you look ravishing."

Lauren curled her upper lip in disgust and hung up the telephone. She did not like being controlled, and Clisson thought he could manipulate her. *We'll see.* She turned her back on the phone and returned to the balcony wall.

Chapter 91

Shane awoke to the ringing telephone. He rolled over to where he expected Lauren to be, but she was not there. His eyes followed the sound of church bells coming in through the partially open balcony door and found Lauren outside talking to someone on the phone. He could not hear what she was saying, but the conversation did not continue long.

Shane swung his legs out of bed and pulled on his boxers. Then he walked to the glass door beyond which Lauren stood leaning on the waist-high stone wall that protected the hotel guests from the sheer drop on the other side. The image was breathtaking. He followed the shape of her back to her waist to her derriere to where her robe was blowing in the breeze and exposing her bare legs. In the background was the Old City of Jerusalem. It was a combination of classic beauty and timeless beauty.

He stepped through the door. "Who was that?"

Lauren seemed startled. "Shane! You should know better than to sneak up behind someone on a balcony."

"I can't see you being afraid of anything. And there's no way you're going to jump."

"Not when I have a guy that looks that good in boxers. That was Clisson. He wants us downstairs."

"He's in a hurry?"

"Who cares what *he* wants? Come look at this view. It's amazing."

Though he was half-naked, Shane could not turn down the invitation. He joined her at the wall.

Shane pointed to the Temple Mount. "In the first century, Jewish culture revolved around this spot."

Lauren gestured to the throngs of people. "It seems pretty much the same today."

"You might think that, but it was much different then. The god of the Jews, Yahweh, stood apart from the gods of other nations. Those gods were gods of the sky and only occasionally visited earth. Yahweh declared himself to be the ruler of earth. The Old City was and remains the Jewish heart, but in the first century, the Temple was the soul."

Shane pointed to the Dome of the Rock. "Yahweh resided where that shrine stands today, in the Holy of Holies of the Jewish Temple. We have nothing today that compares. Imagine what it would be like. God residing on earth. Not just watching everyone from a heavenly throne. Actually, physically, residing in a room. His spirit emanating to fill the rest of the country."

Lauren sighed. "I can almost see it."

"If we were standing here in the first century, the Temple would be about *all* we could see. It was one of the largest buildings in the world. It covered thirty-five acres, with cornerstones weighing one hundred tons. The Sanctuary was fifteen stories high, twice the size of any temple in Rome. Hanging on giant hinges, the polished Corinthian bronze doors to the Sanctuary were sixty feet high. It's said when they opened, the creaking could be heard as far away as Jericho."

"That has to be an exaggeration."

"Perhaps." Shane paused. "But we better get going."

Lauren turned and reacted forcefully. "Clisson can wait. This is a big day for us. Come make love to me again."

Lauren grabbed Shane's arm and pulled him back toward the room. She loosened the belt of her robe and opened the cloth as she walked. The flirtatious look on her face communicated she would not be refused.

Shane was not about to disappoint her.

Chapter 92

"Where are we?" Reese asked his taxi driver.

"This is the King David Hotel. It's one of the nicest hotels in Jerusalem. I'm not sure you can afford it."

Reese ignore the dis because the Frenchmen's taxi pulled up in front of the main entrance. "Please turn in as if you're about to drop me off."

Reese watched the large hulk step out of the taxi. He was carrying a soft-sided briefcase and another small bag. A few seconds later, his smaller companion followed.

While the Frenchmen settled with their driver, Reese opened his door. "I'll get out here. What do I owe you?

He swallowed hard at the amount but paid it without complaint. The Frenchmen entered the lobby, and Reese hurried after them. He soon realized there was little need to rush.

Inside the main entrance of the hotel, the Frenchmen were passing through a metal detector. The briefcase and their other meager possessions were in the scanner at their side. Reese looked away and right into one of the security cameras scanning the hotel entrance.

He wondered whether he should enlist the hotel's security force but decided against it. He was afraid he had so little proof he might attract their attention for nothing. Or they might become uncontrollable and act too quickly. Either reaction would not get Reese what he wanted.

The Frenchmen made it through the metal detector without incident. Reese slowed his pace to maintain distance. He could not help but wonder what they had done with their weapons. A hotel bellboy approached them to take the briefcase. The older Frenchman refused but said something to the bellboy before they headed off together.

As Reese's bag moved forward on the belt, he passed through the metal detector. He pretended to watch his bag, but he never lost sight of the Frenchmen until they entered the hotel storage room and disappeared.

Reese's bag emerged from the scanner, and he said to another bellboy what he assumed had been the Frenchman's instructions. "I would like to store my bag."

The bellboy waved his arm palm upward. "This way, sir."

"Do you have a safe?"

"Of course. Do you have something to store there?

Reese wondered what the Frenchmen had been carrying in the briefcase, but the contents were not his top priority. "Perhaps later."

Before they had gone far, Reese saw the two Frenchmen emerge walking to a sitting area in the main section of the lobby. They sat down facing each other in two large, plush chairs separated by a table.

As they walked, Reese casually surveyed the room for a place to watch the Frenchmen without being seen. He found a spot around a corner behind some large plants decorating the lobby.

They arrived at the storage room, and Reese watched his bag disappear behind the door. The bellboy returned with the ticket, and Reese traded him a few shekels. Reese spun around to leave when he saw one of the hotel's armed guards meandering through the lobby.

The sight changed his mind. He turned back to the bellboy and signaled he had a request. He showed him his badge and pointed to his chosen hiding spot. "Please have your head of security meet me over there."

Chapter 93

Reese stood up when he saw a well-dressed man approach.

"Mr. Reese?" The man's tone indicated Reese was keeping him from something important. "My name is Calev Spielmann. I'm Chief Security Officer here at the King David Hotel. You asked to speak to me?"

"Yes. I'm Detective Adam Reese." He showed Spielmann his identification, but Spielmann seemed unimpressed.

"Detective Reese, the Cambridge Police Department has no jurisdiction in Israel. What do you want with me?"

"I've been following two Frenchmen who committed multiple murders in Massachusetts and Connecticut. They're sitting in your lobby right now." Reese gestured toward the two men. "They appear to be waiting for someone. I'll need your help when that person arrives."

Spielmann twisted his upper torso to look and then turned back to Reese. "Have they committed a crime here?"

"Not that I'm aware of."

"Do they pose a threat to this hotel?"

"Not as far as I know."

"Then you must go through the proper channels and request their detainment and extradition."

Reese's jaw dropped. "You have armed guards here. Can you hold them while I do that?"

"No. We're here to ensure the security of this hotel, not to involve ourselves in international matters. This is a matter for the police."

"These men are dangerous! Don't you guys have some kind of anti-terrorist unit?"

Spielmann's laugh told Reese he was exposing his ignorance concerning Israeli security protocol. "The Shinn Bet is not the police."

"Shinn Bet?"

Spielmann huffed as if the conversation was over. "I really don't have time to educate you in the many layers of Israeli security." He paused. "But since you're a fellow officer, the Shinn Bet is the common name for the Sherut HaBitachon HaKlali. Perhaps you have heard of them by their acronym–Shabak?"

Reese shook his head.

Spielmann's face relayed his frustration. He exhaled heavily before continuing. "They're our country's internal security service, not unlike your FBI. They use informants to capture terrorists, and they interrogate suspected terrorists. Are these Frenchmen terrorists?"

"I wouldn't call them terrorists. But they have committed numerous murders."

"Then it's a matter for the police. It's their job to capture criminals like these men. Our police are very capable. I myself rose through their ranks, and most of my men are ex-policemen."

"So why can't your men help me now?"

"You're not listening. Our job is hotel security. Unless these men cause an incident here, it isn't our job to apprehend them. It would be bad for the hotel's reputation. I'll be glad to call the police for you. The headquarters is here in Jerusalem. I have a friend who's a Chief Inspector."

This kind of bureaucracy frustrated Reese to no end, but losing his temper would just make matters worse. It seemed Spielmann was trying to help him in his own irritating way. Reese's attention shifted to the Frenchmen, who were rising from their seats. He watched them nonchalantly walk in the opposite direction toward a hallway. "Where are they going?"

"They're walking toward a restaurant. Perhaps they're hungry."

Reese's stomach growled in response. He could not remember his last decent meal. "Is there a hotel exit they can escape through?"

"This is a large hotel, Detective Reese."

Chapter 94

Neuville had convinced Al-Jamal to let him take a shift watching for Randall, David, and the others as long as he was accompanied by Ahmad Habib. He could see his Palestinian guard thought him arrogant and pretentious, no more than a weak bureaucrat and infidel. The ruffian had no idea who he was dealing with.

While still passing through security, he glimpsed Andre de Vaux and Raphael leaving the lobby for a side hallway. Seeing them brought Neuville mixed emotions. He had no illusions regarding the Palestinians' plans for him. They intended to use him until he no longer had value and then dispatch him. All he had to do was signal, and his men would come to his aid.

On the other hand, armed guards were ever-present in the lobby. Though he had no doubt de Vaux and Raphael could free him, he could not guarantee there would not be a scene. Now was not the time to engage with hotel security. *I am too close to the prize. I must remain hidden for now. God will let me know when.*

He and Ahmad walked to some potted trees near the lobby elevators and positioned themselves behind them. They remained there several minutes without speaking until Ahmad's nervousness apparently reached a level he could no longer bear. "Where are they? Over half the day is gone. Why are they waiting? Do you think we lost them?"

"No. And I do not know."

On cue, one of the lobby elevators opened, and the Israeli archaeologist emerged.

Neuville's excitement emerged with a hushed quality. "There! Leaving the elevator."

Ahmad saw him. "It is the Jew."

The doors of another elevator opened, and Clisson and his bodyguard stepped out to join the Israeli archaeologist. The three men exchanged what appeared to be uncomfortable pleasantries.

Ahmad grunted a laugh. "They seem very casual for treasure hunters."

Neuville ignored the sarcasm. "Whatever they intend to do, they will do soon. Call Al-Jamal."

While Ahmad punched buttons on his mobile phone, Neuville continued to watch the elevators. Once again doors opened. This time Randall and Lauren Mallory appeared and joined the conversation.

Ahmad handed him the phone and spoke with the tone of a child who had just tattled on a sibling. "Ya Sidi wants to speak with you."

Neuville took the phone. "Allo."

"Ahmad thinks you are wasting our time."

"He is wrong. We should follow them."

"Unlike Ahmad, I believe you. Give me back to him."

Neuville handed the phone to Ahmad and smiled as Ahmad's expression transformed from mischievous anticipation to surprise to anger. He spat his objections into the phone, but Neuville expected the argument would not last long. He understood hierarchy, and the chain of command between Al-Jamal and his men was very clear. He returned his attention to the group in front of the elevators.

Randall seemed excited about something. "That's great!"

David stood facing him. "I know. Eathan says Nathan and Hadasa will remain in the hospital a day or two, but they'll fully recover."

As the two archaeologists spoke, Clisson stepped up beside them with obvious frustration in his face. "What are we waiting on? It's midafternoon."

Randall gave David a look that communicated their conversation must be over. Then to Clisson, he said, "We have time."

Neuville almost laughed out loud watching Clisson about to explode.

"Qu'est-ce que vous dire?" the French aristocrat asked vehemently. "What do you mean?"

Randall reacted stoically to Clisson's bluster. "We need to arrive near closing time. I see you have on comfortable shoes. That's good. We'll be walking a lot today."

"Closing time where?" A subtle gesture from Clisson resulted in his bodyguard taking a threatening position beside him. "Docteur Randall, do not presume I am someone you can manipulate."

Randall raised his hand palm outward. "Be patient. We'll explain it on our way through the Jaffa Gate into the Old City. You'll know everything soon."

Randall led Clisson and the others out the hotel entrance. Neuville turned to find Ahmad still recovering from his conversation. "Call Al-Jamal again. Tell him we are coming out. They are headed for the Jaffa Gate. If we are lucky, we can get there ahead of them."

While Ahmad fumbled with his phone, Neuville walked a short distance away and stood with his back to him as if casually surveying the hotel grounds. *I know where they are going! God has sent me a message!* He reassessed the risk of asking de Vaux and Raphael for help. As Ahmad chattered in Arabic, Neuville pulled out his own phone and sent a message to de Vaux. He deleted the text from his history file and turned back to Ahmad.

Ahmad ended his conversation with Al-Jamal and spoke with authority. "Ya Sidi wants us to join him right away."

Neuville turned toward the lobby. "I do not know about you, but I need to visit the toilette before I return to the car."

Ahmad gave him a funny look, but he ultimately must have thought a visit to the toilette to be a good idea. He followed without comment.

Chapter 95

While Raphael sat with his father awaiting their food, he looked around the restaurant at the wealthy elite dining there. His disgust brought a squint to his eyes and a curl to his upper lip. Most of them were doomed to eternal damnation, the price for ignoring their God to amass earthly treasures. None of them understood the war for men's souls going on every day.

His father must have read his face. "My son, the world is full of hardship. You, as much as anyone, know this to be true. Take advantage of the blessings that come your way."

Raphael nodded, but his acquiescence was false. He did not understand how his father could order food while the Directeur was in trouble.

Again his father read him. "God will watch over the Directeur until we save him. I know this in my heart. As should you."

Raphael took the mild chastisement in stride. He had suffered much worse on numerous occasions. His father's deep faith was one of his most admirable traits. It gave him a purpose and conviction few could match. Raphael prayed every night God would reward his father for all he had accomplished in his service.

Raphael's father's text message tone reverberated like a message sent from Heaven. *Our wait is finally over.*

His father read the message, placed his napkin on the table, and stood up. "We need to go now."

After throwing down enough cash to more than pay for the meal, his father briskly walked toward the restaurant exit with Raphael in tow. He handed Raphael the mobile phone with the message still displayed.

La toilette de hall de l'hôtel maintenant

The Directeur wanted them to meet him at the hotel lobby toilette right now. It was a strange request. Raphael handed the phone back to his father. The lobby was coming up at the end of the hall. They did not have to choose a direction.

Crossing in front of them from right to left was the Directeur. Raphael's father gently grasped Raphael's forearm. It was a simple and subtle gesture to indicate Raphael was to remain calm and still. The Directeur was walking toward the toilette with a Palestinian. His father pretended effectively he and his son were merely being courteous and letting them pass.

The Directeur saw Raphael and his father but gave no outward indication significant enough to raise the Palestinian's concern. He just shifted his eyes in the direction of the toilette as he walked past. The gesture was like a shot of adrenaline straight to Raphael's heart.

After the Directeur and the Palestinian had entered the toilette, Raphael's father released his forearm and took a sentry-like position beside the entrance. Raphael stepped inside.

The room was divided with two stalls and three sinks on one wall and a row of urinals along the other wall. The Directeur and Palestinian were standing at the urinals with their back to the sinks. Raphael's entrance drew the attention of the Palestinian, who turned his head to look over his shoulder. Raphael nonchalantly bent over to wash his hands and face in one of the center sinks. As he reached up for paper towels, he heard one of the urinals flush.

Raphael saw in the mirror the Palestinian walking toward the sink beside him, while the Directeur remained with his back to them. Raphael threw away the paper towels and turned toward the urinals. As the Palestinian passed, Raphael turned more quickly than the Palestinian could have guessed him capable. He grabbed the Palestinian with one hand on his chin and the other hand on the side of his head. With all his strength and quickness, Raphael twisted the Palestinian's head until he both felt and heard his vertebrae snap multiple times. The vibration and sounds sent such ecstasy through every pore of Raphael's body that he continued to hold the Palestinian close, even after his victim's legs could no longer support him. Raphael had felt people die enough times to know when the Palestinian was gone.

"Merci, Raphael," the Directeur said from behind him.

Raphael dropped the Palestinian to the floor. Assisting the Directeur and being recognized for doing so was as great an honor as Raphael could ever attain on earth. He hoped and prayed it would lead to honors and reward in heaven.

"Hurry," continued the Directeur. "We must hide the body."

Raphael lifted the Palestinian under his armpits and dragged him into one of the stalls. Closing and locking the door behind him, he positioned the body on the seat and leaned the upper torso against the back wall. Then he stepped on the front of the bowl and rolled sideways over the stall partition. The partition creaked and threatened to collapse but remained upright.

As the Directeur and Raphael burst from the room in the direction of the lobby, Raphael's father joined them. The Directeur acknowledged him but did not slow his pace. In a few quick strides they were in the open space of the lobby headed for the entrance.

The Directeur gave them matter-of-fact direction. "We must get to a taxi. The professeur and the woman are with an Israeli and Clisson. They are headed for the Jaffa Gate. We need to get there before they do."

The woman! Lost in thought, Raphael could not avoid colliding with one of the hotel's elderly female guests, who had walked too close to Raphael's massive trunk. He barely felt the contact, but the woman went sprawling to the floor.

Raphael did not stop. He saw two hotel guards turning in his direction with their mini-Uzi submachine guns in a ready position. For a moment he feared they would challenge him, but they remained where they were.

Raphael exited the hotel with the Directeur and his father. They had rescued the Directeur, and the bright light of heaven was shining upon them.

The ignorant guards can keep their precious hotel with its façade of safety. They deserve the present I left them.

Chapter 96

Reese knew Spielmann was about to give up on him. Randall's group had appeared and then casually left as if they were on a vacation. Their sudden appearance had caught Reese off guard and unsure of what to do. He had elected not to leave the Frenchmen he knew to be murderers, though now they were calmly sitting in a restaurant eating a meal. He understood very well how the events made him appear.

Spielmann's patience was gone. "Detective Reese, I don't want to be rude, but you have taken all the time I'm willing to give. I'll get you in touch with the police. They can help you with your suspects. Or if you prefer, we can leave them out of it, and you can join your friends and enjoy your stay in Jerusalem."

Spielmann turned to walk away, but he stopped after a couple of strides. The two Frenchmen were rushing back into the lobby. A third man had joined them. The younger hulk followed the two older men, who weaved through the other guests. One of the guests, an elderly woman, fell to the floor, and two guards turned in the Frenchmen's direction. They looked at Spielmann for permission to engage, but with the slightest headshake, the security chief held them in place.

Reese pressed him to act. "Obviously they found who they were waiting for. If you don't stop them, people are going to die in your city."

As the Frenchmen exited the hotel, Spielmann signaled his men to assist the woman on the floor. Then he turned back to Reese. "But it will not be in my hotel."

Reese found what he was hearing to be incredible. "It's not just the potential murders of American citizens. If I know these two guys, they won't stop there. Israeli citizens are in danger as well."

"I believe you, Detective Reese."

"Then how can you stand there and do nothing?"

"You haven't been listening. My job was to eliminate the threat to the hotel. I'll call the police and get you the best help I can arrange."

Reese shook his head in disbelief. "I have to go. Somehow I have to keep them from catching up to the other group." He reached into his pocket and pulled out a card. He handed it to Spielmann. "My mobile number. Please have your friend with the police call me as soon as he can."

Reese turned to leave, but Spielmann called out to him. "Detective Reese, wait."

Spielmann reached inside his suit coat and pulled a Jericho 941 semi-automatic pistol from its holster. Reese feared he was going to detain him.

Spielmann handed him the weapon. "I can't have you getting yourself killed. I really am on your side."

Reese checked the clip and safety and placed it between the small of his back and his belt. He pulled his shirt tail out and over the weapon. At least he now had twelve shots at his disposal–not enough to waste but enough to be effective. *I can't figure this guy out.* "Thanks. If you really want to help me, have your friend call me to arrange backup."

"He'll call."

Reese nodded and ran through the lobby. He burst through the exit and strained against the sun to search for the Frenchmen. He feared he may be too late. Then he saw them. A taxi had just pulled out and was turning to make its way through the hotel grounds. He could see the Frenchmen through the rear window.

"Taxi, sir?" one of the hotel staff said to his right.

"Yes, quickly."

As Reese helplessly watched the Frenchmen driving away, a whistle pierced the air. With his peripheral vision, Reese saw a car pulling up. He reached into his pocket, pulled out a few bills, and handed them to the taxi-caller.

Leaping into the car, he barked at the driver. "Please hurry! Follow the taxi that just left. There's a big tip for you if you get me to where they're going without losing them."

Chapter 97

Chief Inspector Melech Koenig sat in his office in the Israel Police headquarters located in the predominantly Arab neighborhood of Sheikh Jarrah on Mount Scopus in northeastern Jerusalem. He understood why the headquarters was there. The eight hundred twenty-six-meter-high mountain had served as a base for attacks on Jerusalem for thousands of years. Because of its repeated change of control, the area had been the target of many property disputes, with Jews claiming they had legally owned the land since the time of the Ottoman Empire and Palestinians claiming Turkish documents disproved their claims.

Sheik Jarah's name originated from a tomb dating to the year 1201 belonging to Husam al-Din al-Jarrahi, a high ranking sheikh and physician to Saladin. Another tomb concentrated the Jewish occupants of the area. Shimon HaTzadik was one of leaders of the Jewish people following the Babylonian exile. He was best known for a confrontation with Alexander the Great. The Greek general paid homage to Shimon because he had seen the Jewish leader in his dreams before big battles. When Alexander later demanded a memorial marble statue of him be placed in the Temple, Shimon explained such images were forbidden and suggested an alternative–giving all male babies born that year the name Alexander. Alexander liked the idea and left the Temple untarnished.

Koenig was Chief Inspector of the elite unit of the Israel Police known by its acronym *Yamam*, short for *Yehidat Mishtartit Meuhedet*, or Special Police Unit. It was established in 1976 after a failed military operation led to the murder of twenty-one children before the hostage takers could be killed. Arguably the most experienced and capable police unit in the world, Yamam focused on freeing hostages inside the borders of Israel, but it also performed other police duties involving armed and dangerous criminals.

Koenig's office phone sprang to life, and his assistant informed him that his friend Calev Spielmann was on the line. He picked up the handset.

"Calev, good to hear from you."

"Melech, I would like to catch up, but this is not a social call."

"What is it?"

"An American police detective just left my hotel in pursuit of three French nationals. He says two of them have killed multiple people in the United States. They may be here after some other Americans. He seemed quite certain that unless he got help, there would be more deaths here in Israel."

"You have done the right thing in calling me. How do I contact him?"

"I have his name and mobile telephone number."

Koenig wrote down the information. "I'll call him right away."

"Thank you. I'll call you tomorrow to catch up and find out what happened."

Spielmann disconnected. Koenig looked at the paper containing the name and telephone number his friend had given him. As he did so, he was uncharacteristically shaken by a chill. He was not a superstitious or overly religious man, but he did believe in intuition and premonitions. In this case, his intuition told him this assignment would be more dangerous and much more complex than it appeared at first blush.

He read the name on the paper out loud. "Detective Adam Reese. What are you getting me into?"

Koenig picked up the telephone again. Regardless of any personal trepidation, he understood his duty was to call his senior NCO and get his unit ready to move out.

Chapter 98

The people and cars everywhere overwhelmed Reese's senses. "Slow down."

His taxi was approaching a drop off point after having passed through a gap in a massive wall constructed of large light-colored stone blocks. The site had taken his breath away. It was like something out of an adventure story, an ancient fortification complete with notches along its top used by ancient defenders to fire down arrows and stones on their enemies.

The three men he was following were just two taxis ahead of him. After his driver coasted in, he pulled enough cash out of his pocket to cover the fare and the large tip he had promised the driver. But he did not immediately hand it up front. "Just a second."

The doors of the Frenchmen's taxi swung open. Reese hunched down in the back seat and watched the younger Frenchman emerge and assist the other two men. Seeing him with a crowd of Israelis nearby reinforced for Reese just how large the man was. He swallowed hard.

The taxi pulled away, and the three men entered the throng. Reese studied them as they walked.

The two men he had been following represented both ends of the criminal spectrum. The older man exuded intelligence. He was the kind of criminal that hid behind others and covered his involvement with alibis and misdirection. Criminals of that breed were difficult to apprehend and often lived long, affluent lives. The younger man displayed little but animalistic urges and brawn. He was obviously the muscle. In the criminal world, brutes were expendable and replaceable. While Reese sensed a close connection between the two men, he suspected if push came to shove, the younger man would be the one facing danger.

The third man was their superior. Reese had seen group dynamics in every possible setting from high society dinners to gangs on the street. In a matter of minutes he could determine the pecking order with an uncanny accuracy. This man had other people do his bidding. Reese concluded the third man ordered the events in and around Boston and New Haven. He was the man Reese was after.

Reese paid his driver and stepped out of the taxi. He followed the Frenchmen's path through the churning crowd, never walking very far at any one time and often stopping at kiosks and feigning interest in whatever was being hawked. When still, he stood at angles that kept his face hidden. He knew he had to be careful. He had heard stories of grizzly bears sensing they were being followed and circling back to attack their pursuer.

Reese had not followed the Frenchmen far into the crowd before his mobile phone vibrated. A strange combination of numbers filled the display box. Reese stopped mostly hidden behind a stone kiosk and answered the call with a questioning tone. "Adam Reese. Who's this?"

The caller had a strong Israeli accent. "Detective Reese, this is Chief Inspector Melech Koenig. I'm Chief Inspector of the Yamam. My friend Calev Spielmann told me you had a situation. Do you need my help?"

"Yamam? I thought Spielmann was going to call the police."

"I *am* the police."

Koenig explained the role of the Yamam within the Israel Police.

Reese liked what he heard. "You sound like the person I need."

"What is your status, Detective Reese?"

"I'm following three men. I'm convinced they're pursuing an American and his friends."

"And you suspect these men of multiple homicides?"

"I much more than suspect. I was present when one of our own police departments underestimated them. They killed three policemen and a civilian. Later they severely wounded a young woman. I suspect them in the murder of a Harvard professor in Cambridge, which is my jurisdiction. There are probably others."

There was a moment of silence on the other end of the line. Perhaps he had lost his connection. With the Frenchmen were getting farther away, he was about to hang up when Koenig spoke. "You followed them here? Why?"

"I came to find an American I think is involved in this somehow. His name's Doctor Shane Randall. On the way, I stumbled onto these guys again and have been tailing them since. I saw Randall at the hotel, but I didn't approach him because the Frenchmen were nearby, and I didn't think by myself I could hold him and his friends and take on the Frenchmen. I may have made a mistake. My gut tells me if the Frenchmen find Randall, all hell's going to break lose."

"Do you know where you are?"

Before Reese could answer the question, he noticed the three men separating into different directions. They were splitting up.

Koenig called him back to the phone. "Detective Reese?"

"Sorry, we drove a short distance from the King David Hotel through a gap in an unbelievably large wall. Cars are coming and going through the opening. I don't have a lot of time."

"You're at the Jaffa Gate. I'll get my men and meet you there. We should be there in less than thirty minutes. If you move again, call me."

Koenig gave Reese his mobile number and his office number.

Before hanging up, Reese wanted to ensure Koenig understood the situation. "Chief Inspector, don't underestimate these men."

"I heard you the first time, Detective Reese. We'll come prepared."

Koenig hung up, and Reese focused all his attention back on the three men. They seemed apprehensive, like herd animals uncomfortable alone in an open area. They moved increasingly apart but always kept line of sight to each other. They were looking for someone, but they also seemed afraid someone was looking for them.

Reese felt a similar anxiety. At least he had help on the way. *It's about time someone took me seriously.*

Chapter 99

"Where are they?" Hamdi Adwan asked from the back seat.

Al-Jamal did not answer. Ahmad and the Frenchman Neuville had not returned, and there was no answer on their mobile phones. Al-Jamal felt the pressure of time. The archaeologist's group was getting too far ahead.

Milak voiced what all of them were thinking. "Something is wrong. Ahmad would not do this."

Al-Jamal did not have to be told. Ahmad was restrained or dead. Whether the Frenchman was also a victim was impossible to know. All he had to go on was Ahmad's last call. "Hamdi, get up here and take the wheel."

Hamdi rushed to the driver's seat and started the car.

Al-Jamal knew where to go. "Head for the Jaffa Gate. There is a municipal parking lot just outside the walls near the Tower of David. We can enter on foot from there."

As they maneuvered the short distance through the Jerusalem streets, Al-Jamal tried his best to hide his nervousness. *How much of what Neuville told me was true?*

The drive did not take long. After parking their car, Al-Jamal and his two men crossed the space to the Jaffa Gate. They carried no weapons except for small knives concealed in their pockets. Their purpose was reconnaissance, not aggression.

Al-Jamal slowed the pace at the entrance and scanned the crowd for Neuville or the Jewish archaeologist and his companions. "Spread out. Be invisible. If you see them, do not take action. Find me."

They entered the Old City and immediately took different paths. Al-Jamal took a route up the center while Hamdi diverged to his left and Milak to his right. As expected, the area churned with people of all nationalities and all walks of life. In addition to the individuals and couples scattered about, there were numerous tour groups. Finding Neuville would require a miracle. Al-Jamal prayed Allah would grant him such assistance.

"O Allah, I seek help from you alone and ask forgiveness from you and believe in you alone and praise you for all the good things you have given me and are grateful to you and are not ungrateful to you and I part and break from all those who are disobedient to you. O Allah, you alone do I worship and pray exclusively to you and bow before you alone and hasten eagerly toward you and fear your severe punishment and hope for your mercy because your severe punishment is surely to be meted out to the disbelievers."

An armed Israeli security officer passed in front of Al-Jamal. The security officers were there to watch over the visitors and ensure order. The last thing Al-Jamal needed was to get their attention.

As he serpentined through the crowd, he changed his appearance. He hunched his back and exaggerated the bend in his knees. Though he searched every face, he kept his own face pointed downward and skillfully avoided eye contact. He took pride in knowing he could walk up next to Neuville, and the Frenchman would not know him.

Al-Jamal found nothing but frustration. He turned back to where he would meet his men. *There he is.* Neuville was standing to his right surveying the crowd. He was signaling others with subtle gestures. *He has help.*

Al-Jamal hid himself behind others in the crowd. It was now obvious what had happened. Others had come to Neuville's aid. They had either captured or killed Ahmad.

He tried to see who Neuville was signaling, but he could not get into position to do so without exposing himself. He weaved through the crowd to get behind Neuville. *This arrogant Frenchman has no idea how near death he is.*

Al-Jamal stood within a meter of the Frenchman's back. All that remained was to use his knife to end the double-crosser's life. Killing him without attracting the attention of Israeli security would be difficult. Timing and speed would be critical.

Chapter 100

Shane stood with Lauren just inside the magnificent Cathedral of St. James and thought how appropriate it was they were there. He had chosen not to go directly from the King David Hotel to their final destination, and the cathedral lay on their route from the Jaffa Gate to Mount Zion. He could not resist stopping to see it.

As next in line after Jesus, James had inherited his brother's mission and gained the mission of his nemesis Paul. He had captured the words of his brother in what Shane was now calling the Sicarii Gospel, and he had cared for and hidden the treasury of his sect to be used as a war chest upon his brother's return. While doing everything he could to continue his brother's message of peace and love, James had also prepared for the day when his brother would return at the head of God's army to wage an apocalyptic battle. Jewish Christians and non-Jewish Christians, peace and war–James handled the duality and complexity of his mission with such style and grace he was one of the most popular people in Jerusalem at the time of his murder.

Despite James' popularity during the first century, he was maligned through the following centuries by an increasingly anti-Jewish Christian church. An obvious Jew, James was presented as not understanding and even resisting his brother's message. His parentage was questioned when the Roman Church preferred Mary as a perpetual virgin. Historical facts and references, Jewish culture and traditions, and even common sense went out the window to rob James of his legacy as the savior of Christianity. Without James, the light of Christianity would most likely have gone out shortly after Jesus' death at the hands of the Romans. Such was the pattern of history and what the Romans expected.

Centuries after his death, James fell victim to a final act of confusion. He rested in the same cathedral with James, the son of Zebedee. The two disciples of Jesus, one his brother, one potentially a cousin, shared the same common name of Yacov, or Jacob, later converted in Greek to James. James, the rebellious son of Zebedee, was the first of the Twelve to be martyred at the hands of Herod Agrippa I in the year 44. James,

Jesus' brother, joined him in death eighteen years later. Then in the twelfth century their tombs were enclosed within the same cathedral.

The cross-shaped cathedral had undergone significant renovations since, with many of them occurring in the first half of the eighteenth century under the Armenian Patriarch Gregory the Chain Bearer. The addition to his name had come from his wearing a heavy chain around his neck while traveling through Armenia raising money for the Armenian Quarter.

Lauren broke the silence. "Why are we here, Shane?"

"Shhhh." Then he whispered, "It's forbidden to talk inside the cathedral. The monks are watching."

Shane's gaze turned to the ancient oil lamps hanging from the vaulted dome. The oil lamps and candles scattered around the altars were the only sources of light in the cathedral, and the flickering light reflecting off the stone and metal gave the cathedral a supernatural spirituality. Shane could not help being affected.

He looked upward as if to heaven. Over every oil lamp at the end of the ropes connecting the lamps to the ceiling were ceramic ostrich eggs decorated with symbols of the branches of Christianity. While just a traditional decoration today, the slippery eggs in the past served a more utilitarian role. They kept rodents from climbing the walls and descending the ropes to the lamps.

Higher still, the crisscrossed pattern of the arches in the dome high overhead formed a giant concave Star of David unlike anything anywhere else in the world. It reminded Shane that though he was standing in a Christian cathedral, the bones enshrined there belonged to Jewish men.

Looking to the left on the northern wall, Shane found the altar of James, the son of Zebedee. He entered the altar and kissed the golden clam shell that adorned it. With gestures he instructed Lauren to do the same. Christians kissed the shell both as a sign of homage and in hope of a special blessing. *We need all the help we can get.*

He had heard a story, now legend, concerning the cathedral and James, the son of Zebedee. Because of its three feet thick walls, the cathedral served as a bomb shelter for the Armenian Quarter during the 1948 Arab-Israeli war. One night, the bombardment was especially intense with over one thousand shells landing around the cathedral. Not one Armenian died. Later, many Armenians testified they had seen St. James, dressed in white and standing on the roof of the cathedral, using his hands to divert the bombs.

Shane and Lauren walked back to the center of the church where they found the altar and ornate seventeenth century throne of James, the brother of Jesus. Shane thought it understated for the man who shared DNA with Jesus and had laid the foundation for his brother's sect to become the largest religion in the world. If he could go back in time and converse with any man who had ever lived, this man was near the top of his list.

Shane felt himself pulled to the side away from Lauren. It was Gustave taking him to where Clisson stood several feet away.

Clisson was fuming. "This is outrageous. Where is the treasure?"

Shane saw that Clisson had attracted the attention of the monks. He knew his response had to be quick. "Monsieur Clisson, I was just coming to find you."

Clisson gave him a skeptical look.

"Sincerely," Shane assured him. "I'm afraid we're being followed. You should send your man ahead." Shane nodded in Gustave's direction. "I'd like to know our destination's safe for us to enter. If you could have him scout the location and get back to us..."

Clisson interrupted him. "And that would be where?"

"The Cenacle."

Clisson smiled. "Of course. The Upper Room."

Shane knew Clisson would be familiar with the Cenacle. Located on Mount Zion, it had served as the headquarters for the early Jewish Christian church–the site of the Last Supper and where the Holy Spirit filled the Twelve before Pentecost.

Clisson was almost giddy. "I will send Gustave immediately."

A monk tapped Clisson on the shoulder and with gestures scolded him for talking. Clisson expressed his regret without words. He then gave Shane a look expressing his thanks before walking away with Gustave.

Shane returned to Lauren's side. She looked at him with questions in her eyes, but he looked passed her and found Amit nearby. He sent him a quick wink.

Chapter 101

Never losing sight of the Directeur and his father, Raphael's senses scanned the crowd inside the Jaffa Gate. While briefing them on his relationship with Clisson and his capture by the Palestinians, the Directeur had warned them the Palestinians knew their destination. They had little time.

The presence of armed Israeli security officers patrolling the area increased Raphael's already foul mood, but they were not what had set him off. He had learned from the Directeur he had been in the same hotel with the woman, perhaps only meters away. If he had not joined his father for a meal he did not want, she would be in hell. He prayed he would come upon her in the crowd.

His prayer was not answered. *The woman is not here.* Raphael sensed she had been there and gone. *Too late! Merde!*

Raphael checked his father, who looked similarly frustrated. When Raphael found the Directeur, he was gesturing for Raphael's father to rejoin. The Directeur then turned his attention to Raphael, but their eye contact was interrupted when the Directeur reacted to his mobile phone. He looked at the display and smiled.

When they made eye contact again, the Directeur's smile vanished, and his face morphed into intense anger. *Was the message about me? What have I done? What should I do?*

Raphael froze. He was not accustomed to fear, but at that moment he was greatly afraid his world was about to turn upside down. He wondered who his father would support should the Directeur turn on him, but he was afraid he knew the answer all too well. Then in an instant, the order in Raphael's world was restored.

The Directeur was not looking at him. He was looking at someone behind him. Raphael twisted around to see a Palestinian sauntering through the crowd and observing the people as if he was looking for someone. *The Palestinians are here!*

Raphael turned back to the Directeur to get his instructions. The Directeur signaled with his eyes and a subtle movement of his head. The silent communication was all Raphael needed. He turned and stalked his prey.

Raphael thanked God and asked his forgiveness for momentarily doubting his support. At the same time he reached into his pocket and nimbly slid his razor from its phone cover compartment. He kept his hand in his pocket. A simple reflection off the blade could draw the attention of the Israeli security officers. Killing a man in a crowded section of the Old City without being seen and arrested would take all of Raphael's skill. He reveled in the challenge.

Raphael was careful in his actions, but the Palestinian seemed to sense his presence the way an impala senses a cheetah hiding in the high grass. Raphael guessed his movements had mimicked the Palestinian's too closely. The Palestinian's peripheral vision must have communicated a message of danger to his unconscious mind.

Raphael was close enough to the Palestinian to hear the rate of his breathing increase. He was nervous. Raphael assessed where the Palestinian would go to find safety. He slowed down, turned to his left, and flipped his razor open with his thumb. As predicted, the Palestinian broke from the crowd and walked around the back of a stone kiosk in the direction Raphael had just taken. The move was a critical error.

Raphael seized his opportunity. With three long strides he was on his prey.

Chapter 102

This is absurd! Hamdi would do anything Ya Sidi asked of him, but what he was doing now was ludicrous. He was willing to sacrifice his life without question to advance Islam or to free his people from Jewish domination, but what they were doing now amounted to foolish risk. They had explosives and weapons in the trunk of a car in a municipal parking lot. How long could they remain there before they were discovered?

Having had lost sight of Ya Sidi and Milak in the throng of people, Hamdi felt alone. He had no way of knowing if they were still searching or had given up. Perhaps they had already come to the same conclusion–that there was no one at the Jaffa Gate of interest.

I am done with this!

Though ready to return to the car, Hamdi was hesitant to do so without speaking to Ya Sidi first. He began looking for a place to make a call in private. He saw a stone kiosk several meters ahead of him to the left.

A wave of discomfort rolled over him. He sensed a presence nearby. It was just a dark blur like smoke from a flame, but it was enough for him to conjure up the stories of the jinn he had heard as a child. The Qur'an spoke of three types of sentient creatures–angels, humans, and jinn. The jinn, like humans, had free will. Shaytan, or Satan as the Christians knew him, was a jinn. He had enjoyed special privileges in Paradise until he had refused to bow before Adam. After being expelled from Paradise he tempted and tormented humanity.

Like humans, jinn were both good and evil. They lived in a parallel world and were usually invisible or shadowy. Occasionally they took human form to torment or murder their victims. A chill shot through Hamdi's body, and his hair stood up on end.

Calm yourself. You are not a child.

He needed Ya Sidi. He was his rock. He headed for the kiosk and turned to go behind it. With his back to the wall he would be able to see anyone or anything coming toward him.

As soon as Hamdi cleared the edge of the kiosk, he knew he had made a mistake. A shadow engulfed him. *The stories of the jinn are true.* He could not figure out which way to run. He reached into his pocket for his knife, but he was too slow. A giant hand covered his mouth, and another hand slid across his throat. The shadow moved on as if it floated on the breeze, leaving him in pain and spurting blood.

Hamdi fell on his side to the concrete, wide-eyed and unable to scream. He grasped his throat but could not stop his life from escaping through his fingers. The blood pooled beneath him and spread out to the outer edges of the kiosk. A nearby Jewish woman rushed to his side. She kneeled and looked down on him with both concern and helplessness in her eyes.

Hamdi mustered the last of his strength to reach up to her with his bloody hand. He grabbed her arm, pulled her closer, and used his eyes to plea for help. Blood began spurting on the woman, and her face contorted into sheer terror. He heard only the beginning of her scream.

Chapter 103

Raphael did not even break stride. He dropped the Palestinian next to the kiosk wall, slipped the razor back into his pocket in a fluid movement, and continued until he was back in the middle of the churning mass of humanity. He had performed the entire act with such speed and professionalism that only a few drops of blood stained the cuff of his shirt. With nonchalance he pulled down his coat sleeve to cover it.

He had been careful there were no witnesses or lines of sight from the security cameras to capture what he had done. He knew the Israelis would piece together multiple images from the cameras in the area and see the Palestinian go behind the kiosk but not come out. They would also see Raphael passing behind the kiosk without stopping. Though he had been as careful as he could be with the angle of his face, there was no hiding his massive physique. It was likely they would figure out who he was.

It was also highly probable they would assume he had committed the murder. But they would have no proof. Raphael hoped the Israelis would not care enough about the death of a Palestinian terrorist to investigate thoroughly. If they did and if they pursued him, he had faith the Directeur was powerful enough to help him escape any charges.

Raphael was halfway back to the Directeur before high-pitched feminine screams behind him announced the discovery of the body. The crowd panicked. Assuming a terrorist attack, everyone began running to wherever they perceived safety to be. The Israeli security guards converged on the source of the screams behind the kiosk. People ran into each other. They ran into Raphael. Some people stumbled to the ground to be trampled by others. It was pandemonium.

Raphael took no notice. He had one objective. The Directeur and his father were already walking back toward the taxi stand. He needed to get to them without being apprehended. He closed the distance with long strides and merged alongside them as if they were out for an afternoon stroll.

His father noticed the blood stains peeking out from under his coat sleeve. "Are you all right, my son?"

Raphael nodded.

His father put his hand on his arm and smiled. "You are a great help to our cause. God will reward you."

Raphael smiled at the prospect. That was all he wanted–to please his father, the Directeur, and God.

The Directeur picked up the pace. "We must hurry. I know where they are going. This time we will be there ahead of them."

Chapter 104

A couple of meters behind Neuville Al-Jamal stood hunched with the appearance of a man much shorter than his true height. The Frenchman's arrogance was beyond belief. Al-Jamal was standing right next to him, but the Frenchman had not recognized him. Killing him would be a service to the world.

Al-Jamal had not had an opportunity when he felt comfortable shoving his knife into Neuville's ribs. He had hoped Neuville would move to a more advantageous position, but the Frenchman seemed to sense the safety of his current location. The Frenchman was not worth Al-Jamal's freedom or, even worse, his death. *I have a far greater destiny than the killing of one despicable man.* As he watched Neuville orchestrating the actions of other people out of sight, he realized how much he had underestimated the man he thought to be a simple religious bureaucrat.

A short middle-aged man in wire-rimmed glasses walked up to Neuville. *This is his help? Surely not!* The two men watched something happening in the crowd and whispered in French. Al-Jamal understood only one of the words–*Palestinien.*

Screams from a distance pierced the air, and the crowd scattered in panicked confusion. Al-Jamal did not miss the Israeli security guards rushing to the source of the screams. *This is my chance. Allah has created a diversion.* He reached into his pocket and grasped the hilt of his knife. It was not much of a weapon, but it would be enough. Before he could step forward, Neuville and the shorter man began weaving through the running people toward the Jaffa Gate. Unlike everyone else, they remained calm. *They know what happened.*

Al-Jamal carefully followed to one side. The Frenchmen spoke as they walked, but he could not pick out many words. One word that came up multiple times sounded like a name–Raphael. In Arabic, Raphael was the angel Israfil. He would signal the Judgment Day by blowing a horn. *Is that what the Frenchmen think is happening now? I have their judgment.*

Al-Jamal moved in closer to the two men. As he was about to strike, a gigantic man joined them. Al-Jamal cursed himself. Again, he had underestimated the Frenchman. This time it had cost him his opportunity to take his life. *I will not trade my life for his. If Allah wants to send his soul to hell, he will bring him under my knife again.*

Al-Jamal returned his knife to his pocket and searched the crowd for Hamdi and Milak. They needed to get to their car. The Frenchman could hunt his treasure. Al-Jamal and his men would return to their original strategy.

As he changed directions, he heard Neuville use a word he recognized. *Cenacle.*

Chapter 105

The screams told Reese his prediction had come true. The Frenchmen had spilled blood on Israeli soil. He hoped it was not Randall or someone in his group. As the wave of people reached him, he saw the three men rejoin in the middle of the havoc. *They're on the move.* Their course indicated they were returning to get a taxi. *They must have a new destination.* He surfed the crowd and let it push him in the same general direction.

Where the hell is Koenig?

When the Frenchmen reached the taxis, Reese chuckled at their frustration. The taxis were flooded in a tidal wave of tourists and anyone else who did not have a car parked nearby. The roads were congested like Boston at rush hour. No one was going anywhere in a hurry.

The leader of the Frenchmen spoke to the other two men. "Venir. Nous pouvons prendre un taxi quelques blocs d'ici. Si nécessaire, nous pouvons marcher au Cenacle."

Hell! Reese wished his French was better.

The other two men nodded, and the three Frenchmen began walking through the confusion to Reese's left.

Reese guessed they were going to look for a taxi elsewhere. And they wanted to get to a place called *cenacle*. Reese had never heard the term. He did not know if it was a proper name, a geographical landmark, or something else. He needed help.

He scanned the area and found one of the many tour guides nearby. She appeared to be struggling to keep her group together while they waited for transportation. He walked up to the guide, who was instructing her group in German. "Excuse me. Do you speak English?"

The guide seemed upset by the interruption. Reese used body language to let her know he was not going away.

"Yes," she replied in a strong Israeli accent. "Can I help you?"

"I hope so. Have you heard of a place called *cenacle*?"

"Of course. It is the Upper Room."

Reese was even more confused. The look on his face must have relayed his puzzlement because the tour guide looked at him like he was an idiot. She raised her hands in the air and used them to emphasize the words as she spoke them.

"The Upper Room. The Coenaculum. The site of the Last Supper. The room where Jesus washed the feet of his disciples."

Reese strained to pull up childhood memories. Jesus and his disciples met in someone's house for the Last Supper, right before he died. He recalled the painting of Jesus with his disciples spread to each side of him at a table. "Yes. I know the room you mean. But I've never heard it called by that name. That room still exists today?"

The guide's mouth morphed into a wry smile. "Well, there is a room on a site. In Jerusalem we have a site for everything. Judaism, Christianity, Islam–anything you are willing to pay to see."

"Can you tell me how to get there?"

The guide pointed in the same direction the Frenchmen had walked. "Mount Zion. Follow the wall."

Reese knew he had all the information he was going to get. "Thank you."

The guide returned to her tour group like a shepherd gathering and caring for her flock. Reese turned and hurried to catch up to the Frenchmen. At least he knew where he was going.

Chapter 106

Lauren had sensed Shane and Amit had something up their sleeves. Her suspicion of a ruse had been confirmed when she witnessed the conversation between Shane and Clisson. Clisson had left foolishly happy with what Shane had told him.

As soon as they were outside the cathedral she pulled Shane close to her side and slowed their pace until they trailed the others. She looked up at him with a smirk but serious eyes. "You and Clisson. What was that about? And where's Gustave?"

Shane avoided eye contact. "Clisson couldn't stand not knowing where we're going."

"He seemed happy. Did you tell him?"

"I had him send Gustave ahead to scout the Cenacle. I want to be sure no one's waiting for us there."

Lauren wished she had taken more excursions during her visits to Jerusalem. "The Cenacle? I don't recall it."

"It's the re-creation of the room that served as the meeting place for Jesus and his disciples while they were in Jerusalem. It's where he taught them lessons such as when he washed their feet, where he presided over the Last Supper, where he appeared to his disciples after his resurrection, and where the Holy Spirit filled those same disciples at Pentecost. When Jerome translated the New Testament into Latin in the late fourth century, he translated the Greek words for *upper room* into a single Latin word, *coenaculum*. A coenaculum was a dining room located on the second floor. Over time, the Latin word coenaculum became the English word *cenacle*."

"It's a re-creation?"

"Tradition is the Cenacle was on the second floor of the home of Mary, the mother of John Mark. The house was located on Mount Zion. When the Roman general Titus put down the first Jewish revolt, he knocked down every building in Jerusalem and the surrounding area, including the Jewish Temple. The Romans did nothing half-ass. Josephus, who was with Titus, wrote if someone unfamiliar with Jerusalem was passing by, he wouldn't've been able to tell a city had ever been there. The original building housing the Upper Room would've been leveled."

Lauren was getting lost in Shane's history lesson. "I don't understand. Was the building restored?"

"Let me lay it out for you. It's not important that you remember the details. But you'll get the gist of why it's important to us."

Lauren pretended to be hurt by Shane's insinuation. "I'll try to keep up."

Shane laughed. "You know what I mean. The building housing the Upper Room was Jesus' Jerusalem headquarters. It remained so under James and Simon, the subsequent heads of the Christian sect. As we know, before Titus destroyed Jerusalem, Simon led the Jewish Christians to Rihab near Pella. Shortly after the war, the Christians returned to Jerusalem. The tenth century church historian Euthychius wrote he had sources putting their return in the year 73. They found their headquarters leveled."

Lauren eyes widened in reflex. "That must have been a bad day."

"Probably. So on that site they built a synagogue where they could meet and worship. They built it with its length, width, and height in proportion to Solomon's Temple. And in the walls they re-used large rectangular blocks of carved stone from the Temple destroyed by the Romans."

"Some kind of symbolism?"

"It was more than symbolism. They believed using the same materials in the same dimensions transferred the sacredness of the former building into the new one. Adding to the theme of new versus old was the location. From Mount Zion the synagogue overlooked the site where the Temple stood before its destruction. But instead of orienting the synagogue toward the site of the Temple as Jews had traditionally done, they pointed it toward the site of Jesus crucifixion and resurrection, the site where the Church of the Holy Sepulchre now stands. That's one way we know it wasn't a later Byzantine church because they always pointed east. According to the fourth century bishop Epiphanius, after Hadrian put down the second Jewish revolt about sixty years later, the Romans found the synagogue on Mount Zion. Later Christian Romans gave the synagogue the name *Church of the Apostles.*"

Some of what Shane was saying sounded like legend to Lauren. Legends promising treasure were common but seldom produced anything. "How much of what you're saying's fact versus guesswork?"

"We know all this is true because during Israel's War of Independence a mortar shell damaged the building housing the Cenacle, and an Israeli archaeologist named Jacob Pinkerfeld supervised the repairs. While doing so, he removed some damaged marble floor slabs and found the original walls and floor and a niche in the apse that was used to house the Torah scrolls. About five inches below the current floor, he found the plaster floor built by the Crusaders. Then about nineteen inches below the Crusader floor, he found a Roman or Byzantine mosaic floor. Then about four inches below that floor, he found the original plaster and stone floor. When measured from the original floor, the Torah niche was at the exact height you would expect in a first century synagogue."

"I'm confused. So it's not a synagogue today?"

"Yes and no."

Lauren huffed. "Why can't you ever give me a simple answer?"

Shane laughed. "The Jewish Christian synagogue continued for hundreds of years in some form, becoming more Christian as the Roman Empire became Christian. The Christian Roman Emperor Theodosius I built a church next to it, and the complex thrived until the year 614. That's when Islamic Persians conquered Jerusalem and destroyed the building. After that, it was rebuilt and destroyed several times. Rebuilt by the Persians only to be destroyed to the ground by the Muslim caliph Al-Hakim in the year 1009. Rebuilt by the Crusaders only to be destroyed again in 1219 by the Ayyubid sultan of Damascus. Rebuilt by Franciscans monks in the fourteenth century and then turned into a mosque by the Ottoman Empire in the sixteenth century. Pinkerfeld found evidence of each rebuilding project."

Lauren was amazed anyone could retain that much detail. "You really know a lot about this building."

"Of course. It's arguably the most important building in Christendom. The Crusaders built the second floor to house the upper room on top of the remains of the original synagogue walls. And Franciscan monks repaired the roof of the Cenacle, strengthening it with a gothic rib vaulting that's still there today. Then it was the Ottomans who inserted an Islamic, Mecca-facing prayer niche in the wall opposite the Jewish niche. From the Ottomans on, Christians were banned from the building until Israel's independence in 1948. Since then, Mount Zion's been part of Israel, and the Israeli Department of Religious Affairs now administers the building."

Lauren was still confused. "So there are two floors?"

"Yes."

"And the Cenacle's the upper floor?"

"Yes."

"A treasure the size we're looking for would be too great to be hidden on the second floor of a building. Why'd you have Clisson send Gustave there?"

Shane looked at her as if he had said too much and now did not know how to get out of it. Lauren saw motion and realized Amit and Clisson had closed the distance between them and were now facing them.

Amit was smiling. "Tell her about the Tomb of David."

Lauren perked up. *Tomb of David? Now that sounds like a place for a treasure.* She looked from Clisson to Shane and back again. Shane appeared not to know what to say. And Clisson looked like someone who just realized he had been duped.

Chapter 107

Chief Inspector Melech Koenig stepped out of his vehicle knowing he and his men were late. He had heard reports of the murder on his radio. A Palestinian had bled out after having his throat slashed. The news had come after a call from Calev Spielmann. The security chief had a dead Palestinian with a broken neck sitting on one of his toilets. Two murdered Palestinians in locations Detective Reese and the Frenchmen had visited added up to only one conclusion. Reese had been right.

Koenig admitted to himself he had not totally believed the American. Still, he had assembled a very capable unit–a total of ten experienced officers, including two marksmen and two bomb disposal specialists. It was not a full complement of officers for the two modified GMC Vandura vans, but they were a force to be taken seriously.

A young security officer stepped up and greeted him in Hebrew. "Chief Inspector Koenig?"

Koenig nodded. "What is your name, son?"

"Brickner, Aaron Brickner."

Koenig could tell he was stressed. "What is the situation?"

"Everything is calm now. We had quite a panic on our hands for a while. Fifteen people were injured before we could get control. They are getting treatment."

"And the murder? Any progress?"

"We have video from the cameras. The quality is not good, but they show a large black man following the victim behind a kiosk. Only the black man emerges. He walks out in the ensuing panic."

"Was he with anyone?"

"He did walk out with two similarly dressed men.

"Do you know where they went?"

"Not yet. We are trying to piece together video from other cameras."

Koenig surveyed the surrounding area and thought of Reese. If the Frenchmen were here and left, he probably had followed them. *That is what I would do.* "Any sign of an American detective? He was supposed to meet me here."

"No sir. But it has been chaotic to say the least."

Where are you, Detective Reese? Why haven't you called? Koenig pushed the numbers for Reese's mobile phone and listened as it rang. Reese did not answer. When the call transferred to voice mail, Koenig disconnected. *Harah!* Reese had probably set his phone to silent.

Koenig looked at the officer. His eyes revealed how tired he was. Koenig had been where the officer was now. "Help him," Koenig instructed his men. "But be ready to leave. We will be moving quickly when the call comes."

Chapter 108

Clisson did not know how angry to be. "What about the Tomb of David?"

Randall looked disappointed and frustrated, but he gestured for David to continue.

David appeared uncomfortable as if he had let something slip that should not have been said. "The Crusaders added the Upper Room as a representation of where Jesus and his disciples met. They were Bible literalists. The Last Supper, as well as other New Testament events occurred on the second floor of a building. They believed the first floor marked King David's tomb."

Clisson was confused. "Does it?"

"No, not the real tomb. About one hundred years ago, the royal tombs were found on the eastern hill, not the western hill, right where the Bible said they were."

Nothing fits together. "Did they find any treasure in the tombs?"

"No. In ancient times, there were rumors of vast treasure. Josephus wrote King Herod tried to loot David's tomb, but someone had already beaten him to it."

Lauren must have been experiencing similar difficulty following David's explanation. "Why'd the Crusaders think the Cenacle site was David's tomb?"

"We know what happened from a Spanish Jew named Benjamin of Tudela. He wrote a report to Constantinople about a story he heard in Jerusalem. The Crusaders were renovating the ancient synagogue that made up the first floor. While two Jews were working on the renovation, a wall collapsed. Behind the wall was a secret passage that led below ground to a palace with marble columns. They found some gold, silver, and jewels, including a golden crown and scepter. They assumed the palace held the tombs of David and the other kings of Israel."

Clisson jumped back in. "Did they take the treasure?"

"No. According to the story, before they could take anything, a strong wind came out of nowhere and blew them over. The men were so afraid, they fainted. When they woke up, they heard a voice telling them to leave. They ran back through the passageway and sealed the opening."

Clisson could not believe what he was hearing. "And they never went back?"

Randall joined the story. "The two workmen fell ill. After three days, the Crusaders found them in bed, but the workmen couldn't be persuaded to return to the site. They were convinced God didn't want men to go there. The Crusaders believed them. They accepted the site as David's tomb and marked the site with a sarcophagus, now known as the Cenotaph of David because David's remains lay elsewhere."

David continued. "Over time the local Jews and Muslims accepted the legend as history. The sarcophagus is still there, covered in a velvet cloth bearing a star for each year of Israel's independence and two Hebrew inscriptions. *David King of Israel lives forever* and *If I forget you, O Jerusalem, let my right hand wither.*"

Clisson still found the account hard to believe. "That's quite a story. But no one ever dug for the treasure?"

David shook his head. "The Franciscans managed the building as a holy site until 1524 when Suleiman the Magnificent seized control. He banished the Christians saying the prophets buried there shouldn't be polluted by infidels. To keep the Christians out, he declared both floors to be mosques. The site was under Islamic control until Israel took it in 1948. Since the site is revered by three religions, it's one of those sites the Israeli government treats very carefully. Who can visit which floor and which religion controls access have been fought over for centuries. The least thing can stir up a riot."

Lauren accented her conclusion by pointing her finger. "So you two are saying the rumored treasure is our war chest?"

David shrugged. "The story's a legend. No one in authority believes it to be fact. Today the first floor's a Jewish synagogue, and the second floor's open to Christian visitors. An Italian archaeologist by the name of Pierotti confirmed in 1859 there was a cave beneath the sarcophagus, but the Islamic religious leader of the day wouldn't let him go farther than a few steps. It was almost one hundred years before Pinkerfeld in 1951, and Pinkerfeld died before he could do a thorough examination beyond the foundations and walls."

Clisson paced back and forth. "So anyone can walk into a room that may contain the entrance to a treasure cave?"

David shook his head. "No. The cenotaph room is blocked with iron bars. And the entrance to the cave was filled with cement a long time ago. The Israeli Ministry of Religious Affairs had to put an end to the risk from would-be treasure hunters."

Clisson realized he finally had the true destination. He had to get to Gustave and Neuville. "Docteur Randall, enough of this. I assume you have a plan. Let's get to the Tomb of David and put it into action."

Randall stiffened. "All right. But before we go, everyone'll hand over your mobile phones to Amit. He'll take care of them."

Clisson reacted with indignation. "Sur vous quels sont à? What are you up to?"

"It's simple. Now that you know our destination, I don't want the information to get out."

Lauren handed her phone to Amit, but Clisson continued to react as if insulted. "So you are saying you do not trust me?"

Randall stepped directly in front of Clisson's face and held out his hand. "I'm not going to argue about it. You'll hand over your phone." He paused. "Remember, Monsieur Clisson, your bodyguard's no longer here."

Clisson knew he was outmatched without Gustave. "What about Gustave? He is on his way to the Cenacle where you sent him."

"He'll still be able to warn us if our way's not clear. We'll collect him when we get there."

Clisson sighed and relinquished his mobile phone to David, who placed it in his bag.

Randall seemed satisfied. "Now we can go."

Chapter 109

Reese stepped out of his taxi alongside a massive stone fortress with four corner towers, a large conical dome, and a domed bell tower. The perfectly cut rectangular stone blocks in the walls had been left rough on their outer side, giving the structure additional color and texture and adding to its medieval appearance. The taxi driver had said it was the Dormition Abbey, also called the Hagia Maria Sion Abbey.

The complex stood just outside the Zion Gate. In spite of how it looked, it was not a fortress. It was a church marking the site where Mary, the mother of Jesus, had fallen asleep for the last time and where her soul ascended to heaven. Its name in Latin, Dormition Sanctae Mariae, meant Sleep of St. Mary, and a wood and ivory statue of Mary in its basement crypt marked the exact location.

Looking up at the dome, Reese saw a mosaic of Jesus surrounded by women from the Bible. The bell tower rose in the distance far enough away that its shadow could not fall on the Muslim sacred place of Nabi Da'ud next door.

It was toward this adjoining building that Reese with some panic directed his attention. While walking outside the Old City wall, the three Frenchmen had successfully hailed a taxi. It had seemed like an eternity before Reese had found one to follow.

Tour groups moved through the area in front of the crowded building complex like flocks of birds clustered together in a crowded sky. He did not see the Frenchmen. Reese walked up to an elderly man listening to his guide describing the abbey's architecture. The guide spoke in English, and the man appeared to be American. "Excuse me. Do you speak English?"

The man appeared startled and somewhat disoriented. When he refocused, he smiled broadly. "Yes, I'm from Nebraska."

"I hate to bother you. But I'm a little lost."

The man responded in a grandfatherly tone. "Don't let it bother you, son. Happens to me all the time."

Reese's blood pressure was rising by the second, but he managed a smile. "Thanks for understanding. Do you know where the Cenacle is?"

"It's quite impressive." The man pointed to a corner section of the Dormition Abbey. "The entrance is around that corner."

"Thank you very much."

Reese broke into a sprint for the corner, contorting to dodge people in his path. As he ran he reached into his pocket for his mobile phone. *Shit.* He had missed a call.

He scolded himself for leaving his phone on silent but not checking it. The number was Koenig's.

Reese slowed to a walk and called the number. Koenig answered right away. He was not happy. "I'm at the Jaffa Gate. Where the hell are you?"

"Sorry, I've been busy. What took you so long?"

"Where are you?" Koenig repeated.

"I'm outside the Cenacle. That's where they're going."

"We're on our way. Don't do anything stupid."

The line went silent. Reese put the phone away and jogged the short remaining distance. He slowed to a stop and casually looked around the corner and down the wall.

There! The three Frenchmen were walking under an arched entry. The outer portion of the stone arch was about twenty feet high and twelve feet wide and somewhat pointed at the top. Inset was a shorter arch flatter at the top. Four semicircular steps led up to the entry, and two open metal gates swung on hinges to seal the entry when not in use. The men disappeared into a dark interior about twenty feet deep, then exited through a matching arch on the far side.

Reese trotted down the roughly hewn stone wall of the Dormition Abbey and then crept through the entry. On the other side was a cloistered courtyard. It was rectangular with a series of arches attached to the surrounding buildings to form covered walkways along the walls. He searched for the three men.

Where'd they disappear to?

Inside the courtyard, tour groups gathered by the language of their guide. As he walked, Reese sought out the English-speaking guides.

"The hill we stand on is misnamed," said one of the guides. "Byzantine religious pilgrims assumed the larger, flatter western hill must be the site of the original city of David. They called it Mount Zion. We know now the western hill was not incorporated within the walls of Jerusalem until the eighth century before the Common Era. Regardless of the error, the name stuck, and the western hill is still called Mount Zion."

Piss! No help. Reese continued walking.

"The Tomb of King David complex covers an area of one hundred thousand square feet. It is one of the holiest spots in Israel, which makes it one of the holiest sites in the world. Because of this fact, the complex is the home of many yeshivas, which are rabbinical schools. Though the site is administered by the Israeli Ministry of Religious Affairs, three religions are represented in the building. A Jewish synagogue is located on the lower level, which also includes the Tomb of David. The Christian Upper Room site is on the second level. And the roof is Muslim. We will enter the Tomb of David now."

Now we're getting somewhere. Reese stepped into the wake of the tour group. They walked toward the leftmost archway in the southwest corner of the courtyard. Reese subtly pulled Spielmann's handgun from the small of his back and buried it a few inches in a nearby trash receptacle. Then he followed the tour group through the archway and door beyond. Inside the doorway they passed through a security checkpoint.

The guide spoke lowly and respectfully. "We have entered a synagogue. This hallway passes through the first floor of the Crusader building constructed in the twelfth century. It was built on the foundation of an older synagogue dating to Roman times."

The hallway led them to a low, rectangular antechamber with piers and vaulting. Pictures of rabbis and Jewish symbols decorated the walls. Two square doorways framed with colorful tiles led to a second antechamber.

"What's this?" a woman in the tour group asked.

The woman was pointing to a niche in the wall partially hidden by a bookcase. The niche was covered with ceramic tiles, some of which were green and black in geometric designs.

"That is a mihrab," the guide explained. "Under the Ottoman ruler Suleiman the Magnificent this area was a mosque. The mihrab points to the Kaaba in Mecca such that Muslims know the direction to pray. The green and black geometric tiles are patches similar to the sixteenth century repairs performed on the Dome of the Rock."

The woman looked on in wonder. "I see."

"From here," the guide continued, "we will separate by gender to view the Tomb of David. Men and women worship separately to minimize distraction. Women will enter on the left and men on the right. Men, you must show respect for Jewish law and cover your heads. There is a cart with disposable paper yarmulkes if you do not have one. You will be able to view but not enter the tomb."

Reese could hear voices chanting prayers and psalms nearby.

The guide stood in place while the tour divided by gender. "When everyone has viewed the cenotaph room, we'll tour the Upper Room. Please take your time."

Reese attracted the guide's attention. "What if I want to go directly to the Upper Room? How would I do that?"

The tour guide gave him a look that made him feel like an unwelcome hitchhiker. "Go back to the entrance. There are steps to the second level."

"Thank you."

He broke eye contact and retraced his path until he found a parade of people climbing steps. He followed them to a large room with a tile floor and marble columns. Three freestanding columns down the middle of the room and three pillars on each of the two side walls subdivided the room into six naves. Arches connecting the columns and pillars gave each nave its own domed ceiling. Illumination of the room came from lights installed on the capitals of the columns and sunlight passing through blue stained glass windows highlighted with red and white designs and Persian writing.

Upon entering the room he heard another guide addressing her tour. "The Upper Room was constructed by the Crusaders and later repaired by the Franciscans. The architectural style is Cypriot Gothic. The column to the right of the entrance has drawn on it a Crusader shield bearing the name of the German city Regensburg. Carved into the capital of another column are two pelican chicks picking at the breast of a larger pelican. The pelican was a symbol of Jesus' death and resurrection based on an ancient belief that pelican mothers wound themselves to the point of death to feed their young with their own blood. Then they are resurrected."

There they are.

The Frenchmen stood together talking among themselves at the far side of the room. They seemed nervous and very uncomfortable. Reese tried to keep the nearest column between him and the three men while he waited for Koenig.

Who's that? The three Frenchmen were talking to a well-built fourth man. He looked familiar. *Shit! He was with Randall at the King David Hotel. Is Randall here as well?* Reese scanned the room for Randall or anyone else from his group. He found no one.

Something's going on. Reese began suspecting whatever the Frenchmen and Randall were into was about to come to a head. *Koenig, where the hell are you?*

Chapter 110

Clisson had already passed through the security inspection in the Cenacle / Tomb of David building. He stood waiting next to Lauren for Randall and David. David was having an issue. The agents appeared to be taking exception to his bag containing flashlights, night vision goggles, and an assortment of hand tools. They were speaking in Hebrew. As the emotion increased so did the volume. Reinforcements backed the original officers. The highest ranking officer stepped forward in front of David and demanded order. David showed him his credentials, but they had no effect. In fact, they may have made the security personnel even more resolute in their position.

After several frustrating minutes, one of the security officers waved Randall through the metal detector. He passed through cleanly and walked to his friend's side. David was launching verbal grenades at the lead officer. Clisson had seen this kind of situation before. David would soon find himself in serious trouble. Randall seemed to sense the officers were nearing their limit. He grasped David's arm and pulled him away.

Clisson greeted David with a reprimand. "What were you doing? We don't want attention."

David spoke with frustration. "I had to leave my bag. They say I can reclaim it when we leave."

"Don't we need it?"

Randall stepped between them. "We'll improvise. The building closes soon. We need to get Gustave. He should be in the room at the top of the steps. Let's go."

Clisson was not familiar with the layout of the Upper Room, but the last thing he wanted was for Randall and David to walk in on Gustave talking with Neuville. He called Randall back.

"Docteur Randall, perhaps you and Docteur David would serve us better if you remained on this level and finalized our plan. We still have some time before closing. I am perfectly able to retrieve Gustave by myself."

"All right. But don't get any ideas about running off."

"Docteur Randall, you wound me to the quick."

Clisson followed the other visitors up the steps and into the Upper Room. He worked himself through the people there until he found Gustave and Neuville. Two of Neuville's henchmen stood there with them. One of them was a giant with the look of a wild animal. The smaller man next to him had to be his handler.

Clisson put on his best face. "Bonjour, Directeur Neuville. Cet a été un pendant que. It has been a while."

"Bonjour, Monsieur Clisson," Neuville greeted. He pointed to the men next to him. "Monsieur de Vaux and his son Raphael."

Son? "Enchanté."

Neuville got right to the point. "We are here where you told us to go. But the treasure cannot be in this room. Where is it?"

Clisson was matter-of-fact. "Beneath the Tomb of David. I would have sent you the information, but Randall commandeered my phone. He is quite sharp. He may suspect we have exchanged communications."

Neuville looked skeptical. "The legend of treasure under the Tomb of David has persisted for centuries. I hope we are acting on more than legend. Are you saying the Sicarii Gospel has directed them there?"

"That is exactly what I am saying. They have proof."

De Vaux took a half step forward. "The Tomb of David is sealed off, with iron bars across the openings. Even if you were able to sneak in, the only known opening to the cave below is sealed with cement. How do they intend to enter the cave?"

"I do not know. I suggest it is time to find out. We know the location, and we have Gustave and your man there. Randall and David are academics."

Clisson did not miss Neuville's bristling at his implication of academics being weak. He did not care. He would deal with Neuville and his men after they found the treasure. "They are waiting downstairs. I will draw them away from the security station. Then we take them and make them tell us what we need."

He turned to leave, but Neuville hesitated. "And the woman? She has given us a lot of trouble."

Clisson would sacrifice anyone to get the help he wanted. "*Once* we have the treasure, you can have her. Do to her what you want."

Chapter 111

Al-Jamal watched as the Jewish archaeologist and the rest of his group disappeared into the Tomb of David complex. The scientist in Al-Jamal knew the real tomb lay elsewhere, but the Muslim in him revered the site as the prophet David's resting place. The Arabic name for the nearby gate the Jews called the Zion Gate was Bab a-Nabi Daud, the Gate of the Prophet David. The Tomb of David was a sacred site that had been defiled by the Jews since their illegal seizure of the land over a half century ago.

Al-Jamal had deduced the cave under the cenotaph room had to be the target and not the Cenacle. He knew the centuries-old rumors and legends of treasure but had always thought the stories far-fetched, even child-like. Now he thought differently.

Getting this far had not been easy. He had lost two men. Since getting further would be even more difficult, he had called in two more followers–Zeid Eiwan and Sohaib Faisal. Any more men may have drawn the security officers' attention in time for them to ready themselves, even call in help. He needed surprise.

This is it. "Let's go!"

The four Palestinians stepped out of their car in unison. They hid their AK-47 assault rifles under jackets, but they still drew the attention of the surrounding people. Confused murmuring filled their wake, and some of the tourists began hurrying in the opposite direction.

It does not matter. We will not be coming back this way.

They walked with large strides in a straight line through the courtyard and into the building. Upon entering the security station, they pulled their assault rifles and opened fire. The Israeli security officers did not have a chance. They fell backward at odd angles riddled with bullets.

More officers rushed down the steps and through the hall, firing their weapons at Al-Jamal and his men. Bullets embedded in the scanning equipment and whizzed by Al-Jamal's ears. Using the security machinery as cover, he and his men had a significance advantage. After a brief but intense battle, the reinforcing officers also lay dead.

Al-Jamal leaped from behind the scanner. "Come!" He led the way down the hall, with the metal detector alarm blaring behind them. Trapped and wounded tourists cringed behind whatever cover they could find. "Get out or die!"

Al-Jamal's men accentuated the command with gun shots into the floor and ceiling. The people poured past them toward the exit, their panicked screams echoing throughout the building.

Al-Jamal laughed. There were so many of them, they could have easily overpowered him and his men, but no one interfered. They were not warriors. Nor were they committed to a cause worth dying for.

Al-Jamal and his men made steady progress through the chambers to the wall where two barred openings separated them from the Tomb of David. While the others stood guard, Milak kneeled and removed a bag from his shoulder. From the bag he pulled Semtex and applied it to the wall. Then he added a blasting cap and timer. "Ready!"

The four Palestinians ran back into the adjoining chamber and lay low to the ground behind anything they could find. A few seconds later an explosion shook the building. The blast shot debris through the doorway against the far wall, and the air filled with dust. Al-Jamal coughed and raised his shirt to cover his nose and mouth. He examined the walls and ceiling but saw no structural damage to the building.

Al-Jamal led his men back to the cenotaph viewing area. A large gaping hole with rough edges now connected the two rooms. Al-Jamal bent over and stepped through the hole. The sarcophagus was larger than Al-Jamal had expected. It was covered by a velvet cloth and plastic cover, and above it were Torah crowns from synagogues destroyed in the Holocaust. Burn marks dating back to Islamic attacks over a millennium ago still marred the walls. Elsewhere the walls bore dark staining from centuries of smoke from candles.

"Zeid and Sohaib, stay where you are," he commanded. "If anyone comes, you know what to do. Milak, come with me."

He ran behind the sarcophagus and kneeled to examine the floor. In the center just behind the sarcophagus the floor varied in color. The change indicated where the cave opening had been sealed.

Al-Jamal pointed next to the spot. "Milak, here!"

Once again Milak expertly applied a small amount of Semtex and set it to explode. Al-Jamal and Milak ran back through the hole in the wall and found cover. The explosion erupted.

Al-Jamal, followed by his three men, re-entered the cenotaph room and hurried through the cloud of dust to the space behind the sarcophagus. The velvet cloth was torn and shifted, but the sarcophagus had sustained only minor damage. Al-Jamal was not concerned about the cloth. *A Jewish pollution.* He was more interested in the jagged hole in the floor.

Milak handed him a flashlight. Al-Jamal lay on his stomach with his face over the hole. What he saw surprised him. Highly worn stone steps extended downward. *Steps are meant for people.*

Al-Jamal found the discovery both exciting and concerning. The fact that people had used the cave for some purpose gave credence to the possibility of the treasure being there. On the other hand, if a lot of people knew the treasure's location, there was a high likelihood the treasure had been looted long ago.

Al-Jamal twisted around such that he sat on the edge with his legs in the hole. Then he shifted his weight and supported himself on the stone steps. He stepped down the first few steps and bent over such that his head was beneath floor level. He illuminated the cave the best he could and estimated its size as over thirty meters long by fifteen meters wide by four meters deep. There appeared to be a passageway at the far end.

"Get down here!" he cried to his men.

Milak hesitated. "Ya Sidi, we will be trapped. How will we escape?"

"Allah will provide us another way out."

Al-Jamal continued down the steps, followed by his three men. They disappeared into the darkness.

Chapter 112

Neuville was leading Clisson and the others toward the Upper Room exit when they heard the gunshots–too many to count and so close together they had to be from automatic weapons. The gunshots and associated screams were coming from the first floor. Matching screams filled the Upper Room.

People talked frantically among their groups wondering how bad the situation was. Neuville knew. Someone had stormed the Tomb of David. He doubted Randall and David would commit such an act, but Al-Jamal and his men would.

Neuville began walking toward the exit again. He serpentined through the other visitors until he was at the top of the steps. Before he could descend, more rapid fire began. It was followed by more scattered shots accompanied by vibrations in the floor.

In unison everyone in the room feared they were no longer safe from what was happening below. Their instinct to flee overcame any fear of what they might encounter. People sobbed and cried out in terror. A few people broke for the steps, and everyone else followed. The crest of the human wave pushed Neuville forward onto the steps, while the exit bottlenecked the progress of the crowd behind him.

An explosion shook the building. Material from the ceiling and walls fell to the floor. Dust and other small debris clouded the staircase. The panic increased, as did the pressure behind Neuville. A few people stumbled and tumbled past him down the steps.

The explosion confirmed for Neuville the Palestinians had somehow discovered their destination. He found it difficult to believe even they would wreak that kind of destruction on a sacred site.

Another explosion rocked the building, lifting the terrified tourists to yet another level of fear. The torrent of humanity reached the first floor and dropped Neuville to one side.

As he waited for de Vaux and Raphael, screams of a different tone drew his attention to where tourists had stumbled into the slaughtered security officers. Blood spatter on the walls was so thick it still oozed toward the floor. Pools of blood around the bodies were deepening, spreading, and joining such that there was no place to run without stepping in the sticky liquid.

The visitors spewed from the building into the courtyard. Most of them continued to run until they were totally free from the building complex. Others stopped and looked behind them in morbid curiosity. They gathered in small groups as if other inquisitive people standing nearby could protect them from what else might emerge.

De Vaux and Raphael joined Neuville and stood to each side of him. As the last of the visitors rushed by, Clisson and Gustave re-united with them as well. Neuville greeted them with his conclusion. "Randall and David cannot be the cause. It must be Al-Jamal and his men."

Clisson agreed. 'Oui, but where are they. And where are Randall and David?"

"Let's find out."

Neuville began stepping over and around bodies through the hall toward the Tomb of David. He had not gone far before de Vaux and Raphael overtook him and began leading the way. He praised God for their loyalty.

When they reached the cenotaph room, they saw the hole in the wall and destruction within. Neuville knew he had been correct. It was not difficult for him to guess where the Palestinians were now.

De Vaux lightly gripped his arm. "Wait here. Let us check it out."

Raphael nodded and stepped through the hole in the wall that once had screened spectators from the sacred site. His massive frame barely fit through the jagged opening. Before proceeding he turned to help his father through the hole. They crept around both ends of the sarcophagus and rejoined on the far side. They stood there staring at the floor. Their expressions confirmed Neuville's suspicions.

"Monsieur Clisson," Neuville began. "We need to find some flashlights. And have your man retrieve some of the security officers' weapons. This cave has a lot more than bats to worry about."

Chapter 113

Reese stood in the courtyard cursing his luck. Terrorists had chosen to bomb the Tomb of David, and now he had no idea where the Frenchmen were. He had been swept out of the Cenacle by panicked tourists. Once released into the courtyard, he had retrieved his weapon, secured it in his belt under his shirt, and searched in vain. *Shit, Koenig! If you'd got here in time, none of this would've happened.*

Reese was about to reenter the building when another commotion drew his attention. Six Israeli military men rushed into the courtyard with weapons drawn. They took up positions in a pre-specified formation. They were dressed in dark body armor and helmets and carried Tavor TAR-21 assault rifles. Their arrival was the final straw for the remaining visitors, who quickly dispersed leaving only Reese in the open space.

A middle aged, balding Israeli of average height entered the courtyard surrounded by a handful of other men. Like his men, he was dressed in dark body armor, but his head was uncovered. His face looked leathery, and what little hair he had was light gray.

Reese met him in stride. "Chief Inspector Melech Koenig?"

"Yes. Detective Reese?"

"Yes. You're timing's perfect."

Koenig did not react to Reese's sarcasm. "We're here now. What do you know?"

"Not much. I was on the second floor with the Frenchmen in sight. Then there were gunshots and two explosions. I'm afraid the security officers took the brunt of it."

"And the Frenchmen? Were they involved?"

"I don't know. But they're nowhere to be found."

"Let's see what we're up against."

Koenig signaled his men to enter the Tomb of David. Without further direction they moved forward in formation and entered in a pre-determined sequence. Reese and Koenig waited for an uncomfortable several minutes before one of the men emerged and signaled Koenig to join them. "The building is clear, sir. But you need to see this."

Reese followed Koenig past the man into the hallway. Blood and bodies were everywhere. The carnage struck Reese as much more gruesome than it had appeared when he had swept past it. With his adrenaline subsided and the crowd absent, he took in the full depth of the horror.

Koenig and Reese continued down the hall into the antechambers beyond. Koenig's man directed them until they arrived at the cenotaph room. Some of his men were on the near side of the screening wall, and some of them had passed through a hole blown into the wall. They all seemed anxious for Koenig to see what they had found.

The man leading them pointed to the other room. "Sir, please step through."

Koenig hunched downward and stepped through the hole. Reese did the same, followed by Koenig's man. The men in the room stood scattered throughout, with two of them behind the sarcophagus.

The man who had brought them there joined the two men on the far side. "Here, sir. They escaped through the floor."

Reese followed Koenig to the far side of the sarcophagus. There they found a jagged hole blown through the floor. A void extended beneath it.

"They entered the cave," concluded Koenig.

Reese stepped closer to Koenig and spoke lowly into his ear. "The man I know may be down there. We may have both hostiles and friendlies."

Koenig yelled to his men. "I need to know everything there is to know about the cave in five minutes. And fetch the night vision equipment. We're going in."

Chapter 114

Lauren followed Shane and Amit about one hundred yards behind the Tomb of David / Cenacle complex. The area was grassy and shaded from the evening sun, allowing them to hide within the shadows. Upon seeing the grass, Shane had quoted the second treasure verse from the Sicarii Gospel.

"The Kingdom of God is like a treasure hidden in a field owned by a man who did not know the treasure was there."

As soon as Clisson had ascended the stairs out of sight, Shane and Amit had whisked her out of the building, collecting Amit's bag along the way. Shane led them along the walls and out of the courtyard in a direction leading behind the building. After clearing the structure, they half-jogged the short distance to an area void of buildings. It was a small field seemingly out of place amid all the historical, over the top construction. The field was apparently not interesting enough to attract anyone else's attention. They were alone.

They stopped in the center of the field and stared at something almost hidden by tall grass and other wild growth. It was a strange contraption that looked like a cage constructed from steel bars and mesh. It had to be centuries newer than the surrounding buildings, perhaps only decades old.

Lauren was confused. "I thought the treasure was under the Tomb of David. Why are we here?"

Shane and Amit did not answer her. Instead they kneeled and labored over the cage clearing the growth from a section of the mesh. Through the openings in the metal, Lauren could see the cage covered two doors held together with heavy chains and a brass padlock. Someone definitely wanted to keep people out of whatever was in there.

Shane gestured to the cage. "Help us strip away the mesh from the middle bars. I'll explain while we work."

Lauren maneuvered her body around Amit to help Shane pull on the steel mesh as Amit cut it with his wire cutters. The mesh was tight with heavy gauge and difficult to cut and bend backwards.

Shane spoke through his strain. "We told the truth about the legend of the Tomb of David. There's a cave system under the building. In fact it runs under most of Mount Zion. It may even connect to the Temple Mount and all the way under the location of the Holy of Holies. Some people think it's where the Ark of the Covenant was hidden."

"So why are we here and not there?"

Amit cut through another steel wire with a loud snap. "Like we said, the opening into the cave system from the Tomb of David is sealed. And for that matter, the cenotaph room itself is sealed. Clisson may be crazy enough to break into a national shrine, but we're not. Besides, it was only a matter of time before he double-crossed us. We had to get away from him."

"So what's this place?"

Shane alternated removing his hands from the mesh to let blood return to his fingers. "This is the place indicated by the Messianic Seal we found in Rihab. An elderly Greek Orthodox monk led a magazine editor here about fifty years ago. The monk was a hermit, but the editor somehow formed a friendship with him. While visiting the monk, the editor saw some artifacts the monk had retrieved from this cave before the Six Day War in 1967. They were engraved with the symbol they later called the Messianic Seal."

"What kind of artifacts?"

"Just some pieces of pottery and oil lamps."

"And some stone pieces thought to be used in ceremonies," Amit added. "About thirty pieces in total, though most of them have since disappeared."

Lauren still did not understand. "Ceremonies?"

Shane explained while using his weight to spread the mesh. "This cave's thought to be a sacred healing and baptismal grotto associated with the Jewish Christian synagogue next door. Converts would be purified through immersion in water and then anointed with oil. The monk found a marble slab with an Aramaic phrase on it–*For the Oil of the Spirit.* The practice of healing the sick by anointing them with oil in the name of the Lord is described in the Epistle of James in the New Testament. This cave may have been used when the original Upper Room still stood. It may've been where the apostles baptized three thousand converts on the Day of Pentecost, as described in the Book of Acts. And it almost certainly was used by the Jewish Christians when they returned to build their synagogue."

"Did the monk find any gold? Or jewelry?"

Amit shook his head. "No. But the cave system wasn't explored. The Israeli government shut it down. Too much political downside."

Shane released the mesh. "That's enough. Get the bar spreader in there."

Amit positioned another tool between two central bars. Shane held it in place while Amit operated it. It looked and functioned like a car jack. With each crank of a lever the tool expanded and spread the bars a fraction of an inch. Progress was slow and the work difficult, but the bars were giving way.

As Shane traded places with Amit to work the lever, gun shots disturbed the quiet. They were muffled as if from a distance, but they could have come from the Tomb of David complex. After a pause, more gunshots rang out. There was no doubt they were coming from the complex.

Shane looked at Amit. "You don't suppose Clisson would enter the Tomb of David by force?"

"I wouldn't put anything past him."

Lauren had no doubt Clisson would do whatever was required to get the treasure.

Shane completed the switch with Amit and began operating the spreader as quickly as he could. An explosion rang out. It was followed by quiet and then another more muffled explosion. "This area's about to be covered with Israeli security forces. We'd better get below ground."

Amit patted Shane's shoulder. "That's enough."

Shane removed the spreader from the bars, while Amit retrieved yet another tool. This time he held a small but highly leveraged bolt cutter. He reached into the opening they had created and cut the lock from the chains holding the doors together. He pulled the chains free and opened the doors.

Stale, musty air escaped from the cavity behind the doors. Lauren turned away from the smell. When she turned back, Amit was halfway into the opening and Shane was squeezing through the bars.

Amit held up his arm to slow Shane while he studied the cave with his flashlight. "Just a short drop. Then some steps down."

Shane leaned in. “Any spiders.”

“Some cobwebs. But I don’t see any spiders.”

Amit took out his night vision goggles and handed the other set to Shane. He relayed the flashlight back through Shane to Lauren and then disappeared into the cave. Shane maneuvered through the bars and then the doors. Lauren remained where she was for several seconds. Another cave experience was not appealing.

“Lauren!” called Shane. “Get down here. And shut the doors behind you.”

I guess I don’t have much choice.

Chapter 115

Raphael stood silently in the blackness of the stone chamber. It was about fifteen meters wide and over twice as long with a ceiling that stood well above his head. Everyone else in his group carried a flashlight, and together they illuminated a large portion of the cave in front of them. He preferred the safety and comfort of the dark.

Except for a few stones scattered around the floor, the cave was completely empty. The flashlight beams moved haphazardly and rapidly along the floor and walls but ultimately came together in a far corner where there appeared to be a dark opening in the stone. The opening was large enough to be a passageway into another section of the cave system. The concentrated flashlight beams shortened as the Directeur and Clisson crept toward the corner followed by de Vaux and Gustave. Raphael fell in behind.

"Gustave!" barked Clisson in a hoarse whisper.

The bodyguard ran to the cave wall next to the opening. Everyone in their own way readied their weapons. Raphael had spurned an assault rifle for a Glock 19 pistol. He stood back, willing to let Clisson's fool bodyguard take the risk of discovering whether armed attackers awaited them on the other side.

Gustave curved his head around the edge of the opening and back again. Apparently not seeing anyone, he spun a couple of steps through the passageway, expertly pointing both his assault weapon and his flashlight into the void. Nothing happened.

Gustave called back without turning around. "It's a tunnel. It drops downward and connects to another chamber at the far end."

The others in the group lowered their weapons and pointed their flashlights down the shaft. Raphael sensed they were not far behind the Palestinians. He looked over their heads and listened for any sign of what awaited them.

The tunnel was about three meters wide and tall and twenty meters long, widened and squared off by occupants sometime in the distant past. He knew if the Palestinians realized they were being followed, this shaft would be the perfect place to confront them.

The Directeur whispered to de Vaux. "We have come too far to stop."

Raphael's father put his hand on Raphael's arm. Raphael understood he could not follow behind any longer.

He and Gustave entered the tunnel side by side. When they had made it about halfway without incident, the others followed. Gustave exited the far end first, followed by Raphael. They kneeled while Gustave used his flashlight to survey their location and the others joined them.

The flashlights did little to illuminate the giant chamber. It was far larger than the previous chamber, perhaps fifty meters square and six meters high. Man-made fixtures hung in various places on the walls and rotting ropes hung occasionally from the ceiling. Raphael assumed they once held sources of light, such as oil lamps or torches, but in their current condition, they gave the room the appearance of a dungeon.

As the flashlight beams continued their paths across the chamber, the far wall caught Raphael's eye. When the beams joined, the full extent of the structure became visible. Four man-made columns stretched from floor to ceiling and guarded a smooth stone wall with a dark upright rectangular opening in its center. Each column was about a meter in diameter and the doorway was about three meters wide and four meters high. Taken in its entirety, the structure looked like a stone palace that had survived below ground for centuries.

The group separated with the Directeur in the middle, Clisson and Gustave together several meters to his left, and Raphael and his father several meters to his right. As they walked, a strong draft exited the doorway and filled the chamber. It seemed to be carrying a supernatural voice. If the high-pitched sounds were forming words, Raphael could not understand the language, but it definitely sounded like a message from heaven, or hell. They had all heard the stories that God protected the caves. Everyone dropped to their knees.

As the draft and voice dissipated, two shadows rotated from behind the columns and fired their automatic weapons in the direction of Raphael and the others. These were not spirits or angels. They were men intent on ambush.

As Raphael had predicted, the flashlight lenses acted as targets. He took the flashlight from his father's hand and turned it off. Then he pulled his father toward the side of the cave just before bullets ricocheted off the stone floor.

Everyone else went flat. Some of his group returned fire, and for a while the cave was filled with bursts and echoes. Raphael heard a groan to his far left.

"Turn off your lights," commanded the Directeur. "And cease fire."

Raphael thanked God the Directeur did not sound injured.

With the flashlights off, Raphael could not see his own hands, but his other senses compensated. He felt the fine dirt atop harder stone beneath him. He smelled the familiar scent of his father nearby. He heard low groans from his left that told him someone was indeed wounded. And he heard the men still there in front of the door. He envisioned them leaning against the columns and rubbing their backs against the stone.

"Andre!" the Directeur whispered as if the name was a command.

Raphael sensed his father reaching for him, and they clasped hands. "Once again, we must call on you. You must clear our way."

He handed his father the flashlight. Confident he was invisible in the darkness, Raphael stood up and made his way silently to his right until he found the cold stone of the cave wall. Using the stone as a guide to the front of the chamber, he crept without noise, careful to move any objects on the floor with his feet before shifting his weight forward. When he felt the direction of the wall change, he knew he had arrived behind the columns. After taking several more steps inward along the wall, he took out his razor, crouched, and waited.

He did not have to wait long. He heard a shuffle of movement. Then an assault rifle erupted in front of him firing in the opposite direction. The muzzle flare lit up the column and the upper half of the Palestinian like the flash of a camera.

When the Palestinian rotated back into position behind the column, Raphael leaped into him and pressed him against the column. Raphael felt the Palestinian's assault rifle and two hands pinned between his torso and the man's chest. The Palestinian grunted and struggled to escape. Raphael grabbed the Palestinian's head with his left hand and forced it backward into the column. Then with his right hand he slashed at the man's jugular vein with his razor. The man let out a yell, but the spurting of warm liquid against Raphael's shoulder told him he had struck his target. The man crumpled to the ground. He was already unconscious and would be dead in a little over a minute.

"Zeid?" Fear filled the Arabic voice to Raphael's right.

Raphael silently returned to the wall and made his way to the doorway. Not hearing an answer, the second Palestinian would run, and there was only one exit.

Quick footfalls on the stone let Raphael know he was right. He swung out his massive right arm and knocked the running Palestinian to the ground. Raphael heard the assault rifle clang backward on the stone, and he could hear the Palestinian struggling to breathe. Raphael had knocked the breath out of him, a condition he made worse when he dropped his knee and all his weight on the man's chest just below his sternum.

Raphael took great satisfaction from the Palestinian's helplessness. "Pardon moi, mon ami, Votre mort est exigée."

Raphael slashed the man's face, throat, chest, and arms until the Palestinian no longer struggled. He remained on the man's chest with his head bowed until the rush coursing through his body subsided. He stood and found his way to one of the columns. "Clear!"

Three flashlights turned on almost in unison. Raphael guarded his eyes from the beams until they shifted sideways, where they exposed Gustave lying in a dark pool of blood. Raphael walked in his direction. The bodyguard was not dead, but he had taken a round near the top of his shoulder. The bullet had exited his back near his shoulder blade.

The Directeur addressed Clisson. "If you want, you can take your man back. We are moving forward."

Clisson refused. "No. Help me bandage him. He is coming with us."

Raphael looked at the semiconscious man. He knew it would require a miracle for him to survive the day without immediate medical help. Still, he bent down and tore the man's shirt into strips and used them to bandage his shoulder. The man groaned as Raphael tightened the cloth and secured it with a knot.

When he was done, Raphael saw a gleam of confidence in the Directeur's shadowed eyes. While Gustave lived, removing Clisson was problematic. With him wounded and probably dying, the power had shifted heavily to the Directeur. Raphael sat back in awe. God smiled on the Directeur like no other.

Another strong draft circled through the chamber and repeated its haunting cry.

Chapter 116

Shane stood on the cave floor and scanned the spherical grotto. It spanned about twenty-five feet in diameter, arcing to a dome about ten feet high at its zenith. It had been sculpted by decades of human habitation, though it still retained a rough stone texture. To the right was a square pit. Shane estimated the sides at a little over two feet long and the depth at about six feet. Steps led down into the pit. "It's a mikvah."

"A mikvah?" Lauren repeated. "Like a bath tub?"

Amit corrected her. "A ceremonial bath. First century Jews used them for purification. Devout Jews and their religious leaders were obsessed with purity. They injected purity laws and issues of purity into every aspect of Jewish life."

Lauren seemed curious. "I don't think of people of that time as being all that clean."

Amit shook his head. "Purity was on many levels. Only one level was cleanliness. Hands were ritually washed, and bodies were immersed in baths. Another level was the bodily tissue itself. The skin had to be free from blemishes, rashes, cuts, and deformities. Then there was genetic purity. There could be no doubt to the parentage and ancestry of a Jew. If there was, he or she was declared a *mamzer* and not allowed to participate in many Jewish rituals. Blood connected Jews to God. It was so holy it could not be touched or consumed without defilement. Finally, there was spiritual purity."

Shane sighed. "Purity is why leprosy freaked them out so much. There were purity laws about every orifice of the body. Leprosy sores looked like orifices on the skin, but they didn't know how to purify them."

Amit continued. "Because of their obsession with purity, many Essenes were celibate. Those who had sex did so only to have children. They wouldn't enter Jerusalem until three days after having sex because they didn't want to defile the city. And they wouldn't take a bowel movement inside the city walls. Herod the Great built a special gate for the Essenes so they could walk outside to do their personal business."

Shane dropped to a knee to get a closer look. "There's a mikvah very similar to this one at Qumran."

Amit stood beside him but talked to Lauren. "Originally the purification ritual took place in a flowing stream. But life in the desert required a substitute. Mixing rain water and drawn water spiritually transformed the mikvah into a flowing stream. The seven steps into the water represented the seven days of creation. The Torah describes the act of creation as a *gathering of waters*. Immersing in a mikvah was returning to the purity of creation. The beginning."

Shane rose to his feet. "Initially, ritual baths were used to purify Jewish worshippers before entering the Temple. Forgiveness of sin came through purchased sacrifices. John the Baptist and Jesus offered a less expensive and simpler method of purification and forgiveness involving immersion and a direct relationship with God."

The tone of Lauren's voice changed. "So this cave was used by the Jewish Christian church?"

"Most likely," Amit confirmed. "They anointed the sick with oil and prayed over them as part of a healing ritual. New converts descended the seven steps for baptism and immersed themselves fully three times. After each immersion a blessing was recited, or a prayer, or a psalm. After the third immersion, the convert exited a new person and was anointed with oil."

Lauren did not sound satisfied. "So how does this relate to the treasure?"

"It doesn't," Amit replied. "This room's about ritual. We need to find the treasury."

"The *treasury*," Lauren repeated. "I like the sound of that."

Shane searched the walls of the cave and found a crescent-shaped area in the far corner darker than the rest of the stone. "This way."

Shane led them to what he hoped was an opening. When standing directly in front of it, he could see what appeared to be a tunnel, but the entrance was mostly blocked by a circular stone about seven feet in diameter and almost a foot thick.

Amit reached out and rubbed his palm along the surface. "It looks like a burial stone." He kneeled down and brushed the dust from the floor behind the stone. "There's a track. The stone rolls back and forth to seal or open the passageway. The track inclines upward such that the stone has a tendency to close with gravity. It's partially blocked right now by some rubble. That's why it's not all the way closed."

Shane remembered the next treasure verse from the Sicarii Gospel.

"*No one can enter a strong man's house and steal his treasure unless he first binds the strong man. Then he can take what he wants.* It's the next treasure verse."

Amit stood up and seemed doubtful. "So you think the *strong man* is this stone?"

Shane shrugged his shoulders.

Lauren pushed on the stone. "Can we move it? It feels heavy."

Amit began clearing the rubble. "Help me clean out the track. The stone should roll easily enough."

Each of them took a section of the track and worked until it was clean.

Shane stood up. "That should do it. Amit, help me with this. Lauren, grab some rocks to block it from rolling back."

Shane put his back on the wall to his left and pushed the side of the stone as if he was performing a bench press. Amit stood parallel to the stone, gripped it below its center with both hands, and pulled upward and backward. The stone vibrated back and forth and then rolled. After a few feet, Shane groaned downward. "Lauren, now."

Lauren positioned a few fist-sized irregular rocks in the track as far under the rolling stone as she could push them. "Okay. Let it go."

Amit released his grip, and Shane felt the stone shifting in his direction. He kept pressure on the stone until it seemed stable. Then he backed away. "It's holding."

Shane looked down the passageway descending at about a thirty-degree angle. It was about six feet high and four feet wide, and it extended at least thirty yards. It appeared to open to a wider section beyond. "It's down there or nowhere."

He stepped into the shaft and began carefully walking toward the far end. Lauren and Amit followed closely behind. As Shane hunched over, able to touch both sides with his extended arms, he recited the next verse.

"The gate is wide that leads to death and destruction. Follow the narrow path instead. It leads to the treasure of life."

Amit read his thoughts. "You think the verses are clues?"

"I don't know what to think yet. But you have to admit it's coincidental."

When Shane exited the passageway into a clear area about fifteen feet square, what he saw was awe-inspiring. A twenty feet high network of carved, recessed shelves rose above him on all four walls. They were arranged in sections separated by steep steps. There had to be nearly one hundred niches carved into the spaces above the shelves.

In three locations the shelves were interrupted by small tunnels about four feet high and three feet wide. Two of them were near the floor, and one was near the ceiling. They were most likely connectors to other segments of the cave system.

Amit examined one of the lower niches. "It's a catacomb."

Lauren gasped. "We're in a cemetery?"

Shane knew Amit was right. "Yes. A late first century Jewish Christian cemetery."

Some of the recesses were mostly sealed with a thin layer of plaster, while some were completely open. Bone fragments still lay in some of the exposed areas. Faded Aramaic lettering, geometric designs, and what appeared to be graffiti decorated the plaster and other flat areas between the shelves.

"Unlike the Romans," Amit began, "Jewish law demanded burial rather than cremation. Cremation was seen as pagan and a possible barrier to resurrection. There were many rules. Burial had to occur within twenty-four hours of death to maintain ritual purity. The body had to be buried outside of the village where the person lived. The cemetery had to be at least fifty cubits, or twenty-five meters, away. Families were buried together. And so on. If you consider the members of the nearby synagogue a family, all of those criteria seem to be in place here."

Shane knew there was more to the location. "And placing the cemetery here would limit access to what lay on the other side."

"How?" Lauren asked.

Shane understood the first century Jewish psyche. "Purity. Contact with a grave was the worst kind of ritual impurity."

Amit's tone took them back in time. "You can almost see it. Family members preparing the body with oils and spices, wrapping it in linen, and carrying it in a procession through the tunnel into this room where they would lay it on a stone shelf carved into the wall. They would then seal the opening with plaster and write the person's name on it. They might also scribble scripture or a blessing on the walls around it. Following the destruction of the Temple by the Romans, secondary burial into ossuaries went out of style. So the bodies would remain in their stone hollows forever."

Muted, rapid gunshots reverberated through the stone and interrupted Amit. There was no way of knowing how far away they were or how much stone separated them.

Lauren seemed worried. "It sounds like someone isn't getting along. Do all of these caves interconnect?"

Shane did not know. "Not sure. But we better get moving."

Lauren waved her arm in the direction of the tunnels. "There are three ways out," said Lauren. "How do we know which one to take?"

I wish I knew.

Amit had a suggestion. "What's the next treasure verse?"

Shane mentally kicked himself. *Of course. Instead of quoting treasure verses after the fact, I ought to be using them to guide us.* He recited the next verse.

"Do not store up treasure on earth, where moths and worms consume and human hands can take it from you. Sell your possessions, and give the money to the poor, thereby storing up for yourselves treasures in heaven, where moths and worms cannot consume and where no human hand can reach it."

Amit nodded. "The only tunnel fitting that description is the one near the ceiling. It's high off the ground and can't be reached without climbing the steps."

Shane examined the narrow stone steps which curved up and over to the opening. He had no reason to trust them to support him. The average Jewish peasant stood not much over five feet tall and weighed about one hundred ten pounds. Still, he began climbing the steps using both his hands and feet to maintain his balance. Lauren followed behind him and then Amit.

Shane tried to ignore the graves he was passing to both sides. The cemetery represented a major archaeological find, but for now he had to stay on task. As he neared the top, he saw a small ledge in front of the tunnel large enough for them to stand. He pulled himself up on the ledge and turned to help Lauren and Amit.

Lauren nodded toward something on the wall to the right of the opening. "Is that what I think it is?"

Shane saw it too. There was a shape etched into the stone. It was faint but definitely man-made. Shane traced the design with his finger. The top half he confirmed to be a menorah. The bottom half outlined a fish, and the middle was a Star of David.

Shane smiled. "They left a sign."

Chapter 117

By the time Reese and Koenig's team exited the long tunnel connecting the first cave with a second, much larger cave, the shooting they had heard before descending into the cave system had been over for some time. Reese trailed behind and watched the precision movements as Koenig commanded his men simultaneously through his helmet's communication system and with hand signals.

Reese wore a vest and night vision helmet provided to him by one of Koenig's men. Though the cave was empty, he was awestruck by what lay at the far end–stone columns fronting what appeared to be some sort of ancient structure. *That has to be what this is all about.*

Koenig's men spread out throughout the chamber and made their way toward the columns. Reese followed at a distance.

"Over here," called one of Koenig's men through the communication system.

Reese looked up to see one of Koenig's men signaling. He hurried to where the man stood next to a pool of blood.

"Someone was hit," the man said. "There's no blood trail, but you can see where someone was partially dragged in the direction of those columns. He must have been bandaged here and then taken through the opening. We probably just missed them."

A powerful draft blew through the cavern as if it was spewed from whatever lay behind the columns. It carried a haunting moan. After a few seconds, the draft and accompanying voice dissipated as quickly as they had come.

Reese's hair stood on end. "What the hell was that?"

Even Koenig seemed somewhat affected. "The legends surrounding these caves say they are guarded by God. Or his angels. We're not supposed to be in here."

Reese could not believe what he was hearing. "Do you really believe that?"

"I've lived here long enough not to question such things."

"Pakad!"

Reese and Koenig turned to find where one of Koenig's men was summoning the Chief Inspector in Hebrew. He was on one knee next to the center right column. He twisted back around to look at something on the ground. A few more men were grouped behind him near the large entrance to the stone palace.

As Reese approached the columns he saw lighter colored scars in the stone left by bullets. By the kneeling man lay a body surrounded by blood. A look of terror remained etched on the dead man's face. Below his face was a gaping gash in his throat.

Reese recognized the modus operandi. "One of the Frenchmen uses a razor."

Koenig was surprised. "This man is Palestinian. Is there anyone who's not chasing your friend?"

Koenig's men clustered near the large opening parted to give a line of sight from where Koenig and Reese stood. As they did so, the man who had spoken earlier started to explain in Hebrew. Then in deference to Reese he switched to English. "There's another body over there. And it's not pretty. He was slashed all over his upper body. We're tracking an animal."

Reese followed Koenig to the second body. The wounds were horrific. He silently hoped many of them were inflicted after the man had died, but he knew otherwise.

"Another Palestinian," confirmed Koenig.

Reese had seen it before. "It's the big Frenchman. He did the same thing in New Haven. Now you understand."

Koenig addressed his men. "Has anyone seen what's in the next chamber?"

His men remained silent for several seconds.

"We were waiting on your orders," said the same man who had spoken earlier.

"Then form up."

Chapter 118

Gustave let out a muffled groan as Clisson lowered him to the stone and leaned him against the wall in total darkness. Clisson was not accustomed to the physical exertion or practiced in the coordination required to support a wounded man while also carrying a weapon. He would not be able to support him farther, and he was not going to get help. *It is only a matter of time before Neuville commands his dog to dispatch me.*

Upon entering the chamber past the columns, they had seen two flashlight beams in the distance. The cave was larger still than the one they had just left and had been occupied in ages past. Though the Frenchmen had immediately turned their lights off, the beams in front of them had picked up speed.

Clisson watched the beams bounce from position to position at the far end of the chamber. Though he could not see him, Clisson sensed Neuville assessing how to approach the Palestinians. He hoped Neuville was not as bright as he seemed to think he was. He needed him to make a mistake.

He heard Neuville talking from perhaps three meters away. "Silently. Do not let them hear you."

Gustave whispered from where he sat. "Go with them."

Clisson reached for his bodyguard and found his arm. "Would you have me leave you here?"

"You and I both know where I am going, I will stay here and make sure no one follows."

Clisson knew Gustave was right. He would have to fend for himself until he could once again gain the advantage. "You are a good man. Bon voyage."

Clisson patted Gustave's arm and hurried to keep up with the other three men moving forward. He tried to stay near enough to hear them but not so close they turned and attacked him. The lights ahead of them still shined but had long ago stopped moving. *How did I get here? I am not supposed to be walking in the dark with a weapon.*

Suddenly shots rang out. Clisson hit the ground in a panic. The side of his face burned in the rocky soil. He clenched his jaws and waited for the bullets. *Mon dieu!*

He took mental inventory. The bullets had not struck him. He mustered the courage to raise his head and look forward. Neuville and his men were firing away from him. The lenses on the flashlights in the distance shattered and fell to the stone floor. The broken glass was followed by the sounds of footsteps running quickly away from him.

Clisson struggled to his feet. He searched for his flashlight but did not turn it on. He crept forward and was perhaps half way to where the lights had gone out when Neuville and de Vaux turned on their flashlights. The contrast of light after the darkness seemed to brighten the entire cavern.

Neuville and the other two men stood around a marble table. Pieces of two flashlights lay scattered across the table and surrounding floor. There were no bodies. Clisson turned on his flashlight as well. The Palestinians were not there.

Neuville became incensed. "It was meant to delay us. Where did they go?"

Neuville began following the cave wall with his flashlight. He started to their right and followed the rock counterclockwise to his left. He went past what looked like an opening and then pulled the beam back to it. It was not the large doorway type openings they had encountered thus far. It was much smaller, perhaps a meter and a half high and a meter wide. Clisson's heart leaped. A cave chamber on the other side of this passageway would not have been inhabited or used on a regular basis like the caves thus far. But it could have been used for storage, perhaps even the storage of treasure.

Neuville began following the path of his light toward the opening. His two men walked with him, one to each side, and Clisson sheepishly followed in their wake. They had only taken a few steps when a low rumbling noise vibrated along the cave floor. Loose soil and scattered small stones rained down from the ceiling and walls. Everyone froze where they stood and began searching the walls and ceiling for the source. A stone perhaps ten centimeters in diameter separated from the ceiling and struck de Vaux where his shoulder and neck came together. He crumpled to the floor.

Neuville screamed. "Earthquake!"

Clisson kneeled to the ground and shined his light up at the ceiling. There was nowhere to hide. *Merde! What am I doing here?* Then as suddenly as it began, the vibration stopped.

Chapter 119

Shane emerged from the twenty-five feet long tunnel into yet another cave chamber. It was roughly square with each wall about twenty feet long. For the most part it was nondescript, with rough walls and ceiling. The only oddity was that the ceiling angled upward to the right and narrowed to a point well back behind the right wall that arced backward as it rose. Directly in front of them were two tunnels continuing forward in divergent directions.

Shane took a moment to stand upright and stretch. He tried to envision how far they had come and where they were in relation to the surface.

Lauren must have been reading his mind. "We're in a maze. How'll we know when we've gone too far?"

Shane did not know. "You've seen the signs and heard the clues."

Amit kneeled and began using his hands to sweep away loose dirt from what appeared to be shallow channels in the floor. "What's this? Shane, what's the next treasure verse?"

Shane replied, *"The Kingdom of God is like a treasure hidden under a light for all to find."*

Amit appeared perplexed. "These don't appear to have anything to do with light. More like water. They look like gutters sloping downward under the wall back the way we came."

As Amit spoke, Shane experienced de ja vue. A memory was just out of reach. He stood silently trying to draw it from the archives of his brain.

Lauren noticed his struggle. "Shane, do you know something?"

"I think so. But I just can't seem to..." Then it hit him. "The Pantheon in Rome! There's a hole in the top of its dome to let in sunlight. It's called an *oculus* because the combination of the blue sky and the surrounding smooth concrete looks like an eye."

Lauren looked at him like he was crazy. "What does that have to do with gutters?"

"The oculus also allows rain to fall on the floor. The Romans built drains in the floor to carry away the water."

Amit stood up. "That would make sense. If water hit this floor, the inhabitants would've wanted to collect it."

Shane looked upward to the top of the cave. Its strange shape intrigued him. "Lauren, shine your flashlight up at that point in the ceiling."

Lauren did as she was told. Shane positioned himself to see what lay at the highest point of the cave. It was impossible to tell.

Amit moved shoulder to shoulder and looked up as well. "Are you thinking that's an oculus?"

"I'm thinking it might've been. Before a couple of thousand years of building in the city covered it up."

Amit scanned the chamber. "The verse says to look under a light. Should we look on the right side under the oculus? Or on the left wall where the light would hit the stone?"

Shane's heart raced. "You and Lauren take the left wall. I'll take the right."

Shane tried to align himself directly under the narrow formation in the ceiling. He rubbed his hands along the surface and studied every imperfection. He found nothing.

"Shane!" called Lauren. "It's here."

Shane ran to the other wall where Amit described what they had found. "It's similar in design to the Rihab mechanism. It's constructed of metal and extends from the wall about two centimeters. Up here just above our heads is a menorah. The best I can estimate, it's located exactly where the light from the oculus would strike the wall, almost as if lighting the candles."

Shane looked back to the ceiling. "I think you're right. What else?"

"The rest looks like it was meant to complete the Messianic Seal, but it's distorted. The whole thing's about a meter long."

Shane looked at the design and saw what Amit meant.

"If it's like the other mechanism," began Shane, "we need to complete the design. Help me with this right section."

Shane positioned his hands on the bottom right section of the design. Amit traced the edge upward to the left and placed his hands there. As Shane pushed down to the left, Amit pushed to the right. The metal rotated clockwise. After a few inches, it snapped into place. The wall shuddered. Pieces separated and fell to the floor. A section of the wall to their left seemed to pull away from the section holding the mechanism.

Shane stepped back and looked at the shape of the design.

He knew they were on the right track. “Now the left side.”

Shane grabbed the upper end while Amit pushed down and to the right on the lower edge. Again, the metal edge rotated, except this time counterclockwise. When they reached the intended position, it also snapped into place. The result was a completed ichthus symbol.

With a loud grinding noise of stone against stone, a twelve feet long section of the wall to their left fell downward, disappearing through the cave floor. As it fell, jagged chunks crumbled and broke off amid a dust cloud which expanded to fill much of the cavern. The top of the wall suffered most, with large portions falling away. Finally, unable to overcome the friction, the wall stopped with about twelve to eighteen inches remaining above the floor.

As the dust settled, Shane could better see the construction of the wall. It was man-made. Blocks of stone about eight inches thick and high and perhaps a foot long had been mortared together across a natural curvature in the cave. Then the outer surface of the wall had been covered with plaster camouflaged to match the connecting walls.

Amit said what Shane was thinking. "The men who did this definitely knew how to work stone."

Shane's heart pounded the inside of his chest. "Jesus was a stone mason, not a carpenter. Carpenter is a mistranslation of the Greek word *tekton*." He paused. "I can think of only one reason why someone would want to build this wall."

"Shane!' declared Lauren. "Do you think we've found it?"

"Only one way to find out."

Chapter 120

Finding the treasure had not been as easy as Al-Jamal had hoped. Perhaps there was no treasure. Regardless, he had made his play. He would do it again. He was satisfied that he had acted correctly given the information he had. Now he was running out of time. His choices narrowed to only one option–confront the men who followed them.

Only Milak remained, and he had only his backup flashlight to find their way. They were too exposed. He had to find the right defensive position. While scanning the small chamber a low rumbling caught his attention. Milak let out a muffled cry.

"Ya Sidi! It is an earthquake."

The vibration increased through the floor and wall to their right. Milak hugged the wall as dust rained down, but Al-Jamal stood confident. He directed his flashlight upward, but he knew there was little need. Even as the cave continued to tremble, Al-Jamal knew he would not die. He was not destined to be buried alive.

As he predicted, the vibration passed, but it left him with a thought. *The rumbling did not feel natural.* He directed his light to the wall next to them. "Milak, look at this."

Milak stood right next to his shoulder. "What is it?"

"Does that wall look right?"

"Yes. No, wait. Is that mortar filling in between stones?"

Al-Jamal smiled. The wall was skillfully constructed with the appearance of solid stone, but in reality it was manufactured. Overhanging stone edges hid most of the signs of human intervention, but in some places the years had exposed the fraud. Al-Jamal could only assume the false wall blocked a passageway to another section of the cave system, a section the builders did not want people to enter.

That was not an earthquake. Someone is on the other side! "How much explosive do we have left?"

"Not very much."

"Enough to blow this wall?"

"There is no way to know how thick it is."

"Try."

"Ya Sidi, an explosion like that might bring down the roof as well."

"It is our way out. It is the way to the treasure."

Milak nodded and kneeled down to the cave floor. While Al-Jamal provided the light, he pulled the remaining Semtex from his bag and applied it to the wall. "That is the last of it."

"It is all we will need."

Chapter 121

Neuville composed himself and used his flashlight on Raphael still on one knee holding his groaning father in his arms. "How is he?"

"Broken collar bone."

De Vaux struggled to move in his son's grip. "I am all right."

Neuville twisted around and found Clisson still on both knees and covered in the fine dirt from the cave floor. The assault rifle hanging limply made him appear even more comical. Neuville wondered why he had ever thought Clisson formidable. He turned back to his men. "Can you carry your father without endangering him?"

The giant nodded and lifted his father easily as he stood to his feet. De Vaux groaned but seemed to settle in comfortably.

Gunshots rang out in rapid fire near the entrance to the chamber. From the muzzle flashes, Neuville could see Gustave firing on someone entering the cave. Shouts and screams in Hebrew filled the air.

Clisson screamed. "Israelis!"

Gustave continued firing until return gunshots ended his life. Neuville turned off his flashlight. De Vaux followed his lead, but Clisson broke for the tunnel to the next cave. *Coward!* Neuville saw the shadow of Raphael moving to block Clisson, but he was encumbered with his father. Clisson fired a single shot blindly behind him. It effectively stopped Raphael's pursuit. The gunshot gave the Israelis a location, and bullets from multiple weapons immediately sprayed the stone around them.

Neuville froze and prayed. "Father in heaven, please deliver us from this peril. If you choose instead to take my life, into your hands I commend my spirit."

As Neuville prayed, an explosion jolted him to the ground. It seemed to come from the direction Clisson had just run. The force of the blast shot air through the tunnel and swirled it around the chamber like a tornado. *The spirit of God!*

The explosion silenced the assault rifles, but sounds much more terrifying filled the void. The crackling of stone coming apart in the ceiling warned of an impending shower of rock. Neuville covered his head and waited terrified for the worst.

A major section of the ceiling gave way. Like a rock waterfall, the stone fell to the floor for what seemed like minutes but in fact was only seconds. When the cave was quiet again, Neuville rose to his knees. He coughed from the dust cloud and quickly raised his shirt to his mouth. He had no idea which direction he was facing or where he was relative to the fallen stone. He decided to take a chance and turn on his flashlight. What he saw amazed him. A wall of stone now separated him from the Israelis, and the passage to the next section was still open. *Thank you, Father, for this miracle.*

A haunting cry drew his attention. His beam found Raphael sitting on the ground with his lifeless father in his arms. De Vaux had a single bullet hole in the middle of his blood-soaked shirt. Raphael let out a primal scream as Neuville kneeled beside him.

"I am sorry, Raphael. Your father was a good man."

Tears streamed down Raphael's face. "Clisson!"

Raphael's one word response communicated exactly what had happened. Clisson fired backwards at Raphael to secure his escape. The bullet had struck de Vaux.

"We will avenge your father." Neuville assured him. "God has worked a great miracle. We are free to find the treasure. He will not have died in vain."

Raphael let his father slide to the cave floor and stood up. Neuville could see the rage on his face. He stood beside him and lifted his hand to the giant's shoulder.

"Raphael, I know we have not been close. But if you let me, I will watch over you the way your father did."

Raphael responded by pushing Neuville away. He growled and ran for the opening. He did not take de Vaux's flashlight.

"Raphael!"

His plea was pointless. Raphael's father was all that kept him human. Without de Vaux, Raphael would quickly degenerate into the beast of Martinique. Neuville followed him with his flashlight, but the large dark figure disappeared into the blackness. Neuville prayed for God to watch over the young giant and to use him to further his will.

Chapter 122

"Shit!" Lauren exhaled heavily.

Shane could not have agreed more. He stood looking at yet another empty chamber. It was small and rounded, not even ten feet deep at its farthest point. While it had the appearance of a storage area, it was far too small ever to have held the treasure. There was no way of knowing why the Jewish Christians had gone to such lengths to hide the room. Perhaps at one time it held a ritual item or religious relic.

The far wall was smooth and slightly concave. Shane could not see anything to indicate what they should do next. He stepped inside to examine the wall. Amit and Lauren followed.

"Do you see *anything*?" Shane asked them. "A symbol, another mechanism, anything?"

"Not yet," replied Amit.

Lauren shook her head.

They separated to each work a section of the wall. Shane and Amit with their goggles and Lauren with her flashlight put their faces as close to the wall as they could and still focus. They also used their hands to feel the texture of the surface.

"Nothing," confirmed Amit.

Shane was dejected. "What's left to go on?"

Amit stood silent for several seconds before asking, "Is there another treasure verse?"

"Yes. One more. But it's more like a proverb than a direction. *Blessed is the man who perseveres in times of hardship, because when he has passed the test, he will receive God's treasure.*"

Amit appeared to be deciphering the meaning. "Well, it fits. We're definitely in a time of hardship."

Shane walked over to Amit and put his right hand on Amit's shoulder. He hoped his friend had an idea of where to go next and would convince him they were not at an end of their search. He would love to *persevere*, but he could not think of anything else for them to do. They had interpreted the signs left for them, and they had run into a dead end. Perhaps the treasure really was just a hoax to divert the Romans. To continue without an indicator pointing them to the right tunnel would be foolish. It was time to leave and rethink.

Amit looked up at Shane but did not say anything. Though Amit's face was hidden behind his goggles, Shane could sense tears forming in his friend's eyes. "I wish there was something else to do."

Lauren grabbed Shane's arm and spun him around. "What? You're giving up?"

"For now."

"We can't quit. We're too close"

"I'm open to suggestions."

An explosion shook the chamber and immediately shifted their priorities from treasure to survival.

Shane shouted over the rumbling. "Let's get out of here!"

They stumbled out of the empty chamber and huddled next to the wall of the larger cave. Shane looked upward and listened intently for any sign the top of the cave was giving way. Their greatest danger was not from the rocks. "We're about to get company. We need a place to hide."

Amit joined him and pointed across the main cavern at the two openings in the cave wall. "They'll be coming through one of those tunnels."

Shane agreed. "Yeah. But which one? I can't believe they've been using explosives. Are they really that stupid? Regardless, we can't wait here. We have to take a chance on a tunnel. Once inside, there may be other places to hide. Which one?"

Amit gestured with his arm. "My gut says to the right."

"Then let's go. Lauren, stay close behind us."

Shane ran toward the right tunnel and entered it without hesitation. It was only about five feet wide and high with rough sides and ceiling. In the lead, Shane had difficulty maneuvering without hitting his head. He slowed down, but he did not stop. He kept jogging as best he could in his hunched position. *What I would give to be holding my Beretta right now.*

The tunnel dumped him into a small chamber not ten feet deep and high. Three openings, even smaller in diameter than the previous tunnel, marked the far wall and connected the chamber with whatever lay beyond. Shane felt like a hamster. There was real danger of getting lost and never finding their way out. "Let's wait inside the right tunnel."

He crossed the short distance and bent over to enter the tunnel. After taking several steps inside, he stopped and steadied himself by holding both sides of the passageway. Then he lowered himself to a sitting position by twisting around and leaning back on the wall. Amit sat beside him.

Shane was worried. "I don't know, Amit. We have no weapons. We're probably outnumbered. But we can't keep running. We're going to lose our way."

"Let's wait here a while. Then we'll start back."

"I agree. Lauren, are you..."

Shane stopped in mid-sentence. He leaned forward to look past Amit and confirm what his senses were telling him. Lauren was not there.

Chapter 123

Reese sat on the ground and wiped the blood from his forearm. It was more a scrape than a gash and not deep enough to be a concern. The bruise beneath would be more of an issue but not until his adrenaline level diminished. He was covered in dust. Men were moving all around him. If not for the night vision in his helmet, he would have been in total darkness. He was beginning to believe the legends were right. God did not want men in these tunnels.

Reese stood up and found Koenig. He could not tell whether Koenig was angry or just frustrated. His helmet hid too much of his face. His orders to his men in Hebrew were loud and commanding, and his men reacted to each one without question. Reese guessed they had seen their commander in this sort of mood before.

Koenig had lost a man when they stumbled upon one of the Frenchmen waiting for them with an assault rifle. The remaining Israelis had dispatched the Frenchman, but their advance had placed them in almost the worst position possible at the time of the cave-in. Reese and Koenig had barely escaped with their lives. Some of Koenig's men had not been so fortunate. They had just uncovered the fourth man to be buried under the falling stone. Three of the four were dead. The fourth was severely injured and probably bleeding internally.

Reese saw Koenig approaching and waited for the discussion he knew was coming. It was only natural for Koenig to blame him for the loss of his men. If Reese had not come to Koenig for assistance, his men would still be alive, and he would be sitting comfortably in his office or home. The most logical thing to do was to give up. It was exactly what Reese did not want to do.

Reese decided to go on the offensive. "You can't go back. I need your help. I'm sorry about your men, and I know you need to send a couple of the others back with your injured man. But you and a few of them need to come with me."

"Detective Reese, are you under the impression I'm turning back?"

Reese opened his mouth, but nothing came out.

"No one kills my men and gets away. And I surely don't tuck tail and run. I've already given orders to see to my man. And we've found a way through the rubble. If you're ready to go, I suggest we leave now."

Chapter 124

Al-Jamal was jubilant as he crossed over the boundary into the cave system previously sealed. He knew he was close to discovering what had lain hidden for two thousand years. "Stay alert. There is someone else here."

Milak nodded. The cave they had just entered was an extension of the one they had just left. It was round with a domed ceiling about twenty feet in diameter. As Al-Jamal examined it with his flashlight, his jubilation turned quickly to frustration. He had hoped the path forward would be more obvious. Instead, three tunnels led out of it. They were set almost equidistant apart on the far wall.

Which path leads to my prize?

Even in his frustration, Al-Jamal knew only one or two more correct decisions separated him and the treasure. As he walked across the cave floor he silently thanked Allah for his assistance and requested his guidance in the decisions he would have to make in the coming minutes.

Al-Jamal and Milak arrived together at the leftmost tunnel. They directed their flashlight beams into the opening, but after a short distance the passageway turned even more to their left and gave up none of its secrets. They moved to the center shaft. The rough walls extended about five meters in length before emptying into the darkness of yet another chamber. They were about to look down the right tunnel when Al-Jamal heard footsteps coming fast from the cave behind them.

"Do you hear...?" Al-Jamal did not finish his question.

The footsteps rapidly entered the newly discovered cave, and a ring of light engulfed the two Palestinians. Al-Jamal and Milak turned and raised their assault rifles. Before either of them could fire their weapons, a man dressed in a suit covered in dirt sped directly between them. He entered the right tunnel without saying a word or acknowledging their presence in any way.

"Ebn El Sharmoota!" cursed Milak.

Al-Jamal was not unaffected. The man had seemed terrified. Perhaps he had run into one of the jinn said to guard the caves. Al-Jamal pointed his flashlight down the right tunnel, but it curved quickly to the right. The man was gone.

A much softer set of footfalls sounded on the stone behind them.

"Zarba!" exclaimed Milak in a hoarse whisper. "What now?"

Al-Jamal turned and raised his assault rifle, struggling with his flashlight. He was not prepared for what he saw. A dark mass entered the cave chamber and floated swiftly toward them. He had been correct. *It was a jinni chasing the man!*

Milak froze at the sight of the giant shadow, but Al-Jamal fired his assault rifle. The jinni seemed to sense his actions and changed directions to avoid Al-Jamal's aim. Al-Jamal heard a loud noise and saw a spark of light erupt from the middle of the shadow. Milak flew back against him and knocked his assault rifle from his grip and his flashlight to the cave floor. As Milak slid down in front of him, another spark of light brightened the dark mass. Searing pain burned Al-Jamal's chest. He fell backward to the stone floor with Milak still lying motionless on his legs. He could only breathe in gulps accentuated with coughed up blood. A bullet must have cracked a rib and punctured one of his lungs.

What kind of jinni uses a gun?

Al-Jamal felt for the flashlight at his side. After a few tries he grasped it and pointed it at the approaching dark mass. The beam reflected off the eyes of his attacker. They relayed pure evil. *Shaytan!* Al-Jamal tried to push himself away from the oncoming eyes, but he did not have the strength. Two dark extensions reached out and grabbed his head by the hair on both sides.

Al-Jamal rejoiced. He would die a martyr of Islam and be admitted to heaven. *Today I meet Muhammad and rejoice in the bounty provided by Allah.*

Al-Jamal stared into the evil eyes as his head lifted off the ground and then was driven into the stone.

Chapter 125

How could Shane betray me like that?

Lauren had not followed Shane and Amit.

Shane promised to help me. Then he gives up? I thought he'd never give up. Perhaps I should find Clisson. He won't stop. And he has the means to get the treasure out.

Lauren pointed her flashlight at the left tunnel. After a short distance it emptied into another cave. It did not look very appealing. She took a step, then stopped.

What the hell am I doing?

Lauren slowed her breath and forced herself to think clearly. She had just reacted. Her lust for the treasure had overcome her reason.

Now, calmer and saner, she saw her situation for what it was. She was wandering in the darkness with a single flashlight, no compass, and no way with certainty to find her way out. And her only hope was finding in the maze of caves and tunnels a man who could be as lost as she was, a man who could not be trusted.

I must catch up to Shane. I'll make some kind of excuse. He'll understand. We'll come back for the treasure.

She hoped she had not made a fatal error and could find Shane before getting totally lost. She moved to the right tunnel and bent down to enter. Before she could step inside, she felt pressure on her shoulder pulling her back with force.

What the hell!

She was forced upright and an arm stretched across her throat. The muscle flexed and tightened, cutting off her air. She struggled and awkwardly clubbed with her flashlight, but despite her efforts she felt herself lifted from the ground.

She was seconds away from blacking out when the muscle relaxed and released her throat. Her feet struck the stone floor with enough force to send a shock up her spine. Air rushed into her lungs, and blood began flowing again to her brain. Her throat and head ached.

Before she fully recovered, she felt the muscle return around her waist. A powerful tug followed, and she flew through the air like a rag doll. She passed through the left tunnel, hit the floor, and crashed against the far cave wall. The flashlight flew from her hand and clanged to the stone floor with the lens shining its light in her direction. She crumpled to the floor, landing spread-eagled on her back. Once again she struggled to get her breath.

Her attacker stepped into the flashlight's beam, which cast an eerie halo around his form. He was a dark giant, appearing even more enormous in the small cave. His white eyes encircled large dark pupils which stabbed at her like daggers. As he came closer and leaned over her, she thought she had seen him before.

The giant spoke in a strong French accent with hatred on every syllable. "I could easily have snapped your neck." He showed her his semi-clenched hand. "Or shot you." He showed her a pistol before dropping it to his feet. "Or slit your throat." He showed her a razor reflecting the flashlight beam before he folded it and put it in his pocket. "All are too quick. Because of you my father is dead. Because of you I am lost. I will take my time. Perhaps remove your skin inch by inch."

Lauren saw the monster's white teeth as he broke into a smile, the hatred in his eyes replaced with lust.

He lowered himself beside her. "But first, a different kind of pleasure."

Lauren screamed. "No!"

She kicked with her legs to push herself away, but a sweep of the giant's arm brought his backhand across her face. The blow dazed her and slowed her struggling. She lashed out and shouted her determination, but another blow to the side of her head knocked her limp to the floor.

The hulk unfastened his belt, lowered his pants, and leaned over her. With his left hand he grasped her throat and squeezed. Lauren clawed at the hand and tried to reach the giant's face, but his arm was too long.

With his right hand her attacker grabbed the waistline of her jeans in the center and pulled down hard, ripping her jeans and panties from her body. The fabric tore into her skin and left her raw nerves burning in the air. She tried to scream but could not get enough air for more than a whimper. With another sweep of his arm, the giant removed her shirt and bra. Lauren lay nude on the stone floor, pinned there by the giant's massive arm.

She clenched her eyes to clear her tears. Then she mustered everything she had left to try to free herself. She kicked and clawed, but the giant merely tightened his grip on her throat. Nothing she did stopped her attacker from using his knees to spread her legs. She stopped her struggling and gave into her fate. She had nothing left.

Her attacker released her throat to use both hands to bring her wrists together. With one enormous hand he held them above her head on the stone while squeezing her breasts one at a time with his other hand. Saliva drooled from his mouth onto her breasts, and she groaned in her repulsion. Her groan was like gasoline to the giant's fire. He positioned himself over her.

Lauren let out a final sobbing scream.

Then a blur of movement passed over her face, and the giant was off of her. Her wrists were free of his grasp, and she brought her arms down to roll over onto her side away from the giant. She looked up to find her savior.

Chapter 126

Shane hoped the giant's head hurt as much as his foot, but he was afraid he had just made him angry. He had left Amit like a bread crumb behind him and had gone in search of Lauren. When he heard her screams, he followed them to where he found her being attacked. A swift kick removed her attacker from on top of her, but it had not eliminated the threat.

As Lauren rolled over and dragged herself the short distance to the cave wall, the giant rose to his feet. His face was cut and bleeding. *If he bleeds, he's human.*

Shane assessed he had two advantages. First, Shane had night vision, while the giant could only see what was in the beam of the flashlight on the floor. Second, as distracting as it might be, the giant still had his pants down around his ankles and could not take long strides in any direction. Shane had to act before his opponent found ways to offset both advantages. He hoped he remembered his capoeira and tae kwon do.

As the giant reached down to his pants, Shane performed a high swinging kick that connected with the side of the hulk's head. The contact opened the previous gash and released a torrent of blood. The giant roared and rushed forward but Shane performed a low spin move and twisted away from his opponent into the darkness. The giant stumbled forward and fell hard to the stone floor. As the hulk struggled to rise, Shane cartwheeled back into the light while performing a kick that once again contacted the gashed side of the giant's face and knocked him to the ground.

When the hulk rose again he held a razor in his hand. Shane knew this changed everything. The giant would slash him to ribbons if he tried an offensive move. The giant rushed forward. Shane anticipated the tactic and rolled backward in a move that ended with a kick to the chin of the giant. Though Shane's foot made solid contact, the giant reached out and grabbed Shane's ankle before he could complete the flip. Shane found himself upside down until he swung his other leg around directly into the giant's gash. Though freed, Shane knew he had to escape before the razor found his flesh. He spun to his side back into the darkness.

A gunshot echoed in the cavern, and the dark giant flew head first into the stone wall, collapsing face down to the floor. He had another long gash losing blood across the back of his head. Shane looked up to see Lauren holding a Glock. Her hand was trembling.

Shane walked to Lauren's side and took the handgun from her hand. He leaned into her, and she buried her sobbing face into his shoulder. He held her until her tears had run their course. While doing so, he looked for something to cover her.

Since her clothes were useless, he bent down to remove the giant's jacket and belt. Lauren slipped into the enormous jacket and buttoned it. She looked like a child playing dress-up in her father's clothes. Shane handed her the belt and watched her manipulate it until it was usable to cinch the jacket tightly against her body.

"Thank you, Shane," she said in a tone Shane had seldom heard her use.

"Was that sincerity?"

Lauren let a half-laugh escape her already bruising face. She picked up her flashlight and pointed it at her attacker. "Is he dead?"

Shane saw the man was still breathing. "No. But he may be soon."

Lauren spoke through clenched teeth. "Finish him!"

"You know I can't kill someone in cold blood. Not even a monster like him."

"Then give me the gun."

"No. I know you've been through hell, but I'm not going to let you make it worse. If he lives, the Israeli authorities can take care of him. We need to get back to Amit."

Shane grabbed Lauren's arm and pulled her toward the tunnel. He held her hand until they emerged in the oculus cave. A surprise greeted them.

Amit stood facing them with his hands held upward at his shoulders. Behind him stood Clisson with the barrel of his assault rifle buried in Amit's back. His flashlight rested on Amit's shoulder pointing toward them.

"Drop your weapon, Docteur Randall, s'il vous plait." Clisson instructed. "We have much to discuss. And it would go so much more smoothly without the blood of your friend all over both of us."

Chapter 127

Shane dropped the Glock to the cave floor.

Clisson smiled. "Mademoiselle Mallory, be so kind as to bring me the weapon."

Lauren picked up the handgun and carried it to where Clisson and Amit stood. When she reached him, Clisson pushed Amit forward. Amit's eyes apologized, but Shane assigned him no blame.

Clisson reached out for Lauren, but instead of taking the pistol, he wrapped his arm around her waist and brought her in next to him. Never taking his eyes off Shane and Amit, Clisson leaned into Lauren and kissed her on the cheek. Lauren looked repulsed but did not resist. Shane's surprise must have shown through his goggles.

Clisson let out an arrogant laugh. "Surely, Docteur Randall, you know by now that Mademoiselle Mallory and I go way back. When I found out what she did for a living, I knew one day she would be very useful in my quest. And her technical skills were not the only things she brought to our relationship." He pulled her in tighter and kissed her again. "But I think you are probably very aware of her many talents."

Shane broke eye contact but wanted to hear it all. "Go on."

"I intend to," Clisson replied. "Then I trust you will be equally open with me?"

Shane nodded.

Clisson seemed satisfied. "I am how she got into the Royal Art and History Museum. I am an influential benefactor. She is a skillful undercover operator." He stopped to laugh at his pun. "She got me the information I needed. Then she obtained the gospel. When she found you, I knew you would bring in my good friend Docteur David. Mademoiselle Mallory kept me quite informed. That is until you confiscated our phones."

Shane looked at Lauren. "What's in it for you?"

Clisson answered for her. "I offered her a proposition she could not turn down. I needed someone practical. I knew those religious zealots would fail. Neuville is a joke. And Docteur David, I told you that you needed help. Mademoiselle Mallory was the glue that held all of my gambits together."

Shane insisted. “I want to hear it from her.”

Lauren looked genuinely saddened by the turn of events. “Shane, I couldn’t settle for just a percentage of a finder’s fee. This is the chance of a lifetime.”

Shane shook his head. “No matter who got killed or hurt?”

Clisson cut him off. “You were my only wild card, Docteur Randall. And of course those damned Palestinians. But in the end, both you and they were most helpful.” He paused. “Your turn.”

Shane told Clisson about the symbol leading them to Mount Zion and about the entrance in the field behind the Tomb of David. Then he told him about their trip through the cave system and the clues embedded in the treasure verses from the Sicarii Gospel. He finished with the empty cave behind the false wall.

Clisson paced a few feet and back. “There must be more.”

“No.” replied Amit. “It was another promising lead that led to nothing.”

Clisson waved his weapon in a threatening manner. “Show me.” All smiles were gone.

Shane and Amit lead him to the mechanism on the wall. Clisson studied it closely. Then they stepped over the false wall into the empty storage room.

Clisson turned to Lauren. “Watch them, mon cher. I want to have a look.”

Lauren raised the Glock. Shane could see the shame in her eyes, and he doubted she could really shoot him. On the other hand, she had come this far using everyone around her.

Clisson completed his examination but was not satisfied. “There must be another clue. Is there another verse?”

“Yes,” Shane admitted. “One more. But it doesn’t help.”

“Tell me.”

Shane recited the verse: *“Blessed is the man who perseveres in times of hardship, because when he has passed the test, he will receive God’s treasure.”*

Clisson began dissecting the verse. “Blessed is the man. Perseveres. Times of hardship. Passed the test. Receive God’s treasure.”

He stood in silent thought. Shane did the same, but it was Amit who spoke first. “P*ersevere.* What is its definition, some synonyms? We may have missed something after all.”

Shane did not know where Amit was going, but his friend's optimism allowed him momentarily to forget about Lauren and Clisson. "Persist. Remain constant. Continue in spite of hardship. Push through."

Amit moved to the far wall. "That's it. The surface looks odd. Unnaturally smooth. What if it's a final test of faith? What if we're supposed to move the mountain with faith by *pushing through*?"

Shane's heart skipped a beat. Oblivious to the weapons pointing at him, he joined Amit at the wall. "If this works, you're a genius."

They put their hands on the wall about chest high. The position did not feel quite right because of the concavity of the wall. They lowered their hands and found the task easier but still not right. Ultimately the curvature guided them to a flat portion of the wall where they could effectively apply pressure.

"Push!" cried Shane.

He and Amit dug into the cave floor with their feet, leaned into the wall, and pushed with all their strength. Little cracks appeared in the surface, but the wall did not give way.

Shane knew they were on to something. "Again!"

Once more they pushed. This time the surface layer began crumbling away, revealing stone blocks behind. The blocks slid backward but stopped after only inches.

Shane screamed again. "Once more!"

They extended their arms and drove forward with their legs. A section of stone blocks gave way and tumbled into another open space beyond the wall. Once they could make out the blocks, Shane and Amit began clearing them individually to widen the hole. It was obvious that with a little more work, they would be able to clear an opening from that point down to the cave floor. A Roman-style stone arch supported the upper portion of the wall. The blocks filled the space beneath.

Clisson stepped up behind them. "Stand back! I want to be the first to see."

Shane could not believe the arrogance, but he and Amit moved a few steps to the side. Clisson bent over and was about to insert his flashlight in the opening when another familiar voice interrupted him.

"Monsieur Clisson, did you forget about me."

Chapter 128

Shane watched the arrogance evaporate from Clisson's face.

Neuville gestured with his assault rifle and flashlight for Clisson and Lauren to drop their weapons. "S'il vous plaît."

They reluctantly complied.

"Merci, mon amis," mocked Neuville.

Clisson pointed. "The treasure is behind that wall. You are still better off working with me."

"Non, Monsieur Clisson. With the Israelis now involved, the prize will not be as great as I hoped, but it will still be quite substantial."

Neuville's revelation piqued Shane's interest. "Israelis?"

Lauren walked up to Clisson. "What does he mean?"

Clisson cringed in embarrassment. "I thought you knew, mon cher. An Israeli military force followed us into the caves. With them involved, we may have to settle for whatever we can negotiate."

Lauren pushed him away.

Neuville laughed. "Correction, Monsieur Clisson. *I* must settle. Not you. I just need a story. How about I discovered your scheme to remove antiquities from Israel and directed my organization to stop you. We tracked you and the team you employed to help you. You fought back, and I and my man were forced to kill you."

Again Neuville's words pierced Clisson like a dagger. "Your man?"

"Oui. Monsieur Clisson, Mademoiselle Mallory, one last gift for all you have done for me. Raphael!"

The jacketless hulk raced into the room like a crazed wrestler. His once white shirt was now blood-stained, and his head and face were caked in dried blood. He growled like an animal, and his eyes flashed like a demon's. He located Clisson and Lauren and rushed them like a bull with his head down and his arms extended to envelop them both.

Shane leaped in front of Clisson. He stayed low to the ground, picking up Clisson's assault weapon and pulling Lauren down beside him just ahead of Raphael's outstretched arm. As the giant passed, Shane twisted and strafed him with the assault rifle.

Clisson remained frozen in place and took the oncoming giant's blow in his chest. He flew backward into the stone arch. More layers of stone below the arch fell backward, but the arch held. Shane raised himself enough to see Clisson's neck broken and Raphael motionless on top of him bleeding from multiple gunshots.

A couple of bullets whizzed past Shane's head. He threw himself flat to the floor. He signaled Lauren and Amit to stay where they were a few feet to each side. Looking up, he saw Neuville had backed out of the small chamber and had positioned himself behind the cave wall, his flashlight beam searching for them in the darkness.

Neuville taunted them from behind the wall. "Poor Raphael. He had his uses, but it is probably better for all of us that he is gone. And Clisson, what a fool. Always thinking he was in control. All I have to do now is rid myself of you, and I will be the sole survivor to claim the find."

Shane pushed back. "Do you really believe they will buy your story?"

"Your deaths will soon be little interest to anyone. Everyone will be too busy fighting over who owns the treasure."

Shane was afraid Neuville might be right. He looked at Amit and gestured his intent to rush Neuville. At least one of them would remain hidden by darkness long enough to get to him.

"Everyone please put down your weapons!" cried a voice with a strong Israeli accent.

Shane searched for the source of the voice but could not find it.

"I'm not sure who is who," continued the voice. "And it would be embarrassing to shoot the wrong people."

Shane threw his assault rifle forward onto the stone. It was Neuville's move.

Neuville stood frozen and appeared to be cursing himself for taking too long. Shane feared he would opt to sacrifice himself rather than be taken into Israeli custody. Neuville closed his eyes and appeared to be praying.

"Last warning!"

The voice seemed to shock Neuville back to consciousness. He raised the assault rifle in one hand and then set it down on the stone floor. He looked at Shane with a smile on his face. "Dieu me livrera–God will deliver me."

An Israeli commander and four of his men in full body armor entered the outer cave and took up positions around Neuville. "Secure this man."

Two Israeli officers grabbed Neuville roughly and handcuffed his hands behind his back. They stood to each side gripping one of Neuville's biceps.

The commander then looked at Amit. "Are you Israeli?"

Amit answered in Hebrew with his name and a brief explanation of why he and Shane were there. It seemed to pacify the commander.

He pointed to Lauren. "And the lady?"

Shane put his arm around her. "She's with us." He saw the surprise on her face.

Amit confirmed. "Yes, she's with us."

The commander nodded and then raised the volume of his voice. "Detective, we're clear."

Behind the officers, another man entered the cave chamber. He looked like an American. Shane's suspicions were confirmed when the American temporarily removed his night vision goggles and stood staring at Shane with a smile on his face. It took Shane a minute to recall the man's name. "Detective Reese?"

The American nodded and put his goggles back on.

Shane was stunned. "What are you doing here?"

"Believe me, Doctor Randall, it's a long story. I'm glad I get to tell you about it." Reese pointed to the Israeli commander. "This is Chief Inspector Melech Koenig. You owe your lives to him and his men. And believe me, they paid a high price."

Shane nodded. "Thank you, Chief Inspector."

"By the way," began Reese. "Jane wanted me to give you a message."

Shane was shocked and jubilant at the same time. "She's alive?"

"Very much so. She says you better be *homeward bound* very soon."

Shane laughed. He could not believe the news.

Reese sighed audibly. "Now, would you mind telling me what this is about?"

Shane knew his search was finally over. "Come look for yourself. Chief Inspector Koenig, you might want to see this too. We're going to need your help."

Chapter 129

Shane and Amit led Reese, Koenig, and two of Koenig's men to the partially dislodged wall where Clisson and Raphael still lay as if in an embrace. "Help me move them."

The six men moved the two bodies backward and a few feet to the side. Lauren stood behind them almost as if she was afraid to join. Shane made eye contact with her but remained noncommittal on an invitation.

After returning to the wall, the men began using the bottoms of their shoes to clear away more stone blocks. Shane realized the stones shifted with relative ease because when the original builders stacked them, they had used only a very thin layer of mortar. The magic was in the compactness of the stones and the camouflage of the surface.

The construction was not unlike the wall of a Galilean peasant home. Limestone stones were stacked and held together with a mud mortar. Then they were made smooth by coating them with stucco made from the local soil mixed with water and clay. The same process may have been used here except with minimal mortar.

When they had cleared an opening large enough for them to walk through, Shane and Amit stepped inside. Reese and Koenig followed with Lauren in their wake. What lay in front of them looked like a scene from the Arabian Nights' Ali Baba and the Forty Thieves. The chamber was over one hundred feet square and perhaps twenty feet high. Cases of gold bars and silver bars were stacked at odd angles in many different places around the cave floor. Between the stacks of precious metals were other cases containing jewelry, stacks of garments, gold and silver objects of various kinds, and jars that might still contain oils and perfumes.

Amit screamed in triumph. He looked at Shane and ran through the cave from case to case before composing himself. "I never let myself completely believe."

Shane acknowledged his friend with a wide smile and a nod. Waves of both relief and joy poured over him. He saw Lauren off to the side. "We would never've found it without you."

Lauren eyes watered until a single tear released down her dusty cheek.

Reese walked to one of the cases of gold, bent over, and tried to lift one of the bars. His first try with a single hand failed. He tried again with both hands and groaned as he brought it up to his waist.

Shane watched his struggles. "That bar is called a *talent.* A gold talent weighed about ninety pounds. The weight was determined by the amount of gold one man could reasonably carry. It was worth three thousand shekels. Today it's worth about two million dollars. The silver talents weigh about half as much."

"Are you saying I'm holding two million dollars?"

"With some difficulty from the looks of it."

Reese set the bar back into place.

Shane laughed. "The contents of this room are probably worth fifteen to twenty billion dollars."

Reese froze in place. Koenig apparently thought he had misheard. "Fifteen to twenty billion dollars?"

Before Shane could answer, Amit returned to where he and the others stood. "Chief Inspector Koenig. We need help securing the area."

"I figured that out myself, Doctor David. I'll leave a couple of men and call for help as soon as we get out of here."

Amit continued in his excitement. "We also need to contact the Israel Antiquities Authority immediately. They..."

Shouts and gunshots interrupted him.

Shane gestured to Lauren. "Stay here."

All six men rushed back to where Koenig had left Neuville in custody. They found the two Israeli policemen returning from the tunnel previously taken by Shane and Amit. One of them began speaking quickly in Hebrew to Koenig. Shane did not know Hebrew well enough to catch every word, but he knew an apology when he heard one.

Koenig seemed embarrassed. "Director Neuville escaped. He broke for the tunnel when my men were distracted. They fired on him, but they didn't bring him down. His hands were handcuffed behind his back, and one of my men thinks he hit him. They found a short blood trail and tracked it until it disappeared. We'll find him one way or another."

Shane was not as sure. *He'll become one of the spirits haunting this cave system.*

Chapter 130

Raphael heard the gunshots and opened his eyes in a start. He lay face down and could smell the earthy odor of the stone. He inhaled and exhaled with great difficulty, and his body burned with each attempt. He could see nothing.

Am I in the grave? Am I in Hell?

He struggled to turn over on his back. He slowly reached out with an arm but felt nothing. The burning and nothingness answered his question.

I am in Hell. I am apart from God for eternity.

Tears began pouring down his cheeks. They stopped when a glowing halo of light radiating from under an archway caught his attention.

I am not in Hell. I am in Purgatory. I am outside Heaven's gate awaiting God's grace.

Raphael began dragging himself slowly toward the archway.

I am God's servant. He will let me in.

While Raphael was still a meter from the archway, a woman emerged. The light in her hand revealed enough for him to recognize her.

She is the succubus who is Satan's whore. God is giving me a gift. Raphael prayed. *Lord God, please give me the strength to perform one more task. Let me pay back she who has harmed me. Let me be avenged for the loss of my father.*

Raphael felt energized with God's power. He stood to his feet and took one stride to where the woman stood as if waiting for him.

I will end her.

By the time the woman sensed his presence, one of his massive hands already grasped her throat. He pulled her to him and brought his other hand to her throat. If she was struggling, he could not feel her. He could feel nothing.

We will embrace in death.

"Stop!" a voice said to his side.

Raphael looked to see a black man holding a Jericho 941 semi-automatic pistol. He did not let go. Simultaneously, a muzzle flash, an explosion, and a bullet ripping through his throat registered in his brain. He stood motionless for a moment before releasing the woman and dropping to his knees.

God, I have failed you. Father, I am sorry.

The black man handed his weapon to another man standing beside him. He spoke in English. "Please return it to your friend Calev Spielmann with my thanks."

Raphael fell backward to the stone floor. He was again in darkness.

I am in Hell.

Chapter 131

Cardinal Armand Vichilieu loved his job. As prefect of the Vatican Secret Archives, he directed the operation of thirty archivists who preserved, catalogued, and otherwise cared for millions of documents in fifty-two miles of shelves. Founded five hundred years ago by Pope Paul V, the archives were not intended to be truly *secret.* They served as the *private* repository for the records of the popes—state papers, letters, trial documents, and many other historical documents.

Since the late nineteenth century, the Vatican had granted access to about one thousand scholars each year as long as they requested the specific document they wanted to study. Very recently, the Vatican had reacted to public criticism and conspiracy theorists by opening the archives to broader access by journalists and other public figures.

Cardinal Vichilieu had entered the heavily guarded concrete bunker behind St. Peter's Basilica and descended the stairs leading to the lower of two basement levels added in 1980. He carried a parchment file case containing a document. Though the Vatican had publicly insisted there was nothing *secret* to the Secret Archives, Cardinal Vichilieu knew that was not totally true.

He walked to the far end of the lower basement and hit a button on a remote control device he carried in his hand. A section of the floor gave way, exposing yet another stairway to a third basement. Cardinal Vichilieu descended the steps. As he did so, a motion detector turned on lighting to illuminate his path.

Once on the floor, he walked down a central aisle separating climate-controlled rooms each containing rows of shelf racks. Unlike the metal shelves from the two floors above, these shelves were wooden and dated to the sixteenth century.

Cardinal Vichilieu walked directly to a door two thirds of the way down the aisle and entered the security code. When the door released, he proceeded to a row of racks labeled in block letters.

Apocrypha

Cardinal Vichilieu turned in front of the row of shelves and walked to a point near the far end where there was space on a shelf near the top. He put the parchment case in the space as he had done with so many documents before. He read the label on the case.

The Sicarii Gospel

Epilogue

Shane had just finished his last class and was walking to his car when he felt his iPhone vibrating in his pocket. The familiar Indiana Jones ringtone soon followed. It brought to mind the whirlwind that had been the last four months–regular trips to Israel, appearances on four continents for interviews, and meetings with his publisher about the book he was writing on the treasure and his associated theories. In some circles he had become as famous as his movie archaeologist idol.

The Israeli government had been less than generous with their finder's fee, but it was still substantial. They had maintained the treasure was on Israeli soil and had been found without appropriate authorization. Shane had divided the finder's fee into four equal shares. Shane and Amit each had taken a share, and in spite of Amit's objections, Shane had insisted Lauren get an equal share. After all, without Lauren, they would have never found the key that led them to the treasure. She had also brought him the closure he had not found over the years since their time in Texas. Though they continued to bump into each other for a couple of months, their relationship was not the same. Her appearances had gradually decreased, and he had no idea where she was.

The fourth share Shane divided among Detective Reese, Jane, Chief Inspector Koenig, and Koenig's men, including the families of the men who had died. Jane had completely recovered and still ran Shane's lab. And though much of Amit's time was spent working with the Israel Antiquities Authority on the care and display of the treasure, he still escaped to work in the field. The Israeli government had renovated a small building on Mount Zion to display the find. Shane's multiple trips there had kept him and Amit in constant contact. Reese had become a close friend and had often joined them as a third musketeer.

What the Frenchmen had done with the attaché containing the Sicarii Gospel was anyone's guess. Everything the Frenchmen had taken to the King David Hotel had vanished. Shane's translation was now merely words without proof, and his images could not be authenticated. Without the original document for validation, the Sicarii

Gospel at best would remain just another apocryphal gospel never to be taken seriously. At worst, it would be considered a hoax. The true source of the treasure would be doubted forever.

The disappearance had not lessened the significance of the find. In fact, the Israeli government had been more overjoyed because the lack of religious clarity eliminated, or at least significantly reduced, the associated politics. At the same time it heightened interest and the associated tourist revenue. Several countries had laid claim to the treasure–Palestine, Jordan, Italy, the United States, even the Vatican, but ultimately Israel did not relinquish a single piece.

Shane answered the call. "Hello, Detective Reese."

"You know I'm not a detective anymore."

"But it's your calling. A man shouldn't ignore his calling."

"You may be more right than you know. I received a call from the FBI today. They have an offer for me, and I'm considering it. I want to run it by you."

Shane knew Reese and his wife had recently reconciled, but their marriage was still far from perfect. "What do your wife and son think about it?"

"That's part of what I want to talk about."

Shane laughed. "I'm not sure I'm the best person to be counseling anyone on relationships."

"You know, Shane, if I take this job, I may want to call on you for help now and then."

"Not sure what help I'll be, but call away. Now tell me more about the job."

www.ingramcontent.com/pod-product-compliance
Lightning Source LLC
LaVergne TN
LVHW020527100826
845148LV00010B/1363

* 9 7 9 8 9 5 0 0 7 2 0 8 6 *